BRINGER OF LIGHT

THE COMPLETE ALLIE STROM TRILOGY

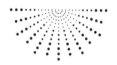

JUSTIN M. STONE

ELDER TREE PRESS

BRINGER OF LIGHT
by Justin M. Stone

This is a work of fiction. No people known to the author have as of yet destroyed Samyaza, so be warned. Please consider leaving a review, and tell your friends about *BRINGER OF LIGHT.*

Thank you for supporting my work.

Join my Newsletter.

www.JustinMStone.com

DEDICATION

To Brendan, Verona, and Ella.

You all inspire me.

BOOK ONE

ALLIE STROM AND RING OF SOLOMON

THE NECKLACE

Allie Strom stared at the eerie blue glow of a small necklace on the floor of her bedroom closet. She knew that necklace well. Her whole life it had always hung from her mom's neck. Yet here it was, while her mom was half-way across the world.

While searching for her favorite pleated skirt, Allie had first noticed the necklace. Starting seventh grade in a new city made her decision about what to wear especially significant.

She shuddered at the memory of sixth grade, when her stupid friend Crystal had betrayed her for the cool kids. All it took was for Allie to tell her she was moving, and maybe it hadn't helped to bring it up during Crystal's birthday party. The cake frosting in her hair took forever to get out, but the feeling of betrayal wouldn't leave with a year's worth of scraping.

No, this year she was determined to make sure she started off right. She would get in good with a group of friends and form her own crew of soccer girls. For the past few days she had thought of nothing else, aside from the occasional annoyance at her mom's absence, once again. Regardless, finding the necklace had thrown Allie off guard.

Even more so now that it looked like the glow was starting to pulsate, a strange magnetism drawing her toward it. She knelt, hand going for it. Her ears rang, a sound like her mother's voice echoing from all around.

A knock on the door startled her, and the effect of the necklace was suddenly gone. Instead, it was simply a stone on a necklace again. Could she have imagined everything? She nudged the necklace into the closet with her toe, alongside the skirt and T-shirt combination she didn't want her dad to see. She paused at the mess, realizing that in spite of having moved here nearly two months ago, her unpacking job of throwing everything in the closet hadn't magically fixed itself.

"Honey, can I...?" her dad's deep voice came from the other side of the door, more hoarse than usual this morning.

"Um..." She checked the other clothes on her bed to make sure they were to her dad's liking. He was a great dad and meant well, but that didn't mean he would let her wear whatever she wanted to school. He still had the idea that she wasn't independent until she turned eighteen, and even that seemed like a stretch. Now, if her mom were here, that would be a different story. She was the one that had noticed Allie buying the pleated skirt and pretended not to see it. She would probably help Allie pick out an outfit, tell her everything a girl needed to know when going into Junior High, when becoming a young woman. But, like always, her mom was deployed with the Army. Off trying to improve the lives of others instead of focusing on her own daughter like she should have been. No one cared about Allie's life. Where was Mom this time, Afghanistan or something? One of the Stans, Allie remembered that much.

Allie turned with a smile as she heard the door open. "Yeah?"

Her dad stepped in hesitantly. He was the kind of dad that seldom lost his cool and wasn't going away for work all the time. Usually, he was clean-cut and dressed well for his job at Nintendo, testing games or doing computers or something, Allie wasn't sure. But years back and couldn't convince herself to trash them quite yet. The idea of her brother being cool needed to be wiped from her brain, but that appeared harder than she would've thought. He would always be her big brother, after all.

For now, she had a priority. She pulled out the necklace and watched the stone glimmer as it twisted on its chain. The rest of her room was dull in comparison. The necklace had always intrigued her, always there, shining from her mom's neck. Now, holding it inches from her eyes, she stared into the silver lines in the blue stone. The little patterns on the stone reminded her of maps she had seen, maps of the world, but of so much more, too. Maybe the universe?

She pulled it up to tie it around her neck again but paused, surprised to see a clasp on the chain where it had been broken before. That was strange. Neither her dad nor Ian would have even known she had found it, let alone sneak into her room and replace the clasp. That would be ridiculous. The only explanation, then, was that she had imagined it being broken before.

A soft warmth emanated from the stone when it touched her skin. She closed her eyes, overcome with a feeling of relaxation, but when she opened them again a flash of light burst forth from the necklace and suddenly she was younger, lying in her mom's arms. Her mom's hair tickled as it brushed Allie's cheek. Those soft blue eyes stared down lovingly, the warm summer breeze tingled as it caressed her skin, carrying with it the scent of strawberries. The warmth of the stone engulfed her like a bath and, for a moment, she saw only the bright light as it flared again. She smelled fresh air, like a forest after the rain. Was she floating? The pleasant sensation drifted through her body and she was in the passenger seat of her mom's car, her mom driving while calm music played in the distance.

"Allie," a soft voice said. "Allie…."

Tap. Tap.

The light flashed again and then gave way to darkness. A cave or a tunnel, rolling darkness as if it were alive, twisting and weaving through her limbs. She wasn't herself. Her hands were too big and something felt different. She wore Army fatigues and was running. Menacing laughter echoed through the darkness from behind. Her boots thudded on moist stone. The scent of scorched metal, a sour taste in her mouth. Her mom's voice sounded distant, but at the same time inside her head, saying, "Run, run!" She tore the necklace from around her neck and placed it on the ground before her, glowing. "Protect it, at all costs," her mom's voice said. Her large hands lifted a rock and then with an echoing smash the necklace was gone. Scorched blue marks were all that remained where the stone of the necklace had been moments before.

Tap. Tap.

Darkness and a lingering scent of honey. Allie was in her mom's arms as a child, falling asleep.

Tap. Tap.

With a jolt, Allie was pulled from her mom's arms, kicking and screaming. She wanted to stay in that comforting embrace forever, but when she opened her eyes she was back in her room, the necklace around her neck. She tried to clear her head. It was heavy. A light sweat dampened her temples. Somehow she had ended up lying on her bed. She sat up and saw someone in the window. Could it be?

"Mom?" She stood and approached the glass to see that the morning sky was still dim. The image she saw was her reflection. Had it all been a dream? Perhaps it was something more, her mom calling to her in desperate need of help. But that was impossible. Allie wanted to scream in confusion.

The tapping sounded again, from her door.

"Allie?" Ian's voice called out from the other side of the door. "Dad wants to know if you'll need a ride today."

She held her head, trying to figure out what had happened.

"Allie?" he said again.

"Leave me alone!" she yelled, then fell down on her bed. Her eyelids grew heavy. She thought she heard her mom whispering to her, or maybe calling from far away. But it didn't make sense, she convinced herself as her eyes closed.

"Allie," Ian called. "You're going to be late!"

Her eyes flickered open and she saw the morning light streaming through her blinds. She must have drifted back to sleep. She jumped from bed to get ready for her first day of school. Whatever had happened, the strange dream or whatever it was would have to wait.

2

THE LIBRARY

A drop of rain followed Allie's bangs, ripping along her forehead then down her cheek. She reached her destination and paused for a moment to wonder if this could really be a school. The hedge walls surrounded the perimeter and came together on each side of an arch above her with a sign that read, "Vigil Junior High School." It was more like a fortress straight out of one of her brother's games. Her elementary school back in Hartsville had been no bigger than a small church and had one-hundred students making up all six grades. Compared to that, this new school was enormous.

Kids scurried around like an army of ants. Parents dropped off their kids and a school bus pulled up nearby. A spray of water from a puddle barely missed her as a car pulled off.

Unsure what to think of this place, she held her backpack straps tight with her left hand. Her right hand fidgeted with her mom's necklace, which lay hidden beneath the top of her shirt.

Near the sliding glass doors, a couple of boys shoved a younger one between them. Allie stood for a moment, watching in shock, sure a teacher would step in any minute. The boy's eyes met hers and she was about to say something when a group of older girls walked by, giggling. One looked her way as if waiting to see what Allie would do. Allie quickly about-faced and made her way through the doors.

This was something she would have to get used to, she decided. In her old school there were so few students that everyone was friends with someone, so picking on anyone would mean picking on a friend's friend. Everyone but her that is, and that hadn't been until the end of the year, when Crystal found out Allie was changing schools. Her betrayal had been a political tactic and maybe she would have done the same in Crystal's shoes.

But here in this new school, Allie wanted no part of the bickering. With a subtle side-step, she ducked into the library. It was the only resting place, the only room in the whole vicinity without kids everywhere.

The library was unlike anything she had ever seen. Massive pillars supported a domed ceiling. Paintings covered the walls, similar to ones they had tried to teach her about in sixth grade, like those in churches. She walked among the towering bookshelves, amazed at how ancient it felt. A dusty scent drifted in the air and she felt at home. She had never cared much for history or science, but a good fiction book got her skin tingling.

She turned a corner to see a boy ducking behind a shelf. She wondered if he was also hiding from the chaos in the halls. When he turned her way, she saw it was the young boy from outside. He was about two inches shorter than her and wore a Sylvester and Tweety t-shirt. A thin line of red trickled from his nose. He looked up and attempted a smile.

"You got a little...." She motioned toward the blood.

The boy cocked his head and then, understanding, wiped his nose with the base of his shirt.

"Thanks." He turned to leave.

"Wait." She didn't know why she had said it. He wasn't the coolest looking kid, but he was the only one there. The only one who had talked to her so far.

"You skipped the tour?" he asked when he drew close.

She turned away slightly, unsure what to say.

"You live in Valleyview Apartments, right?" he said after a long, awkward silence.

"What?"

"Yeah, I noticed you. We're neighbors."

"You spying on me?" She had seen this before—at her last school she was captain of the soccer team. She had had her share of boy stalkers, before the other girls turned on her. Sure, it was a soccer team of fourth through sixth grades and most of her stalkers had been two years younger than her, but still.

"What? No, I—I just saw you moving in a couple months back, and—"

"So you've been watching me for two months?"

"I…." He looked around, his face bright red.

She sighed. Of course he hadn't been stalking her, but the idea of someone knowing about her gave her the squirmies.

"What's this tour?" she said.

"Oh…. Yeah, the eighth graders are showing the kids around. You *are* new, right?"

"I suppose."

"Seventh grade?"

She nodded.

"All seventh graders are new." He smiled as if very proud of his observation. They stood there for a moment before the boy finally stuck out his hand. "I'm Daniel, if you have any questions."

She looked at his hand with a smirk. "Allie. Thanks."

"Yeah, well." Daniel put his hand in his pocket and looked to the doorway in another awkward moment of silence.

This boy reminded her of someone she knew a few years back. Ben Davis. The curly haired son of one of her mom's colleagues. They had spent hours trying to figure out how to take things apart. The worst was his dad's television that had stood as tall as her. But when they hit fifth grade and Allie had the opportunity to hang with the cool kids because she could run and kick, Ben soon faded from her life. It hadn't helped that he had asked her to be his girlfriend—she just hadn't been ready for that. And the fact that her self-perceived coolness hadn't lasted more than several months didn't change a thing between them. The guilt still ate at her. Who throws away a friend like that? No, she couldn't go through that again, and didn't want to make this clingy kid suffer either. Best not to get too close.

"You coming?" Daniel asked.

"Not yet, I think I'll linger and check out some of these books." She grabbed the nearest one and smiled.

Daniel turned to go. "Have fun."

She looked down at the book in her hands and cringed as she dropped it—a taxidermy book with a picture of a crazy-looking wolverine on the front.

She turned to explore the library, amazed by its beauty. On the floor in the center was a bronze map of the world, which she walked across in awe. Outlines of the countries glimmered in gold trim, catching sunlight from the skylight above. She bent down and traced the map, feeling the rough relief of a mountain range against her fingers.

"Ever been there?" a raspy voice asked. She looked up to see a man in his sixties with smile-wrinkles lining his eyes and mouth. "Central Asia. Kyrgyzstan?"

"I, uh…." She glanced down to see she was squatting immediately west of China. She knew that one. But this was the first time she could remember hearing about Kyrgyzstan. Or was it? She hadn't paid much attention when her mom had said she would be deploying again. Allie had grown so used to it all, the constant deployments, Christmas, birthdays, everything without a mom. When her mom had sat her and her brother down to give them the news, Allie remembered leaning back and glaring, but not much else.

She turned to find Daniel, but he was gone.

"I haven't traveled much," she mumbled.

"Perhaps you'll have a chance soon," the man said, then turned and limped away.

Allie stared after him, thinking how much he reminded her of the pictures she had seen of her grandpa, or what he would have looked like if he had lived past thirty. She had not known her grandpa on her mom's side, since he died when her mom was only nine, but she had seen many pictures and wished she had the chance to know him. In the pictures, he was a young version of what a grandpa should look like, with a big nose and gentle eyes. Her mom had always said he was great, the kindest man in the world.

Allie decided at that moment that she liked this librarian.

She glanced back at the map once more, curious as to why the man had thought she may have been anywhere but America. She had traveled to Canada once for a camping trip, a whole two-hour drive, but that was the extent of her international travel. The idea of leaving a perfectly great country, with every food one could possibly crave just around the corner, didn't appeal to her. For now, she would skip the rest of the tour and any more awkward interactions, and instead find a nice fantasy novel to curl up with. She hid in a corner of the library beside one of the oddly too-intricately-designed pillars, and lost track of time as she delved into a story of a female werewolf searching for a cure to her curse.

"Ahem," someone said and Allie jolted.

She looked down to see she had almost finished the book, then looked up to see an older girl, about thirteen, Allie guessed, standing in the aisle beside her. Was she the same girl who had looked at her earlier, when Daniel was being shoved around? She was a pretty girl with straight brown hair and none of the freckles Allie had always been self-conscious about.

"New kid." The girl motioned her over. "Yeah, you. Tour's over, come on. It's lunch time."

3

PRINCIPAL EISNER

The older girl didn't say much as they walked down the hallway, but Allie felt the girl's eyes boring into her. Except that, every time Allie glanced over, the girl was staring straight ahead.

"There you go," the girl said as they entered a large room. She pointed to a line of students by metallic counters lined with food. The smell of grease and cold-cut sandwiches was overwhelming.

"Thanks."

"Big kid lunch for me." The girl winked and walked off to join her friends.

Allie found a slice of cheese pizza and smothered it in parmesan and crushed peppers, got a side of ranch, then paid and turned to face the lunchroom. She groaned – Daniel was seated nearby, already looking her way.

"Allie, hey!" he called.

She almost went to him, but noticed the older girl

glance back her way. No, Allie couldn't be seen with Daniel in the lunchroom, not by that girl. She had to play this right. On TV they called it political capital, and she figured if she were to monetize it, she had enough to buy a cool friend and salvage herself. What did he expect anyway? That they would become best friends simply because they lived in the same apartment complex? She turned to her right, away from him, and pretended not to hear.

"Allie?" his voice trailed after her.

She sat facing the trophy wall, which was past the older girl and what appeared to be the cool kids. Over glass cases, she saw pictures of students throughout the years who had made their school proud, and above that a banner of pastel-blue that read, "Vigil School Pride." She smiled at the color, the same as her shirt, then dipped her pizza into the ranch dressing and told herself she had done what was necessary regarding Daniel. She had to focus on getting her picture on that wall—one of her scoring the winning soccer goal ought to do it. Allie smiled and looked around to see if she could guess who the soccer kids would be.

A scraping sound sent a chill through her chest as a tray slid across a table. Out of the corner of her eye she saw Daniel approaching.

She scanned the room for an escape route. Rain barraged the glass double-doors that led to the courtyard, so that wasn't an option. A retreat to the girl's bathroom was an option, but she was pretty hungry. But something had to be done, the eighth graders and the girl from the tour were in the middle of the lunch-room and they would definitely see her with Daniel.

Allie stood and started walking, her mind made up. She would go and sit with the older girl who she had met at the library. Maybe they would accept her. She passed a thick-boned kid who was staring at her chest. This gave her a moment's pause—she had heard of boys staring at girls' chests, but it hadn't happened to her. There had been no reason to. She glanced down and realized the necklace was visible. When she covered it she glanced back and the boy had turned away. Perhaps it was nothing, she thought.

Then she heard a loud thump and a yelp.

When she turned, she saw Daniel lay sprawled out across the cafeteria floor, holding his face. A large boy loomed over him. He had spiked hair, wore all black, and had a pimple on his nose like a rhinoceros horn. He beckoned the kids nearby to applaud as he knelt over Daniel.

"The girl wants to be left alone," the boy said. "Little piggy."

Daniel glanced her way and she realized this was about her!

Allie stood there, watching this bully pick on the boy slightly smaller than herself, the rest of the students pointing and laughing. She wanted to run over and help him, but come on. How was that her responsibility? Her palms started sweating and she could feel her breathing growing heavy. Her first day in a new school, and now this? She looked around, desperate for anyone else to take action. None of the other students were stepping forward to help him. None of them even cared! She glared around at the students, challenging them to do something, but they were all busy waiting to see what the big kid would do next. She noticed several students dressed all in black staring hard in her direction and whispering among themselves. She was too upset to pay them much attention, and Daniel's eyes were burning a hole in her heart.

Allie couldn't take it anymore. With a deep breath, she turned to the big kid and stomped her foot. "Back off!"

The big kid raised his eyes to hers. He smiled. Another boy stepped out to his side, arms folded and slightly shorter than the first, but in every other way his clone.

"Mind your own business," the first kid said. "We were just helping you out."

"I…." As she feared, everyone was looking at her. She was done for. "I didn't need help."

"Oh?" the boy said as he stepped toward her. "So you and this kid, you got something going on? Little Daniel's your boyfriend or something?"

"No!"

"Uh, huh." He turned to his slightly shorter companion. "Looks like we got ourselves a real Romeo and Juliet here, huh Vince?"

The boy smiled at his companion. "Looks that way."

"Hmmm," the bigger kid said, then turned and

pulled Daniel up and to him. "And what you gonna do about it, little girl?" He punched Daniel right in the stomach and Daniel crumbled to the ground again.

"Stop it," Allie said, her anger growing now. Friend or not, her mom had taught her to look out for those that need help, for those smaller than herself. Well, Daniel wasn't much smaller than her, but he certainly needed help.

Vince made a move for her and pulled her by the hair, in spite of several calls from nearby girls to cut it out. "What do we do with wise-mouth little heroes, Chester?"

"Same thing we do with their boyfriends," Chester said, leering at her. "Throw them in the swamp."

A couple of nearby kids cheered at this and Allie felt herself about to panic. Daniel made a growling sound and lunged for Chester's calf, biting as hard as he could. Chester yelped and Allie used the moment of distraction to break free of Vince and throw herself at Chester, putting all her weight into it like her brother had taught her – of course he had taught her how to tackle when wearing pads and playing football, so she yelped out in surprise at how much her shoulder hurt.

But the mountain of a boy had the worst of it. He fell backwards, his head smacking the lasagna Daniel had spilled on the tiled floor.

"You little snot!" Vince reached out but she ducked away.

Chester scrambled to his feet with cheese sticking to the back of his hair. He grabbed Daniel by his scraggly brown hair, pulling him close. "You'll regret that."

Allie moved out of Vince's grasp, debating her next move when—

"Enough!" an older woman said. The students moved aside like displaced water, flowing out of her way as she strode forward. She glared at Chester. "Just what do you think you're doing?"

"Principal Eisner," Daniel said. "We were just, um...."

"Nothing, ma'am," Chester said, stepping back. "We were getting to know each other."

"Try putting the food in your belly next time," the principal said. "Instead of in your hair."

"Sorry, ma'am." Chester vanished into the crowd. Students around them snickered and Principal Eisner glanced at Allie.

"Okay, new girl, you and your friend with me."

"Daniel," Daniel said.

"Excuse me?" She looked at him as if he had broken the first rule of Vigil Junior High. But her eyes softened when he pulled back. "Yes, you and Daniel in my office. Now."

"What?!" Allie turned on Chester and Vince, pointing. "But they—"

"In my office, now." She nodded to the crowd. The librarian stepped forward to grab Vince and Chester by their shirts. "They'll get their punishments."

Daniel followed first and looked back at Allie with a shrug and a half-smile, eyes full of gratitude. Allie glared in return and followed him with her eyes to the floor. She knew the whole lunchroom was watching, memorizing her face so they could laugh at her later— the girl that allied herself with the nerd of the school on her first day. Great! She had made her choice and sealed her fate. She was doomed.

In Principal Eisner's office, Allie and Daniel sat in small chairs while the principal sat behind her oak-desk. Her fingers formed a steeple. She looked at them from under her silvery hair with her dull gray eyes, as if waiting for them to start talking. Finally, she leaned forward and smiled.

"You two are friends?" she asked.

"We just met," Allie said, perhaps a bit too quick.

Principal Eisner nodded, then picked up an old pencil sharpener and started sharpening pencils, not looking up. After a few minutes, she cleared her throat. "Why'd you stand up for him?"

Allie looked at her hands, only then noticing she had been picking at her fingernails. "No one else would."

"I see." She glanced up at Allie. "And that necklace?"

"What? What's my necklace have to do with this?"

"I feel I've seen it before."

"It was a present."

For a split second, Allie thought she saw the necklace glint sky blue as a reflection in Principal Eisner's eyes, but when she looked down it was normal. No shining, no pulling memories of her mom. She shuddered as she remembered the morning.

Principal Eisner returned her gaze to the pencils.

"And today you decided you'd step in to help another. How convenient."

Daniel stood from his seat. "I didn't need help, I—"

"Sit down." Principal Eisner motioned with a pencil. "I'm sure you didn't."

Allie looked at him in a new light, standing up for himself like that. Now that she thought of it, he had attacked Chester back there, even if it was a bite in the leg. A punch or kick would have been more impressive, but she had to give him credit.

"I didn't..." Daniel murmured.

The principal motioned for the door. "Daniel, you may depart."

"What about her?" he said.

Principal Eisner set three sharpened pencils into her pencil holder and stood. "Worried about her? Don't be, she's not in trouble either. Go on."

"But...."

The principal cleared her throat and Daniel stood with a shrug to Allie before leaving. Allie allowed a smile.

The principal turned to Allie. "So, Allie Strom, welcome to our school."

Allie's smile faded. She felt uneasy under the principal's stare. "You, um, had something to talk to me about?"

"More of a warning. I want you to be careful, okay? And if you ever need anything, I'm here to help. The librarian can be a great help too, that's what he's here for."

"Okay," Allie said with a frown, unsure what this lady was talking about. Where was this coming from?

"I hope you enjoyed your morning." Principal Eisner handed her a slip of paper. "Your afternoon classes, since you somehow missed the part of the tour where everyone introduced themselves and was assigned class schedules. I hope this will be to your liking."

Allie took the paper and sighed to see History class. Seeing that the Principal had turned to sharpen another pencil, Allie stood and showed herself out.

In the hall, Daniel came over to her. "Can you believe that? I mean, we didn't even get in trouble!"

"Yeah, sure," she said. She looked at him, thinking of what she had done. This political capital thing may have already been used up, thanks to this kid. She turned and started walking down the hall, her brain too scattered to process what class came next.

"Hey, since you live so close, I was thinking, I mean, if you want, maybe after school—"

"No." She turned and saw his hurt expression. "I mean, what?"

"I don't know, I was thinking we could hang out, you know?"

She stared at him. How did they deal with situations like this in the movies? Drive off the little dogs that wouldn't leave you alone? Oh yeah, rocks. She would try to be gentler.

She stepped close and lowered her voice when she said, "Listen, there's no *we*, okay?"

He stared at her, eyes wide. "But...?"

"I didn't ask to come to this crummy school, but since I'm here... I got big plans."

He frowned, blinking without comprehension. She wasn't sure she even knew what she was saying. But it was out, no turning back. With a deep breath, she about-faced. She walked off as her conscience rose inside her. It pulled at her heart and balled her stomach so the pain of guilt overwhelmed her. She clenched her fists and kept walking. She had done what was necessary.

4

DODGEBALL

By the time Allie found history class, she was feeling horrible. As always happened in the end, her conscience had won. That darn gnawing feeling deep down where she tried to hide it had managed to bubble up and eat away at her. She could see her mom looking at her with those judging eyes, wondering how Allie could have let her down. Her parents had taught her better than this and she knew it.

She found a desk to the back left of class and dropped her bag with a clunk. How had she let herself lose it so badly? He seemed all right, but not her style. He had to understand that. But all of her self-justification had floated away between the hallway and the moments it had taken to sit down. It didn't help that the room smelled like stale oranges – now she was guilt-ridden and annoyed at the stinging in her nostrils.

The door opened and two girls entered, Daniel behind them. He walked directly toward Allie, not seeing her yet. His eyes stayed on the ground, his bangs hanging over his face like a closed curtain. When he saw her, he left-faced and continued to the opposite corner.

He wore a look of rejection on his face because of her. She had been trying to play the game, but maybe it was time she grew up. Maybe it was time she stopped being such a jerk.

She tried to catch his attention with a smile, but he picked at his fingernails and didn't seem to notice her. On the one hand, she wanted to apologize, on the other she wanted to stay seated as far as possible from the click-click-clicking of his nails.

"Good afternoon students," the teacher said as she entered the class. Her hair flipped up in a fun, seventies style way. She introduced herself as Ms. Aldridge and stood behind the oak desk facing the students.

Ms. Aldridge then turned and outlined a shape on the board that Allie thought she recognized. But from where? She stared for a moment and listened, suddenly attentive. Ms. Aldridge went on about border crossings and something about a coup, but Allie couldn't take it anymore.

"Excuse me," she said with a raised hand.

Ms. Aldridge turned with as much surprise as the rest of the students. "Yes?"

"Um, what is that you drew there?"

"Miss Strom, is it?" Ms. Aldridge said, stepping closer and folding her hands before her. "I have been discussing the importance of history with current events, and for about five minutes now I've been talking about Kyrgyzstan here."

The class giggled but Allie was too busy thinking over where she had heard of Kyrgyzstan before. Then it hit her. The map on the floor of the library.

"Oh, bordering China!" she said.

"That's right." Ms. Aldridge nodded in approval, apparently surprised at this bit of knowledge so early in the year. "And also bordering Uzbekistan. A large portion of the people living in the southern half of Kyrgyzstan are Uzbeks, a fact that exists because of borders drawn in the time of Stalin. Does anyone know why this southern population of Uzbeks is of relevance today?"

Everyone turned to Allie to see if she had an

answer. She did not, because she had never cared before. And now the chair couldn't get low enough as she shrunk down into her seat and waited for the teacher to answer her own question. Her eyes darted to Daniel, who quickly looked away.

"It was not long ago that a major clash broke out between the Kyrgyz and the Uzbek people," the teacher said. "And, by some accounts, over four-hundred thousand Uzbeks tried to flee across the border within two days of the outbreak of violence."

Allie found her attention span wavering, but she heard Ms. Aldridge go on about the danger these families had to face, and how homes were burned and even children were attacked. However, Allie decided she disliked history class more than ever, because while in the past it had bored her, now it was making her sad. She wondered why she couldn't worry about her own troubles and let more experienced people, like her mom, worry about the problems of the world.

That thought struck a nerve. Her mom was always off saving the world. Allie's whole year of third grade had been chaos as her mom was deployed and her dad had scrambled to make sure Allie and her brother got to school on time and had lunches aside from leftover pizza (though leftover spaghetti was never a problem). Where was her mom this time? She had talked about somewhere full of mountains like Ms. Aldridge was saying, an area that used to be along the Silk Road. And then Ms. Aldridge said "Central Asia" and Allie felt her heart jump. That had to be it.

But why had she been drawn to that spot on the map in the library? And was it a coincidence now that the first country her teacher chose to discuss was this one in Central Asia? She gulped and looked around, searching for an answer, but the rest of the students were back to their own worlds, none paying attention. None except Daniel, who stared straight ahead, taking notes. For a moment, this little act of his made Allie wish she had been nicer to him. He cared. He wanted to learn about a subject with which she suddenly had a connection.

The feeling of confusion faded by the time the bell sounded, and Allie decided it had been one big coincidence. After staring at the map for half of class, she now knew there was Afghanistan, Pakistan, Uzbekistan, Tajikistan, Kazakhstan, Turkmenistan, and Kyrgyzstan—who knows which one her mom had gone to? She wasn't even totally sure that her mom had gone to Central Asia this time. Or was that before? Her mom had probably gone to Southeast Asia, or Africa this time. Why did she have to go to so many places and make this so confusing? The bell rung and Daniel brushed past her at the door without so much as a glance in her direction.

In the hallway, Allie looked at her schedule and smiled—PE class. Finally, something she kicked butt at. She could enjoy at least part of her day. That is, until PE class came around and she saw the tiny gold shorts they gave her to wear.

"You gotta be kidding me," she said, but Ms. Trallis,

the unnaturally large PE teacher, faked a smile and nodded to the locker room.

After changing into her PE clothes, she walked into the gym, constantly pulling at the legs of the shorts to stop them from riding up. The boys didn't have to wear such tiny shorts, so why should the girls? It got even worse when she noticed an eighth grader looking at her legs. She quickly turned away from him and hid behind some other kids. Then she saw the girl from earlier, the older girl from the library. She wanted to talk to her, but decided to observe instead.

At her old school, grades and even sexes had been separated during P.E., so she wasn't sure what to think of this. Her wandering eyes stopped on Daniel, alone again.

He always seemed to be alone, and each time she saw him like that, she felt terrible. But it wasn't her fault! She glanced toward the older girl, then bit her lip with the realization that no, today she would not be earning cool points. Today she had to go talk to Daniel and apologize for earlier.

Halfway there she stopped. Someone else was approaching him and she looked around with dread. It looked like she would have to step in and help him out again. But when the boy reached him he said something and they started laughing. They even pounded fists.

As if in a moment of understanding, she realized she may have misjudged this Daniel boy. She was the only one at this school without any friends, and that thought stung. It didn't help that his dimpled friend with smooth blond hair was cute.

She stood there staring until a whistle sounded and Ms. Trallis emerged from the locker room with a large green bag. Ms. Trallis dumped the bag on the ground and two dozen large red balls bounced across the gym floor. Within minutes, the class was divided into two teams for dodgeball. Allie found herself on the same team as Daniel. His buddy was on the other side.

It wasn't until that first ball whizzed past her face that she noticed that the two guys from earlier, Chester and Vince, were also in her class and on the opposing side. Chester ran for a ball in the center. The older girl from the tour was on Allie's side and reached the ball first, but Chester shouldered her out of his way and took it. He threw right at Allie, but missed. Ms. Trallis's whistle blew repeatedly as kids were hit out, then called back in when their teammates caught balls. Allie grabbed a ball and focused on deflecting the myriad balls flying at her from Chester and Vince – it was like they'd completely forgotten about Daniel.

So had she!

She looked around for him. He was dodging like all the rest and moving like he'd been born to throw big red balls. Half the whistle blows were due to his well-aimed attacks. A ball slammed right into Vince's gut and the whistle blew. One of her assailants had to step out until someone would bring him back in.

Chester wasn't done though. He yelled as Vince abandoned him, then threw with all his might right for

Allie's head. Helpless, she stared at it coming her way, unable to move. She was sure the velocity of that ball would split her nose in two.

But out of nowhere the older girl appeared, red ball in hand, to bounce Chester's ball aside and return the favor. Everyone was watching. Allie stood beside this older girl and the two of them were on the assault, throwing balls like nothing else mattered. Kids were getting whistled out left and right, and before she knew it there were only two guys on the other side, Chester and the cute boy that was Daniel's friend. But when Allie looked at her own team, she saw only the older girl and Daniel beside her. The rest of the crowd was stuck in the out-boxes, cheering them on.

The older girl lunged forward and released, but it wasn't good enough. Chester caught it and Vince was back in the game. They moved close with their shoulders together, each with a red ball, deflecting the attacks. Allie ran and threw until her whole body was sore, and neither side gained ground. Then, while the girl ran for a ball Chester stumbled with his eyes on her, and before he could recover, Allie threw all her weight behind the tossing of that textured red ball. She watched with amazement as it went straight for his groin. The whole auditorium cringed with "oohs" as Chester collapsed, his eyes rolling up to the ceiling.

But no whistle blew.

The teacher stood there with a look of stupid shock on her face, her mouth open and the whistle at her lip.

Vince hadn't stopped and his eyes glared at Allie. He

ran forward, grabbed two balls at once and crossed the line to heave them at her. She didn't have time to react. One slammed into her gut as the other hit her in the forehead. She looked as if she would fall back and crumble forward at the same time. She stood there dazed, confused at the ringing in her ears and the yellow and red circles floating around the auditorium.

The whistle blew and Ms. Trallis called both her and Chester out.

"What?!" Allie yelled back.

"You heard me, you're out," the teacher said.

Daniel stepped forward, hands out wide in protest. "He was over the line!"

"And she hit the big kid in the crotch, neither was fair so both are out. Get moving."

Allie couldn't believe it – first the teacher was making ridiculous calls, but even crazier, now Daniel was standing up for *her*? What kind of world was this? She wouldn't have it.

"No," she said and stood her ground.

"Out, young lady," Ms. Trallis said. "Nobody plays until you step into the out-box. Nobody wins until you learn to behave like an adult."

Allie adjusted her shorts and looked to the older girl for assistance, but she was ready at the line, focused on the resumption of the game so she could take Vince down. Daniel shrugged and moved to find a ball. He too was giving up on her.

"This is junk!" Allie said.

A ball sat five feet in front of her, with Vince not far

past it. For the first time she smelled that fresh rubber scent. The goose-bumpy skin of the ball felt like part of her. The lights of the gymnasium shone like this was her moment. She was sick of her first day at school, confused and disoriented. Such injustice! With a giant step toward the ball she lifted her right leg back, up in the air, then brought it down to connect the instep of her foot with the ball.

TWANG!

It shot across the short distance to smack right into Vince's cheek, knocking him onto his butt.

"Tell him *he's* out!" she shouted, pointing at Vince. She stormed off to the locker room to the students' calls of "All right!" and "Ooohhh" behind her.

Allie slammed the locker room door but it shot back open. Ms. Trallis stood looming in the doorway, clipboard in hand and whistle at her side. She stared down at Allie like a giant ready for its meal.

"And what was that, young lady?" Ms. Trallis asked.

Allie stared, refusing to back down. Refusing to answer, because she too had no idea what had come over her back there. How had she become the bad kid, the one that loses her cool?

"Very well," Ms. Trallis said after several moments of the staring game. She lifted her clipboard and scribbled down something, then looked down her nose at Allie. "This will be on your permanent record."

And with that Ms. Trallis returned to the gymnasium and Allie heard the whistle blow. The shoes squeaked on the floor and kids yelled again. But she wanted to sit on the bench in the locker room and be alone. She wasn't even totally sure why she had lost her cool, to that degree anyway. Regardless, they shouldn't have been forced to play dodge ball. It was a stupid game!

"Agh, whatever," she said and threw her clothes on over her gym suit, along with her necklace.

As she walked into the hallway, she looked at her necklace and it sparkled like a teardrop. It brought her a moment of comfort, a reminder that her mom was out there somewhere, thinking of her. A left turn brought her back into the auditorium, leaving her unsure of where to go. Her next class didn't start for another fifteen minutes, but she didn't want to stand there by herself. She was about to go find the library, when a pair of eyes caught her attention – the older girl, still in her gym clothes.

The girl approached and nodded. "Nice moves there."

Allie looked around to make sure the girl was talking to her. "Thanks."

"Hey, you gotta win, right? Do whatever it takes."

"I don't think I was worried about winning. Is this what it's always like?"

"You mean those punks? They're part of, well, how do I say it? You saw the kids walking around in black here?"

"I guess so." She remembered seeing some kids in black in the auditorium and lunchroom, but wondered what they had to do with this.

"This school's super weird, but you just have to go along with it sometimes. Stay away from them. They think they're some secret society or something, the Strayers they call 'emselves. Twelve fights in one day last year, you wouldn't believe it unless you saw it."

"Seriously?"

"Yeah, those two weirdoes back there claim to be part of the group. Don't think about joining, they're a bunch of idiots."

"I wouldn't."

"Of course not. They make their new joins do stupid stuff like picking on other kids, stealing stuff, you know. Typical immature boys if you ask me. That's why they were picking on that friend of yours during lunch."

"Yeah well... He's not my friend." Allie fidgeted with her bag then looked back to the girl. "So you saw that too, huh? In the lunchroom?"

"Twice in one day. They're gonna be out for you." The girl assessed Allie for a moment then shrugged. "That was some kick though."

"Yeah?"

"I'm Paulette, by the way."

"Allie."

"I play goalie for the Angels, I don't suppose you—"

"Goalie?" Allie couldn't believe it. "You mean—"

"The soccer team. Cute right? Vigil means protector, so we figure since we're Vigil Junior High, we'd call ourselves the Angels, like guardian angels. Ever played?"

"I might've played a few times." She didn't want to appear too eager.

"Well Allie, give me your phone, I'll shoot myself a text on it so you'll have my number."

Allie dug into her pocket for her cell phone and then handed it over. A smile spread across her face. This school was starting to look a little less crummy. Now she had to see if she could hang. But the next stop was, once again, the principal's office.

And the rain had stopped, leaving a void that felt too silent.

Allie paused, eyes searching their surroundings. She turned to Daniel, who was also spinning and looking. Where fog had been moments before, now a rural darkness surrounded them. Stars filled the sky with an intensity Allie had never seen in city skies. The evergreens of the school grounds were replaced with firs, small red flags tied to some of the branches. A violent wind shook the branches and pushed the flags about, while Allie had to lean in to Daniel to be heard.

"Don't be scared," she said. "All this, it…. I think it's a dream."

"We're not sleeping, Allie."

She ducked as the wind blew a branch her way, nearly colliding with her head.

"We have to be." Allie wrapped her arms around her torso and rubbed, trying to stay warm.

He looked at her with skepticism.

"What?"

"If you know what they were talking about, if you can explain this to me," he motioned toward the necklace and their surroundings, "now's about the right time."

She stared at him in disbelief. For a moment she considered telling him everything about how her mom never left the necklace out of her sight, and how that morning she had seemed to have visions that she was now starting to doubt had been a dream. But instead she shook her head and said, "Daniel, I have no idea."

He squinted, as if trying to read her, and then shook his head. "Fine. So where are we?"

"At school," she said, but she wasn't so sure. "We just need to—"

"Allie…" a voice carried on the wind. A whisper, but one she knew all too well. Her mother's voice. "Allie…" it said again.

The images of that morning returned, of the dark tunnel and the horrible sense of being ripped away from her mother. Somehow this was all connected.

"Hello?" Allie said, spinning, eyes searching to pierce the fog. "Mom?"

"What are you talking about?" Daniel looked at her like she was crazy, but she held a finger to her lips to shush him as she listened.

"MOM!" she yelled out.

"They're going to hear you!" Daniel said, stepping toward her. "Quiet."

But Allie didn't respond, because she was focused on something that had appeared in the darkness, like the peak of a small mountain, or perhaps a dark tower, past the woods.

She motioned for Daniel to come close. "Do you see it?"

This time he didn't question her, but asked, "How'd it get here?"

"Or how did we get here?" she asked. "Wherever here is."

With a slight pulse of the blue glow from the shape in the distance, like a glimpse of a heartbeat, Allie heard the whisper once again as it said, "It's up to you now, Allie," and then it was gone, along with the fog. Allie stumbled backward and nearly fell in the mud, but Daniel caught her.

Daylight returned as if the sun had been eclipsed and was back to normal.

"You saw it?" she asked.

He nodded his head.

"You heard the voice, my mom?"

He nodded again, his eyelids showing a slight twitch of fright. For a moment, they stared at each other. If this was happening, then the images of that morning were most likely not a dream either. The rain began its pitter-patter again as it trickled through pine needles, and soon it was pounding them, pouring into the streams that threatened to cut them off from the school grounds visible beyond the trees.

"Come on," she said. "We can't stay here."

They ran back to the school, jumping the gate to avoid Chester and Vince. The first door they reached was to the library, and they darted in, happy to escape the torrential downpour. Allie shook herself dry, then watched Daniel as he looked down the nearby aisles of books to make sure they were alone. His hands were shaking, whether from the chill of rain or the craziness of what had just happened, Allie could only imagine.

"So?" he said as he turned his gaze to her and then her necklace. "What was that about?"

It was then that Allie realized she was shaking too. She held the necklace so she could inspect it, but it

6

NEW EDUCATION

Allie and Daniel stood with Gabe in Principal Eisner's office. Allie's head was spinning, her mind reeling with the news that Principal Eisner had just told her—that her mom was missing.

"But no, I—I just Skyped with her like, two weeks ago."

"And when did you find the necklace?" Principal Eisner said. "Or rather, when did it find you?"

"What's that have to do with my mom missing, and how do you know this?" She looked at them, flabbergasted and annoyed. "This isn't funny." She stood to go, but the librarian stepped in front of her.

"Please, listen," he said. "For the sake of your mother."

Allie paused. Of course she couldn't argue with that, if indeed there was some truth to what they were saying. None of it made logical sense, but if she were to accept the images from that morning or what had just happened in the woods, if all that had really happened, then she had better at least hear them out.

"Allie," Principal Eisner said, her voice stern. "Please sit." Allie obliged and Principal Eisner assessed her with great, caring eyes. "The necklace. When?"

Allie rubbed the stone of her necklace uneasily. "Early this morning."

Principal Eisner and the librarian shared a worried look. "Then there still may be a chance, at least."

"A chance?"

"If you act soon, my dear. Your mom is in some sort of danger, that's all we know. She wouldn't have passed on the necklace unless something was wrong, and the necklace wouldn't have followed the blood line unless you were ready." Principal Eisner took a moment, staring at the necklace, and then shook her head as if waking from a spell. "It's just so hard to believe it chose one so young."

"Brooke was much younger when it chose her," Gabe chimed in.

Principal Eisner nodded slowly. "Yes, but Samyaza was a mere shadow in the corner in those days. This is a different time, Gabriel."

Allie suddenly stood, knocking back her chair. "Will somebody please tell me what exactly is happening?"

Principal Eisner sighed, as if she had wanted to avoid this. "That sign there, on the necklace. You wear the seal of King Solomon."

"The Star of David," Daniel said. "We got that."

"No, not just that. I mean the actual stone that came from his ring. Now it belongs to you."

"So?" Allie said, dismissive of what seemed to be yet another history lesson.

Principal Eisner raised her brow at this, but Gabe put a hand on her shoulder.

"Legends say he controlled angels and demons with his ring," Gabe said. "This exact stone."

"It belonged to your mother's father before her," Principal Eisner continued. "And who knows how many generations before that."

"And it does some kind of magic or something?" Allie asked. "It showed me where my mom was?"

Gabe nodded. "Not exactly magic, but yes. It answers to a higher power."

Allie took a moment to process this. She had seen something out there, and heard her mom's voice. And there had been the vision that morning, but... magic? No way. But what then? A hallucination? An undigested piece of pizza dipped in rancid ranch sauce that was causing her to imagine everything?

"I don't know what you're talking about. And I don't have to sit here listening to this ridiculous—"

"Allie," Principal Eisner said. "You have a responsibility now."

Gabe smiled, warmly. "You are a Bringer of Light."

For a moment, Allie considered everything they were saying. Perhaps she could really be some fighter against evil. Could there actually be angels and demons? A ring with some kind of magic? All of those days with her brother and his role-playing games, and now these two were trying to tell her some of that was real. She wasn't some kid that could be manipulated, she was smart enough to know reality from make-believe.

Allie laughed—what other response was there? "I'm not some Bringer of Light or whatever else you want to tell me I am. I'm a teenage girl. Or... will be, very soon."

She spun on her heels and stomped out of the office, closely followed by Daniel, who up to then still hadn't said a word. She wasn't going to sit around wasting her time and listening to these lunatics. There had to be a better explanation.

The rain was starting to come down harder as Allie and Daniel walked home. For some reason, forty-five minutes east in her old city, the rain had not been so annoying, so incessant. Neither of them said a thing until they reached their apartment complex, where Daniel turned on her, soaked.

"Well," Daniel said. "Today was crazy, but I'm with you, whatever happens."

"Yeah?" Allie asked.

"That's what friends do, stick together. So, of course."

She hesitated, then smiled. "Yeah, I suppose we are. Friends."

He looked up hesitantly, then held out his fist for a fist-bump. She hesitantly pounded back with a smile.

He turned to go home. "Have a good night, Allie."

With a wave of his hand, he went into his apartment that, Allie was surprised to learn, was only three down from hers. She turned to the big brown building she called home, but stood there, listening to the pitter-patter of raindrops on the cement and smelling the fresh scent of rain. The water cleansed her spirit, reminding her of camping trips her family used to take on Mt. Rainier.

She had no idea how the day turned out to be so weird. Highs, lows, and so many crazy moments. When she moved to this town she had no idea what was to come, but hadn't expected to be kicking balls at people, running through woodlands in the rain, and especially not being told she was in charge of rescuing her mom. No, she decided. It couldn't be true, none of what had happened in the woods could have been real, and her principal was delusional. That was the only realistic explanation. Was Daniel in on some prank? She couldn't believe that, but had no idea what to think anymore. Her dad would know, and she would make sure to figure this out before she lost her mind, if it wasn't already too late.

Something in the sky caught her eye and she looked up to see, way in the distance above, an eagle soaring, barely visible among the grey clouds. It let out a mighty screech, sending shivers down her spine.

A car drove by with a hiss of rubber spraying water, and then stopped nearby.

"Allie, where were you?" her dad said as he exited the car. I wanted to surprise you and pick you up."

Allie continued to stand in the rain, letting it wash her clean of the day.

"Come on, dear," her dad said. "Let's get you dry."

Snapping out of it, she ran over to him and, under the shelter of his umbrella, went indoors. At first, she considered telling him everything, about what the Principal had told her, but she couldn't. Somehow, voicing it would make it real, and she wasn't willing to accept that yet. A haze filled her thoughts like a dream, settling in her gut with a darkness that made her want nothing more than to curl up in a ball and cry.

She made it through dinner, but then slid into bed with a picture from a drawer in her nightstand. It was a picture of her mom and dad, holding each other and smiling. Her mom wore the Army fatigues, a duffle bag thrown over her shoulder, and a rose in her left breast pocket. It had been taken at the airport the day she deployed.

And that silver chain hung around her mom's neck. The necklace.

Perhaps Allie's was a fake and everyone was wrong? She caressed the stone, then tapped it with her fingernail.

A knock on the door and her dad entered with a full laundry basket. Allie tucked the necklace beside her leg.

"You have anything you want washed?" He smiled, but she could tell something was off.

She shook her head. As for the necklace and her mom, it was best to leave him out of it. She wanted to be alone, but wasn't sure how to tell him.

"Honey...."

"Dad, not now, okay?" she said. "It's just, everything's been too crazy lately."

"You have to know, I can't keep it in."

She looked up at him, surprised to see the determination in his eyes. Was he going to start talking to her about Bringers of Light and King Solomon, too? Did he know about all this after all?

He sat beside her, placing the laundry basket on the floor. "I received a message from your mom's command."

She hated the hesitation in his voice. She knew the answer before she asked, "And?"

Her dad breathed deep. "They haven't heard from her for a couple days now, and, well, that's not normal."

So her mom was missing? Allie couldn't accept it. "Dad.... Do you know where she is? Do you know what happened?"

He held her gaze, his eyes sad and helpless. No, he didn't know any more than she did—less probably.

"She'll be back soon," Allie said, as much to herself as to him.

"I hope so honey, but we won't be able to Skype with her tonight, so I wanted to make sure you understood." He kissed her on the forehead. "No laundry then, kiddo?"

Allie shook her head.

"I can't do this alone." He heaved up the laundry and closed the door behind him, leaving her to wonder what he'd meant by that.

When Allie got up to use the bathroom later that night she heard a sniffling sound from her dad's room. She stopped and peered in through the crack of his door. The computer screen cast a soft glow on his face, reflecting the tears in his eyes. He wiped his arm across his face and clicked off the computer screen. Even in the darkness, she could tell his face was in the palms of his hands, his shoulders shaking.

She turned and rushed to the bathroom, closing the door gently so her dad wouldn't hear it and know she was up.

Why was he crying? No way—the rough man she knew to be her dad never cried. He was too strong for that. But she had seen his tears, they had been real.

She turned on the cold water and splashed her face. If her mom's command hadn't heard from her in a few days that was one thing, but what if her mom were in some real trouble? What if she were…. Allie couldn't bring herself to think it, it was too horrible. Worst of all, what if Allie really did have the key to saving her mom, but was wasting time debating the reality of it?

Allie gripped the edges of the porcelain sink until her fingers hurt, sure she was going to tear it right off. No, she told herself, her mom had to be alive. This not knowing had to stop, and whether the Bringer of Light mumbo-jumbo was real or not, Allie had to act. Even if that meant believing in magic, believing in a reality that went against everything she had known to be true for her whole life. Her mom would come back, and Allie was going to figure out what role she played in making sure of that.

7

A DOOR

The next day at school was going well enough, except that Allie couldn't focus on a single thing her teachers said. She couldn't stop thinking of her mom's voice whispering to her from that shape she had seen through the fog, or the images of the dark tunnel she had seen when she found the necklace.

Math class was so bad Allie had to get a bathroom pass just to escape and clear her head. She ducked down the hallway, avoiding Principal Eisner's office because more of that talk right now would overwhelm her.

She needed to breathe and be alone, but noticed several kids dressed in black looking at her. They weren't returning her forced smile. After another turn she found the bathrooms, but just as she was about to enter she heard a low humming nearby. It was too odd not to investigate, so she followed the sound to a door, opened the door, and found herself at the top of a descending staircase. After ensuring that no one was watching, she began the descent.

With each step, the humming grew louder. Soon it became more of a chant. She reached the final stair and retracted her hand from the cold wall. The noise came from a hallway to her left. Two layers of curtains covered a red door. The door, chipped from years of neglect, had been left slightly ajar.

Candlelight flickered through the crack in the door. When Allie leaned in, she saw a room full of cloaked figures, none of their faces visible. Some sort of circle pattern covered the floor where they stood. They each held out their left forearms, waiting for a particularly tall hooded character in the middle who paused at each one with a special chant. With each pause, the darkness increased and the flames in the candles seemed to wither.

Realizing she'd been holding her breath, Allie slowly exhaled.

A pair of eyes found her, then the rest of the hooded figures turned.

"Grab her!" one yelled.

Allie fled back into the hallway, her legs shaking. She collapsed, but picked herself up at the base of the stairs and climbed. A hand clawed the back of her shirt. They had her hair. She screamed and the grip loosened, but then someone had her arm. She pushed and then pulled, but fingernails dug into her skin as she broke free.

The yellowish lighting of the hallway was dull, but

that moment filled her with hope of escape. She made it and closed the door behind her, but there was no way to fasten it. Desperately she threw herself through the nearest door she could find. Trapped in darkness, she fumbled with the door to lock it. She collapsed to the floor and pulled her knees to her chest. Yelling sounded outside, and then the pounding of fists on the wooden door. She held her necklace tight.

A song sounded from somewhere. Her phone!

She pulled it from her pocket and pressed accept as the closet door flew open.

"Help!" she shouted into the phone, and then a bright light took her. Allie cringed, holding the phone to her ear and waiting for the hooded people to take her.

No one came. When she opened her eyes, she saw the mossy green of the forest beneath her. She raised her eyes and saw she was in the woods, with Daniel standing in front of her. He looked at her with wide eyes. He held his phone to his ear, his hand trembling.

"How did you...?" He looked around, trying to figure something out.

She stared at him, stunned.

"I wanted to check these woods again," he said. "See if I could find anything. Then I thought I better see if you wanted to join me, and.... Are you okay?"

She jumped up and threw her arms around him, nearly sobbing and very relieved to be with him, regardless of how she had gotten here.

A crack of a tree branch pulled Allie to her senses. She pulled back from Daniel, eyes searching the woods.

"I think we need to go see Principal Eisner," she said.

They ran back to the school and it wasn't long before they found the woman. They led her to the door Allie had taken down to the weird room, but when they reached the spot, there were no stairs, only another broom closet. Allie checked the door she had hidden in and, sure enough, it too was a broom closet.

Allie turned in exasperation to Principal Eisner. "I don't get it. They were right there."

Principal Eisner's eyes darted up and down the hall, then she leaned in and said, "This is worse than I thought. Are you ready to listen?"

Allie nodded.

"Good, come with me."

They made their way to the library, where Gabe stood waiting. He held in his hands a massive book with the title "History of the Bringers of Light."

They sat around a table and, after briefly explaining everything to Gabe, he nodded, his expression solemn.

"But the door," Allie protested, "How...?"

"You may soon learn that doors don't always lead to the same place," Principal Eisner said. "You are too young, but maybe soon you will begin your training and you will enter such a door. It is unfortunate that the first door you entered was one of theirs."

"But why do they need this door?" Daniel asked.

"The doors open from cities throughout the world,

and often lead to the training facilities on our end, but the Dark Ones use these doors for other purposes."

"So they could show up anywhere?" Allie asked. "Cult followers of some dark power, out to get us, and they're everywhere?"

"In theory, yes. The ones you must have seen, they most likely don't all reside here. But they must have one on the inside, a teacher, or perhaps a student, or the door could never have been opened. We will have to keep a better eye out for these Strayers."

For a moment, they sat there in silence. Allie eyed the floor as she tried to process all of this. Finally, she looked up and made eye contact with first Principal Eisner and then Gabe.

"What do they want?" Allie said, feeling her hands begin to sweat and clam up.

"The Strayers have been after the necklace," Gabe said. "But there is something larger at stake here. What your mom went to Kyrgyzstan for in the first place." He opened the book he held in his hands. Turning the page, he stopped at a detailed drawing of a warrior in glowing armor, his head haloed in gold like a saint. "There are those of us on the good side, the Bringers of Light, and then…."

Principal Eisner cut in, "There is a dark force at play, one the Strayers follow. One they call Samyaza."

"These tired eyes have lingered long over the old books," Gabe said. "The pattern written is clear. When the Ring of Andaleeb is united, formed as one, the Tenth Worthy will stand against the dark forces with the shield of faith, the helmet of salvation, and the sword of the spirit."

"The ring of what?" Daniel interrupted.

"It is another word for the ring of Solomon. King Solomon."

"And what does that have to do with us?" Allie asked.

"The Tenth Worthy is destined to stop the fallen one, Samyaza, and keep light in the world." Gabe opened the book to a page of a winged shadow with eyes of fire. "Unless Samyaza gets to these items first, as he hopes to do. If indeed he's able to wield them this time."

"This time?" Allie said, her head spinning.

"He wasn't always bad, he wasn't always called the Dark One, or Samyaza. He was once like us, a Guardian. But he envied the Bringers of Light, and his heart began to rot as his lust for power grew. He meant to make the ring his own. He took what had not chosen him, and was corrupted in the process. He was banished, turned into a mere shadow, and almost ceased to exist. But he stood his ground and called on darker forces to aid him. If he gets the ring now, he will be an evil not easily defeated, as his power is great."

Allie stared at them, baffled. They were talking like her brother had when playing his RPG games, only these people were much older than him, and they appeared to be quite serious.

"I was once one of you," Principal Eisner said. "I once carried a symbol like your own. The Bringers of

Light. Now we are but Guardians. There are many of us, possibly more in this very school. Bringers of Light, those fighting and searching, and Guardians, the ones that support. But there is one that is chosen, one that must bring an end to Samyaza and the dark forces he represents. That one is the Tenth Worthy."

"And that one is my mom?" Allie asked.

Gabe shook his head and pointed to the necklace. "We had thought so."

"But not anymore?"

Principal Eisner shook her head. "As I said in my office, Allie, the necklace chose you. Are you ready to accept this?"

"And if I'm not, what then?"

"Then no one can save your mother."

Allie's hand instinctively gripped her necklace. "But you said there are others, the Guardians. Right? Can't one of them—"

Principal Eisner waved her question off. "The Guardians support the Bringers of Light. Only one Bringer of Light, the so-called Tenth Worthy, the one with that stone, can stand up to Samyaza when he comes out of the depths." She leaned forward and put her hand on Allie's shoulder. "Your mother depends on you."

"I...." Allie searched for a response. "I'm going to need time to think."

Allie stood and walked out of the library and soon found herself breaking into a run. So it was all real? It was more insane than she could have ever imagined, yet somehow, it was starting to feel real. That was the scariest part—that somehow she believed all of this. She turned a corner and slammed right into someone. The collision threw her back onto her rear, and for a moment she had to clear her head before she saw it was the girl from earlier, Paulette. Then Allie noticed a sparkle from down the hall and reached for her neck— the necklace had been knocked free by the collision.

As Allie locked eyes with Paulette, Daniel came jogging up.

Paulette stood, brushing herself off. "Allie, hey. And...?"

"Daniel," he said.

"Yeah, gottcha." Paulette turned and spotted the necklace. She reached for it. "Looks like you dropped something."

"Thanks," Allie said as she thrust herself in Paulette's way and pocketed the necklace.

"You feeling okay?"

Allie and Daniel shared a look, not knowing what to say to that.

"Well," Paulette continued, "listen, me and some of the girls, well, we're thinking of getting together for soccer practice after school. What'ya say?"

Allie couldn't believe it when she answered with a "No, no thank you. Not today."

That afternoon, Principal Eisner gave Allie and Daniel a ride home from school. Principal Eisner explained that she didn't want to risk any more trouble with the Strayers. She told Allie how she had worked with Gabe to look out for them after the incident, but so far had not identified any particular kids that could be Strayers, and Chester and Vince seemed to have ditched their classes.

Principal Eisner opened the door for them to exit, with a glance around. Her smile wrinkle creased down in worry. "Remember, if you need a ride tomorrow, let me know. And don't forget, Allie, you have it inside you, the strength to win over this thing." In response to Allie's look of doubt, she said, "You just have to have faith." With a wink, she returned to her car.

"But…" Allie tried to protest.

"You hold tight, the necklace will reveal the path when you are ready."

Daniel walked Allie to her door as the car drove off. He paused and, without a word, turned to go.

Allie reached out. "Don't leave."

He paused and then turned to her, unsure.

"She was deployed, my mom, for part of some developmental assessment in the Middle East, or Central Asia, my dad tells me, and…. Maybe all this craziness is part of that? Maybe it's true?"

"Like the librarian said?"

The necklace sparkled around Allie's neck. Allie's eyes lowered to it. "If this is really happening, I'll need you here, with me."

He reached and their hands touched. "I promise."

Allie stared at him, feeling the sidewalk heave from side to side. The air tasted stale and her lungs struggled for breath. She hadn't asked for any of this, but she had heard her mom calling out to her. She would have to answer.

Daniel stared into her eyes. "If you're in some kinda trouble, of course I'm going to help you. That's what friends do."

"Thank you," she said. Cars whizzed by and a little bird flew nearby and landed on a tree branch that reached out across the sidewalk, and seemed to watch them.

"But, just to get this straight," Daniel said, his brow furrowed. "There's this ancient evil, some sort of demon or fallen angel or something called Samyaza, and he has a group of followers, called the Strayers, and they go around doing his bidding in an attempt to bring him back to power?"

"That's about the gist of what I got from all that."

"And now you are somehow involved, because your mom is missing?"

Allie swallowed, her throat dry, and she slowed her pace to keep herself from falling.

Daniel walked beside her for a few moments in silence, but then he asked, "Why can't they just call the cops?"

At first, she thought about this, but then couldn't help but laugh. "What would they say? Hey, these people believe in some sort of demon and worship it or something, arrest them."

"Oh," Daniel smiled at the silliness of that idea. "Right, freedom of religion and all that?"

"And freedom to not sound crazy, I guess."

Daniel thought about it for a moment and then said, "Well, it looks like we got our work cut out for us. Have a good night, Allie."

"Good night."

She turned and walked back to her apartment, trying to make sense of it all. Just yesterday she thought all this stuff was the creation of imaginative nerds, like her brother or like she had been for a while. Now, she almost believed it could be true. She could even start to believe she had some role to play in saving her mom.

8

THE WOODS

Allie waited expectantly on the couch, rocking back and forth, the necklace held between her hands. She figured this was a talk better had between her and her dad. What would her dad do when he found out? She imagined him jumping up and down for joy, like a child on Christmas morning. And then what? Somehow, he would know what to do. She was sure of it.

Her dad came home later than usual, his eyes heavy and focused on the ground before him. In the entry-way, he sighed and pulled out his phone, stared at it longingly, then looked up to Allie with a half-smile.

She ran to him, the news exploding from her mouth. "I found her!"

"What?" He took a step back, colliding with the open door.

Ian came in behind him and paused at the awkwardness, eyes shifting between the two.

"Allie?" her dad said.

"I know where Mom is, or, I know how to get there anyway, you see—"

"You feeling alright, pipsqueak?" Ian said.

Allie rolled her eyes at him. "I mean, I didn't see her, but her necklace took me there, to where I'm sure she is."

"Her necklace?" her dad said. "How would you have that?"

"And there were trees surrounded by fog," Allie motioned around, as if the trees were still there. "And this place in the distance, and—"

"Wow," Ian said, holding up both hands in mock surrender. "She's lost it." He closed the door and leaned against it, watching for their dad's response. "She finally lost it."

Her dad stood staring at Allie, his breathing loud and his eyes unfocused. Finally, he shook his head and blinked hard. "Honey, this isn't funny. Junior High can be tough, I get it. And with all this going on…. Listen, we went out to Ft. Lewis today, trying to get an answer, but there aren't any answers, okay?"

She held her hands together, pleading for him to listen to her. "I'm telling you—"

"I'm sorry. Why don't you get some rest?"

"Dad, wait!" She followed him as he moved to his room. "I'm telling you the truth!"

Her dad stopped in his doorway and turned, shaking his head. "Let's just pretend that this isn't one of your games, that you haven't reverted back to your ways when you were eight or nine, and that for some reason you believe this. Well, you're wrong. What you're saying is impossible."

"It's the truth!"

"No, it isn't." He closed the door.

She reached for the doorknob, then paused, hand extended. She slowly let it fall, along with her hopes. She turned to Ian, desperate, but he chuckled as he walked past her to the kitchen. How could they not take her seriously? She was twelve now! She stomped into her room and slammed the door. Sure, her mom could be a real pain sometimes, but at least *she* never treated her like a child.

How could Allie convince her dad to believe her? Their family depended on it. The love of his life was at stake and he closed the door in Allie's face! She was going to have to find some way to convince him, some way to show she was telling the truth. After all, she couldn't be expected to save her mom, whatever that entailed. That was a job for a dad. She considered trying to get Ian to help her. If she could convince him…. But no, she knew the futility in that. The last time he had sided with her on anything was when they had both wanted to drive to Aunt Betty's for Thanksgiving, and that was only because Aunt Betty had a next-door neighbor whose daughter Ian thought was cute.

No, he would be no help.

She moved to the side of her bed and threw off the sheets with a scream. She fell to the mattress with her eyes stinging. The rain splattered against her window, sending rivers of water down the glass. The mood of it all, the dimming night sky and the pounding rain, made everything worse. She couldn't do this alone, she was sure of that. Daniel said he would help, but two twelve-year-olds? No matter how grown-up she thought she was, she knew the realities of that idea. She still had her ten-o-clock curfew. Traveling to weird, foggy places was surely out of the question.

It wasn't dark outside, but she lay in bed, hoping to fall asleep. She needed to clear her head, but she couldn't stop trying to piece everything together. Her brain hurt. She closed her eyes and rolled into a fetal position.

A dream started to form, one of her on an airplane, reclining in the seat and eating peanuts (though she had never been on a plane). The smell of lasagna baking pulled her out of it. The last time her dad had made lasagna he'd had a bad fight with her mom, so Allie imagined he was feeling guilty this time for not believing her about the necklace. She wasn't going to be able to sleep with that delicious scent filling the apartment, so she lay there staring at the darkness outside.

Water continued to cascade against the outside of Allie's bedroom window. Somehow, the weather in Hartsville hadn't felt so invasive. She tossed and turned in her twin bed, wishing the rain would stop so she could fade away to the happiness of her dreams. Generally, her dreams were pleasant, and she still remembered the dream of flying over Mt. Rainier, surrounded by friends.

Sixth grade had been bearable, nothing like seventh grade so far. Having only gone to Silver Road Elementary School for one year, Allie hadn't become too attached but had made several friends, at first. On her birthday, they had come over for pizza and cake, and they had even invited her to go over to their houses more than once. Not that she had ever enjoyed playing with dolls or gossiping about boys. A day of soccer won out every time as far as she was concerned.

When Ian was younger, he would even kick a ball with her occasionally. Her friends had teased her and called her a tomboy, but at least she had friends back then. At her good-bye party, seven girls had come over and played in the backyard, girls that had laughed at her only a week earlier, thanks to Crystal… who hadn't bothered to show. At the end, they all hugged as if it would be the last they ever saw of each other. Perhaps it had been and, if so, now what? All she had was a brother who had stopped playing with her as he grew older, a missing mom, and now a dad that didn't even trust her.

Well, she had Daniel.

She threw her feet over the edge of the bed and onto the beige carpet. Rummaging through her closet, she found her fluffy green jacket and threw it on, then grabbed the yellow rain boots with red eagle patterns, on her way to the door.

"Hey, squirt." Ian stood in the hallway, apparently waiting for the bathroom—his dance wouldn't have made sense otherwise. He had gotten all dressed up in his pea coat with gold buttons. As if that wasn't bad enough, he also wore a checkered brown scarf wrapped around his thick neck to make him look like he was bundled up to enter a blizzard. Blizzards didn't hit Washington in September too often, but he wanted to study music and painting and called his style 'artistic expression.' Ridiculous.

"Got a date?" she said sarcastically. She knew he never had dates.

"Where you think you're going?"

"Out."

"Is that Allie?" her Dad's voice called from behind the bathroom door. "Tell her dinner will be ready soon."

"Looks like she's all ready for the rain," Ian said, still blocking her path. "Maybe it's *you* who has a date? With your new friend in the apartment nearby?"

"Shut up," she said, then called out to her dad, "I need to clear my head, maybe explore our new apartments. Just for a bit, before dinner?"

"We need to talk dear," he said. "And besides, it's all wet out there."

"Please?"

"Ian, why don't you go with her?"

"Dad, come on," Allie said. "I'm not some little kid anymore."

"Yeah Dad, she's human now, not a baby goat anymore." Ian snickered. He always thought the same old jokes hilarious. "Besides, I kinda have to use the bathroom, so if you could hurry up, that'd be amazing."

"Ack, all right," her dad said. "Go have fun, but stay out of trouble and come back in twenty minutes, okay?"

"Promise, Dad," Allie shouted as she dodged under Ian's arm and ran into the chilly evening air. She paused at the doorway, surprised at the amount of rain pounding the sidewalk. She hated to be seen using an umbrella, but she grabbed the black one by the door and decided to suck it up. As long as she wasn't trapped in that apartment anymore, where the walls echoed her negative thoughts and no one believed in her.

She looked down the gloomy streets covered in increasingly large puddles. There had to be something special about this place, anything to distract her. But she saw nothing, only normal chestnut-brown two-story apartment buildings in the middle of nowhere. She pulled the necklace from under her shirt and caressed the silver star for a moment, wondering if it had all really happened. Could stress cause such delusions?

Incessant rain met her umbrella in a rhythmic taunt as if saying, 'Figure it out, Allie.' Amidst the sheets of rain, an opening appeared between the brown buildings. Hemlock trees rose up on each side of an overgrown path, giving it the look of a welcoming entrance to a kingdom in the forest. She imagined a sheltered paradise of star-shaped cookies hanging from the trees and dancing fairies—a latent memory of her three years of attending a hippie school on Whidbey Island. They had all lived there, together, a whole family, without a single deployment. One time she had spotted the end of a rainbow in the backyard of their two-story farmhouse and had been ecstatic. Ian helped her chase it down, but the rainbow had faded before they reached its end. That was before Ian became too busy for her. She still remembered the days running through the woods on the other side of that field, building forts and hunting mice.

These woods in Portsdale enticed her with the potential of reliving the past. She had her rain boots after all, so why not have an adventure? Using her umbrella to push aside branches, Allie took her first cautious step into the woods.

It was a different world. A canopy of the trees blocked nearly every drop of rain from reaching the ground. Rays of light shone through an opening in the north where the grey clouds parted. Orange and yellow rays of sunset sifted through shadowed wings, perhaps an eagle flying high above the branches. Allie was in heaven, an upside-down bed of green, covered in tiny rainbows where the sunlight met the moist air. It was a treasure all for her. No fairies or cookies, no end to the tiny rainbows, but the scent of fresh Washington State air and the beauty inspired a momentary sense of belonging.

She meandered along the path, glancing up occasionally in hopes of seeing the eagle perch on one of the tall evergreens. Huckleberry bushes boasted their red berries and she considered snacking, but contemplated her chance of being wrong, the berries possibly poisonous. Her cousins had always picked the berries and her aunt would even make pies out of them, delicious pies and great memories. But for now, Allie would wait for her dad's lasagna.

Maybe this Eden could be her fortress from the world? She closed her eyes and breathed in deep, spreading her arms as if to hug the forest. A swoosh sounded to her left and she spun, eyes open. Perched on a low hanging branch a great eagle stared at her, its damp feathers glistening. It was the most beautiful thing she had ever seen. The eagle was so close that she could see her reflection in its eyes. She took a step and reached her hand out, as if to touch it.

The illusion of solitude was ripped apart by a recurring thump nearby. Allie's eyes searched for the source, and when she turned her head back, the eagle was gone. Still in a sense of wonder at what had happened but annoyed at the thumping for ruining it, she set out to discover what caused the noise.

Following a narrow trail, she found herself at the edge of a stream. Not far on the other side, she saw a shape among the trees, and then the shape, which she realized must have been a person, noticed her. Why was she here in the first place, she wondered, and wanted to be home, curled up in bed.

She jumped up and sprinted toward the opening she had come through. The rain appeared in front of her and the ground took on its sleek, muddy form, which she knew meant safety. There it is, the opening and the curtains of rain. She could hear the splattering of water on dirt. Almost there.

"Allie!" she heard a voice call from behind, but as she turned to see who it was, her feet slipped in the mud. Her body lunged forward with no control. A hand attempted to save her, but was too late. Mud splashed like the waters of a still pond when a large pebble is dropped in its midst. A sharp pain hit her lungs and she tried to yell, but she could not.

She lay on her back, rain falling on her face and mud beneath her. A round face with red cheeks and startled brown eyes appeared in front of her. Daniel.

"You okay?" he said.

She groaned, more out of embarrassment than pain.

"You gotta be more careful." He reached down to offer assistance.

She looked up at his concerned face and felt her blood rushing into her cheeks. Determined to go back in time and erase everything that happened, Allie picked herself up with the help of her umbrella.

"What're you doing out here, anyway?" she asked.

He shrugged and looked around. Only then did she notice a soccer ball in his hands. "I needed to clear my head, and," he held up the soccer ball, "I thought I'd give it a try, since you seem to love it so much."

In spite of now being in pain and covered in mud, she smiled at him. She groaned. "My dad's gonna kill me."

"Come on," Daniel said as he walked past her. "We can go to my place for a bit to lie low."

She laughed. "Thanks."

THE CHASE

Allie followed Daniel into a small bedroom, tiptoeing past his dad. The man seemed to be fast asleep on the couch, so they were careful not to wake him. A blue comforter lay tossed across the bed and video games were scattered across the floor.

"Some place you have here," she said.

"I'm sure." He smirked. "Whatever, I'm a guy. I don't have to be clean."

"Huh," was all she could say to that.

"So, no luck with your dad then?" he asked.

Allie's sour mood returned. "I thought if I just told him...."

Daniel leaned against his television stand and Allie noticed something behind him.

"Is that a present?" she asked.

He turned and sure enough, he picked up a small package in blue wrapping paper.

"What is it?" she asked.

"Oh, yeah, this. Just a present from Chris." At her quizzical look he added, "My friend from P.E. class."

She stared at him. "It was your birthday?"

He blushed. "Day before yesterday. I would've invited you, but...."

"But you didn't know me."

"Exactly."

From the wrapping paper he pulled a book, "Aesop's Fables."

"Besides," he said. "I always get these weird presents I have to pretend to like."

"I remember this book." She reached out and he tossed it over. She started flipping through the pages. "Yeah, it's a classic."

"Yeah?"

"Back in my old school, we read all about that sort of stuff, it was some hippy school, teaching us about religions and mythologies from around the world and whatnot."

"Now that sounds cool."

"I only went there a couple of years. My mom wasn't around much then
either."

They shared a somber moment, but it was interrupted by a crash from the other room. Daniel's eyes flared and he glanced around, then to the window. The rain had stopped.

"Come on, I'll show you something." He opened the window and started climbing out.

"Are you serious?" Allie said, then heard a muffled yelling from the other room.

"I don't wanna stay here. Are you going home, or can you come with me?"

She followed him, almost falling in the darkness, but Daniel caught her.

They kneeled below the window, still touching, when Daniel said, "That's how he gets, ever since..." and then the door creaked from inside.

"What the hell?" they heard Daniel's dad yell. "Boy!"

Daniel motioned for Allie to be silent. They crouch-walked past the window and took off running back to the woods.

They reached the entry point from before and Daniel held back the tree branches for her to enter.

"Back in there?" she asked. He nodded, stern, and she figured it was better than going home again.

The moon lit the path now, and soon they found themselves past the stream and in a little clearing.

"This is where I come," Daniel said. "When I need to be alone, or to think."

The clearing glistened with the fresh rain, silver leaves rustling in the breeze. Allie wrapped her arms around herself, realizing how cold she was. She hadn't fully dried from earlier. She was about to say they should head back when Daniel said, "She died."

"What?" Allie said.

"My mom, a couple of years back. My dad's been like this ever since. I mean, I can't blame him." Daniel kicked a tree. "That's why I need this place."

"I'm so sorry," Allie said.

He stepped toward her and reached out. She wasn't sure if he was going to brush her cheek with his hand or what he was going to do. Her breath caught as his hand went to her necklace. He held it up so he could see the blue stone in the moonlight.

With a release of the stone, his eyes rose to meet hers and he said, "Don't let your dad get like that."

"It was real, right? We were there, in the fog, with the trees?"

"We have to figure out how to get back." He looked into the trees, as if an answer lay just beyond the branches. "Whatever it takes, it's up to us now."

"My dad thinks I'm nuts."

"He might be right. But if you are, so am I."

Allie reached up and put her hand on Daniel's. "Thanks."

He looked into her eyes for a moment before pulling back awkwardly. "So how do we make it happen?"

"I don't know." She stared at the necklace, considering. But she couldn't focus. "What about your mom.... What happened?"

He looked away.

"Sorry," she said. "You don't have to tell me."

"No, I want to." He took a moment, then closed his eyes as he said, "A drunk driver."

"I.... That's horrible."

"But, Allie...." He made eye contact again, and she could tell he was trying to look strong, to be there for her. "Me and my dad, we'll be okay, eventually. For now, let's get that necklace glowing. We're gonna get your mom back."

She took his hand and forced a smile.

"So what do you suppose we try first?" he asked.

Again, she held out the necklace. A glimmer of light hit the silver to turn the stone a brilliant blue—nothing else.

"Well, before, how did it happen?" she asked. "Tell you what, I'll go over there and you call my name, then see if it brings me to you?"

"Ah, like with the phone. Might as well try everything."

And they did. First, they ran around in the trees, shouting for each other. Then they rubbed the necklace like a genie bottle, and Allie even tried dancing while holding the necklace up in the air. She climbed a tree and held it to the moonlight, but nothing. Her shoulders slumped and she looked back down through the tree branches, realizing the climb down may not be as easy as the climb up. Then she noticed something out of the corner of her eye – the eagle. Could it be the same one as before? When she looked again, it was gone. The necklace sparkled, and Allie climbed down.

Allie and Daniel found a dry spot under a tree and sat, each holding the necklace with their hands clasped around each other's. Their eyes met and a moment of embarrassment flashed across their faces. Allie scooted back and leaned against the tree as Daniel let his hands fall.

Allie stared sullenly at a wet pinecone nearby, images of her mom floating through her mind, just out of reach. "She took us camping once. I hadn't wanted to go, I never seemed to like it much. So my mom got us a cabin, for the girls, you know, and we stayed up late drinking hot chocolate and she told me all about her brothers and sisters, all kinds of crazy stories."

She looked up at Daniel, who put a hand on her shoulder.

"She even said there was this one time that she became a bird at night, soon after my grandfather's death, and she thought she could fly to heaven and find him."

Daniel laughed, then tried to hide his smile. "Your mom sounds really cool."

"She was. I mean, she is." Allie turned to Daniel with fright in her eyes.

"No Allie, don't even think it. She's gonna be fine, and we will find her. Something's got to work."

They had called it a night after attempting all conceivable options—more calling out, more holding the stone to the sky, and even praying—and Allie snuck into her room and had changed before her dad barged in to find her in bed with her eyes closed. She couldn't imagine how frustrated he was with her, considering everything that was happening. But when he sat down beside her and caressed her hair, all he said was, "We'll find her, don't worry." He kissed her on the forehead and left, while she continued to pretend to sleep. It hurt that her dad didn't believe her, but she probably wouldn't have believed her either, so she couldn't hold it against him. He was right though, they were going to find Allie's mom. Somehow.

The next day at school Allie had made up her mind to demand Principal Eisner and Gabe give her more information, and she would go talk to them right after history class. Through the windows of her classroom, she could see the black clouds forming outside and a thick rain pouring at a forty-five degree angle. She shuddered, glad to be inside. She glanced at Daniel in the seat nearby, and they shared a look of hopelessness.

Five minutes late, Ms. Aldridge entered the class. Allie liked the way the teacher flipped her hair to the left and wore thick glasses. Ms. Aldridge took a dry-erase marker and started drawing squiggly lines on the whiteboard.

"Today," the teacher started, "I thought we would talk about ethnic violence. Remember, contemporary issues are the history of tomorrow." She drew little mountains in her outline, oblivious to the lack of attention from the students. "Kyrgyzstan, with a coup and then intense ethnic violence, I want you all to write down that name, got it? This is a map of the country, and here," she turned on a slide projector. "Suleiman Mountain, or the mountain of King Solomon, some would say." She made direct eye-contact with Allie, who let out a yelp when she saw the picture in the slide. She looked at Daniel and he had seen it too – it was the same shape they had seen in the fog in the woods. They had seen Suleiman Mountain.

"In the city of Osh," Ms. Aldridge continued, "Southern Kyrgyzstan, some say he was even buried here."

They both leaned forward to take notes, hanging on her every word—probably the only two in class that seemed to care.

When class was finished, Allie and Daniel walked together into the auditorium, heads close, whispering in excitement.

"That was definitely the place," Daniel said. "So—"

Allie grabbed his arm. "We have to find Principal Eisner and Gabe, they'll know."

But something caught her eye. On the other side of the auditorium, Chester and Vince stood in the shadows, wearing cloaks. Chester nodded to her and grinned wickedly. The shadows around them seemed to dance, moving to reveal cloaked figures in the hallway. The Strayers. They filed into the auditorium, staring at Allie with eyes surrounded in black paint. Chester and Vince walked among them, also in black.

Allie stumbled as she took a step back. She looked over to see that Daniel hadn't noticed the impending danger.

The Strayers closed in.

Allie pulled his wrist.

"What the—"

But then he saw them coming and he was running with her. They ran faster now, trying to make their way to the principal's office, but she was hit by the sudden realization that it was in the other direction. Everything was backward as a low chant echoed from the walls, a fog of darkness closing in. Each turn brought her to a place she didn't recognize. Each hallway grew darker and longer. The footsteps from behind grew louder.

Sprinting around a corner, Allie saw a door. She flung it open and pulled Daniel in behind her. She closed the door and locked it, then turned to see brooms and mops, and shelves full of cleaning supplies.

"I've got to stop running into closets!" she hissed.

The sliver of light from the door, the only light in the room, hit Daniel's wide eyes. "We're trapped."

CRACK!

The noise came from the door as someone kicked it.

"Ouch," Daniel said, and Allie looked down to see she was still holding his wrist tightly.

"What do we do?" she said, releasing his arm to bang on the walls.

"How'm I supposed to know?"

"Think, Daniel!" she screamed. They stared at each other.

"Allie?" a girl's voice echoed faintly.

Allie jumped, searching. The voice hadn't come from the other side of the door, but somewhere else.

"Allie, is that you?" the voice said again.

"Hello?" Daniel said as he tapped the walls.

"It's me," the voice said, "Paulette. I can hear you through the wall, are you okay?"

"The walls?" Daniel said as he followed her voice.

He knocked and found a spot that seemed hollow. He turned and found a mop handle, picked it up, and slammed it into the wall. Sure enough, it made a hole in the plaster.

"Help me," he said, and started kicking and pulling at the plaster. Allie followed and was surprised to find a narrow corridor on the other side.

Allie stooped to crawl behind Daniel. The corridor was barely tall enough to allow them to crawl easily, but dust caked the walls and felt like dry snow on their fingertips.

"Can you hear me?" Paulette asked. "This way, keep coming."

They crawled and sneezed, the metallic smell filled Allie's nostrils and soon she began to feel like she was in a coffin, a long, narrow, dirty coffin. Daniel was ahead of her, she had to remind herself of that fact several times – she wasn't alone. She focused on her breathing. In, out. In, out. When she was sure she was going to lose it, her head slammed into something soft like a pillow. She looked up to see she had bumped her head right into Daniel's butt.

"What're you doing?" she said.

A loud crash came from behind and they heard the door burst open. Then lights were flickering through the corridor. The kids behind her must have been using their cell phones as flashlights.

"There's a vent covering here, but..." He tried kicking it. "Screws!"

"Hold on a sec," Paulette's voice came from the other side, and they heard a scratching noise.

"Wait," Allie whispered, pulling Daniel by the leg. "Can we trust her?"

"Do we have a choice right now?"

She realized he had a point, and moments later the vent was open and they were clambering out.

"Quick, put it back up," Daniel said. He helped Paulette hold it in place. She got one screw in with her keys as a screwdriver, but then it was too late. A foot sent the cover flying.

"Run!" Allie pulled Daniel to her right.

"No," Paulette said. "This way!"

Allie froze. She looked up to see a face appear through the vent, a boy with wild eyes and scraggly hair. She didn't have time to question Paulette, only to follow. Their legs ached as they ran, turning down hallways until Paulette jumped left to shove open a door. Allie and Daniel followed, finding themselves in a musty room.

"We can't wait here," Allie said. "They'll find us."

"Don't worry, I have an idea." Paulette took out her phone and shone it around the room until the light landed on a spherical object in the corner. She stepped closer and the faint glow of her cell revealed a chest-high globe. When Paulette reached out and caressed it, Allie was surprised to see no dust. Paulette spun the globe and then turned to Allie.

"You have that necklace?" she asked.

Allie hesitated. "What?"

"We don't have time." Paulette turned to the globe that still spun, increasing in speed. "Grab your necklace and come here."

Allie grabbed her necklace and stepped toward the globe. "How do you...?"

"In here!" a voice called from the hallway.

"You must grab the globe, now!" Paulette said.

Allie stepped closer and felt her head rolling, her eyes fading in and out of focus. She couldn't explain what was happening, but that was becoming the norm for her. She held her necklace tight, searching for Daniel in the darkness but not finding him. She called out to him and then felt his hand on her shoulder. She grabbed the spinning globe and everything stopped, frozen in a silent moment of utter darkness.

10

THE THRONE OF SOLOMON

A light shone, growing and pushing out slowly from Allie's chest. It moved to her hand, pulsating as it sent tingles of warmth through her body. With a crack as if the air were a whip against the earth, the light expanded as far as the eye could see and then was gone, leaving the natural light of day.

She stood atop a small hill behind the brick remains of a house, Daniel and Paulette at her side. They were in a sprawling city of brick buildings and trees surrounded by mountains and foothills. The sun shone bright, doing nothing against the cold chill of the air on her skin. Her hair danced in the wind and she felt Daniel's hand on her shoulder, but also jagged rocks beneath her. She looked over and saw him, his eyes wide and his bottom lip trembling.

"Come on," Paulette said as she ran past. "There's no time to waste."

Allie shrugged at Daniel and ran after her, eyes

wide with awe at the city. It was like nothing she had ever seen before. Houses of red brick with sheets of metal for roofs surrounded them, stuck together like thousands of toy blocks. They ran under arches and turned back once when they came upon a brown river, battered tires and unused chicken coups on its bank. Paulette ran, glancing around as if searching for something, while people in colorful garments walked past as if not seeing them.

"What..." Allie said between breaths, "are we... doing here?"

"We only have a bit of time," Paulette said. "Your necklace isn't powerful enough to hold the charge for longer than twenty minutes, I would guess."

Allie stopped and held her necklace, it was glowing again. "How do you know this?"

"You aren't the only one to ever have one." Paulette turned back and grabbed Allie, pulling her forward. "You just happen to have the most powerful one I've ever seen."

"I don't understand," Daniel said, finally catching up. Allie stared, dumbfounded at the thought that Paulette had known about her necklace all along. It was becoming clearer that somehow Paulette was involved.

"Neither do I, not fully," Paulette said, pointing at the chain around her own neck that led to some sort of stone beneath her shirt. "They all work differently and are connected in some way. But we have to learn to use them. Mine tells me where things are, and it says there's something here. Somewhere."

"Why didn't you tell me all this before?" Allie asked, hysterically. "I mean, if I'd known—"

"Save your breath. I had to be sure you were chosen."

"Chosen?"

Paulette paused to look down a side street, and then turned and played with her wavy hair. "Yes, just because you wear a symbol doesn't mean it answers to you. We know now, yours does. But until you learn to properly use it, the charges won't reach their full potential."

"So this thing can make me travel and stuff?" Allie asked as they started walking again.

Paulette shook her head. "Kinda, but it's not just that. It's like it takes you to another plane. We're here together, so we don't have a problem." She paused and pointed. "There."

Through the streets, they saw a massive rock extending from the earth. The greenery was sparse on the hill leading up to the rocks. Clouds streamed into the sky from its peak.

"Is that…?" Allie said.

"The Throne of Solomon." Paulette smiled and took off at a jog.

Allie stared in amazement. Paulette had done it, she had brought them back. She turned to Daniel. "We need to find out as much as we can from her, if we're going to find my mom."

They followed in a jog, two out-of-place kids running through the streets. Daniel turned a corner and nearly collided with an old woman in a zig-zag patterned blue dress, washing her feet by the side of the road.

"Excuse us," Allie said, shooting Daniel a look of caution.

But the woman didn't even look up. Daniel leaned in close and waved his hand before her. Nothing.

"She doesn't look blind."

"Maybe it's that different plane thing Paulette mentioned?"

They continued on and soon reached the base of the rocks and Allie turned to look back the way they'd come. It was an expansive city, with brown and white hills in the distance and patches of trees between the many houses. Sunlight covered the city as if reflected from a rippling lake, sparkling like the entire city was blanketed in a swathe of gold.

"Where'd Paulette go?" Daniel asked as he took the last step to join Allie. He turned to the view and stood with his arms on his hips, his chest heaving. "Wow."

"I don't know," Allie said.

Daniel wiped a light sweat from his brow. He looked up at the rock to where a red flag with a bit of yellow in the middle flew in the wind. "This is definitely Kyrgyzstan, like she said in history class."

"Solomon's Throne." Allie looked up at five peaks of limestone. She could almost see how one of the peaks was shaped like a throne.

"Come on, we gotta find her," she said as she began climbing a steep path.

Daniel darted up the rocky slopes, struggling to stay with Allie. A group of tourists passed, like everyone else, not seeing them. The path was narrow with jagged rocks and wisps of long brown grass. No trees or buildings were on this side of the hill, so the harsh wind whipped around the rocks. In September Washington wasn't cold, but the biting air on this hill made Allie wish she had something on over her white sweater.

When they reached the top, there was still no sign of Paulette. Daniel caught up with Allie and she turned to see him join her but paused, then froze. The light over the city was dimming, in spite of the sun's position in the center of the sky. Past the city, night crept toward them. A dark shadow moved along the earth and sky, consuming everything in its path. As if it all vanished into complete nothingness, if black was nothingness.

"You're a weird friend to have," Daniel said as he stared at the darkness that approached them like a tidal wave of night.

"Something tells me we shouldn't wait here for whatever that is."

Daniel looked back and nodded vigorously. "I agree."

Allie scrambled toward the other side of the hill, looking for the way back. She wasn't sure where they should go. She knew they shouldn't stay there, but the approaching darkness seemed to captivate her, pull her in, as if she could watch it forever. Still, she sensed something terrible would happen if she stayed in this spot.

She attempted to step across a gap but a dirt clot beneath her foot crumbled and she slipped, falling fast. She screamed and flailed. As she felt the air whipping around her and she knew she was falling, Daniel grabbed her wrist.

"Got you," he said, then looked past her with excitement. "Look what you found!"

He gestured in the direction she was falling. The drop didn't continue too far, sloping off at a forty-five-degree angle, five feet down into the rock.

Allie looked into the sky and saw the darkness growing close. The sun was starting to turn orange, the edge of it purple. "We have to get into hiding."

"What about your friend?" Daniel said, looking around frantically.

Allie nodded. "Let's pray she found somewhere to hide."

The rock was gritty and provided easy traction as they lowered themselves into the cavern. A cave opened up before them, but somehow the cave's lack of light was nothing compared to that darkness they had seen approaching. Its damp coolness welcomed them with the scent of untouched pools of water, which reflected when Allie opened her phone for some light.

"Let's move," Daniel said, and they started into the cave.

They kept walking and as they went deeper, the walls narrowed. Daniel expressed his worry more than once, but Allie assured him there would be no bears or snakes in the cave.

Something snarled ahead. Allie gulped and dropped her phone, but a light still shone. A light from her necklace reflected into the eyes of a wolf as it drew close. She bent down to retrieve the phone. More snarls rose around them, creeping through the cold air to chill her spine. The first wolf, with scraggly greying hair and paws the size of her face, began to circle her.

"Come to me, Daniel," she said. He did, and she held out an arm as if to shield him. She reached with her other hand, and the wolf took a step back. A wolf to her right snarled and leaped into the air. It came at her, claws outstretched, teeth bared. She thought it was over for her and Daniel, then—

THWACK!

The beast fell back, rolling across the rocky ground. Allie looked to Daniel, but he still stood behind her looking scared and a bit curious. "What happened?"

"I don't know," he said. "It's like he hit a wall when he jumped for us."

Allie inched forward, ensuring Daniel was behind her. She faced the wolves and watched as the larger one nuzzled the first one that had failed in its attack. A third wolf came from behind, but approached the other two and lay on the ground, its shining eyes watching Allie and Daniel patiently.

"Just keep moving," Allie said as they left the wolves in the dark tunnel behind them, moving deeper in.

The cave curved down deep, always descending.

She couldn't hear anything behind them, but she was sure they were there. One time she almost went flying onto her face when she unexpectedly came across a stair, but she leaped into the air and caught herself on the tunnel wall. Daniel wasn't so lucky, but he only banged a knee. The deeper they went, the more her necklace glowed. That or her eyes were adjusting, she couldn't be sure. Either way, she was able to make out the surrounding walls. There were hundreds of carved patterns. Kings and queens, angels and demons lined the walls, an intertwined knot tracing the ceiling.

"Are you seeing this?" Daniel hissed. He grabbed her shoulder and she jumped. "I can't keep running, slow down."

"But they're coming!" she said.

"Who Allie? Who? No one's coming!"

She paused in the silence, hearing only an indistinct dripping of water somewhere in the distance. The light from her necklace began to glow brighter, increasingly illuminating the tunnel. Reflecting on the walls, the light revealed a relief of a man on a giant throne, surrounded by animals at his feet and angels above. Allie wanted to stay and inspect the intricate artwork, but at the same time, she wanted to run. The sandstone felt soft to her touch, brittle. Her slightest contact made it crumble. At that moment, the light from her necklace became a single ray of light that shot through the hole in the rock wall that her finger had made.

With a glance at Daniel, she pursed her lips and raised her hand, palm flat against the wall. When she pushed, the wall gave way. It crumbled to reveal an arched entrance. Daniel stepped in first and she followed. The smooth rock walls rose into a broad dome above their heads, while on the floor the rock was carved to form an ancient map of the world – like in the library at school. Allie spun in amazement, then stopped as the light from her necklace reflected back brightly against what appeared to be a wall of solid gold. The gold wall rose to a plateau too high for them to see, but Allie's necklace pulled toward the wall as if it were alive and its home was at the top.

With a flash, the light became so bright they were forced to shield their eyes. Allie saw the white behind her scrunched eyelids, the reflection of gold from the wall, and then it was gone. They were back in the school, in the dark room with the globe. Among the color circles she could barely make out Paulette, staring at them expectantly.

11

RISK

Allie blinked, trying to clear the light blotches visible in the dark room. Daniel rubbed his arms, as if to make sure his whole body had returned. Whatever had happened, Allie was more certain than ever that her necklace was the key to figuring everything out, and her mom hadn't simply been on some development mission.

"Did you get it?" Paulette asked.

"What could my mom have been doing there?" Allie asked, ignoring Paulette's question.

Paulette raised an eyebrow.

"It's some Indiana Jones stuff is what it is!" Daniel said. "I mean, did you see those carvings? And then the room!"

"You found the room?" Paulette stepped forward and started patting Allie's pockets. "What was in there, what'd you find?"

"Stop it," Allie said, stepping back. "What are you doing?"

Paulette took a step back and leaned against a nearby wall, her expression discouraged. Footsteps pounded in the hall. The doorknob turned. "Listen, we have to get you back there, I don't know what it was, but we were meant to find something. Something very important or my necklace wouldn't be telling me to help you. But for now, we have to get you to safety."

They were in a room with only one door, which at the moment was rattling as someone from the other side was trying to break the lock. Paulette looked at the floor and around the walls for vents, but there was no other way out. Then she saw a dim light from a corner of the ceiling. She ran over and beckoned Allie and Daniel to follow.

"I'll give you a boost." She held out her hands, locked together for one of them to place their foot.

Allie looked at her apprehensively, then back to the door when it shuddered with a heavy clash. She ran and stepped into Paulette's hands for a boost up. She felt herself rise to the ceiling and pushed hard on a square ceiling tile. She crawled up into the ceiling as she heard the door's lock breaking with a clang. Daniel pushed past Allie and scampered away from the hole. Loud banging on the door drove Allie to poke her head back down to find Paulette struggling to keep the door closed.

"Go on, get help," Paulette said as she held the door tight. "I'll keep them away."

"It's not safe," Allie said, but she saw that it was too late. The door was open and someone pulled Paulette through.

Allie placed the floorboard back where it had come from. Allie started crawling along the narrow passage, Daniel ahead of her. When they reached a tile above them that budged, they kicked it up and found themselves in a fluorescent-lit classroom, with posters of rocks and a large map of the earth.

"How fitting," Daniel said, his breathing heavy but his eyes returning to normal. "History class."

"We have to find help."

He nodded and they ran into the hallways, trying to re-orientate themselves.

"She's right though," Allie said as they ran. "There was a reason we were there. We've got to go back."

"Allie, I don't know if you noticed," they turned down a hallway to the left, "but the sky was turning black in the middle of the day, we ran into wolves, and then that crazy necklace was shining all over the place."

"We have to find whatever it is we were meant to find. It has to be the key."

Daniel stared at her. He nodded. "Okay. But we have to research that place. I'm going to find out about Osh and Solomon's Throne. You get someone to help Paulette, then figure out how we can travel back there. We've got to make sense of all this."

"Thanks."

He nodded. "Meet me in the library after school."

After he took off, Allie ran to find the principal, or

maybe the librarian. But when she turned down a hallway she stopped short of running right through Paulette.

"I'm fine, I escaped." Paulette looked ragged, her eyes bloodshot.

"But how?" Allie asked.

"Those fools aren't as quick as they think they are. I simply slipped through them, tripping one on my way so the rest had to stumble over each other." She grabbed Allie's arm. "Go on with your day, pretend like everything is normal, we'll meet back up soon. And... I shouldn't have to say this, but don't mention it to anyone. Especially not Eisner. Got it?"

"What, why?"

Paulette blinked as if the question didn't make sense. "Trust me," she added, then walked off, glancing around as she went.

Did Allie have any reason not to trust Principal Eisner? All of it was so confusing, but she still wanted to check in with an adult and try to get some semblance of reality. But Paulette had made it back okay, and Allie wasn't sure what to believe. So instead, she followed her friend's advice.

Allie did her best to get through the rest of her classes and when the final bell struck she dashed for the library. Gabe the librarian gave her a nod when she entered, then motioned toward the far wall. She found Daniel back there, rummaging through a pile of books.

"So?" she said when she reached him.

He didn't bother to look up from the page. "This Solomon's Throne thing, I don't think you understand what we stumbled upon."

"Yeah?"

"This place is like this big tourist attraction in Osh."

"Okay, and?"

Daniel flipped through a large book, showing her pictures of the mountain named The Throne of Solomon – definitely where they were.

"Well, it was rumored that King Solomon used to travel through Osh, so he may have actually founded the city." Daniel closed the book and looked at her. "And some reports even say he may have been buried under those hills."

"Wait, you don't think...?"

"Yes, I think that room we found, it was his tomb." He grabbed the book and headed for the front desk. "Come on, back to my place."

For the first time on their walk home, the sun decided to peek out from behind the clouds, but Daniel and Allie were too excited to notice. They went over what had happened, with the people in Kyrgyzstan being unable to see them, and then the darkness moving as if alive. And now this, the discovery of a long-lost tomb. Allie hadn't been into this Dungeons and Dragons or Warcraft type-nerd-fest stuff for a couple of years, but now she found her heart pumping and her words flowing out in excitement.

The first thing Daniel did at his house was turn on

his laptop and start typing, leaving Allie to look over his shoulder and tell him to click on different links she thought sounded interesting. After searching for a while, they found they were no closer than when they began.

"Have you heard from Paulette at least?" Daniel asked.

Allie checked her phone and clicked on a text. "Paulette says she's working on something, she'll meet us at school in an hour or so."

"Great. Let's keep looking for now then."

"We tried everything. What has this done for us?"

"Well, at least now we know what we're dealing with."

"We do?" She fell backward onto his bed. "All I see is a bunch of Wikipedia junk saying this and that about Solomon's Throne. What's this have to do with my mom? Some ancient guy who controlled angels and demons with his ring?"

"Sounds pretty awesome to me."

"Where do we draw the line? How do we know what's myth and what's reality?"

"Welcome to the study of history."

"Get serious," she said. "Don't you realize how important this is?"

"I am serious. That's how history works, you can get as close as primary sources, firsthand accounts of how it happened and all that, but then who do you trust? How do you know how to interpret the facts? Because some 'expert' says so, that's how."

"You are *truly* a nerd, you know that, right? Seriously, how old are you?"

"Whatever."

Allie let out a long sigh. "This is all useless anyway."

Daniel swiveled around in his chair, his eyes determined. "If we've come this far, we'll get back there. Otherwise, what's the point of all this?"

Allie fumbled with her necklace, agreeing with him but still completely confused and frustrated. "But we have no idea how to control this thing."

"If you don't want to wait for it to do its magic, maybe we could buy tickets and fly?"

"To Kyrgyzstan? How much would we need for that?"

He turned to the computer and clicked through a website. "About two-thousand, each, this time of year."

"How about we take the more realistic route, I grow wings and we fly. You can sit on my back." Allie allowed a smile and Daniel laughed, a nervous, uncertain laughter. Allie stood and started pacing, the way she saw her dad pace when he was upset. "How do we know we can even find our way back when we want to? Maybe it's like Narnia or something."

"Or ask Paulette if she can figure it out."

Allie scrunched up her nose. She wasn't sure what to think of Paulette, but wasn't ready to go that route. Not yet. At the moment, she felt like the only person she could truly trust was Daniel.

Focused on his computer again, Daniel pointed to the screen. "Maybe this has some connection. Look, legend has it that either Solomon or Alexander the Great founded Osh. Alexander was one of the Nine Worthies. Solomon wasn't, but maybe there is a reason the two are connected here."

Allie turned to the window and placed her hands against the windowsill, her forehead against the cold glass. "The Nine whats?"

"The Nine Worthies, historical figures determined to be of great spirit and—"

"I know we established this, but you truly are a nerd."

Daniel ignored her. "I don't know, it's like I was born to read about this stuff, you know? These Nine Worthies, all this stuff it makes me want to jump into battle and win the day for good, you know?"

"Wow."

"Wait, I remember a map of Alexander's empire, like it reached toward the area where modern-day Kyrgyzstan would be. Maybe Alexander went there for a purpose, to find something. Something of Solomon's!"

Allie turned to him, a spark of hope in her eye. "Could this have something to do with my mom? I mean, her necklace took us there, and all this stuff sounds so crazy, but maybe?"

Daniel smiled at her then looked to the window with surprise. Staring in at them was Chris.

"Perfect timing," Allie said, sarcastically, as Chris disappeared from the window to head for the door. "What's he doing here?"

"Give him a chance," Daniel said as he moved to the door to let Chris in.

She waited for them to return, then frowned to see Chris carrying a board game.

Chris smiled at her. "I was hoping me and Danny-boy here could finish our game from his birthday, but you can join, I guess."

"So you have nerd in you too?" she said. "We don't have time."

"I mean, we do need a break." Daniel looked at her and shrugged. "Maybe clearing our minds would get the juices flowing."

He had a point. How much longer could they look at Wikipedia? They were going in circles, and she could think of nothing else to try before meeting Paulette.

"Allie?" Chris said. They both stared at her, waiting. Something about the way Chris's green eyes gleamed when he looked at her made her want to forgive him, to play this dumb game with him and Daniel.

"Well...."

"It'll be fun."

"We have forty minutes, then we have to go," she said and sat on the bed. With a hint of scorn, she watched them set up the little soldiers on the map. She had never played Risk before, though she had heard her brother talk about playing it with his friends. When it came to sports in the family, she was the one to go shoot some hoops with her dad. She never thought that when she moved to a new school and started seventh grade, she would be sitting with two boys playing one of the many games she made fun of her brother for spending his Saturdays on.

Still, she enjoyed herself as they got into the game. Thirty-five minutes into it and she already owned South America and had moved over from Australia with plans for Asia. And Chris could be a real charmer – he had the sort of laugh that caught on in seconds, and more than once the three found themselves rolling on the carpet, holding their stomachs and cracking up.

After a quick break for Goldfish crackers and Cokes, Chris picked up his three white dice and smiled wickedly at Allie.

"I'm attacking in Asia," he said. "Let's see… From here to here."

"Jerk," she said playfully as he picked up four men and placed them at the border of China and Afghanistan, where she defended with three. "See if I care. I'll come back and crush you from India."

She rolled her two dice: a five and a four.

Chris tilted his head and rolled his three attacking dice. They hit the floor beside the board: six, six, six. Allie frowned and reached to pull her two dead men away, while Chris reached to move his men into her territory.

Her hand paused as she saw a glimmer of blue hit the board.

"Allie!" Daniel stood up, excited. "Your necklace's glowing again!"

Chris continued to reach for the board, his sleeve creeping up his arm, and Allie's eyes followed it with terror. At the bottom of his sleeve, she first saw a bit of black. She now realized it was the same pattern she had seen on the floor in that mysterious room with the slayers. As the sleeve retreated further it was evident the black formed a pattern, the three circles and a serpent.

THE RETURN

C hris's smiling face grew bright as the necklace's glow increased, the blue mixing with the red of his eyes to form a purple that then became shadows, shadows that reached out, shadows that moved around the room as if attempting to escape the light.

Allie turned to Daniel in horror and saw his eyes rolled back in his head. He fell, but before he hit the ground Chris lunged forward and the light flashed blindingly to fill the room.

Then the room was gone, her so-called friends were gone – it was only her, floating through the sky like a spirit. Could she be dead? The wind passed right through her. Clouds parted before her, the sky seemed to welcome her coming.

But she wasn't dead. She knew this when she saw the mountain, the Throne of Solomon in the distance, and below her the city of Osh, Kyrgyzstan. But it wasn't the same as before. Now, where there had been sturdy houses, bricks lay scattered, wooden walls eaten by fire. Sunlight reflected on the fragments of glass from shattered windows, and people walked the streets in an eerie silence. She sensed things were different, or perhaps this was a vision of things to come if fate went unaltered.

With a turn of the wind, she flew toward the mountain. The red and gold flags flapped hard before her, twisting and turning in the chaotic sky. The Throne beckoned her forward, like a marker of a time long gone that longed for more.

She stood with the solid rock beneath her feet, at the top of the Throne. With a flash of her necklace, Daniel was there before her, collapsing to the ground. She rushed to him and cradled his head to stop it from slamming into the rock, just in time. His eyes fluttered white, then returned to normal.

"W—What's going on?" he asked weekly.

"I don't know."

"How?" He struggled to sit, holding his head and taking in his surroundings.

"We're back, but I don't think we want to be." Then she saw it, the darkness approaching from the hills, like the last time. "We have to find the cave again."

She helped Daniel to stand, but as they moved for the cave the darkness approached fast, accompanied by distant chanting sounds, similar to those made by the Strayers she had seen in that dark room at school. And then it was too late. Darkness surrounded them, completely, except for the brilliant light shining from the stone around Allie's neck.

She turned, aware of eyes on her from below. Sure enough, at the base of the Throne, she saw dark forms spread in the darkness – an army of shadows. They began to take form. The shadows twisted around the figures, transforming into black robes with full armor, their hollow eyes focused on the ground at their feet. Hands of bone gripped spiked spears and jagged swords.

One figure stepped forward from the rest, his human face turned up toward Allie and Daniel – Chris. The pattern on his arm glowed a purple-black as he pointed to Allie.

Other faces turned up as they materialized, faces she thought she recognized from the groups of Strayers at school. Then, like a swift-moving storm cloud, the darkness surged forward.

Allie opened her mouth to yell, but like the worst nightmare, no sound came out. A moment later Chris was inches from her, his hand on her necklace, his eyes shining red.

The chain broke with a snap.

The darkness faded along with her surroundings and she reached for Daniel. Her hand went through him as again his eyes went white, his body limp. He fell to the ground as the darkness took him.

All was darkness.

The light returned, but it was simply the dull buzzing light of Daniel's bedroom. Allie stood with her hand outstretched for Daniel, but he was gone. She was alone in his room. Pounding came from the door. In a daze, she turned to the window and slid it open, clumsily pulling herself over the sill and then falling in the dirt on the other side.

She pulled herself up and stumbled toward the street, the sky above a storm of swirling gray clouds. The pounding continued and she realized it was in her head. She stood in the parking lot, hands to her temples, spinning in circles.

A low whimper escaped her lips, "Daniel?"

The sky glowed red, the clouds growing darker. She didn't know where to start – the necklace was gone, along with her mom and now Daniel. Chris had seemed fairly normal, until this. She didn't even quite understand what *this* was yet, but she knew that it meant she had no idea how she would save her mom.

Amid the pounding and confusion, Allie racked her brain to figure out what she could do next. She ran to her house and flung the door open, calling for her dad. But there was no sign of her dad or brother. Was all hope lost?

Paulette!

She was supposed to meet Paulette at the school. It was clear now that Paulette knew something about the necklace, and Allie had to figure out what that was. How did Paulette's necklace tie into all this?

Heck, she had her own! And what about the others at school? Maybe Principal Eisner could help? But would they still be there? She began to walk, pulling out her phone to dial Paulette on the way.

"Pick up, Paulette! Pick up!" she whispered into the phone as she began to jog. There was no answer.

Drops of rain began to fall around her, but she pushed forward. Dark faces appeared to leer at her from every shadow, not quite there but watching her nonetheless. The trees loomed out over the sidewalk, sending sheets of water down on her as the sky thundered. Soon she found herself in an all-out run, the puddles beneath her of no consequence. She was sick of losing people in her life! Her thoughts focused only on reaching the school. After that, she would figure everything out. Somehow.

The school stood tall as a beacon in the rain, dimly lit windows like a lighthouse, guiding her. But she arrived and was hit with a wall of sudden doubt, a fear that she would find no answers here. She moved into the courtyard and shook the locked gate of the main entrance. How could it be closed already?

"Paulette!" she screamed.

But something clanged around the corner. She ran, hopeful, sure it was Paulette waiting with some answer. The hedge wall stood in her way, but she wasn't going to be stopped by shrubs. She stood back and ran, vaulting herself as high into the bushes as she could, then climbing the rest of the way. No amount of scratches from those branches could dissuade her. She reached the other side and ran in the direction she was sure she had heard the noise. When she turned the corner she saw it was Gabe, the librarian, books on the ground.

"I dropped these," he explained. "Looking for something?"

"I…"

"Since you're here, perhaps you can help me?" He gestured to the books. "Listen, I have to take care of a leak." He tossed her the keys and winked.

She didn't understand. She bent down and began collecting the books. A thought hit her: hadn't Gabe said something about traveling to Central Asia? In the library, on orientation day. Had he known there was some connection? She stood and ran, but there was no sign of him.

In confusion, she returned to the library and managed to work the key in the door while holding the pile of books. She burst through the doors, arms full and clothes drenched. The map on the ground was dark, shadowed from the clouds over the skylight. She took a step back, a sense of terror gripping her.

But her mom needed her. Daniel needed her.

She set the books down on a cart and looked over the library in awe. The marble pillars stood over it all like guardian angels, the paintings fluctuated between dark and light. In her sense of unease, she reached for the necklace, forgetting it was no longer there, forgetting Chris had ripped it from her neck.

She missed her mom, and she was scared for Daniel. She knelt down with her eyes closed.

"Help me, Mom, where are you? How do I save you

and Daniel?" A gust of wind touched her cheek and she opened her eyes, staring forward. Something was off about the painting directly in front of her. In the center of the painting a man stood above the rest, pulling her attention toward him. She approached the painting, reaching up to touch the face. Then she remembered the stone carving on the wall in the cave of Osh, under the rock known as Solomon's Throne. She remembered the face of the king on that rock before it crumbled, and now that face was right before her! She touched the face, knowing it held some mystery. But what?

The man had been painted in extravagant clothes of red and gold. Deep brown hair covered his face and head, a gold crown at the top. But his eyes did not look forward. She followed his gaze to the left, where his hand pointed. Among the many other faces on the wall, she saw a line of eyes, starting with the king's, curving around the painting. She followed them around to a spot where it ended on the opposite wall – here the painting to the left looked down and right, to where their invisible lines of sight formed an upside-down triangle.

These men in the painting were telling her something. She traced the triangle with her finger, hopeful for a crack to appear, a crumbling wall, anything. But nothing happened. She took a step back and then saw it – as if the triangle pointed to it, there on the ground was one stone different from the rest. She hadn't noticed it because her shadow had covered it, hiding the slight discoloration. The other stones around it were white or grey, but this one stone took on a dusty brown color. She knelt down and inspected the spot, then stepped on it. Nothing happened. She jumped up and down on the stone and again nothing happened. She pounded her fist on it, but nothing. She threw herself on the ground, staring up at the stone ledge above her.

At this rate, anything could be happening back in Osh, at the Throne of Solomon. For all she knew, it was too late.

Then she remembered the tunnel, and again thought about the wall that had crumbled. She hadn't pushed against that wall or pounded it. She had touched it ever so gently. She rolled over onto one knee and reached out her left hand, gently feeling the cold stone against the tip of her finger. Vibrating gently, it sunk an inch into the ground. She smiled, awash with relief.

A gushing sound came from the map in the center of the library and Allie shrieked to see the stone turning to rusty water. The water spun, thick and brown. She didn't want to enter but when she approached and looked into the great whirlpool she saw a rippling image of gold at the bottom. It had to be a test of faith, and she knew what she had to do. With a yell, she ran and jumped, expecting at any moment to be surrounded by cold, muddy water.

But the water never touched her.

THE RING OF SOLOMON

She looked around, instantly recognizing where she was. Before her stood the gold walls of Solomon's throne, beyond the wall that had crumbled. She was back in Osh.

Footsteps echoed from the rock tunnel behind the crumbled wall. Allie turned, looking for somewhere to hide. Ready for anything except, to her surprise, when

Paulette poked her face through the opening, panting and sweating.

"What happened?" Paulette asked. "How'd we get back here?"

"I… I found another way." Allie stepped back and looked at the massive golden wall, too tall to climb. "You?"

"I don't know, I was on my way to meet you and my necklace started to glow, and suddenly I was in the tunnels, scared. But I heard something, and knew it was you."

Allie shook her head, trying to clear it. This was all too much. "Daniel is out there, we have to save him. And Chris. He isn't himself."

"They're here too? This can't be good."

"What do you mean?"

"Allie, tell me exactly what happened."

Allie told her as Paulette circled the room, inspecting the walls and ceiling. When Allie finished and explained how she had returned, Paulette nodded knowingly. "The Strayers must be behind everything. Their magic must be hiding their presence at school, and it seems they've gotten to everyone, if they got to your friend Chris. Unless we do something they're going to take Daniel as one of their own."

"So what do we do?"

"The secret to saving him must be here, in this very room. Come on, we gotta find it." She turned, ready to go, but paused.

"Paulette," Allie said. "I'm glad I'm not the only one."

Paulette smiled and put a hand on her shoulder. They shared a moment of eye contact before shaking it off and getting back to work. They explored the darkness to find only a square room, with nothing but the gold wall. The floor seemed solid. Allie searched the dark corners and noticed Paulette running her hands across the smooth gold, knocking occasionally.

"It's solid," Paulette said with wide eyes. "Do you realize what this would be worth if someone could get it out of here?"

Allie stared at the ceiling in desperation. "I doubt we'll be able to buy Daniel back from them." She stepped back, craning her neck. "There's definitely a ledge up there. There's got to be a way to reach it. If Daniel were here…. Wait, I remember reading something at his place, about Solomon's Throne, about the six steps, and at the base were a lion and an ox made of gold."

She ran to the side. There was nothing but stone. The stone closest to the steps was a different shade, beige, like sand. She pinched it and it crumbled to reveal gold beneath, worn and dull, but gold nonetheless.

"You found it!" Paulette said as she ran to the other side and found a similar spot.

They chipped away at the sandstone until two gold statues stood before them: one a lion, the other an ox.

"Great, now what?" Allie said. This couldn't be what they came for. Paulette looked equally confused. Allie searched around the statues, hoping she could use the same trick from before. She caressed the statue, hoping a gentle touch would win its secrets.

"He's out there, possibly dying and we just sit here playing with gold statues!" Allie said. She kicked the statue and leaned against the leg of the ox. It began to tremble, with her on it. A golden step rumbled as it moved out from the wall, the leg of the ox lifting her to its height.

She scrambled onto the step and watched as Paulette did the same with the lion.

They found themselves on the first step, where this time the statues were of a wolf and sheep. Allie tried the same tactic, but it didn't work. Paulette finally climbed onto the sheep's back to try reaching higher and when she did so, smaller steps opened in the ledge before them.

This continued on each level. The next was a tiger and a camel, a lever of which was a tooth in the tiger's open mouth. Then came an eagle opposite a peacock, a cat opposite a rooster, and a sparrow-hawk opposite a dove. At the sixth step, two large eagle wings spread down, which Allie and Paulette climbed upon and were lifted to the ledge where they froze in amazement.

Before them was a throne of pure gold, surrounded by ancient writing inscribed into the walls.

"Can you believe this?" Allie said.

"It's like a dream," Paulette said.

Allie searched around the throne, hoping to find something. "Why would we do all that only to find a throne?"

Paulette looked around and then smiled at something on the far wall. "Look, over there!"

Allie strained her eyes and indeed saw a ledge on the far side. But it was at an equal height as the throne, some twenty feet from the ceiling. Below it was emptiness, nothing to climb.

"And what good would that do?" Allie sat in the throne, facing the ledge, and when she sat, a switch triggered and a golden rope uncoiled from the shadows above. She ran forward, but the rope recoiled and was gone.

"You stay here while I sit," Paulette said. "I'll keep the rope down."

Allie waited, and as soon as Paulette sat on the throne the rope shot down and Allie grabbed it. She gave it a hard pull, then turned to Paulette. "Here goes everything."

Paulette held up crossed fingers and smiled. "Good luck."

Allie ran and, gripping the rope with all her strength, jumped from the ledge. She swung across, reaching with her toes for the opposite ledge. She felt stone, but it was too dark to see. Hoping blindly, she let go. Her other foot landed, but only half on the ledge. Her arms flung about in the darkness and she thought it was over. Screaming, she overcompensated and fell forward, smacking her head into something hard.

"Ouch!"

"Are you okay?" Paulette asked.

"I hit my head, that's all. It's so dark over here!"

"You have your cell?"

Allie hadn't thought of that. She pulled the phone out and flipped it open. Before her, the faint light reflected on damp stone, cut smooth and shaped into a rectangular box. It had a lid, and as she looked closer, she saw deep patterns carved in the stone. She pulled back, her breath catching.

"What is it?" Paulette called from the other ledge.

Allie breathed deep, unsure what to do.

"Allie?"

"Um," she managed, then pushed back her fear. "I think I found the tomb."

"Solomon's tomb?" Paulette ran forward, leaning over the edge from the other side. "You've got to open it, see what's inside!"

"Are you nuts?" Allie yelled back. "What if there's a dead body? Bones? Or worse, bugs?"

"Think! We're here for a reason and so far as I can tell, the only possible reason lies before you. Don't let it slip away because you're scared!"

Allie gulped and stepped forward. She pressed on the stone top but it didn't move.

"It won't budge!" she shouted into the surrounding darkness. Although she had noticed a slight echo before, it didn't bother her until that moment. She wanted to find the rope and climb down, to leave this place. But she couldn't, and then Paulette gave her the reason why.

"Your friends need you." Paulette's voice carried

through the stale air like words lost, barely there, but stinging in Allie's ears.

She was right. They needed her. Allie searched and found the wall was only two feet away from the tomb on the opposite side. Holding her phone for light, she put her back against the wall. She lifted one foot and then the next, placing them against the stone top of the tomb and then pushed with all the muscles in her legs. It budged. She pushed again and it moved far enough for her to stand and look inside.

The stench of death did indeed come from the opening in the tomb, like rotten eggplant, but when she held her phone above the opening, not wanting to look in at all, she was surprised to see, instead of slimy bones, the glisten of the light's reflection on metal. A ring rested on the curve of a shield. She reached in first for the ring, pocketing it, and then tried for the shield, which she managed to lift with surprising ease. While the ring was simple bronze with an empty spot where a stone would be, engraved on the shield she found a knotted tree set in the green-clad metal. A circle of old runes surrounded the engraved tree. The shield scraped against the stone as she lugged it out, sending piercing echoes through the cavern.

"What'd you find?" Paulette called over.

"Just this," Allie said holding the light of her cell phone to the shield so Paulette could see.

"What are we going to do with a shield?" Paulette paced the ledge. "Nothing else?"

Allie pulled the shield with both hands then

attached it to her arm. It must have weighed at least twenty pounds. "Throw me the rope."

Paulette looked up. "I don't see it. Check if there is anything else, there has to be something."

"There was nothing else." Allie fumbled with the ring in her pocket, not sure why she wasn't telling Paulette the full truth. "You have to sit on the throne to bring down the rope."

Paulette stood staring across the gap, but Allie couldn't see her eyes. "Fine," Paulette said. She turned and sat on the throne and the rope fell, but it was on Paulette's side. Paulette ran, grabbing the rope and jumping before it could recoil. But it began to pull back up anyway, and she heard the ceiling groan.

The rope gave way, and Allie heard Paulette smack into the floor. She ran forward.

"Are you okay?"

A groaning noise came from above. A crack of light began to form in the ceiling, growing as rocks tumbled down upon them. Allie held the shield above her head and yelled, hoping Paulette could hear her. "Get below the ledge!"

More rocks fell, the mighty room crumbling away, the whole wall falling outward to reveal the open air. Rocks smashed the gold, and the gold crumbled into dust as the sunlight from outside shone down upon it. Then, with a final massive tremor, it was over.

Allie stared at the destruction in a moment of disbelief. She turned, looking for Paulette, then saw the open sky and the dark army one-hundred feet from the fallen wall. They spotted her and the darkness seeped into the room, blocking out the sunlight in a dense shadowy mist.

"Paulette," Allie whimpered.

A muffled voice answered from below. The rocks had piled up beside the ledge Allie was on and she was able to climb down. She strapped the shield to her back and started the descent, almost losing her balance more than once. The second time she said 'forget it' and tossed the shield to the ground.

"Where are you?" Allie said. "We have to get out of here!"

She tried shoving rocks aside, working her way to the opposite side of the room. A clatter of metal told her the army had begun its approach.

"Paulette!" she screamed again.

Then she spotted her, arms around her head, cowering under the ledge. She was alive, but her left leg's pants were torn and lines of blood showed. Allie lifted her up and held her by the waist, then pulled her toward the tunnel they'd come through. It was blocked by the fallen rocks.

"We only have one way out," Paulette said. She turned on her own and looked toward the darkness. Allie heard the roars of the army and saw the spear tips glinting in the purple haze as they drew closer. She wished nothing more than to be back home with her mom and dad, tucked into bed and listening to a sweet bedtime story. Only her mom was here somewhere, relying on Allie to save her.

"Get down!" Paulette said as a whistling filled the air.

Allie dived for the shield, raising it in time as black arrows scattered across the ground and dinged against the green metal. A moment later, another volley of arrows struck the ground around their feet.

"This isn't going to work!" Paulette screamed as she grabbed Allie and pulled her up. "Let's move!"

They ran, Paulette with a slight limp, past the wall and out of the fallen rocks. They dived behind a small outcropping just outside the Throne of Solomon. Breathing heavily, Paulette poked her head over a large rock to see what was happening. Allie followed, holding the shield up below her eyes, ready to raise it.

The army marched forward, the Strayers' faces visible among them. They all walked in a daze, their skin grayish and the darkness weaving around them to make up their robes and weapons. As they walked the shadows escaped into the air, twisting and twirling, then formed before them into some sort of shape. The darkness formed thick arms and legs and eyes blazing with midnight-black fire. The shadows melted into the skin of this ten-foot tall demonic giant, leaving an oily flesh that glistened and dripped as he walked.

The giant leaned back with massive arms spread and roared into the dark sky. It raised its fists as the army around it fitted arrows to their bows. Then, with another roar, the giant brought its fists down, slamming them into the ground. A wave of fire burst forth and shot towards Allie and Paulette, the volley of arrows following.

Instinctively Allie dropped the shield and reached for the ring in her pocket. She turned her eyes skyward, the ring now on her hand.

Energy surged through her limbs and exploded from the ring – it pushed outward, a great ball of light deflecting the wall of flame and myriad arrows.

Paulette looked at her with excitement. "That's what I'm talking about!"

Allie collapsed to one knee, her energy drained, but exhilarated. "I don't know what came over me." The feeling didn't last when she lifted her eyes to the enemy – the giant lunged sideways as it walked, and at that moment she saw Daniel. He was hovering off the ground, a red glow around him, his eyes white. Allie yelled out, then looked to Paulette with eyes that pleaded for her to do something.

"There's only one way we can defeat a force such as this," Paulette said as she ducked back behind the nearby rocks.

"Anything," Allie said. "Just hurry."

"We have to use their power against them."

"How!?"

Paulette pulled her necklace from beneath her red blouse and Allie saw that it was a simple triangle. But Paulette pulled the triangle and the lower half became a blade. She grabbed Allie's wrist and pulled it to her, taking the blade and cutting deep into the flesh of Allie's forearm.

"What are you doing?" Allie yelled as she tried to pull her arm back. "Ouch!"

She struggled, but Paulette's grip was too strong. She pulled hard, watching Paulette's glowing eyes as she cut the shape of three circles into Allie's arm. The struggles were useless, but Paulette stopped mid-cut. Her eyes were on the ring on Allie's left hand, the one from the tomb.

"So that's how," Paulette said, dropping the blade. "You did find it."

Allie tried to pull her hand back, but Paulette's grip was like the vice of hell, her other hand reaching for the ring.

"Wait," Allie pleaded.

A power surge coursed through Allie's arm, the one with the incomplete pattern. It tingled. Her arm glowed purple, then rippled with energy. It blasted Paulette into the opposite rock wall. Something burned inside of Allie's stomach. She felt the urge to puke.

Paulette shook her head and looked up, her eyes red now. Her fingers tightened around Allie's ring. "It's my play, Allie." Paulette spit blood, but she smiled, kneeling beside the mountain. "You've lost."

DANIEL AND THE GIANT

Allie lifted her arm and desired the power again, the intense force that had shot at Paulette. All around her, the rocks of the mountain seemed to fade into darkness, the sky smothering her in a thick black mist. The power came, coursing through her fingers to blast Paulette in the forehead. Instantly Allie felt her insides churn and found herself on the ground coughing up blood. She heard laughter and looked up to see Paulette's face shadow over and her eyes turn a fiery red. Paulette turned toward the army and broke into a run.

Allie stood, clutching her stomach. Blood dripped down her arm and chin. Paulette sprinted towards the giant, her hand held high, the ring between her forefinger and thumb. Then Allie saw another face she knew. Behind the giant, Chris ran for Paulette, Allie's necklace in his hands. He grinned wickedly. An aura glowed from the ring as the two drew close, surrounding the dark forces as if they all emanated from the ring. Something told Allie she could not let the ring and the necklace be united, not by those two.

But utter hopelessness took over. She knew she couldn't reach them in time. She fought back tears, refusing to be afraid of death. But Daniel...

A screech sounded and Allie looked up to see an eagle circling the darkness, rays of light cutting through the thick clouds. Allie recognized the eagle from the woods by her house; she was sure it was the same one. This was the moment to act. She pushed herself forward, running all out. Daniel appeared, still unconscious and rotating in the black shadow before her. She would save him or die trying.

Allie gained on Paulette, but she wasn't fast enough. The eagle screech sounded again, and Allie was moving faster than she knew was humanly possible. Was she flying? She looked up to see a fifteen-foot wingspan, and she thought for a moment she had grown wings. But no, it was the eagle, and it was carrying her. Its wings spread wide, chopping through the purple haze and dark shadows, carrying her forward.

Chris's eyes opened wide, his mouth yelling curses she couldn't hear. Paulette turned, her hand almost touching his. Allie crashed into Paulette. The ring flew into the air. The eagle grasped it in its talons, delivering it to Allie before circling into the sky.

As Paulette and Chris stared in horror, Allie placed the ring on her finger. Then she turned to the stone from her necklace in Chris's hands.

"That's mine," she said as she pounced and snatched her necklace away. At the same moment, the spell around Daniel snapped and he fell to the ground by a nearby stream, coughing and rubbing his throat. The army froze. The giant turned on Daniel but then paused, looking back at Allie.

"What're you doing?" Daniel mumbled, his eyes slowly opening. "What's going on?"

Everyone turned to Allie. Pulsating light surrounded her. She felt its warmth coursing through her flesh, flowing between her fingers and tossing her hair, covering her in a dim glow. It grew bright, emanating from the objects in her hands, pulling at each other like magnets. They joined with a bang and an explosion of light. When the light faded she held the ring, the rock firmly in place in the ring's center.

The Giant roared and turned on Daniel, picking him off the ground before slamming him back down. Allie ran, dived under the giant's legs and grabbed hold of Daniel. Paulette and Chris moved in, but Allie was lifted in the air with Daniel, about to be slammed by the giant. She closed her eyes and held up the ring, willing to be saved. A bolt of light blasted from the ring to the giant, Paulette, and Chris, knocking them all onto the ground like an outward circle of dominos. Allie reached for Daniel and grabbed his arms, rolling with him when they hit the ground. She pushed herself up, but he lay motionless.

"Wake up," she yelled. "You have to wake up!"

She held him close, her eyes darting between him

and the approaching enemy. She closed her eyes and willed him to get up, with all her spirit. A low humming sounded all around her. She felt warm, relaxed. She imagined her mom's smiling eyes, her gentle hug good night. And when she opened her eyes she saw that indeed streams of light encircled them. She felt more refreshed, healed.

Daniel slowly opened his eyes, but the Giant still lumbered towards them.

"What's that?" Daniel said.

"What we have to defeat to find my mom," Allie said.

She stood, head high and fists clenched, and then charged the giant. A swooshing sounded from her right and she dodged as the giant's fist smashed into the ground beside her. She searched for any sort of weapon, noticing the army slowly backing away as if unsure what to do. The giant lunged for the attack again, but this time—

THWAK!

Something hit the giant and it stumbled back.

Allie looked back to see Daniel reaching for a rock. She couldn't believe it – all those times she had made fun of baseball, how she had called him a wuss for only being into that sport, and here he was using it to fight a giant!

"Keep 'em coming!" she yelled.

Then, as if from nowhere, Paulette lunged at Daniel and had him by the hair, and at the same moment, the giant charged at Allie. Her ring glowed bright and out of nowhere, she had the shield that she had left behind. She stared at it for a moment, then lifted it in time to block the giant's strike. The force slammed her across the dirt and onto her back, but she was mostly unhurt. She stood to see the giant charging again, this time a red-glowing mace held in each hand, the spikes as long as her fingers.

She stood and held out the ring, beginning to understand what was happening. The air pushed her into the sky, up and over the giant. She landed with a kick to Paulette's stomach, freeing Daniel. Again she willed herself into the air, this time with Daniel's hand in hers. They flew right over Chris and past the giant a second time, but it turned and hurled a mace at them. She saw it coming in mid-air and deflected it with the shield.

They landed and she felt a tingling on her arm. As if the marks on Chris were talking to her marks. The shadowy serpents reached for each other, intertwined, and began to pull her and Chris together. Her body flew forward, faster now. The giant lumbered past, pausing in confusion as she flew between his legs. The giant had lost her, but Daniel was still in its sights – it regained its composure and, with thunderous steps, lunged for him.

"Allie!" Daniel called, eyes wide.

She tried to stop her movement, but the force on her arm pulled strong. But her other arm, the shield… she yanked her arm from the strap and flung it with all her might. To her surprise-and delight-Daniel caught it. She watched as he braced himself for the impact with the giant. Allie embraced the pulling force and ran for Chris. Better to be done with him quickly. She tackled him to the ground, regretting it instantly. The shadows engulfed her. Her arm burned and she felt the internal fire traveling through her blood. A feeling came over her and she knew that at any minute now she would become like Chris. Whatever dark power of Samyaza had taken over him would soon have her as well.

"Daniel!" she screamed, trying to turn and see how he was faring. Surprisingly he was dodging left and right, maneuvering the heavy shield with ease to block the giant's maces. Snarls came from her left and she twisted to see the wolves charging only feet away. They had escaped the caves. She focused her energy and punched Chris hard across the mouth, blood and spit flying across the already red dirt. She tried to stand, but her body was stiff as if caked in dry mud. The wolves charged and knocked her sideways.

Instead of fangs biting into her flesh, she felt a slobbery tongue. Chris was standing, backing away as two wolves turned on him, snarling and baring their fangs.

She didn't waste an instant and turned on the giant, blasting light with her ring. It was like a child's shove and barely caused the giant to blink.

"Move Daniel!" she said and blasted again. This time the giant stumbled, turning on her with bared crooked yellow and grey teeth.

Paulette laughed as she grabbed Daniel from behind. "Finish him," she told the giant.

But the giant was already rushing at Allie. Paulette cursed the giant and tossed Daniel to the ground as the wolves dashed between the giant's legs and leaped at her.

Allie couldn't see what was happening. She looked up at the giant's massive ten-foot frame, its muscles stretched tight as he lifted one of his maces into the air and howled. But in an instant the wolves appeared, saliva flying as they tore at his flesh. Allie rolled to her side as his clumsy strike landed with an explosion on the rocky ground. She stood and threw herself backward as another strike missed her nose by inches. She blasted the giant as hard as she could. It screamed and she saw the blast of golden light had assisted the wolves, but the giant would not give up so easily. It raised both maces into the air, blocking out the sky and everything else from Allie's view.

"Duck Allie," Daniel yelled, "get down!"

Instantly she was on the ground, covering her head. Through a sliver between her fingers, she saw Daniel push away from Paulette, a small stone in his hand. He aimed, pulled back the rock, then let it fly. It hissed through the air, but the giant moved left, dodging with ease. The giant had to halt his strike to move, and Allie had her chance to run. Again, Daniel let a rock fly, this time it passed right over her head but she heard it miss the giant and clatter against the dirt.

The eagle screeched a warning and half a second

later Paulette plowed into Allie, knocking the breath out of her as their bodies slammed into the rocky surface. The eagle dove, clawing at Paulette with its talons. It barely fazed her. As her hair was torn and blood flew, Paulette focused on Allie, slamming her head into the rocks repeatedly.

The pain surged in Allie's body and she writhed like a dying snake, but the blows kept coming. Everything was red, her mind flashing in and out of consciousness. She felt herself flittering away, her eyes willing to be closed. Paulette lifted Allie's head and Allie knew it would be the last time before darkness took her. She saw Daniel, heard him scream out, and watched as he flung a third rock at the giant.

Allie turned to see the rock flying, its trajectory sure. Without understanding her actions, she raised her hand and pointed the ring so that a ray of light connected with the rock. Glowing red, the rock increased in size, a trail of fire behind it, and a moment later it exploded in red and blue flashes of light at the connecting point of the giant's eyebrows.

The giant grunted as it stumbled back, blinded and wounded. It reached for Paulette as it fell, and for a moment the darkness faded. The ground shook as the giant fell, lifeless.

All else seemed to have frozen in that moment, but then the darkness returned and Allie became aware of Paulette's screams. Paulette ran for the giant's corpse, forgetting her assault on Allie. She knelt to caress the giant's form as bit by bit it began to wisp away in the wind, like dark sheets being pulled up from the monster and carried into the sky to swirl over Paulette's head.

A clatter behind Allie showed that the army pushed forward, moving again as if a wall had dropped and now they had the freedom to attack. Paulette stood to face Allie as the army formed a circle around, weapons at the ready.

"Aghhh!" Paulette shouted as she blasted a purple fire at Daniel, who only barely survived thanks to Allie tackling him out of the way.

"Hold on!" Allie said as she closed her eyes. The ring emitted bright lights in bursts, as all around them darkness closed in.

Paulette walked slowly toward them, her eyes glowing red. She approached and her body dimmed to a pitch-black, along with everything else but the circle of light from Allie's ring.

"Come on!" Allie screamed and concentrated on the ring harder. "Take us home!"

She opened her eyes to see Paulette raise her arms above her head. The darkness converged on her. And then the darkness shot from her eyes and mouth, straight for Allie.

"Now!" Allie screamed, holding Daniel's hand tight and focusing with all her might on being gone from that spot. The light enveloped them and filled them with healing warmth. The air around them seemed to shatter like breaking glass. Thunder filled her ears.

When she opened her eyes they were no longer in Kyrgyzstan and there was no dark army.

As if in a dream, she saw the pillars, the paintings, and books lining the wall of the school library. The light faded and she felt herself growing dizzy. The floor reached up to smack her in the face. Darkness.

15

FLAPPING OF WINGS

"Allie!"

Allie stirred, sure she had heard someone calling her name. She imagined opening her eyes to find herself on her bedroom floor, having fallen out of bed. But no, the smell of musty old books filled her nostrils, and then there was someone calling her again.

"Allie," Principal Eisner said, and Allie opened her eyes to see the principal's warm face, her silver hair framing the deep lines around her eyes.

Allie became aware of the principal's hands holding her head and intense pain running through her left leg. She tried to move.

"Wait," Principal Eisner said. "Rest a moment."

"Wh-what happened?" Daniel asked, recovering beside Allie.

"It's still happening," Principal Eisner said. "You aren't finished."

"You know?" Allie asked.

The principal nodded. "Unfortunately, though we never would've suspected Paulette."

"What happened to her?"

"It appears a dark force is at work, something may be corrupting her, the one they call Samyaza. He became a shadow, one without form. None of us could have known he had become powerful enough to take over someone's body. Unless she was one of them, one of the Strayers. Yes, it's all making sense now. Come, stand. You have been chosen to fight the dark powers."

"And you know this because you were with the Bringers of Light?"

Principal Eisner nodded.

Daniel rose to his knees and turned with confusion at the shield now lying beside him. "And this?"

Principal Eisner held up a hand, finger tracing the

tree pattern on its front. "You have already begun." She turned back to Allie. "You've saved your friend, but you aren't done. The path has been passed to you."

"And my mom?"

"Solomon's ring has chosen you. The stone wasn't as powerful by itself, in the necklace. But now it has found its other half, what your mom was searching for. The stone and the ring are united, as Samyaza hoped they would never be. United, and under our control. With the ring you have the power to destroy the dark forces. You may be able to succeed where your mom never could, where none have before." She smiled at Daniel. "The potential is unimaginable."

Allie looked at her ring, a new awe building within her. "But how?"

"Focus! It may not be too late. Trust in yourself. Faith is the power that leads to light. Normally it's just the one, but... you two are so young."

"Wait, me too?" Daniel said.

"She's going to need your help. You've already begun." She nodded toward the shield. "It's part of a set of armor, very special, and doesn't work for everyone. If the dark forces were to ever get their hands on the ring and the armor, we wouldn't stand a chance."

"All of this is up to us?" Daniel stared for a moment in disbelief, then turned to the shield and slung it on his arm. "We already got the giant, let's finish this."

The principal smiled at Daniel. "You don't have much time."

Allie looked between the principal and Daniel, then

reached out for Daniel's hand and closed her eyes. She felt her body surging like at the end of a rollercoaster.

When she opened her eyes, they were once again surrounded by a dark fog, the army standing somber as Paulette kneeled over the spot where the giant had fallen. Smoke rose where only a shadow remained.

Murmurs rose from the army and Paulette turned slowly, her eyes glowing red now, black tears streaming down her cheeks.

"You dare to return?" she said, her hands glowing in purple flames. "You dared to deny me my desire!" She motioned and the army of darkness moved in, forming a dense circle around them. "Now you will SUFFER!"

Paulette raised her hands then thrust them forward. Black and purple flames shot out at Allie but Daniel threw himself into the flames' path, shield braced. The flames licked around the shield and over their heads.

Paulette screamed and ran forward, motioning the Army to charge. "Bring me that ring!"

The Army of darkness roared and advanced, their swords and spears held at the ready.

"Lead the way," Daniel said, his eyes wild but determined.

Allie saw a dim path of light leading toward the collapsed hillside of Solomon's Throne, emanating from her ring. "She's there, she's in the tunnels."

"But how do we get there?!"

She looked to the sky, where the eagle from before circled high above. It gave her an idea. "We fly."

She grabbed the back of Daniel's shirt with one

hand, her ring pointed down to the ground with the other. "Brace yourself!" she yelled and concentrated her energy into a focused beam of light. It burst from her ring, hitting the ground and propelling her and Daniel into the sky so that they flew right over the army as spears and bursts of dark fire narrowly missed them.

A stream of black fire appeared, flying right for them. Daniel spun and lifted the shield in time to deflect it. The light of her ring subsided, bringing them down to a soft landing at the base of the collapsed entrance to the cave. The army roared in pursuit.

Behind them, Paulette threw fire around her with no care for who she hit and sent more than one Strayer running in flames.

Allie pulled Daniel with her, running to the rocks where the stream of light showed a path through – as they ran, the light blasted the rocks apart and a tunnel formed.

"In there!" Allie said.

As they reached the entrance Daniel turned and yelped, raising the shield barely in time to block a massive boulder. The force threw him backward so that he collided with Allie and sent her sprawling.

She jumped up and pulled down the shield. With a burst of energy she sent a final blast of light toward Paulette, then turned and motioned for Daniel to follow. However, instead of running with her through the dark tunnels, he stood at the small opening with the shield, determined.

"You go, you find her," he said.

"I won't leave you!" she replied.

Something clanged against the shield from outside the tunnel and he braced himself. "Go!"

"But…" She couldn't argue. She saw that if she were to make it without being pursued, this was the way.

"Go, find her, I'll block them off!" he said again, and this time she ran.

"I won't be long!" Allie turned and held the ring before her as she ran, a glowing trail leading from her ring down the cave tunnel.

She fought through the darkness, pushing herself forward with the thought of finding her mom. Concentrating all of her energy on that thought. She stumbled on a loose rock, then caught herself on the rock wall. She breathed deep, taking in the depth of the darkness, the impossibility of it all.

It was up to her. No one would find her mom if she didn't, she had to push through.

So she took a step forward, reaching out with her hand to follow the wall, but with the second step the ring began to glow, and with each successive step the light increased, and soon she could see the rock floor beneath her and about five feet ahead. Then she was running, calling out for her mom.

Before long she saw a large pile of rocks ahead, blocking her path. The glow hit the rocks, sparkling, and gleaming. This was the spot.

"Mom!" she shouted as she began to move the rocks aside, one at a time. "I'm coming, Mom!"

She moved more aside, and then she came across

one she couldn't lift. She heaved and grunted, but it wouldn't budge. Struggling with the stone, she fell to her knees, shoulders forward, in defeat.

A small whimper came from the rocks – her mom's voice! Allie had no doubt.

She stood and pulled at the stone, and as she did so the light around her grew bright.

"I'm coming, Mom!" With a burst of light Allie pulled the stone free. As it moved, the rest shot off down the tunnel.

Where the rocks had been moments before, her mom lay, weak but alive. Her frizzy hair fell around her thin face, large yellow bags of skin under her bloodshot eyes. She cringed at first to see the light, then her vision adjusted and her eyes fell on Allie. Her left hand reached weakly for her daughter.

Allie rushed forward to help her mom sit up. "I knew you'd be alive, Mom, I knew you wouldn't give up on us."

Her mom smiled up at her daughter and caressed her face. But she paused, eyes frozen on the ring on her daughter's finger. "You, the Ring of Andaleeb, of Solomon…. How?"

A crash echoed through the tunnel and Allie knew Daniel needed their help. "Not now, mom, we have to get you home."

They struggled through the tunnel, Allie attempting to support her weakened mom. The echoes of clashing metal on metal continued to pound through the rock walls around them, the source of it growing close.

Almost to Daniel, the darkness surged around them and then pulled back like a great wind. The rock wall to their left lifted away, rocks flying into the distance.

Allie stood in the tunnel, now exposed to the army and the fog of darkness. In the center of the army stood Paulette, her hands in the air. Darkness swirled like a tornado over her head. She smiled wickedly when she saw Allie.

"Not this time!" Paulette called out, her voice deep, a mixture of Paulette and a much darker, more powerful force.

"No..." her mom said, her voice halting, her eyes unbelieving. "Samyaza, he's taken her."

"How about now, Ms. Strom, how about when your twelve-year-old daughter is all that stands between me and victory? Her and her little friend..."

Paulette moved her hands toward Daniel and a streak of black lightning fell from the sky upon him. Allie let out a scream and pulled her mom toward his collapsing form. Her body wavered under her mom's weight.

Paulette faced them with fiery red eyes, a gloating smile across her face. She lifted her hand to strike again.

"Daniel, no!" With a final burst of energy, Allie pulled herself and her mom to Daniel's side. She fell to her knees. The dark lightning filled the sky. Her mom shrieked and grabbed her daughter in her arms, but the darkness hit nonetheless.

Allie felt her head falling, aware of its weight, aware

of the softness of Daniel's chest as her head landed on him with a thump. She couldn't move, she couldn't think. All she could do was see the frail frame of her mom, reaching...

"Get up," her mom said, kneeling beside her daughter. "You didn't come all this way for it to end like this."

Allie's head rolled back. High above she saw the Eagle, again darting through the clouds, pushing them apart to reveal a ray of light.

"Take me home," her mom pleaded.

Allie, eyes to the heavens and using all her energy, lifted her ring. A smile met her lips, but her eyes slowly closed.

Her eyes burst open as the streaming light careened over the rocks of Solomon's Throne, overtaking the mountain like a sunrise come to life. The light intensified, speeding towards the darkness. Light and dark met in an explosion of color. In golds and oranges Allie saw faces, heard the swooshing of wings.

Then there was a face she only remembered from pictures, her grandpa, barely visible, and her mom was smiling up at him. His thick voice filled the air, "Go Allie, go!" The flapping of wings intensified a thousand-fold, and the light surrounded them like streamers, capturing the dust and reflecting like diamonds.

Allie felt her strength returning. She managed to lift her head to see the Army retreating, followed by Chris and the wolves. But Paulette ran for Allie, her hand outstretched, her mouth in a silent scream.

The ring glowed bright and the darkness whipped

back toward Paulette, around the retreating army. It enveloped Paulette like the shadow of the mountain taking solid form, like a net that pulled her back.

"Noooo!" Paulette screamed as her eyes flickered between fiery red and their normal green of the girl that may still have been somewhere within.

The light became too bright and they saw nothing but explosions of gold and white. Were those smiling faces in the light? As the light began to fade, she no longer knew where she was. Someone was saying her name, softly.

She blinked and could make out blurry pillars, then blinked again and saw she was in the school library, laying in the middle of the school map. She remembered the day the librarian had asked if she had traveled, if she had been to Central Asia. She wanted to laugh at that question now.

She turned, rotating onto her elbows. Her mom and Daniel lay beside her, smiling back. She reached for her mom and their fingers touched. Allie wanted to jump up and hold her mom, but she felt the blood rushing to her head and the room spinning, and then the walls seemed to shift in size and dimensions. They blurred and went black as her eyes lost focus.

"Allie," her mom called. "Allie..."

She was on the ground, feeling her consciousness returning, then fading out again. A knot in her stomach felt like it was clawing its way out. Someone approached, as if running at an angle, but Allie realized it was her perception. She forced her eyes open long enough to see Gabe the librarian, and then she felt herself fading out again.

She woke in the school nurse's office, someone caressing her cheek. The smell of sterility filled her nostrils like cut metal. Her vision blurred again and she saw her dad's loving face, inches from her own, worried. Her eyes closed and reopened to reveal her mom and dad holding each other. She was in a real hospital, her mom with a tube in her arm connected to a bag that hung from a metal bar. But she was alive and standing, and her dad caressed her mom's hair. They kissed as Allie lost consciousness once more.

16

DESTINY

Although Allie had been allowed to sleep in her own bed the night of their return, a week had passed before her mom was discharged. Army commanders from a special unit waited at the hospital to explain to everyone that asked how they had found her mom and brought her back just in time. Allie suspected they weren't exactly real Army at all. The doctor told Allie that an average person could go for only a few days without water, but the damp caves had been kind to her mom. And she was strong, she had put up a fight.

Making up a story for Allie was much harder, and then there were the missing children. The Strayers had vanished. Cop cars were everywhere, but no one had answers. Regarding the bruises and scrapes on Allie and Daniel, they found a simple enough explanation—they were beaten up by the bullies, Chester and Vince. Since no one could find Chester or Vince, the story held up. Allie imagined the parents of those two were losing their minds with worry, but she also wondered if maybe there was more to the picture—like maybe Chester and Vince weren't exactly meant to be there to begin with?

Principal Eisner gave Allie the week off school to spend at her mom's side. Allie would talk for hours with her mom, something she couldn't remember ever doing. She never realized how beautiful her mom's laugh was, or how firm her grip was as they held hands. But they always avoided the topic of what had happened—until the day of her mom's discharge.

"We have to talk," her mom finally said when her banana-pudding was done.

Allie simply nodded, understanding by the tone of her mom's voice that this was serious.

"Do you know what you wear?" her mom asked, glancing at the ring on Allie's pointer finger. "Has anyone told you?"

Allie nodded and said she knew. Principal Eisner had filled her in a bit more, told her about the eagle and spirit animals, and the "Bringers of Light," a group dedicated to protecting those around them.

"I see," her mom replied. "Yes, listen to her, she came here for you. And Gabriel, the librarian."

"We know all this, Mom."

She smiled. "He was so pleased to take that position, imagine Gabriel surrounded by books all day." She chuckled and stared out the window at the trees blowing in the wind, losing herself in thoughts.

"So all of this… the army?"

"All a cover story," her mom replied. "My involvement, anyway. My purpose was always to guard the light."

Allie grinned. "You're like security for electric companies, yeah?" She held up her hands and chuckled. "Joking."

At this her mom couldn't control herself and burst into hearty laughter so loud the nurse ran in. Her mom held out her hands and told the nurse she was okay, then calmed herself and turned back to her daughter once the nurse had left.

"More like the protectors of all that is good." She eyed Allie, debating. "You know, Eisner wasn't a principal before this year. When I was transferred here, the Guardians sent her and Gabe to watch over you. I insisted it wasn't necessary, but it seems I was wrong."

"But now you're back, right? So everything can go back to normal?"

"No, it has chosen you. We never know who it will be, or why. In this case, I can only think it was to save me, but perhaps that's too self-centered a way of seeing things. I don't know. The ring, Solomon's ring, it holds light, or rather it calls upon the light when you need it most. But it isn't for your enjoyment. It serves a purpose so much larger than you or I. The Bringers of Light work to stop the evil forces of Samyaza, the foretold bringer of darkness. You may not be ready for all this, God knows I wasn't. Samyaza meant to bring the world to a place his followers claimed it should have always been—in darkness. If we don't stop him, the world loses hope, the world loses life."

"And your work is part of this?" Allie couldn't believe it. She had seen a couple of war movies, on the TV when her dad wasn't in the room, and always wondered how her mom could be crawling through the jungles, riding ships onto beaches as bullets rained down. Now she knew the truth of it, but she understood it so much less.

"Not anymore dear." Her mom took Allie's hand and placed her other hand over the ring. "Now my job is to support you. The ring has chosen you. There are others—rings, necklaces, all sorts of symbols that contain the power of the light or the power of darkness, but none more powerful than this ring. However, it depends on you. It only works when you need it, when you have true faith and a true need."

Allie pulled her hand back and stared at the ring, unable to believe it. Slowly her hand dropped and her eyes rose to her mom's.

"Why me?" she asked. "Why now?"

Her mom shook her head. "I have no idea, and honestly, it worries me. But seeing you in action out there, I know you have it in you."

"I can't, I...."

"Allie," her mom sat herself up in the hospital bed. "Of course you can, you saved me."

That same day, Allie's mom was finally allowed to leave the hospital. She was met in the waiting room with big hugs from her dad and brother. They laughed and sang along with 70's songs the whole way home, and when her dad opened the door he turned and picked up his wife to carry her through the entryway.

"Here's to us spending more time together," he said as he lowered her feet to the floor.

Her mom smiled and caressed his cheek, then looked to Allie, who had run to the kitchen to pour her mom a glass of water.

Her dad followed her gaze. "All of us."

Her mom smiled and wiped her eyes. "I'll never leave your side again."

Her dad pulled his wife in close and kissed her forehead. "I was never truly at ease when you were out there, but this time..." He turned to Allie. "And this little one never gave up, she never lost faith in you."

Allie looked to her mom, wanting to ask if she had told her dad. But her mom shook her head in a way that said it wasn't the time. When her mom tucked Allie into bed that night, she held her tight then looked into her eyes.

"We'll tell him, someday," her mom said later. "I don't think he's ready to believe, okay? One day he'll be ready to accept that his little baby is facing the dark forces of the world, but not yet."

Allie smiled and said she understood, all the while wondering what made anyone think she was ready. She certainly didn't think so.

The next day, after her first full day back at school, Allie went to the baseball field where Daniel said he'd be. She couldn't believe her eyes. There he was indeed, on the pitcher's mound. He leaned forward, assessed the boy at the plate, wound up, then released the baseball with more speed than any twelve-year-old kid should have been capable of.

"Strike three!" the umpire yelled and the students went wild, rushing Daniel.

Students surrounded him, giving him high fives and jumping around. She couldn't believe it. Was this the same boy she had met only a couple of weeks before? The nerdy boy she had been sure would ruin her reputation? Now he had more friends than the entire student body of her last school!

The sun sparkled in his eyes when he saw her. He waved bye to the other kids, apparently making some excuse for why he had to leave, then ran over to join her at the lonely side of the bleachers.

"Hey," he said.

"Hey." She smiled at him, checking out the baseball uniform. "So you made the team?"

"Yup."

"Nice uniform."

He blushed, then lowered his baseball cap. "Sorry, you know."

"What for?"

"I know you wanted to make the soccer tryouts."

"I used to… I don't know, being by my mom in the hospital felt more important, you know?"

Daniel smiled. "Yeah, I get that." He motioned to the stands and an older man in a camouflage jacket waved. "My dad came to watch me play."

"That's your dad?"

"Yup. I don't know what came over him, but he insisted he buy me my first glove and come to all my games."

She looked at his dad and at all his new friends out on the baseball field. Sure, she was a bit jealous, but she had her family, and at least one really good friend.

Daniel's face lit up. "I thought of something."

"What?" she said, hesitantly.

"Well, Paulette was the goalie, and she's gone, right?"

"Yeah?"

"And my dad mentioned he knew the coach, on the way over he was saying it was too bad because now they had to find a new goalie, and well, maybe I could have him tell the coach about you?"

"Seriously?!"

"Yeah, think you can play goalie?"

"Of course I can!" she jumped over, arms around him. "Oh my gosh, you're the best!"

He stared back, his brown eyes wide and confused under his blue baseball cap. She stepped back, holding her arms behind her and smiled awkwardly.

"Um…." Daniel looked around then took off his cap and fanned himself with it. "I'll take that as a yes?"

"Thanks, I mean…" She felt her cheeks flushing now, unsure why she had acted so silly. "I would love it."

Daniel's dad gave them a ride home. After talking about school and everything she had missed, she lay with Daniel in the grass outside their apartments to relax. Rays of light broke through fluffy white clouds in the perfectly blue sky above.

"It's so weird without Paulette and Chris around," she finally said.

"And there are others too," Daniel said. "You should hear everyone talking about it. They all have their own theories about what happened. UFOs, the rapture, an exodus in preparation for a flood.... And half the parents are claiming government conspiracy, others suing the school. They have the police scouring the woods, the lakes, everything. Only we know the truth, but they wouldn't believe it."

"The things kids come up with." She smiled, but it faded quickly. "What about Chris's mom?"

"She's over every day, getting consolation from my dad. I can't imagine what she's going through." Daniel propped himself up to better see Allie's face. "Do you think Principal Eisner knew so many of her students were Strayers?"

Allie paused, unsure how much to tell him. If not him though, could she trust anyone? She smiled, excited to share what she had learned from her mom in the hospital. "Most of them didn't go here, they came from all over."

Daniel raised an eyebrow. "Wow, I never would have guessed. But that makes sense, there were so many of them, more than have gone missing from here."

"There's a whole war going on, and we're caught in the middle of it."

"A war?"

"You bet," she stood then, hands on her hips. "But don't worry, I'll protect you."

Daniel guffawed and threw a piece of grass at her. "This isn't my war."

"Hmm," Allie squatted, unsure. "But you were there with me, and…"

"Chris used me to get the necklace, right? That's all."

"Maybe." She still wasn't convinced. Something told her Daniel had a role to play yet. But for now, she didn't want to worry about it. She looked over and saw Daniel was smiling like a buffoon.

"What?" she said.

"Dad's cooking beef stroganoff tonight, first time he's cooked in ages.... Allie?"

"Yeah?"

"Thanks. I'm happy you moved here, I'm glad we're friends and, you know."

She leaned over and hugged him. "Thank *you* for helping me save my mom."

Daniel blushed, then hugged her back. "Don't mention it," he said as he pulled back and stood, his face blotched with red.

"No, I will mention it." She stood and cupped her hands, looking into the sky and yelled, "DANIEL HELPED FIND MY MOM AND IS MY BEST FRIEND IN THE WHOLE WORLD!" She turned with hands outstretched and a proud smile.

He stared back, shocked. She chuckled. He giggled. Then it was unstoppable – they broke into laughter.

When they were done laughing Daniel figured he'd best see how his dad was doing with dinner, and Allie agreed because she swore something smelled like burnt hair. She walked him to the entryway and gave him a hug good-bye. He turned and opened the door, then turned as if remembering something.

"Wait a sec," he said.

"Huh?"

"I got something to show you."

Allie noticed the shield she had found, hanging on the wall. "They let you keep it?"

"Oh, yeah. Funny thing, most people can't see it, you can only see it if you believe, something about another plane. So my dad sees a drawing I did in class of a tree."

"Yeah?"

"I guess since I'm part of this whole world now I can see it."

"I'm glad you are," she said. "But Chris…."

"That's what I wanted to show you. Remember the present he gave me for my birthday?" He pulled his blue backpack from the wall and took out a book, *Aesop's Fables*.

"What about it?"

"Well, I thought nothing of the book until we got home last week. I was about to throw it away, or burn it, I don't know. I was pissed at Chris. But then I picked it up and noticed a couple of pages were all dog-eared." He held it out to her. "And well, look."

Allie looked at the page, a sketch of a wolf. Behind it rose a mountain, very similar to Solomon's Throne in Kyrgyzstan.

"How...?" she asked in amazement.

"Exactly. It's a fable of a wolf that craves power, only in the end to find his hunger controls him and his power causes destruction over everything he loves."

"Could it be possible?"

"That Chris knew something was happening and somehow couldn't control himself? I know Chris. Not only is it possible, but there's no way he would have betrayed me unless something was controlling him."

"And the wolves! That must be his spirit animal."

"Huh?"

"I don't know exactly, but I asked Principal Eisner about that eagle, when she visited us at the hospital, and she said that maybe it was my spirit animal, and well.... What if Chris has one too but it's a wolf? Maybe he sent the wolf to warn us in the caves. They defended us against the giant, and then followed him when he ran with the army."

"So he may not be completely lost after all!"

"No, perhaps not."

"I'm going to need some time to process all this."

Allie shook her head, bewildered at the ways of the world – not the normal world, but the new world she had somehow stumbled into. She paused in a moment of realization.

"And then we're going to have to save him," she said.

"I suppose so."

Allie walked home in a daze, unsure how to take everything that was happening, unsure what to think of the past couple of weeks. She reached her home and entered to see Ian reading on the couch with their mom beside him watching the television. Allie smiled and jumped in between them, snuggling up against her mom. For the time being at least, she could be a little girl again, if only for a few minutes.

Her dad entered with a large bowl of popcorn. "Feeling up for a movie, Princess?"

Allie smiled up lazily. "I wouldn't miss it for the world. Anything but action."

Her mom squeezed her lovingly and Ian grabbed a handful of popcorn as he sat up. Their dad put on the movie, then sat beside his wife.

He lifted the remote but paused, then turned to Allie. "Thank you for never giving up hope."

Allie looked lovingly from her parents and then to Ian as the opening music to their movie began. Ian smiled back and ruffled her hair. She frowned at him and the ring on her finger glimmered before returning to normal as she giggled.

That night she slept soundly, the most relaxing sleep she ever had.

BOOK TWO

ALLIE STROM AND THE SWORD OF THE SPIRIT

BACK TO SCHOOL

llie Strom felt the walls pushing in, rocks crumbling around her as the smell of sulfur told her that something terrible was on its way. A deep voice called her name, pulling her close, and then the shadow of a being was in front of her with eyes of fire.

"Allie," a distant voice said. "Help me…."

She woke with a start and dashed from her bed as she yelled, "I'm coming, Mom!"

Allie burst into her parents' room, ready to do whatever it took to protect her mom again. Prepared for the worst. Instead, she was confronted with the groggy and confused faces of her mom and dad.

"I got this," her mom said, and led Allie out of the room.

"You're okay?" Allie said when they reached her door.

"Honey…. This is, what, the third time this week?" Her mom held Allie by the shoulders and looked into her eyes. "I get that you've been through a lot, and believe me, I know how it feels. But I'm back, you saved me and I'm safe, okay? We're all safe."

"For now," Allie mumbled.

Her mom took her in a hug and caressed her hair. Before her mom had gone missing earlier in the school year, Allie would have pushed her away and been annoyed. At the moment though, after yet another one of her crazy dreams, Allie leaned into the hug.

"You and me, we're not so defenseless." Her mom walked her to bed and tucked her in. "But I tell you what. Next time you have the dream, you can come sleep with your father and me, okay?"

"Yeah, right." Allie smiled and turned over in bed. "I may get scared, but I'm twelve. Get serious."

Her mom left, but Allie couldn't sleep. After an hour of tossing and turning, she gave up. She wondered if

Daniel was having similar issues. She rummaged around the drawer of her nightstand for a few minutes, found her cell, and texted him. While she waited, she found an outfit for the day, a hoody with long sleeves over a red T-shirt. She glanced down at the dark pattern on her arm, like a tattoo, but with some deep magic that she didn't understand. It had been carved into her arm by Paulette, right before she revealed herself to be possessed by the evil spirit Samyaza.

Allie had been too scared to tell anyone about what had happened to her. She still hadn't told her dad or anyone else about the craziness of her being a Bringer of Light, or Daniel a Guardian. She hadn't started a blog about her progress toward her supposed destiny of becoming The Tenth Worthy. And when questioned about Chris's whereabouts or anything related to the battle at Solomon Mountain, Allie just shook her head and said she had no idea.

Maybe telling people would have been the better way to go, but she didn't want to seem crazy or put those around her in danger.

A tapping on her window pulled her from her thoughts.

"About time," she said as she moved aside for Daniel to crawl in.

"For five in the morning, I think I did pretty good." He took a seat on her desk-chair and swiveled back and forth.

"Pretty well," she corrected, and instantly hated herself for it.

"Are you sure?" He sat at her desk and had a look around her room. "Finally got to cleaning, I see."

The boxes that had occupied most of her closet were finally cleared away, and she'd decided that the nerdy posters and fantasy figurines—gifts from her brother—maybe weren't best for her walls. Not when she was trying to maintain her sanity and think of anything but giants and magic and grand destinies.

"Yeah, well…. When you have nightmares all the time, what else is there to do?"

"Aside from waking me up?"

"Sorry."

He waved her off. "Honestly, I haven't been sleeping too well either. I keep seeing that giant with fiery eyes and the way Chris looked at me, as if we'd never met."

Allie shuddered. "Yeah. Back to school, yay."

"Think the police will still be around?"

"They get to you yet?"

"Don't worry, I stuck to the story." He cocked his head like he was some sort of hero.

Allie smiled at the thought, thinking he definitely was a hero. They had worked together to defeat Paulette, or whatever the deal was with that Samyaza demon-character taking over Paulette's body, and in the process they had rescued Allie's mom. All Allie wanted in life was to be a normal girl, but with the Ring of Solomon now in her possession, she knew that wouldn't be the case. She would never be normal again.

"How about you?" he asked. "What'd you tell the cops?"

"Somehow I've still managed to avoid them."

"Good luck with that."

She shrugged and they sat in silence for a bit before she suggested playing Minecraft together. He didn't object, although he reminded her that they were a bit old for it.

"Eh, you're never too old for an awesome game," she said. "Well, so Ian says anyway."

"But he's a nerd."

She laughed. "Welcome to the club."

"Speaking of clubs…. Today's the big day, right? Soccer tryouts?"

"I totally forgot!" She couldn't believe it had slipped her mind, after how much it had meant to her when preparing for seventh grade.

"Get your head in the game, Allie," Daniel said. "Mine's one hundred percent in the world of baseball, I promise you that."

"Deal," she said, and they shook on it.

At around seven, Daniel snuck out the window to ring the front doorbell.

"It's for me," Allie said as she ran to get the door. "I invited Daniel over for breakfast."

"You two are spending a lot of time together," her dad said, reading the morning news on the couch.

"Is that a bad thing?" she asked, opening the door.

He smiled at Daniel with a wave. "No, of course not."

The look her dad gave her mother was too obvious for Allie to miss. Whatever. She knew what he was thinking, and yeah, she had thought of boys that way—Chris for one, before she knew he was a Strayer. But her and Daniel? He was amazing, in that fun friend-who-helps-save-the-world kind of way. So yeah right, no way.

Allie's older brother, Ian, was in too much of a hurry to sit and eat, so he grabbed a granola bar and a banana on his way out the door.

"How's being back at school?" her dad asked, shaking his head at his son's quick departure.

Allie shrugged and returned to her cereal. It was like that lately, his questions and her awkwardness. Daniel noticed, and when they headed off to school, he asked her what was up.

"I don't know," she said with a glance back to her apartment. Her dad was looking out the window after them, his arm around her mom.

Daniel was still staring at her. "It seemed like you were a bit cold to him, is all."

"Can we drop it?"

"Of course."

They walked on, neither saying a word. The silence was horrible. A cool breeze blew by, making Allie wish she had put on a sweater over her shirt.

"Fine," she said. "It's…."

"Yeah?"

"Ever since we got back, with my mom and all, it's been like that with him." She looked at the gray clouds forming in the distance, annoyed to be opening up right now. But if she couldn't talk to Daniel, that left nobody. "It's like, if I can't tell him about the ring and all, it's keeping secrets, you know? And I've never kept secrets from my dad before. It feels like lying."

"Of course you're feeling weird. It's like you're pushing him away, right?"

"Yeah, I guess."

"You can't push away the people that matter most. If you do, who else will be left?"

"Right." She glanced over at him, thinking how serious he was. Such a grown-up, always talking about feelings and watching the History Channel. Once again, she asked herself how she had ended up best friends with someone like him. Not that she would change it for the world.

When they reached school though, a lump formed in her throat. The police were back, and they were waiting in front of the main entrance with Principal Eisner. Allie was sure they were waiting for her.

"Come on," she said, pulling Daniel around the hedges.

"It's like a Band-Aid," he said. "Just get it over with."

"I don't think so." She pulled him in the other direction, but nearly collided with a tall boy who looked to be a year or two older than her. She hadn't seen him before, and she would have remembered if she had.

"You okay?" the boy asked, stopping to look back and tuck his wavy black hair behind his ear.

"Yeah, um, thanks." She stared after him, forgetting herself until she heard Daniel clearing his throat. She spun on him. "What?"

Daniel frowned, and then nodded to her left. When she turned to see what it was, a badge was inches from her face. Officer Dunlop. Great.

"There you are, Allie," Principal Eisner said. She walked up beside Officer Dunlop and smiled in her way that said *keep to the story*. "I'm sure you won't mind giving the officer a bit of your time."

"Of course."

"Right this way, ma'am," the officer said.

He led her to the principal's office and closed the door once his partner had joined them. The interview was quick and painless, though, and she didn't trip up when telling them the story of getting beaten up by Chester and Vince, and that she had no idea where they or any other kids had gone. Still, it wasn't easy, and every lie she had to tell brought back memories of Paulette and her eyes glowing like fire, or the army of Strayers in their black cloaks.

Allie darted out of the office as soon as the cops said she was dismissed, but collided with Principal Eisner in the hall.

"You must be more careful," Principal Eisner said as she straightened her hair. "Especially with everything going on this week."

"This week?" Allie asked, her heart pumping. Seeing how Principal Eisner had been involved in the whole Bringer of Light and the Tenth Worthy stuff, if she said it was going to be a big week, this was going to be huge.

"You've been assigned a new gym class." Principal

Eisner handed Allie a piece of paper with a room number on it.

"That's all?" Allie asked.

"Sure," the principal replied with a smile. "That's all."

With a glance at the paper, Allie saw that it was her first class of the day. Great, she would already be late. It was bad enough that she had missed more than a week of classes while she was out saving her mom and then recuperating.

The paper said class was in the basement, room 001. Allie hadn't even known the school had a basement. But after she asked around, a teacher pointed her to the far end of the hall. It took her outside to where a door led to the basement. Here goes, she thought, already looking forward to the distraction of P.E. class and the chance to forget about her recent adventures for a while.

P.E. CLASS

Voices came from a staircase to Allie's right, a good sign in this gloomy corner of the school basement. The walls were all dark brown wood, just shadows in the dim light streaming in from narrow windows where the ceiling met the walls. Cobwebs covered the corners at each turn. Floorboards creaked. As the smell of old wood grew stronger, the voices softened.

Everything felt wrong, and Allie started to wonder if she was in the wrong place.

She was about to give up when she turned a corner and found a door in her path. Room 001. She waited, her hand shaking as she reached for the doorknob. Why was she so nervous? For a moment she wished Daniel was there with her, sharing the dread of the first day in a new P.E. class. But hey, at least with this new class she wouldn't have to deal with Ms. Trallis again.

She pushed at the door. The sun shone bright, blinding her momentarily. A fresh scent of wet pine drifted in and she saw clear skies—a surprise since the morning skies had been full of swirling gray clouds.

Twenty feet of hardwood floor spread out before her, and other students that looked to be her age talked nervously. Between them and the tree line of a forest was a large circle of dirt where older students performed breathing exercises. Great, Allie thought, wondering if she was enrolled in some sort of hippy kung-fu P.E. class. She looked around and saw the boy from outside the school, the one she had almost bumped into.

Then a thought registered—how was this possible? She had walked down several flights of stairs and should have been directly underneath the cafeteria. This sunshine-filled sanctuary didn't seem to belong at all.

A shadow fell over her and she turned to see another girl had just joined her, standing at her side. The girl wore a nervous smile and a brown sweater that matched her long brown hair.

"What do you think?" the girl asked, gesturing to the kids in the circle and then to a yellow wall to the right that Allie hadn't noticed. The fifty-foot wall went out as far as the dirt circle, and then curved away from them to where, if Allie craned her neck, she could just make out two marble pillars that framed snow-white translucent drapes. Through the drapes she could just about make out a door tall enough for a giant.

"It's a little intense," Allie finally replied.

"Intense?" the girl said with a laugh. "Yeah, I'll say. The name's Brenda."

"Allie."

"I'm a Guardian. How about you, Guardian or Bringer?"

Allie couldn't believe it. "You mean...?"

Brenda smiled as if sharing a secret. "You must be new. This is where the Guardians and Bringers of Light train."

"You're telling me this P.E. class is like our warrior training or something?"

"Uh," Brenda looked at her like she was slow. "That's what I just said."

In the circle of dirt in the midst of the clearing, the older kids were moving their hands in time with deep breaths, stepping in sweeping circles. Allie thought she recognized forms, similar to the *katas* she had learned from her one month of karate when she was younger. She didn't want to tell Brenda that she would rather be playing soccer. Something about the girl bothered her. Maybe it had to do with recently being burned by older girls she had met—namely Paulette.

"So, you must be new then?" Brenda asked. "Not a transfer?"

"Yeah, just moved here with my mom," Allie said. "Well, a couple months ago."

"I mean a transfer Guardian. You're just starting?"

"Oh, yeah, that."

"Allie!" a voice said, and she turned to see Daniel

standing behind her, all smiles. He had entered with someone else—the boy she'd almost bumped into outside of the school that morning.

"Can you believe it?" Daniel continued. "I get to train with you!"

"That's awesome," she said smoothly, not wanting to look too eager in front of this older boy.

"Another noob?" Brenda asked, and the older boy nodded. She sneered at Allie and Daniel. "Don't worry, you guys will catch on fast enough, I'm sure."

Allie heard the sarcasm in her voice, and Daniel must have too, because he said, "We've had our fair share of excitement."

The older boy turned to Daniel with a look of interest. "Like what?"

But before Daniel could get out another word, Brenda said, "Me and Troy here are always the best at obstacles, you'll see. If you need any pointers, just ask."

"They'll do fine," Troy said. Brenda scowled at him and crossed her arms.

After a silent moment, Daniel noticed a short Japanese girl standing nearby, seemingly listening in.

"Hi," he said, "What's your name?"

"Yuko," the girl said, avoiding eye contact. She blushed and walked off.

Brenda, apparently bored with the teasing, left as well.

"Don't worry about Brenda," Troy said. "That's just how she is."

Allie was contemplating a witty remark, something

to show him how funny she was, but suddenly all of the students were silent, looking over to the marble pillars where a man had just emerged with a group of older kids behind him. The man gave the kids a nod and they ran off to the trees. Turning back to Allie and the others, he said "Form your classes," and took a spot in the circle closest to the pillars.

His red hair shifted lightly in the wind—Allie wondered if it was a toupee. He barely had eyebrows, they were so light, but his eyes shone like two sapphires. If she weren't so nervous, Allie might have laughed at his white t-shirt tucked into blue Levi's.

"First-years, hurry and get changed and meet back in the circle. The rest of you, through the doors. Hustle now."

Allie shared a what-have-we-gotten-ourselves-into look with Daniel, and then hurried off after Brenda to the locker room. She noticed Troy and some of the older students lining up in front of the teacher as she went.

In the locker room, Allie quickly changed into her gym shorts. They weren't so bad, but she still would have preferred to wear sweats or jeans. She tried to ask what they'd be doing, but Brenda just told her that she'd have to wait and find out, and when she asked Yuko, all she got was a nod before the girl turned to finish dressing.

When they were all back outside in the circle, Daniel standing beside her, the man with red hair returned from the tree line and looked over them, assessing each student.

"So you are my seventh-graders huh? My first-years. Go ahead, have a seat in a horseshoe around me. I am Mr. Phael, Raphort Phael. You there, what's your name?"

"Tom," a small boy said. He wore plaid shorts and his hair curled in a swoosh at the front.

"Good name. Tom here is a strapping young lad, ready to take on any challenge that comes his way." Several girls giggled. "And what is it, do you suppose, that brings you all together here, Tom?"

Tom looked up from commenting quietly to his friend. "Uh, we're all first-years?"

"Not exactly, Tom. Something more. An endless potential. You each have something that drives you. You each have the ability to channel that energy, like the boys and girls you saw practicing here before class started. And I will expect you all to practice often as well, to practice channeling your negative energy into positive energy. Do you understand what I'm saying?" He stared right at Allie.

"No, Mr. Phael," she said.

"You look familiar, what's your name dear?"

"Allie. Allie Strom."

"Indeed." His look told her he must have known her mother at some point. "Each of you will be learning wonderful things. You will guide others, teach them, bring out the best in them. It's not important that you understand clearly today. What's important is that you keep an open mind. Can you do that for me?"

Several boys and girls nodded, but Allie just wondered what the heck he was talking about.

"Allie," Daniel hissed. She looked over to see him motioning toward the teacher with his eyes. "He just called on you."

She looked up at Mr. Phael, and saw he and everyone else was staring at her. "Um, what was the question?"

"I asked if you would like to volunteer," Mr. Phael said.

"Do I have to?"

"You do now. Come, beside me."

Reluctantly, she stood and went to his side. His silly smile reminded her of her dad for a moment, always making her do stuff she had no interest in. But sharing toys with her brother or wearing his old jackets wasn't nearly as bad as standing up in front of all these kids. She hoped they couldn't see her cheeks flushing to match the teacher's hair. She stood with her hands folded in front of her, waiting.

"Come with me," Mr. Phael said, leading her to a spot in the dirt next to him. "Now, I don't want to get those nice shoes of yours too dirty." He smiled at her grungy high tops, one still lightly caked in mud.

"Try to follow what I do." He stood with his hands at his sides and faced the sky with his eyes closed. His eyelids flashed open, and with a quick breath, he moved his left foot back and his hands in a sweeping arc.

Mr. Phael's moves were smooth and fluid, but Allie followed along at a slower, jerky pace. He swept his leg around and brought it in close to his other, shooting his hands out and clapping them in front of him. The movements continued, growing more complex, and Allie tried her best in spite of the giggles coming from several of the other seventh-graders. When she was finished, a light layer of sweat cooled her lower back. She smiled.

"How do you feel?" Mr. Phael asked.

Now that he asked, she realized that the whole time she was performing the actions, all her tension had seemed to disappear. It was as if her heart had released all of its worries into the universe, leaving her with pure peace and joy. She smiled and blushed, feeling a little silly about having such a strong reaction to the odd dance.

"Fine," she finally answered.

"Well, Allie is apparently shy," Mr. Phael said. "She performed like a natural. All right, the rest of you now, form two lines behind the two of us, and we will walk you through it."

Allie groaned, not at all excited to be the focus of attention again. But she took her spot beside the teacher. The other boys and girls formed their lines and, with a muttering and a look to the sky, the movements began again. This time she embraced the feeling of her lightened heart and the flow of blood through her veins. She started to smile, not caring if the other kids were watching.

She wasn't the only one feeling that way, though; when they were done, Mr. Phael was smiling like a proud father at all the beaming kids. A silvery glow seemed to have settled over them, as if moonlight shone through their skin to join the sunlight in harmony.

She shook her head, trying to wake from the dream, and several other students did the same. When she looked up again, Mr. Phael was running toward the forest.

"This way class," he yelled over his shoulder. "Hustle!"

The students ran after him without the slightest hesitancy, Allie included. She felt wonderfully self-aware—her senses tuned to a new frequency. Her shoes met the soft cushion of grass effortlessly, as if she were running on clouds. She turned and laughed to see Daniel and Brenda running beside her, all racing into the woods, their skin still glowing. At that moment she knew she loved her whole family, and thought that maybe moving to a new school wasn't all that bad.

"Halt," Mr. Phael said when they were deep in the forest. A series of logs led away to their left, a small swamp to their right.

"That's just a taste of what is to come," he said, nodding at them as they gazed around the forest in wonder. "It's as simple as allowing your minds to clear and let the love from your heart flow. If you were able to feel the change, if you performed your movements and pattern accurately, that's a sign that you are destined for wonderful things to come. But you must practice, you must keep it up. Now, it's time for part two of P.E. class. Are you ready?"

Allie was doubtful and confused…. But intrigued.

19

DOUBT

Mr. Phael led Allie and her classmates to logs arranged like an exaggerated playground that disappeared beyond the trees.

"What we have here is your typical obstacle course," he said. "It wraps around the woods, finishing with clearing the swamp on the other side. Your first few P.E. classes will consist of practicing the patterns of movement and the obstacle course. When you are ready, one by one, you will be called upon for higher training."

He explained the obstacle course in more detail, then blew a red whistle. Allie was in the fourth group to start. She ran across the first logs, falling only once when she stumbled on a branch. The monkey bars were too much for her, but when it came to the final sprint before the swamp, she passed up three kids that had been ahead of her. She reached the swamp and looked around for a way to cross, but was surprised to see none.

"I don't know how I'll be able to do baseball today after all this," Daniel said between heaving breaths as he came up behind her. "Think... they expect... us to swim?"

At the moment, soccer was the furthest thing from Allie's mind. She caught her breath as she looked around for a way to cross the water.

"Maybe there's a rope or something?" she said.

One boy with a square face and high cheekbones jumped into the swamp and started swimming, but Allie took a step back, refusing to go that route.

"We don't have to go through the swamp—there!" She pointed at the trees growing out of the water. Leaning against the trees were narrow planks. She looked around in the brush and found a similar plank. She lifted it and looked back to meet Daniel's eyes. He shared her smile.

The plank sat easily against the first tree at a forty-five degree angle. It was slippery, but Allie climbed it with little trouble while Daniel held it steady. The problem came when she was at the point in the first tree where the branch went out and she had to pull up the second plank. It was too heavy, and she almost dropped it more than once.

"It's not working," she yelled back. "The water is weighing it down!"

Daniel looked around for another option. "We may just have to swim."

The other boy was already halfway across the swamp, wet moss clinging to his hands. Allie shuddered. No way was she getting in that water.

Other students, some that looked like they were from Africa, Latin America, and even Asia lined up behind them for their turn. Distracted from the obstacle by the growing group behind her, she wondered for a moment at the diversity of these classes. But even more distracting was the fact that Troy was among the observers in one of the other groups, staring right at her.

She looked at the sturdy tree supporting her, analyzing the branches. It might work.

"Daniel, come out here," she said as she shimmied up to the next highest branch.

"What's she doing?" Troy called after Daniel as he crossed the first plank.

"I don't know," he said. "But I don't have any better ideas."

"There," Allie said, pointing at the plank below. "Now you grab it and feed it up. If you can just get the end to me, together we can lift it and place it on the next tree. Then I stay here and steady the plank while you cross."

Daniel fed the plank up just as she instructed, and to her surprise, it actually worked. They leapfrogged the planks, allowing the other students behind to follow in their path.

Everyone was cheering and clapping her shoulder when they reached the other side of the swamp. Troy smiled and Allie felt herself beaming. In the magical forest light, he had the same majestic glow as that first time she had spotted him at the school entrance. Her hands were a bit sore from so much work with the planks, but it was worth it. She couldn't remember being treated so well since she was in first grade and had beat up a second-grade bully. And this time she didn't have to explain a black eye to her father.

The thought of her mother and father scolding her so many years ago brought a longing for the simpler days, but then the sun caught Mr. Phael's red hair, or wig or whatever it was, and she was back among her new friends.

"One of you is wet," Mr. Phael said. "What happened here?"

"Allie figured out the boards, and we followed her across." Daniel beamed.

"That may be right, but that wasn't my question. If the rest of you made it without getting wet, why did one of you fail?"

Daniel turned to Allie with a shrug. The wet boy had gone ahead of them, on his own. What were they supposed to do? Stop him? Was she responsible for everyone there?

"Let that question linger," Mr. Phael said. "The planks are only one of the possible paths across the swamp, and you'll have plenty of opportunities. Three more today, as a matter of fact. You'll learn to work as a team. You are not ordinary students, you are in my special class because each of your principals has deter-mined you worthy. Now, let's not let them down."

"Each of our principals?" Allie asked. She glanced at Daniel, but he looked just as confused.

"You didn't figure that part out yet?" Brenda sneered.

Mr. Phael gave her a scolding look, then turned to Allie with his pleasant smile. "Perhaps I forgot to explain it. You see, each of you has been selected from around the world to come here and train."

"But I didn't go anywhere, just through the basement."

"Me too," Daniel said.

"As you all did, or some door somewhere in your home schools. This is a place of great mystery. Only by portals can you reach it, and only when we want you to."

Allie remembered her own travels across the globe to Kyrgyzstan through similar means. The doorway that had led to a storage closet, and then led her to stumble upon a strange meeting of figures in black hoods.

"Like the Strayers use," she said.

The other students turned to her with looks of shock, some of them obviously familiar with the term.

"Yes, Allie," Mr. Phael said. "Like the Strayers, but nothing like them. Remember that point. And just as we cannot find their doors on our own, so too, our magic protects us against them."

She nodded, glad to know that at least here they

were safe. But she had found a door on her own, the one with the chanting Strayers. Maybe her ring made that possible, or maybe there was some other reason?

Another group of students came charging down the path and Mr. Phael motioned for his class to stand clear while the others started the obstacle course. One tall girl looked Allie up and down as they passed. She had a slight smile and the long slender legs Allie saw in magazines—Allie secretly hoped to one day be able to show off legs like that instead of her little chicken stumps (as her brother liked to call them). They joined with Troy's group, leading Allie to assume that the other class must have been more eighth-graders.

Allie saw the girl again their second time through the obstacle, when they approached the swamp. The girl stood with her maple-brown hair pulled back into a ponytail, her hands at the waistband of her pink shorts as if waiting for something.

"We're supposed to help you," the girl said. "Nice ring."

"Thank you," Allie said, turning the ring over so the seal wasn't visible. She looked around and noticed Troy was back helping Brenda over a wooden wall. She probably didn't even need the help, Allie thought, before turning her gaze back to the older girl.

"Seal of Solomon, eh?" the girl asked.

"Huh?" Allie was surprised to hear someone else say it.

"That star, the triangle pointed up placed upon the

triangle pointed down, some call it the Seal of Solomon. But I imagine you know that?"

Allie looked down and fumbled with the ring. "It was a gift. No big deal."

"Well, I'd be careful with it around here. Symbols, especially ones like that, should never be taken lightly."

"You're telling me," Allie said, remembering her travels to Kyrgyzstan.

Allie frowned and looked back to see Troy and Brenda joining her side. Daniel was still talking with the teacher.

"I'm Karen, by the way," the older girl said.

"Allie."

"Nice to meet you, Allie." Karen pointed to the swamp. "Watch for the particularly dark areas of lily pads. They're made to look like the rest, but are actually on firm ground. Watch your step. You don't want to be covered in that gunk."

"Thanks," Allie said.

Karen winked and turned, bouncing across the swamp.

The rest of P.E. class consisted of one more time through the obstacle and a final pattern exercise in the dirt. Allie felt bad for the wet kid, whose once-white sneakers became caked in mud as he moved in the circle. When it was all over she turned to join the others heading up to the locker rooms, but Mr. Phael intercepted her and beckoned her to follow.

"You showed great promise today, Allie," he said, standing by one of the monstrous columns.

"Okay...." She felt the sudden urge to run out of there.

"I want to make sure you know that we'll teach you skills in this class that not all students will learn. This is voluntary, but we expect much out of you."

"Why me?"

"Perhaps you don't understand yet, but you will," Mr. Phael said. "You've already proven your desire and ability to help others. Sometimes it may be at your own expense, and you must stand up and make the choice."

Allie stared into blue eyes that seemed to peer into her soul. "What exactly are you talking about?"

"The hunt." He leaned in close, lowering his voice. "We're going after Samyaza, or will when we figure out a way forward. It has to be you that takes him down."

She looked at him, sudden cold flooding her veins. Her left arm itched, the one with the carved pattern, and she resisted the urge to touch it.

"Oh. Okay... I... I gotta get to my next class."

Allie turned and walked briskly to the locker room, looking back to see Mr. Phael watching her with arms crossed. The class had been exciting, definitely different from the P.E. classes she was used to. And okay, so Samyaza and his forces were out there, but surely someone else could handle them. She would train and she would help if she had to, but she wished everyone could stop expecting so much from her.

Her first stop was to the bathroom, where she quickly locked herself in a stall and pulled up the sleeve of her shirt. She cringed. The magic, black mark was still there, where Paulette had carved into her. It seemed to writhe before her face, and for a moment it burned. She covered it, stumbled to the sink and splashed cold water across her face.

How could any of this fall on her? It wasn't fair for them to expect a seventh-grader to save the world, especially when she had her own problems to deal with.

20

TIME WITH DAD

Allie wanted to skip the rest of her classes, but knew her conscience would eat her up if she did. Plus, she hoped to see Daniel in the open-air hallways and talk about P.E. class—he'd disappeared while she was talking to Mr. Phael, and she wanted to make sure he was okay. But as the hours progressed, she saw no sign of him, not even in history class.

Clouds gathered with the last bells of class for the day, and a slow pitter-patter streaked the windows of the auditorium where Allie waited to see if Daniel would show. The soccer tryouts and baseball practice had been postponed due to the bad weather, so she had nothing better to do than wait... And maybe Mr. Phael's talk had made her paranoid, but something within told her Daniel needed her.

Troy walked by, carrying Brenda's books. Allie hadn't even realized Brenda went to her school. Troy handed the books over and smiled widely as Brenda wrote her number on a piece of paper for him. Allie thought she would puke at the googly-eyed look in Brenda's eyes. Allie's dad had always told her to wait until she was eighteen to give her number to boys— twelve was much too young.

On the other side of the room, Troy pocketed the paper from Brenda and departed through the automatic glass doors, running through the rain with no umbrella. Allie had purposefully not brought one, herself. Umbrellas in Washington State were for the weak, she always said.

It was apparent Daniel wasn't at school. Allie sighed and waved at Brenda as she headed for the door, but Brenda just played with her brown hair and looked at the ceiling as if Allie weren't even there. Allie had seen her type before, in her old friends from sixth grade. Not a single one of those 'friends' had bothered to call her all summer, and she had learned her lesson.

The rain formed streams and puddles along the path from school to the parking lot. She waited patiently under a gray awning, counting the change in her pocket. Gray clouds hovered behind an off-white stone church that rose above the green and brown roofs of the suburban city. She stared at its beauty, wondering where Daniel could have gone off to.

A horn sounded, and Allie looked up to see her dad in his car, Gabe the librarian in conversation with him.

"Training's off to a good start?" Gabe asked.

She nodded, hopping into the car's passenger seat. Gabe said his goodbyes and headed back to the school.

"What's going on, Dad?" she asked.

"With this rain, I figured I'd come give you a ride," he said. "Did you know Gabe and your mom are friends?"

Allie just nodded.

Her dad frowned. "How're you holding up?"

The guilt about not being able to be honest with him made her stomach twist. She wanted to tell him about her P.E. class today, and about everything that had happened with her mom and the Strayers. But her mom had asked her not to, for his own protection.

"I'm fine," she said.

He looked at her, worried, but smiled. "I've been thinking about you a lot lately, and I want you to know I'm always here for you. Whenever you need me, I will be here."

Did he sense something was off with her, that she wasn't telling him the full truth?

"What about your job?" she said.

"I took the day off, and you know, they hired another person to work under me. A nice old lady, said she can watch the place whenever I need her to. I know you need your father.... You're not doing drugs or something, are you?"

She laughed. "No, Dad, of course not."

"Okay," he said with a ruffle of her hair. "But know that I love you and am here for you no matter what."

She heard him, but her attention was elsewhere. They had come to a red light just outside the school parking lot, and she saw Daniel at the bus stop. A group of boys and girls were walking toward him, and she was sure they were Strayers. But how could they be moving on him now? Hadn't they all disappeared with Paulette? Or maybe they could travel, like with the P.E. class door. And these were new Strayers. She didn't see Vince or Chester among them, and those were the only two she'd really known.

The light was taking forever—she looked at her dad, then back to the bus stop where Daniel waited. The kids were surrounding him.

"Allie?" her dad said.

"Sorry," she said as she opened the door and jumped from the car. Another car pulled up beside her dad's and she had to jump to avoid getting hit. She heard cars honking and her dad calling her name, but she had to get to Daniel.

She reached him at last, scared it was too late.

He sat on the bus stop bench, surrounded by three boys and two girls. Their eyes gleamed with a red tint, but Daniel's eyes were rolled back into his head. One of the boys held a knife and was etching a pattern into Daniel's head—just a half-circle so far. The boy gave her a malicious smile and leaned back in to complete the pattern. The rest of the Strayers turned to Allie ready for a fight.

She charged them, remembering the way she had fought in Kyrgyzstan. She dodged their fists, catching a boy in the stomach with a kick. She slammed her arm across a girl's face, knocking her to the ground. A punch caught Allie across the jaw, but she recovered in time to twist around to the boy who held a knife. She kicked him so that he sprawled forward, his knife clattering to the other side of the bus stop.

She didn't stop to think. She grabbed Daniel under his arms and hefted him onto her back. She felt heat surge from her ring, coursing through her limbs, and she felt powerful. Her legs carried her and Daniel away from the bus stop, and with a glance back she saw her dad pulling his car over to the side of the road. He got out and yelled at the kids chasing her, and presumably pursued them.

He could handle himself, but she needed to protect Daniel. She turned her attention back to running. Each step felt like it would be her last, but soon she was sure she had lost them. Looking around, she saw trees, a playground past them. The added energy from her ring was gone, leaving her exhausted. Daniel was barely breathing, and for a moment Allie wondered if he was dead.

Instinctively she pulled out her ring and closed her eyes, focusing. But nothing happened. She tried again, concentrating on her memories of Daniel, laughing with him, searching the woods, saving her mom…. but nothing worked.

Her mind searched frantically for some idea, some inspiration, and she remembered the odd movements from P.E. class—the way she felt after, as if the rays of the sun coursed through her body, improving her mood. Maybe there was some healing power involved? She stepped next to Daniel's limp body and looked to the sky. She moved her foot and her hands, breathing deeply, trying to focus. She completed the form, but nothing.

In the distance, she heard her dad calling for her. A bit of relief came to her in the sound of his voice, even as it grew distant.

Why wasn't this form working? Maybe it only worked in class? But then what would be the point! She found herself growing frantic.

"Daniel! Wake up!"

She shook him by the shoulders, then checked his breath by placing her cheek by his nose as she had seen in movies. He was still breathing. She wiped the blood from the cuts on his forehead. This was worse than she could have imagined.

"Daniel!"

With a glance around, she realized something. She had done the forms just now on the sidewalk, on cement. Maybe she had to be in contact with the earth for it to work. She stepped to a patch of dirt in the grass on the other side of Daniel. She stood and breathed deep, telling herself to remain calm. To have faith. She looked to the sky, noting the fluffy white clouds and the sun shining brightly in rays across the treetops surrounding her.

This had to work.

She moved with confidence, performing the forms perfectly. The sun shone brighter, the air around her sparkled, glittering. Then it was done.

She felt better, relaxed and full of energy, but Daniel

looked the same. Looking back at the circle, she saw it was still glowing, and suddenly she understood. She rolled Daniel into the circle she had created in the dirt with her feet. It shone brighter, and for a moment he seemed to stop breathing, his skin going pale. Then he glowed, and he woke up coughing. His eyes returned to normal. She leaned over him and held his head off the ground, watching as the markings on his forehead cleared, the blood vanishing.

"What happened?" he asked.

"I figured it out," she said. "I understand the patterns."

He looked at her with confusion. But he was awake, and he was safe. She didn't care if she made sense to him right now, he was safe. She hugged him tight.

They walked home when he felt ready, Allie looking over her shoulder from time to time. She hoped to spot her dad, to get a ride with him and tell him she was okay. No such luck, unfortunately.

"This is all happening again, huh?" Daniel asked, his eyes on the pavement.

"I don't know if it ever stopped," Allie replied.

Daniel looked at her with a smile. "But hey, at least this time they're training us, right? I mean, if we could stop possessed-Paulette without a clue about what we were doing, we're going to bring the noise now."

Allie laughed. "That's one way of looking at it."

Her pocket vibrated, and she checked her phone to see a text from her father. 'Are you okay?' it said.

"Oh, no…" she said.

"What?"

"My dad was running after us, but... is probably worried sick. I gotta call him back."

They were nearly home, so she called her dad and apologized. Oddly, he didn't seem to be too bothered.

"As long as you're okay," he said. "We need to report those kids, but for now... I'll pick you up at Daniel's, yeah? I want to spend some time with you."

"Okay, Dad," she said, even though she was still worried about Daniel. She walked him to his front door and gave him a hug, then waited for her dad on the steps while Daniel went inside to rest from his encounter with the Strayers.

Her dad took her to a coffee shop and bought her a warm apple cider with extra caramel. It had been her favorite when she was ten. She tried to apologize again, but he held up a hand and smiled. "I saw them. There's no need. I know how school can be."

She smiled, blushing, wishing he really did know.

"Do you want me to talk to the principal or something?" he asked. "I mean, is it serious?"

She shook her head. "Thanks for... for the cider."

He looked hurt, and she knew he could tell she was holding something back. They talked in generalities, about how her classes were going and how his work was treating him, until she finished her cider and had to go to the bathroom. On the way back she received a text from her brother and realized another reason why her dad had looked hurt.

'Don't forget today's Dad's birthday' the text from Ian said.

She stopped by the counter and ordered a cupcake, which the emo guy at the counter quietly agreed to put a candle in. When she returned to the table, she smiled and shrugged.

"I'm sorry I forgot about your birthday, Dad. I do love you."

She looked to the emo guy, who brought out the cupcake and helped Allie sing happy birthday. Her dad smiled and hugged Allie, then shared the cupcake with her.

"I know you love me, honey," he said. "But it's good to hear it sometimes."

She smiled up at him, remembering how great it felt to be close like this, not pushed apart by her secrets. And now, with what had happened to Daniel, she decided the only reasonable thing to do would be to find Samyaza and defeat him as fast as possible. To do that, she would have to train as hard as she could. And starting tomorrow, that was the new plan. Samyaza and his dark forces had better watch out, because she was coming for them.

21

THE NEXT LEVEL

Allie took a step back with her right leg, holding her hands together at her side as she watched for Mr. Phael's next move. She coughed as the dry dirt floated around with the sweeping circular motion of her right foot. A momentary loss of balance worried her, but she caught herself as she lifted her left leg before her. She felt better already.

Half a week had passed with too much homework, the occasional hanging out with Daniel, and more P.E. class. Nothing as far as leads on Samyaza or the Strayers. Allie became quite good at the obstacle course and the patterns of movement Mr. Phael had them perform, especially now that she had seen their effects firsthand.

Brenda whispered something to Troy. Allie eyed the two and saw they were looking in her direction. No wonder her ears burned.

"Focus," Mr. Phael said.

Allie blinked and returned to her movement. She felt a tingling inside her. Where was her focus? Now that she was committed to the hunt, she couldn't understand why they weren't out there fighting bad guys. Why were they waiting here? They could be strategizing or something. Or maybe they were, or were already fighting, but just hadn't told Allie, leaving her out of it. That would be the worst.

She pursed her lips and focused on the motions, moving her hands as if a large beach-ball were between her palms and then pushing out with one hand in each direction. She found herself growing angry, anxious to be doing battle instead of practicing forms. Her focus shifted, her body jolted and the tingling became a pulsing of her blood, throbbing up her chest and toward her hands.

A sharp pain coursed through her arms and then through her fingertips, dissolving into a soothing warmth.

Someone yelped behind her.

Allie opened her eyes, staring at the gold specks of dust reflecting in the sunlight that surrounded her.

"Troy?" Brenda's normally snotty voice sounded almost worried.

Allie shook her head, feeling it clear as if waking from a dream. Troy lay on the ground, his eyes blinking as he tried to stand. He collapsed twice before Mr. Phael assisted him up.

Brenda looked from Allie to Troy, confused. "What happened?"

Troy reached out a shaking hand, pointing at Allie.

"I didn't do anything." Allie took a step back. The gold sparkles remained where she had been standing a moment before.

"Look at the ground Allie," Mr. Phael said.

She looked down to where she had stood. Through the sparkling gold dust she could see a circle drawn in the dirt, lines crossing and curving across it, each one shining as if emitting the sun itself.

"What the...?" She felt faint.

"It's what I've been teaching," Mr. Phael said. "Although, we will have to work on your focus."

"But how?" She had understood the healing pattern, because somehow magic happening when she was most desperate was beginning to make sense. But what was this?

Mr. Phael left Troy to maintain his own balance. He walked to the heavy curtains between the columns, motioning for Allie to follow. "You are the first, Allie. Follow me, and we'll see if you are truly ready."

She looked at her classmates, several of who stepped back. Their eyes were filled with terror. A fear gripped her heart as she remembered the fight with the giant demon and Paulette. Had she done something similar to Troy now? Perhaps the mark on her arm had caused it, she thought. Was she some sort of monster, or maybe possessed by demons herself? She pulled her sleeve down to cover the dark marks, faint, but still visible from where Paulette had carved the pattern. If anyone had noticed, would they know what it meant?

She certainly didn't, not exactly, anyway. Only that it was bad.

Allie took a step toward Mr. Phael, her legs moving on their own. She wanted to ask for help, to tell him she was afraid of what she was becoming. But she didn't know how she would say it, or whether he would understand.

"Someone needs to get that freak out of here," Brenda said.

Silently, Allie agreed. Perhaps Mr. Phael had uncovered some great evil in her, and now he was going to destroy her. She took control of her legs and clenched her jaw, walking up to Mr. Phael and standing before him with a determined look.

"I'm ready," she said.

He laughed. "I don't think you are, but I'm glad to hear you say it. The rest of you wait here, I'll be back shortly."

He pushed aside the curtains and pounded on the door three times, each knock resounding through the courtyard. She was scared, but forced herself to stay strong. The door swung inward with a loud grinding of stone on stone.

Mr. Phael turned to her, beckoning her forward. "Now you begin your training."

"My training?" Hadn't she been training already?

She stepped through the door and gasped at what lay before her. A golden-domed ceiling engulfed a circular room with seven levels of open-walled training floors. In the middle of the room was a circle of dirt like outside, where boys and girls were each performing their own movements. She watched in shock as one girl completed a movement and seemed to explode in a burst of light, the kids around her falling back. Moments later the girl stood smiling at their center. A boy to her right regained his footing and completed a movement in the dirt that sent him leaping into the air and onto one of the higher levels. Allie couldn't see what was going on up there, but she heard kids shouting and laughing amid the clanging of steel.

A lion roared to her right, and she nearly peed her pants. It charged past her, disappearing into the welcoming arms of a blond girl not much older than Allie.

"I believe you've already had some experience with spirit animals?" Mr. Phael asked, bringing back the memory of an eagle carrying her in the fight against Paulette, how it had come to her aid when she needed it most, when Paulette had taken the Ring of Solomon.

"You have already begun to learn the patterns, which you will continue to practice in the circle here from now on. As you grow and learn, you will move up the levels—if you succeed that is. You must prove yourself, Allie."

"Prove myself?" Her mind reeled with all the questions that she wanted to ask.

"You're off to a good start," he said. "Your heart has gone through a change, as it must when confronted with great adversity. You've already grown. That's what gave you the ability to perform the Pattern of Light outside, unfortunately against your own classmate."

"I don't understand," she said.

"Some of those kids out there may never make it to this stage. They will continue to train, never accomplishing a thing, always wondering what became of those like yourself. Others will make it, and fail. I hope you will be one to succeed."

Allie looked at the blond girl and watched a lion grow before her, from cub to full-grown in a matter of seconds. It nuzzled the girl and then circled her in a protective, proud walk. She looked to her left and saw a row of swords, spears, and armor and two lines of boys and girls practicing with the medieval gear. Beyond them was a pool of water, and in its midst a raised marble with a glass case at its center. She wanted to go to it, to see its contents. But no, she still didn't believe any of this.

"Believe," Mr. Phael said as if he had read her mind. "Come, I'll introduce you to your new teachers."

"You aren't going to teach me?" she asked.

He smiled, leading the way toward the glass case. "No dear, I'll be guiding those on the outside, assisting the others in finding their path."

The kids paused in their training, nodding reverently as Mr. Phael passed. A brilliant side room rose up before them as they grew closer to the pool. Within it, marble steps led to a giant throne, large enough for three grown men to sit on comfortably. It glowed as if the sun shone upon it, but there was no sunlight in here, no windows whatsoever. Allie felt the urge to bow her head and close her eyes.

"Raphort!" a deep voice said. "How good of you to finally join us."

Mr. Phael smiled and strode eagerly toward two men at the steps of the throne. One wore slacks and a grey-striped dress shirt, the other she recognized by his smile—Gabe the librarian!

"Allie," Gabe said with hands outstretched. "We're so glad you've made it! And first in your class, what an accomplishment. Then again, it's not like there was ever any doubt."

Allie didn't know what to say, and stood silently, taking in the room. Mr. Phael whispered something in Gabe's ear.

"Allie," Gabe said. "I understand you attacked another student?"

"I think I did, but I didn't mean to. Am I in trouble?"

"You must understand something about your power. It is fueled by emotion. While it is meant for good, it can just as easily be turned against your best of friends."

"My... my power?"

The man in slacks walked forward with slow, halting steps. Layers of skin hung around his sorrowful eyes. He pointed a shaking finger toward twelve chairs at the base of the marble steps. The chairs were polished wood, but one among the rest seemed to be decaying, covered in dust.

"You will learn soon enough, young one." The man

guided her forward with a hand on her shoulder. "See this chair, look upon it and its rot. This is the power, the power to maintain or the power to destroy. And you will learn to harness this power which is already inside you."

"Michael, always laying it on deep." Gabe said. "Isn't it too early?"

Michael turned to Gabe and smiled. "Yes, perhaps it is. But after everything you've told me about this one...." He looked down at Allie, his eyes boring deep into her. "I sense an urgency, a need to know sooner than later."

Allie hung her head, as if she had done something wrong. Perhaps she had attacked Troy. She had been mad about her situation, and with him standing closest to her.... He and Brenda had been talking about her, she knew that, and maybe her irritation at them had caused the attack. She thought back to what happened, the sparkling pattern in the dirt and Troy lying there, pointing at her with his trembling finger. She almost wanted to run and hide.

"Enough for now," Gabe said. "Mr. Phael, thank you. We will take it from here."

After Mr. Phael had left, Gabe agreed to show Allie the training grounds while Michael monitored the rest of the students. Gabe led her past the twelve chairs to the giant throne at the top. Here he turned and gestured toward the sky. Allie looked up and saw an elaborate painting on the ledge above the throne.

"What is it?" she asked.

"It's the story of why you will train to become a Bringer of Light, Allie."

Her blood boiled. "I saved my mom, I brought back this stupid ring…." She played with the ring, wanting to throw it into the water. "Haven't I proven myself?"

"You're eager, which can be a blessing… or a curse. There have always been Bringers of Light and Guardians, even before there was a need. You see, the will of a man or a woman is often enough reason for one to emerge. But now we have a darker threat." His eyes darted to the decaying chair, then back to the painting. He pointed to an image of a muscular man in chains. "See this man here? He was once one of our greatest Guardians. He protected someone destined for great things, but in the end he sacrificed her to gain power for himself. His will turned evil, and now he's been cast out from among us."

"Samyaza?"

"The same." Gabe sighed and began to walk down the steps toward the pool. "Guardians are like angels, in a way. But if they earn their wings, it's usually at a point in their lives when they're so devoted to their task that to think otherwise is nearly impossible."

"Wings?"

"Come, I will show you."

She felt an urge to hang back, but her curiosity won. She followed him to the edge of the pool, where she could see inside the glass case. It was empty, except for a sword sheath and what looked like a pair of tar-covered, once-white wings.

"The wings," he said, "as you may guess, belonged to Samyaza."

"The one I defeated?"

"Not exactly." Gabe's expression turned cold. It was clear he didn't like talking about this. "What you defeated was more like a shadow of him, one of many shadows that may lurk in the world. We mean for you to find the rest and destroy him."

Allie stared at him, dumbstruck.

Gabe looked at her a moment longer, and then back to the wings. "When Samyaza betrayed his post, when he was cast out of our halls, he was stripped of his wings. What you see here is evidence of his wrongdoing, and he is not finished yet. He is seeking The Sword of the Spirit, the Helmet of Salvation, the Breastplate of Righteousness, the Belt of Truth, the Sandals of Peace, and the Shield of Faith. They were once within our protection, but taken from us long before Samyaza abandoned his duties with us. Until the armor is restored, the Tenth Worthy cannot be proven, and until the Tenth Worthy is named, Samyaza cannot be stopped. He knew this, and knowing that the Tenth Worthy must reclaim the armor, his spies are scouring the world for each of these items. If we are not victorious, and he takes the power of the Nine, we will be defeated. You must not allow this, Allie."

"Me, but how?"

"Your friend Daniel will help you, and perhaps one day earn his own wings. He will help you prove yourself as the Tenth Worthy, if this is indeed your destiny.

Samyaza has a dark plan, one to take the powers of the past Nine Worthies for himself. We don't have all the answers, but we trust you will be the one to stop him, because the Ring of Andaleeb—Solomon's Ring, if you will—has chosen you. It is that very ring that would give him the power he desires, and it is the same ring that can defeat him."

Allie shook her head, trying to take this all in.

"So why are we spending our time training when we could be out there attacking?"

Gabe's expression darkened and he looked at the tar-covered wings. "I wish it were that simple, but we don't yet know where he or his people are. We're working on it."

Allie looked to the doors, wishing for a minute that she could run off and leave this all behind. But then she made up her mind.

"Well, work faster," she said, walking over to the rack of spears.

"What are you doing?" he asked.

"Aren't I here to train, so I can defeat him when the time comes?" She picked up a spear, surprised by how heavy it was but refusing to show any weakness. "Let's get to it then."

Daniel was sitting at a table with Troy and Brenda, talking in low voices about the obstacle courses and everything they'd been learning in the training grounds. How different from when she first met him, Allie thought, remembering how she had been the only one in the whole lunchroom to stand up for him. Now she was alone, and here he was chatting it up with his new friends.

"Hey guys," she said as she pulled up a chair.

To her horror, Troy and Brenda were suddenly silent and shared a look. Had they been talking about her?

"Sup," Daniel said.

Yup, that confirmed it—he never talked like that to her unless something was up.

She stood to leave, but then Troy flashed a smile and she paused.

"Hey, no hard feelings," he said. "What's behind the doors?"

"I, uh…." Now she wished she hadn't sat with them.

"Come on," Brenda added. "You can't just disappear like that and then not tell us… Especially your best friend."

Allie looked at Daniel, then the other two, and motioned for him to follow. Brenda and Troy glared as she walked off, but she was happy to see Daniel join her.

"What's going on?" he asked.

"You all are acting like this isn't important," Allie said. "You forget we have a world to save?"

Daniel looked around anxiously, then motioned for her to be quiet. "You want people to think we're loonies?"

"You want Samyaza to win?"

His expression grew hard and he leaned in, eyes determined.

"I got your attention?" she asked. "All this, it's way more serious than we thought. I can't tell you everything, but, just…. Train as hard as you can, okay?"

"Yeah, sure, Allie." He assessed her as he worked some food out of his teeth with his tongue. "Other than that, you doing okay?"

"I don't know where to start with that."

"Maybe we need to go to Eisner?" he said. "I mean, won't she do something?"

Allie shook her head. "She knows. Gabe's in there with the others, training. No, I guess we have to wait…. But be ready, right?"

"Right." He glanced back at the table, uncertain, then turned back to her with a determined look. "Come on, grab your lunch and join us."

"I don't—"

"Allie, we're going to need all the allies we can get."

She couldn't argue with that.

That night she collapsed on her bed, exhausted and mulling over the same question—when was she going to get a break? Preteen girls were supposed to have fun, playing sports and checking out boys and studying to get into good universities… not kicking and punching and making magic circles all day.

She reached into her nightstand, hoping for a book that would take her away from all this. The only book there was a childish one her brother had given her when she was younger—Teddy Bears in Monsterland. She glanced at the silly cover and then tossed it aside.

What was she doing? Was this what she was meant for?

A knock sounded at the door, and a moment later her mom walked in.

"Honey…." Her mom looked at her with concern. "I heard about P.E."

"You did?" Allie wasn't sure she wanted to be having this conversation, but she wanted to hear how much her mom knew about it.

"When I was your age… I never had to deal with any of this. And I can't imagine how hard it is."

They sat in silence for a moment, and then her mom sighed. "They're having a vigil, you know? For Chris and the others."

"A what?"

"They think he's—they think he's not coming back. For all we know, it might be true."

"I refuse to believe that."

"But maybe you can go? For his mother?"

Allie saw the pleading in her mother's eyes, the horrible sense of guilt and sorrow at the thought that it could have easily been Allie that had never made it back.

"Of course, Mom."

Her mother stood and went for the door, but Allie cleared her throat.

"Why me?" Allie asked.

"Why someone else?" Her mother put an arm around her. "I had those same questions when it was my time, and the best I could come up with was that it was my destiny, my fate. I know it's not enough, but it's what I had to accept if I was going to save lives. To make a difference and stop the bad guys from winning."

"I just want to go to school and be a normal kid. I don't want to save lives."

"I'm sure that's not true, honey. And I'm sorry, but being a normal kid? You're too special for that."

Allie hugged her mom and smiled as she received a kiss on the cheek. She hated to hear the truth, but she knew that's what it was.

22

SWORDS AND MAGIC

Allie thrust the training dummy with her sword. The steel felt good in her hand, as if the rest of her world paused while she practiced her sword attacks. Each strike with the sharp blade put her nerves to rest.

P.E. class was a nice relief after the sorrow of the event held to say goodbye to Chris and the others that had disappeared. Deep down in her heart, she knew she would find them and save them, somehow. But that didn't stop her chest from feeling like it was going to explode when they showed a video of Chris when he was younger. It didn't stop the tears from forming in her eyes when she saw Daniel crying.

She lifted the sword for another attack when three loud knocks echoed through the training hall. She paused, wondering what it could be.

Metal scraping on marble sounded as the main doors opened. Troy and Brenda walked into the room with wide eyes. Allie remembered the feeling of astonishment and doubt at seeing people jumping up to seven stories, shooting light from their fingertips, and creating animals out of thin air. Now she was one of the students training to perform these feats. She had learned two more form patterns and was working on the jumping pattern now—she had been able to push herself ten feet off the ground earlier. When she had asked about the animals, she was told to wait patiently and her time would come. Meanwhile she was to focus on the basic patterns, and combat.

Practicing with swords and spears seemed a bit odd, but she did it nonetheless—it was more exciting than playing volleyball.

"So this is what you've been up to?" Troy asked Allie when she approached the newcomers.

"Welcome to the next level." Allie smiled and held out her sword in a dueling stance.

Brenda scoffed. "Please, what would you do with that?"

Mr. Phael entered the room behind them. "It sounds like we have a perfect opportunity to show off what you have learned, right Allie?"

"Mr. Phael," Allie said, bowing her head as she had seen others do on her first day. She ignored Brenda's second scoff.

"Come, let us find you a partner to demonstrate." Mr. Phael waved to Gabe and led the seventh-graders to the circle. He cleared the area before pointing to Karen. "You'll help Allie put her skills to use."

Karen nodded, eying Allie soberly. She grabbed a sword and stepped into the circle. Mr. Phael stepped out.

"Um, what am I supposed to do?" Allie asked. She hated the smirk on Brenda's face from the sidelines.

"Just let it come naturally," Mr. Phael said with a wink.

A flash caught Allie's eye as Karen's sword tip swung inches from her face. Allie jumped left, away from another strike. She parried.

"What're you doing?" Allie yelled. "You're going to kill me!"

Karen smiled and lunged. Allie dived to her right. She looked up to see Mr. Phael and ran toward him, hoping he would stop the fight, but he caught her and turned her around with a gentle shove. Karen's eyes were dead serious.

Why was no one stopping this?

Allie looked at the encouraging faces of the other students gathered around. None of them looked nervous, none of them had the look of blood lust. It was normal, like somehow they knew no one would be hurt. She breathed deep, and turned to Karen to attack.

But Karen wasn't there. In the dirt where she had been was a glowing pattern of a zigzag through a crescent moon.

Allie heard a sound above her and looked up just in time, raising her sword as Karen landed with a strike from high over her head. Steel met steel with a clang and Allie fell back. Her heart stopped for a split-second, but then she regained her faith. She jumped up and quickly performed the pattern of light she had learned. She shoved her hands forward and the light caught Karen, turning her in the air and halfway across the circle. Karen pushed herself to one knee and smiled. She nodded slightly, as if to congratulate Allie, but then she was running with her sword raised.

Allie couldn't move fast enough. The steel was solid, sharp. She anticipated the blow, her body shaking. It never came. Everything was dark. She opened her eyes to see the hilt of the sword held in front of her, the blade deep inside her chest. But at the same time, it wasn't.

Mr. Phael stepped forward and raised Karen's arm in the air. "Winner!"

Everyone clapped. Allie stumbled backward, clutching her chest. There was no hole, no blood. "Mr. Phael?"

Mr. Phael turned and smiled. "Sorry Allie, we should have explained." He took Karen's sword and stabbed downward, into his own foot. It looked like it had stabbed him, but when he removed the blade there was no blood.

"We're not affected by our own weapons. They've been blessed." He held the hilt for her to examine. "You see, the pattern there is one of protection. When embedded onto an object, the object can no longer cause damage to another person."

She looked at her own sword and saw the same pattern. It looked like a circle with an aloe plant growing from it. She felt like she wanted to laugh and cry at the same time.

"That was amazing," Troy said. Even Brenda was staring at her wide-eyed.

She turned red. "Really?"

"How'd you learn to fight like that?" Brenda asked.

"You will soon find out," Gabe said as he approached. Allie bowed her head and Gabe nodded. "Allie, keep training while I show your friends here their new P.E. class. When I'm done, I expect you to teach them the basics of a jump pattern."

"But I haven't—"

"You will," Gabe said. "Just practice."

Troy shook his head in bewilderment and followed Brenda and Gabe toward the twelve chairs. How long had it been since she had been assigned this class and taken that same tour? A month? She had learned so much since then. But the jump pattern was complicated. She had to move her arms in alternate directions while bending her knees and maintaining balance before a leap and a sweep of her foot, and if she messed up one part the whole thing didn't work.

She tried, and failed. She looked at the sky, folded her hands and tried again. This time she was able to jump over an eighth grader who was practicing, but that wasn't enough. She was distracted, weighed down by the pressure of knowing she was supposed to save the world somehow, and rely on Daniel to help her. Of the Strayers, and Samyaza. She watched Mr. Phael's red hair bounce as he walked by, wondering if any teachers really knew the full truth and they just weren't telling her everything.

She got in position to try again and caught Karen's gaze. Her doubts about the older girl had been bothering her, too. Was Karen to be trusted? So-called friends like her had turned on Allie in the past. And now Troy and Brenda were in the training hall too, and were they any better? Allie shook her head and tried the pattern again. A wave of energy swept her into the air, then seemed to give out mid-lift. She fell and landed hard on her rear end. She groaned and arched her back in pain.

A hand was before her, reaching to help her up. It was Karen. Allie smiled, thinking of everything she had been going through lately. Maybe this was the time for friends, for trust. She took Karen's hand and they shared a smile.

Later, when Gabe asked Allie to demonstrate the jumping pattern, she felt strangely calm.

The burst of energy caught her, a warm caress as it propelled her into the sky. It felt as if she were flying, as if wings had sprouted from her back to carry her wherever she desired. Slowly she drifted through the air, watching as she passed the different levels of the training hall with their bursts of light and flowing spirit animals. She felt her toes touch the ground lightly, and turned to see Gabe's proud face. She had finally performed the jump pattern.

"Very well done," Michael said from nearby. "It appears you're ready for the doors."

She looked at him inquisitively, and then followed. He led her up a spiral staircase at a bend in the marble walls, one that led past several floors. By the time he stopped, she was panting for breath.

"All this training, and a few stairs do you in?" he asked.

"There're no stairs in the obstacle course."

He nodded, then motioned to the floor where they had stopped. This floor wasn't exciting like the others. It was simply an empty hall, with the right side an open space where she could see the others training below and the left was a series of doors.

"What is it?" she asked. "More training halls?"

"In a way," he said, opening the first door.

She paused to look at the symbol carved beside the frame of the door—a flowing line like an intricate "L," with three dots to the upper left.

"This is Mr. Phael's domain, where he comes from." Michael nodded for her to proceed and she stuck her head in. A warm breeze accompanied the chirps of birds, and pools of steaming water surrounded a bed of flowers. Not far off, a group of students, all with red hair like Mr. Phael's, turned her way and nodded. Michael waved back, and then pulled back and shut the door.

Allie looked at him, stunned, and followed him to the next door. This one had a similar flowing symbol, only it was more like a pointed "M" and the three dots were at the top.

"Brace yourself," Michael warned, and when he opened the door a cold gust of wind sent a chill through Allie's bones.

A quick glance showed a dazzling display of snow-covered ground, snow blowing through the air, and students that looked to be fighting. With a quick wave, Michael closed the door and was about to head to the next one when Allie asked him to wait.

"What is this?" she asked. "Why are you showing me these?

"If I'm not mistaken, you've seen doorways like this before, no?"

Remembering the Strayers, she threw open the

door with the snow—alert for any sign of their black cloaks. But this time it opened on a blank wall.

"You can call it magic, but that's not quite right." Michael closed the door and opened it again, to show the snow. "You see, it's all about what you're ready for. If I grant you power to the door, it will open here, to the training lands of the assault. The other one, Mr. Phael's land, is where you learn advanced healing. The others include advanced protection, elementals, and many more. You will gain entrance to each as we progress."

"But...." Her insides churned, making her queasy. "The Strayers, and Paulette, they used a door like this. Can't they come here if—"

"No," he interrupted, his eyes narrowing. "They can make their own passages, but only when invited can they use one of ours, and of course they will never be invited."

Allie sighed, hoping she could believe him. "But then how can we follow them?" She walked to a third door and opened it, revealing the wall behind it. "Doesn't that mean we can't use their gateways unless they invite us as well?" She opened the fourth door, and just as she did, a strange light shone from her ring onto the wall.

She looked to Michael for an answer, but he seemed as stumped as she was. The wall before her began to glow as the light filled it with color like liquids mixing, and then there was a bright blast. The light cleared, revealing a path of grass with towering trees on each side.

"This isn't right," Michael said. He slammed the door shut, but the light continued to shine from it. When he opened it again, the path was still there.

He looked to Allie and her ring, and his eyes lit up, hopeful. "I'll gather the others. If your ring is doing this, it can only mean one thing.... The ring has found a connection to this place, and unless I'm wrong, that means either one of the six pieces of armor will be in there, or Samyaza himself."

23

THE HUNT

Although it had been a bright day where they'd just come from, here the sky was a dark gray. Trees bent above their heads, looking as if they would fall to crush Allie and the group at any moment. A strong wind blew Allie's hair around her face, causing it to whip at her cheeks. She glanced over to Troy and Michael, jealous of their short hair at a time like this. Not that it mattered—they all had bigger problems coming than just the wind. They were on the search for one of the legendary pieces of armor, and would more than likely encounter Samyaza, or at least his Strayers.

She wished Daniel could've come with them, but he was a Guardian. Michael and Principal Eisner had agreed that, for this mission, only Bringers of Light would be going. When they'd stepped through the doorway, Allie felt as if she were leaving her defenses behind, but arguing for Daniel to come had been met with a simple "No." They thought it was too much risk, given where he was in his training, and didn't bother to consider that he'd already faced Samyaza with Allie once before.

Ahead, the path turned. They pushed their way through overgrowth and palm leaves, and then stepped into what must have been an ancient temple. Ruins lay scattered across the field of grass, with a temple in the shape of a small pyramid at the far side and what appeared to be ocean just beyond it. The scent of fish on a salty breeze confirmed her guess that it was indeed the ocean.

"Where are we?" she asked.

Michael offered a smile, though his worry was still evident behind his eyes. "First time to Mexico, perhaps?"

"Not me," Troy said, but he looked just as confused as she was.

"Well this is Tulum, the site of ancient Aztec worship, I believe." Michael paused. "Or was it Mayan?"

"Aztecs?" Troy looked at one of the carvings with fascination. "Weren't they the ones that played a form of polo with human heads from their enemies?"

Michael replied with a glare.

"Tulum is Mayan," Allie said, quite sure of it. She had done a research paper on old pyramids the previous year, and for some reason that information stuck with her.

"Thank you, Allie," Michael said, "for the helpful input."

He led the way down the path and past one of the mounds of ruins. Some of the stones were worn by wind or touch, others still showed off their carvings. She saw animals, a serpent here and a rooster there. Others were carvings of human faces.

"So...." Allie gulped. "Why are we here?"

Michael pointed at the pyramid-shaped temple. "Something tells me it has to do with that. If we're where I think we are, then that temple was used to make an ancient calendar. The one people got all funny about in 2012, writing about the end of the world and whatnot. Trust me, when the world's going to end, no one will know it."

"That doesn't exactly answer my question," Allie said.

"The way the temple worked is a light would shine through a hole on the other side of the temple at a specific time of year. This let them set their calendar. Given the stories that they also used to practice human sacrifice here at this temple, I have a feeling we'll find more than just a light for a calendar in there."

The group made their way forward, then climbed the stone steps of the temple. Allie jumped at a slithering noise and nearly fell backward down the steps, but she was relieved to see it was just a lizard. Another bonus if Daniel had been allowed to come along, she would have had someone here to keep her sane.

They entered the temple through a low entrance, just tall enough for her to walk through without having to crouch like the others. Large cut stones made up the walls, and nothing about the room struck Allie as particularly odd. It was a simple temple, old and in ruins, and for a moment Allie started to think they had come here for nothing.

Then her ring began to vibrate and glow, and she knew they were in for an adventure.

The sunlight shone through a rock at the far end of the temple, casting an eerie yet beautiful glow of orange and red across the stones of the room. The group stood there in awe for a moment.

"What now?" Troy asked.

Michael was looking around the room, and Allie realized what he was searching for. She followed the shaft of light and saw it was highlighting a stone on the wall. It couldn't be that easy, she thought, but as she approached the stone she saw it glimmer and appear translucent.

"Over here," she said.

She had experience with odd stones, and she pressed carefully on the sparkling stone, but nothing happened.

"Use the other hand," Michael said.

She held up her ringed hand and saw that the ring was glowing brightly. As she moved it closer to the stone, it began to pull toward the rock like a magnet. When the ring touched the stone, the whole room shone like sunset amplified with mirrors, all the stones shining pink, orange, and red.

Allie turned to face Michael and Troy, then pulled back in fear. At least a dozen other faces stared back at her. They weren't solid like Michael and Troy, and they wore old leather skins and loincloths and carried hatchets and daggers.

One let out a war cry and they attacked. Allie held up her hands, but they moved right through her, charging through a solid wall.

Michael studied the wall for a moment, then gestured for them to follow. He disappeared through the stones.

Troy shrugged with a look of queasiness. "Guess that means we have to go through, too."

"Does it?" Allie asked, but Troy was already walking through, reaching back to pull her along, with the others following.

They found themselves in a narrow tunnel that made Allie think of a secret passage in an ancient castle.

"Where are we?" Allie said as she followed closely behind Troy.

"The spirit world." Michael held a finger to his mouth and then pointed left at a fork in the tunnel. "When we cross through passages, we find ourselves on another plane, one where anything is possible."

"Like a girl summoning a giant of black wisps from thin air?" Allie asked, remembering her battle with Paulette.

"For example," Michael said.

Before them, a warm glow highlighted the stones in lavender.

"We're close," Michael said, moving past Allie and Troy to lead the way.

"What exactly are we close to?" Allie asked, but when she turned the corner, she saw for herself.

The spirits had formed a barrier between her group and a large cavern. The walls arched to form a dome overhead, and nearby she could hear the waves of the ocean lapping against rock. Past the spirits, the small frame of a girl no bigger than Allie showed dark, the silhouette highlighted by the object beyond her—the object that was causing the glow.

Allie's first thought was of Paulette, but the girl didn't seem tall enough. It didn't matter anyway, because before Allie had a chance to look, the girl had taken the glowing object and concealed it within her jacket. Then, with a twisting of glowing light that engulfed her, the girl was gone.

"This can't be good," Troy said, as the spirits began their advance.

"We were too late," Michael said. "Retreat!"

And then they ran.

24

THE WATCHERS

The weird excursion to Tulum left Allie full of questions. How could Michael have let someone else make off with the item? How had someone else happened upon it at the same time as them, just one step ahead?

She had told Daniel about it, in spite of Michael's request that she keep this secret. He was her best friend now and deserved to know.

"It couldn't have been Paulette," Allie insisted for what felt like the billionth time. "I would have known."

"Fine," Daniel agreed. "Then it looks like we have another girl our age turned bad guy…. Hey, wasn't Paulette a Guardian?"

"Yeah." Allie wasn't sure she liked where he was going with this. Still, she couldn't help thinking of Brenda immediately, and wondering at her true intentions.

Daniel's eyes lit up with his thoughts. "So, doesn't it

follow that this girl could be a Guardian too? Or even one of the Bringers of Light? I mean, Samyaza has good reason to target those on the inside."

"You want me to start questioning everyone in our training classes? How'll that make me look?"

"Like a paranoid freak, I guess. Shouldn't Michael and the rest of them be taking care of this?"

Allie sighed. "They say they are, but I haven't seen any progress. It's like they're keeping me in the dark."

"Well, let's keep our heads about us," Daniel said, then at a look from her he added, "I mean, let's just keep training and stay focused."

Allie nodded. She didn't like it, but there didn't seem to be any other options.

Frost lined the locker room windows in sharp angles, like the web of a frustrated spider. Allie changed into her P.E. gear, thinking about how this school year was turning into a roller coaster of craziness. Her friends treated her like she had always belonged. Well, Daniel and Troy at least. Karen was always nice to her but seemed withdrawn. And Brenda, well, she was still Brenda and wanted little to do with Allie.

Allie finished changing and walked through the doors to P.E. class, where she was welcomed by the scent of nutmeg and cinnamon. It took a moment before her mind registered the buffet before her. Three tables sat neatly on the ground floor, weighed down with piles of ham, turkey, mashed potatoes, and stuffing. She had forgotten that Thanksgiving was next week.

"You've been doing well, first-years," Michael said. "It's time you were rewarded."

Allie's stomach growled with anticipation, and she darted straight for the pumpkin pie when Michael finished with his 'be thankful' speech. She figured the rest could come after she made sure to have plenty of the good stuff. Thanksgiving was perhaps her favorite holiday. Something about the rich buttery scent of the stuffing, or the way the cranberry sauce complements a juicy turkey.

"This is amazing," Daniel said from beside her. He had a turkey leg in his hand, grease running down his chin.

"Much better than we'd get at home, huh?" Allie surveyed the food, wondering how she could cram as much as she could into herself and not feel guilty about it later. She supposed the training made up for it.

She looked around the room and saw Gabe smiling back from one of the twelve chairs. Usually, the teachers only sat in those chairs when they observed training. But perhaps they made an exception for the holidays?

Allie finished her first piece of pie and decided it was time for mashed potatoes. A wooden bowl had some with leeks mixed in, and she spooned a pile onto her plate. She ate a few bites, then saw the eighth-graders piling into the training hall. Her eyes furtively met with Karen's. She was one of the only students who openly knew her secret. For sure about the ring, and maybe that she could be the Tenth Worthy. She hoped the others didn't know.

For some reason, the eighth-graders weren't joining in the feast. Instead, they lined the training wall, observing.

Allie caught Brenda's eye and nodded toward the walls.

"What's this about?" she said.

Daniel joined them. "Think it's something to worry about?"

Allie saw a bright flash wink from behind one of the eighth-graders. Something didn't feel right. She scanned the seventh-graders around the table. There were seven of them now that had been admitted, and all of them but Allie and Daniel were still around the table stuffing themselves. It was a test.

"Get a weapon," she said.

She dropped her plate on the table, spilling food. But she didn't care, she was running for the wall opposite the eighth-graders. Out of the corner of her eye she saw Michael smile as he watched her, his hand raised. She looked back to see Daniel following, then Michael's hand dropped. The eighth-graders brandished weapons and roared in unison like a monstrous lion. Allie reached the far wall, prying a long spear from its hooks. She turned to see Daniel running back to the circle, two weapons in hand. She followed, and watched as a sword appeared through one boy's chest.

He wasn't hurt, but Gabe was at his side yelling him out. The boy's look of surprise turned to sorrow when he placed the food back on the table and waddled off to sit on the sidelines.

Daniel had reached Brenda and tossed her one of the spears. Allie joined them. They stood ready. Most of the eighth-graders were dealing with the unarmed new kids, but six of them turned on Allie's group.

"Hold tight," she said.

"You do what you want," Brenda said, "I'm getting out of here."

A large girl with short brown hair appeared to Allie's left, and she saw two others flying through the air with push patterns. It was time to be tested. She heaved the spear to her left to block a strike from the large girl's sword. The strike pushed Allie back. She attempted a roll, to get behind the girl and attack, but when she went to stand her stomach lurched—she had eaten too much.

The girl kicked Allie and then came down with the sword, but Daniel leaped in and whacked the sword from the girl's hands. A hand spun him around and a blade fell through his neck. Allie shuddered at the thought of it actually cutting him, and watched as he exited the circle with a glance to her that said 'sorry.'

That left Allie and Brenda alone. Allie found herself fighting off two eighth-graders, and she saw Brenda giving four of them some trouble. She was small and nimble, dodging between attacks. She probably hadn't eaten much, trying to stay skinny. (A bit too skinny, in Allie's opinion.)

Allie swept one of her attacker's legs into the air and struck the boy directly in the chest. She turned on the big girl, ready to take her out, but the big girl had regained her sword and charged Allie. Steel met oak, and Allie was pushed back. She resisted, but it was no good. The other girl was too strong. She tried to divert the girl's strength and use it against her, but by the time Allie had done so and then pulled her spear around to attack, the large girl had regained her footing and struck.

The silver blade struck Allie on the side, and she could see the steel slice down and through her body. Gabe called her out.

"Over here, Allie," Gabe said. She jogged over slowly, feeling the food in her belly swoosh with each step.

"That wasn't fair," she said to Daniel, who smiled and nodded.

"Ain't over yet," Daniel said, pointing to the circle.

Brenda was the only seventh-grader left. She dodged between the tables, using food as a weapon, frustrating the eighth-graders. Karen was attacking with five other students, while the rest of the eighth-graders stood on the sidelines and watched. Brenda maneuvered a beautiful jumping pattern, flying into the sky and out of the way of a sword strike. She smiled at Daniel as she landed, turning to prepare to run again.

Karen lunged forward with her own jumping pattern and tackled Brenda's legs out from under her. She climbed up her body and knelt, sword raised, then brought it down fast into Brenda's chest.

"Not bad," Karen said, helping Brenda to her feet.

Brenda brushed off her shirt and sneered at Allie. "I suppose it wasn't bad, considering I lasted longer than Allie, right? And isn't she supposed to save the world or something?"

Allie froze. Everyone was staring at her. If they hadn't known before, they did now. But who had told Brenda? Allie felt lightheaded. She would have to get to the bottom of this.

She waited until Gabe had finished explaining moderation, the problems with gluttony and how one should always be ready. When he was done, she ran over to Brenda and pulled her by the arm away from the rest.

"Ow," Brenda said, resisting. "Stop that!"

"Shut up," Allie said. "What were you talking about back there?"

"Everyone knows about you and this stupid Tenth Worthy business."

"Well, they do now," Allie said. "But that's not what I mean. What were you saying about saving the world?"

Brenda smiled. "How do you think the Tenth Worthy is supposed to get this name? By just being a cool dude or dudette? No, according to the prophesies, the Tenth Worthy will cast the last vessels of evil from this planet. The fallen angels, the Watchers…. Doesn't any of this mean anything to you?"

"You mean like Samyaza?"

"I mean *exactly* Samyaza, and the rest of the two hundred fallen. Samyaza won't rest until he has taken human form and has been declared the Tenth Worthy. If that were to happen, the world we know would be a second hell. Haven't you read anything?"

Allie's head hurt. She looked back toward Gabe and Michael. They both seemed to be watching her, their faces unreadable. Why hadn't they told her any of this? Well, she supposed they had told her some of it. But the fate of the entire world? She had thought facing Samyaza was more like just taking down a bad guy, like when the police arrested a serial killer or something.

"Are you for real?" Allie asked.

Brenda nodded smugly, and Allie could tell she had enjoyed teaching Allie something she hadn't known.

The rest of training went by fairly quickly. Daniel had finished his obstacle courses and weapons training for the day, and headed back through the doorway to his next regular class. Allie stayed behind while Michael treated them to a lesson of Spirit Animals and imbued objects. After a half-hour of watching Michael and the students pull horses, lions, eagles, and stags from mid-air and play with light swords and healing shields, Allie felt a little like she was lost in one of her brother's roleplaying games. It was too much.

They heard a loud crash outside, and Michael stopped the lesson. He looked to the doors, and then

Allie heard a scream. The doors burst open, and Mr. Phael's stark blue eyes shone with worry.

"Gabe, Michael," Mr. Phael said between breaths. "The school is under attack."

Michael held out his hand toward the students. "You stay here." He rushed to follow Gabe and Mr. Phael through the door.

Allie looked at Karen and Troy. They seemed to be thinking the same thing. Allie was among twenty students or so to dash for the door, and was certainly one of the few that wished she had not.

In the outside training area, thirteen students lay unmoving in the dirt. A mixture of grey and yellow swirling clouds blew across the sky. Allie's legs carried her forward in spite of her mind willing her to stay back and hide. The white exterior walls of the training hall were covered with dark shadows in long wisps, like strands of cloth formed into moving humanoid shapes. She had seen this before, when Paulette had formed a giant out of thin air. The shapes scraped against the marble, their scratching claws making her blood feel cold.

"Damn Strayers," Gabe said. He reached into the air and pulled a fiery sword, then rushed the walls, striking down the shadowy beasts. As they fell, they were swept into the slowly forming upside-down whirlpool of clouds.

Michael was beside Gabe in moments, his sword sending blasts of light-blue fire. "Raphort, go inside and make sure they have not summoned any

Watchers to the school," Michael said. "We will join you shortly."

The school. Daniel was in the school. She had to save him. She felt the numbness leave her legs—she had been frozen in place by the battle. She hurried through the open yard, the dark shadows jumping from the walls, ignoring Gabe's calls for her to come back. She ran as fast as she could for the far door, feeling the icy sheets of shadow caress her face, but it was like waking from a deep sleep—her body didn't want to respond, her mind groggy.

A blue blast exploded nearby, and suddenly she was free. She lurched forward and grabbed the handle of the door, pulling outward. Above her, the dark shapes circled, losing in their fight against Gabe and Michael. There were so many of them. She saw wings unfold, a glistening red scythe, and then it was gone with the strike of Gabe's sword.

Troy pushed her through the door, landing on top of her.

"What are you doing?" he yelled as he pulled her back to her feet.

"We have to get to Daniel."

Troy took a frustrated breath, but his eyes were determined. "Alright, let's do this."

They ran through the halls, jumped the stairs at the end, and found their way out of the building and into one of the open-air halls. Wisps of black fog led from all directions toward the large dome in the middle of the school, the auditorium.

That's where they're heading, Allie thought.

Shrieks rose from the dome as they approached. A thick muck like rotten bananas clung to the normally clear glass of the auditorium, but Allie didn't hesitate. She charged forward, kicking the door, then fell backward onto her butt. Troy shook his head and almost smiled.

"It says 'pull' right here," he said as he opened the door and held it for her.

"Ladies first, huh?" she said as she scrambled to her feet.

Charging through the door, she wished for a moment she had stayed in the training hall. The auditorium smelled of burnt liver and was hotter than a sauna. Students ran like scared cats, a group to the left toppling tables to hide behind, some streaming through the doors in retreat. Then Allie saw why.

On the far side of the room, right beside the cafeteria, a group of students in black were bowing to a dark, growing shadow. It rose toward the ceiling as the dark shapes from outside flowed into it like a deep well. The wisps of dark cloth formed a giant being, one far worse than anything she had seen back in Kyrgyzstan. She felt she was looking into never-ending space.

Its eyes were the worst. They seemed to come from nowhere and to observe everything at once. They burned, but their fire was even darker than the shadow creature itself.

The creature roared, causing several students to faint. Then it started to laugh. It lifted a leg from a dark opening in the floor, and Allie realized she had only been looking at half of the creature. Faces contorted throughout its substance, like a thousand souls captured within. She wanted to be anywhere else at that moment.

But then she saw Daniel, and she heard Troy mutter his name, pointing beside her. He had noticed Daniel too, unconscious, directly in the creature's path.

Allie had to act. She clenched her fists and bit her lower lip, running with all her might. She dove, grabbing Daniel by the back of his shirt and pulling him up like a mother lion does to its cub.

Her ring glowed and she willed it to respond, as it had when fighting to save her mom, but the glow fizzled out. She stared at it in confusion. The creature paused and turned her way—it must have sensed the ring! The pause was just long enough for Michael to burst through the doors and throw himself in the shadow creature's path. Allie heard fighting and girls screaming, but all she cared about was getting Daniel to safety. Troy stood with arms outstretched, yelling for her to hurry. When she reached him, Troy threw himself under Daniel's right shoulder and helped carry him to the far wall.

A blast of black fire hit the exit and it crumbled. Troy cursed and kicked a table, grabbing Allie and Daniel and shoving them behind it. He plopped down beside Allie, and it was only then that she noticed the tears streaming down his face and the sweat seeping through his shirt.

She heard Gabe's voice as he joined the fight. She sat terrified, her hand clenched in Troy's, Daniel's unconscious body before them. She had done it. She had saved him. But she had to make sure Gabe and Michael were alright, too. She turned, her eyes peeking barely above the edge of the table. Her heart threatened to beat right through her shirt, but she didn't care. She was past the point of fear.

Mr. Phael had a ring on his hand that was emanating a bright light around the three teachers. Gabe and Michael were striking the creature with their swords of fire. It seemed to feel no pain, but it could not advance, not with them blocking it. The Strayers were long gone, and the creature moved its head from side to side, as if looking for something but unable to find it.

"Be gone with you, Watcher," Michael said as he raised his sword. "Back with you, Grigori, betrayer of all that is holy. Be gone, to the second plane of Mount Hermon!"

He thrust the fiery blade into the black and white checkered auditorium floor. A blast of white fire circled around him, rising to the ceiling and then striking like lightning at the foot of the Watcher. The ground began to swirl, spiraling down into a red and black haze. The Watcher paused, then shrieked like a thousand dying men and women.

Allie covered her ears. Sweat stung her eyes, and she stared as the Watcher was swept into the ground. It reached for Michael's sword one last time, but only grasped thin air, as if it were no longer in the same world as Michael.

It shrieked again, its screams sounding like threats, and Allie knew it wasn't being destroyed, just being exiled. And then it was gone.

She collapsed against Troy, only then releasing his hand. "It's over."

He smiled at her, the wild look in his eyes slowly fading. They had survived, and Daniel lay safe beside them.

2 5

DOUBTS

The days that followed the attack went by like a blur, and soon became weeks. Everyone now understood the seriousness of their training, and Allie was more eager than ever to begin the attack on Samyaza and his followers.

Allie landed from her jump pattern on the other side of the swamp, bowing as she did so. Troy clapped politely for her, then began the pattern himself to follow her across. It was the first time they had run the obstacle course since the attack, and now they were allowed to use their jump patterns—it made quite the difference.

"Well done Allie," Mr. Phael said. He had joined the class after his students had either moved on to the training hall or failed out and returned to regular P.E. Gabe and Michael stood beside him.

"What's next?" Allie asked.

Gabe motioned to the training grounds. "Next is you keep training."

She balled her fists but kept her complaints silent. After days of inaction, she had learned that nothing she said could change the fact that no one seemed to know where to start in the search for Samyaza or the armor they needed.

Troy landed beside her, slipping on the damp grass. She steadied him.

"We always train," Troy said. "Don't we ever get wings?"

Gabe laughed. "Keep complaining and see if that helps."

"Well, what about those animals, the spirit animals, when can we try that?"

"You two are so eager." Gabe shook his head. "Patience and wisdom are some of the most important virtues in this life. Haven't I told you that the spirit animals choose you? Ask Allie here."

She blushed as Troy looked at her inquisitively.

"Well, I hope it's a dog," Troy said. "I've always wanted one of those."

Gabe's eyes seemed to darken.

"What?"

"Let's hope it's not a dog," Gabe said. "It's never happened and would strike me as quite useless. The closest you can hope for is a wolf, and if a wolf chooses you…"

"What?"

Allie leaned in, suddenly very interested. She and

Daniel had surmised that Chris had spirit animals in the form of a wolf, or multiple wolves, after the wolves had been helping them in Kyrgyzstan.

"Let me explain to the class," Michael said. "I think we'd better have a discussion. Raphort, would you please bring the students into the class when they are finished?"

Mr. Phael nodded, and told Allie and Troy to go on ahead.

When the rest of the students had gathered in the classroom, Michael paced before them with his hands behind his back. "There are many things we have yet to teach you. This is for your own good, so you are not overwhelmed, and so you can develop your spirit without distractions. But there are some things you should know to look out for. You have seen patterns, but have you seen them used for evil as well?"

Allie felt him looking her way, and she nodded.

"What can you tell the rest of the class about the evil uses of patterns, Ms. Strom?"

Allie looked at the rest of her class hesitantly. "I… well, there are the Strayers."

"The Strayers?" Brenda said. "Everyone knows they're a bunch of punks. They have no real power."

Troy cleared his throat. "Shut up, Brenda."

"Please continue, Ms. Strom," Michael said.

"Well, I have seen them on more than one occasion trying to use their patterns."

"Indeed," Michael said. "And the rest of you saw this at work when the Strayers conjured a Grigori, the

Watcher. That was done with patterns, and we changed the memories of the others with a pattern as well."

"I knew it!" Allie exclaimed. She sat back, blushing at her outburst. No one had seemed to remember what had happened, and the news said the attack on the school had been an earthquake.

"Did you?" Gabe said. "I'm not surprised." He reached into the air and pulled a fiery sword as if from nowhere. "With this sword, I carved a pattern into the floor. You cannot see it, as is the nature of this fire, but it is there. Likewise, I can call upon this sword because of a pattern here." He pointed to an infinity symbol on his belt with the shape of the sword through it. "The heavens gave us these patterns, and we can use them to perform good. But there are some who would inscribe these patterns onto the flesh, which also brings power, but it's a power that rots, that corrupts." He held the sword in the air and let go. The class gasped as it vanished.

Allie would have been impressed, but she was too busy pulling her sleeve down to cover the pattern on her arm.

"And that brings us to today's lesson," Michael said. "Spirit animals. I have told Allie, as I have told others here, spirit animals choose you. But that is only if you are patient. Another way to call upon a spirit animal is to inscribe the pattern of the appropriate animal into your flesh. The first Guardian to ever try this fell from the light within a week, and the boy he protected was devoured by the wolf he conjured. If you walk in the light, there are four main animals that may choose you: a horse, a stag, an eagle, and a lion. And breeds such as birds and whatnot. None is more powerful or more honored than the next, and they each have their strengths. But those that call on the shadow animals, they are met with wolves, serpents, or, in rare cases, insects or bugs. You must never allow your heart to crave the assistance of such foul creatures. You must never inscribe your flesh with a pattern of the heavens. Any questions?"

None were asked, and the students were dismissed.

Allie bit her nails as she walked through the halls towards her history class. How could she hope to succeed at all this? It was so complicated.... And it wasn't like she was the first. Others had come before her, and others had failed to protect.

How far back did it go? Maybe her ancient relative had failed to protect Hector at Troy, or Leonidas at Thermopile. The day before, she had learned about their defeats in history class, and suddenly the class seemed to take on a personal note.

26

CALLING IT QUITS

Allie heard Daniel's voice, loud and panicked. Racing now, she turned a corner, trying to pinpoint where she'd heard it from, then it came again. She spotted him just outside, past a half-open door.

"Dad, I didn't mean to... No, Dad!" Daniel was saying into his phone. He looked up at her with wide, moist eyes. "They have him, they have my dad."

"What?" She ran to him and held the phone. On the other end, she could hear someone laughing, and Daniel's father's voice telling them to stay back.

"He called to say he was in trouble," Daniel said. "That he went looking for me when I wasn't home, but then they found him."

"Who? Who found him?"

"He was yelling. People dressed all in black robes, with marks on their arms—the Strayers. He told me not to come, to stay away, because they wanted me...."

Allie stared at the phone, and then at her friend. "We have to get to him."

Daniel wiped away a tear and stared at the ground. He breathed heavily and then looked up at her. "Let's do it."

She held the phone in front of her and grabbed Daniel's arm with her ringed hand, closing her eyes and wishing with all her being that they were with his Dad. The ring grew warm, pulsating with a bright light she could see behind closed eyelids. Daniel shouted in surprise, and then everything went black. When she opened her eyes, they were in the woods near the school, at the edge of a hill. At the bottom of the hill were a dozen people in black robes. And just past them Daniel's dad, Burt, was running, holding his phone to his ear.

"Dad!" Daniel shouted.

Burt lowered the phone and turned, his eyes full of terror.

"Daniel," he yelled, "I told you to stay away!"

The entire group of Strayers turned toward her and Daniel. But she didn't care. She looked at Daniel and was touched by the look of determination in his eyes.

"Shall we?" she said.

"Lead the way," he said, glancing at her ring.

She nodded and charged down the hill, Daniel behind her and the Strayers running to meet them.

"This happens too much lately," Daniel yelled from behind, as the first group of Strayers met them.

Allie smiled and held out her ring at a lanky girl in

black robes. The girl snarled and pulled back a fist. Allie concentrated on her ring, willing the blast of light that had defended her against the giant in Kyrgyzstan.

Nothing happened.

The air left her lungs as the girl's fist connected with her chest. Someone was laughing, and then Allie was in the air. She looked down to see a boy of about sixteen with his hand on her shirt. He slammed her onto her back and stood over her, still laughing. She tried to breathe, but her lungs wouldn't allow it.

What was going on? Why wasn't the ring working? She turned her head to see a foot swing inches from her face, striking Daniel in the stomach. He doubled over, coughing.

"Daniel!" Burt yelled, but it sounded so far away.

Allie tried to stand, but the girl from before pulled her by the hair as an older girl with wide shoulders prepared to strike. The fist connected and the bitter taste of blood filled Allie's mouth.

She had to remember her training. She wasn't useless without the ring. She hoped.

She lifted her arms to block the second strike like she had been taught, then jumped out of the way of a kick. But there were so many of them. Daniel had rolled up in a ball, and Allie caught a glimpse of his dad trying to reach them.

"Get away from him," she yelled, and charged a boy about to kick Daniel in the head. She tackled the boy and used the edge of her hand to whack him in the throat, then turned to sweep a girl's legs into the air.

The girl landed with a thud and instantly Allie was on top of her, ready to strike again. But hands grabbed her arms and pulled her back.

"Enough of this," she heard an older boy say. "All we need is him."

"No, take me!" she yelled.

The boy laughed and put his index finger on her forehead. "Wouldn't that be grand?"

Allie struggled, but her arms wouldn't budge. She heard a smack and the back of her head stung. The green trees shimmered with reds and blues, everything swimming in circles. Her eyelids started to close, and just before everything went black she saw the Strayers lifting Daniel into the air as they waved their weapons at him. She heard his dad yelling, but it was useless.

"Not yet," she heard someone whisper.

She groaned, tasting the dirt and grass, rotating her head to see the sky. Dark, almost black eyes stared at her from beneath a hood. She recognized those eyes.

"Come on Allie," Vincent said.

She winced to see that face again, one of the bullies from before who had joined the Strayers and fought her in Kyrgyzstan, but then she realized he was helping her up. "What..."

"Hey," a girl yelled as she grabbed Vince's robe and pulled. "What're you doing?"

"Now!" Vince called out. He pulled down his hood and grabbed Allie, running for the edge of the woods.

"Wait," she managed. "We have to save Daniel."

A roar sounded from ahead, in the direction Vince

had yelled. At the top of the hill a lion appeared with two figures beside it, one with long blond hair and a leather jacket, the other stooped with gray hair blowing in the wind. The sun shone from behind them as if the trees were on fire, and bright rays of light cast upon the Strayers below.

Gabe and Michael, Allie thought, sighing a breath of relief.

One by one, Allie's P.E. class gathered behind the two teachers. Mr. Phael, his red hair flipping in the wind, joined them.

"Charge!" Mr. Phael yelled.

Her rescuers streamed down the hill like an army defending the shores of its land, except they were only there to save her and Daniel. She couldn't believe it. Vince fought, supporting Allie on her feet until Gabe finally reached her, kicking back a Strayer as he did so.

The Strayers fought for a few moments, the older boy holding onto Daniel as if his life depended on it, but the Guardians and Bringers of Light were too much for them. Allie turned to join in the fight, but Gabe pulled her back, pointing to the boy holding Daniel. The three teachers had him surrounded, many of the Strayers already fleeing, and then the lion pounced.

The boy fell beneath the lion's weight, letting go of Daniel, and only then did Gabe release Allie. She ran for Daniel. Many of the Strayers were being held to the ground, but some were escaping into the woods. Vince had removed the robe and was chasing them along with several other students, but Allie just wanted to hug Daniel.

Daniel's dad beat her to it. Burt wept, holding Daniel's head to his chest. "I'm sorry," he kept saying repeatedly.

"How did you all…?"

"We have a special connection, us Guardians and Bringers of Light," Gabe said. "You will learn to use it someday. We sensed you were in danger and came."

Vince returned, smiling, two smaller boys in his grasp. He tossed them to the ground before Michael.

"Well done," Michael said. "You've earned your spot."

"What spot?" Allie said.

"There aren't just us and the Strayers in this world, Allie. There are those that would assist us, those that we must learn to rely on when we need help. We call them friends."

Allie laughed, but she could tell Michael was serious.

"I saw Vince with the Strayers, but could always tell he didn't want to be there," Michael said. "The other one wasn't interested, thinking he was too important, but in Vince, I saw something, a willingness to help others."

She looked to Vince and he nodded.

"I agreed to pretend to be one of these Strayers, to find out what they were up to," Vince said. "I only discovered today that they wanted to take Daniel's dad as a way of getting to Daniel. We checked on your family, Allie, but they're safe."

Allie gulped, realizing it could have been her dad in this situation.

"What would they have done with me?" Daniel asked.

Vince looked at Michael for confirmation and then continued. "I don't know the whole story, but I overheard this one." He gestured toward the older boy on the ground, who was now whimpering as the lion's drool hit his face. "He was saying something about their lord needing to take the form of a boy, and that they had found the boy. And then we were to move, and someone said they found the boy's dad and was going to use him as bait. I guess it worked, but they didn't expect this."

Allie turned to Daniel, wide-eyed, then to Gabe. "Samyaza wanted to what, possess him?"

Gabe's eyes narrowed, but he didn't answer. He waved his hand and the lion disappeared.

"We'll get you all, none of your families are safe!" the older boy shouted.

Gabe knelt beside the boy and held him down with a hand on his chest. "You serve Samyaza, the bringer of death?"

The boy's eyes narrowed. "He will return, and I'll be waiting. On that day, you will all grovel at his feet, and I'll spit in your face."

Gabe sighed and stood back, watching as the boy scrambled to his feet and sprinted away.

"You're just letting him leave?" Allie said in exasperation.

"We can do nothing but hope," Gabe said. "We cannot make him choose his path; we can only help those that allow us."

"So what is to stop him from attacking again?"

Gabe raised his hand and gestured at the students that had come to help. "They will, Allie. And you will be there to lead us all to victory."

Talk about pressure. Fight, sure. But lead?

She looked at the group of students, and they all smiled or nodded in agreement. Daniel's father still had an arm around him, and she saw in his eyes a fatherly love. But moments before, he could have been taken by Samyaza…. Possibly never to be heard from again. And that boy had threatened all of their families.

She couldn't allow her family to be put at risk again, not because of her.

"Sorry," she said as she handed the ring to Gabe. "You'll have to find someone else."

And with that she walked off, leaving behind all this Guardian and Bringer of Light talk. If being the Tenth Worthy and saving the world meant possibly losing her family, someone else could fill the role. To her, it wasn't worth it.

27

AWAKENED

Allie found herself walking along Pacific Highway, where the Party City sat opposite an old diner. This would have been her favorite spot, had she been able to live a normal life here. There was a time when going to Party City right before Halloween had been the most exciting moment of the year. Halloween had been right up there with Christmas and hanging the lights with her family, or maybe even Thanksgiving when all the pies would get served—her favorite was pumpkin, of course. But regardless, that moment around Halloween, when the whole store felt like a giant haunted house, was once amazing.

Now? With all the magic and Strayers and shadowy creatures, she doubted she'd ever want to see the holiday again.

She wandered over to the mall, considering seeing a movie. But the idea of sitting alone in a dark theater gave her the creeps. What if one of the Strayers were sitting right behind her, or lying on the floor, in the dark spots where you can't see?

Instead, she bought a frozen yogurt—tangy with blueberries and mochi—and found a seat in the food court. A group of older girls, probably high school, walked by on their way to shop after school. Allie almost laughed at how ridiculous that was. People were fighting for the safety of the world just twenty minutes away, and here these girls were without a care. Of course, they didn't know... but still.

Her phone chirped. Allie glanced at it, but just licked her frozen yogurt instead of answering. It was Daniel, and right now she didn't want to be judged. She didn't want a lecture, or to be convinced to go back and join the fight against darkness. She wanted to just be a normal girl, whatever that meant.

When she finally got up to leave, she saw a face she definitely did not want to see—Brenda.

"We've been looking everywhere for you," Brenda said with a glare. "Do you think of anyone other than yourself?"

Allie just stared, and then walked off.

"Don't walk away from me," Brenda said as she caught up with Allie. "Seriously, Troy and Daniel, Principal Eisner and Michael, they're all out there looking for you. This isn't some game, you know."

Allie spun on that. "A game? You think I don't know it's not a game?"

"I—I just...."

"I almost lost my mom, okay? Now Daniel's dad

was attacked, and who knows how many others will be at risk before this is over. What, I'm supposed to suffer so others don't have to? Well, screw that!"

This time when she walked off, Brenda didn't follow.

But when Allie reached her house, her mom was standing by the kitchen table with the ring in the palm of her hand.

"Lose something?" her mom asked.

Allie stared, wondering how best to deal with this, and then simply shrugged.

Her mom placed the ring in a cabinet drawer and nodded. "There, out of the picture. That's what you want?"

"Out of our house would be better," Allie said.

"I hear you, I do." Her mom said as she took a seat and began peeling a banana. "You know how many earthquakes we used to get? When I was fighting the Strayers in Asia, there were so-called earthquakes all the time...."

"We both know this wasn't an earthquake at our school." Allie sat opposite her mom.

"Of course we do, and neither were those.... And neither was the one they just had in Japan, did you hear of that one?"

"What's it have to do with me?"

"Allie, imagine if you hadn't had the ring, or joined your friends fighting that day. What would have happened to Daniel?"

The image of Daniel's limp body flashed through

Allie's mind. She imagined for a brief moment that he had died, and the friends that would have gathered at his vigil.

"You know it has to be this way, honey." Her mother stood and retrieved the ring, holding it out.

Allie took it and retreated to her room. "I'll think about it."

She closed the door behind her and stood, staring out the window, considering the ring in her hand. How could something so small cause so much trouble, and yet be the clue to saving everyone? She returned to her bed and decided to read that teddy bear book her brother had given her, finding herself lost in the adventures of children. Before she fell asleep, she slipped the ring onto her index finger.

Hands shook Allie's shoulders. Her eyes snapped open and she was nearly blinded by the light next to her bed.

"Come on, you have to go," her mom said.

"Go where?" she asked, still fuzzy with sleep. "What's going on?"

"It's Samyaza, they've found a way to track him and he's on the move. He must have located another piece of the armor, in Scotland. You have to go, tonight."

"What do you mean, tonight?" Allie sat up, wide awake, and brushed her mom's hands aside. The red glow of the clock on her wall said it was only three in the morning. "I have school tomorrow."

"No dear," her mom said. "It's time."

Her mom pulled her out of bed and threw some clothes over her pajamas, zipping up the thick jacket and then adding a beanie for the final touch. She guided her to the living room where Daniel stood, shield at his side, along with Principal Eisner and Gabe the librarian.

"Is she ready?" Principal Eisner said.

Allie stared at them. What were they doing in her living room?

"We have to go back," Daniel said, pulling the shield up to his side.

Allie's mom turned, full of pride. "Back to defeat the dark forces of Samyaza." Her mom breathed deep and knelt. "I had been searching for the ring, as was Samyaza. I knew that if I found it first, I'd have the advantage. But only one person every thousand years can truly wear the ring and harness its power. The light has chosen you."

"I refuse," Allie said, taking the ring from her finger and throwing it to the ground. "Let him do what he wants, but I'm done."

Daniel reached for the ring, but Gabe held out his wrinkled hand and stopped him with a shake of his head.

"The time of the Tenth Worthy is upon us," Gabe said. "The pattern is before us. You are to be the Tenth Worthy, the ultimate Bringer of Light. You will restore the balance of our world. Tonight we learned that Samyaza knows of the armor and has found the helmet. With their power, he cannot be harmed, except by one weapon. The Sword of the Spirit, which we think is why his troops are in Scotland. The two of you must find it before he does, or allow darkness to reign."

Allie glared at Gabe, then turned to her mom who stared back with a look of determination. Daniel's eyes quivered. Allie could tell their words scared him as much as they scared her, but the words were true. She trusted that. The next step on their journey was laid out before them, and the adventure would start that night. There was no more running, no more doubt.

"How do we begin?" she asked.

"Take his hand," her mom said. "The shield will lead you on your journey; it longs to be united with the rest of the armor. But it will only take you to the general area. The rest is up to you."

"The two of you must succeed," Principal Eisner said.

"Wait," Allie said. "None of you will be coming with us?"

"We are simply guides," Principal Eisner said. "Here to help you on your way. We have limited abilities, such as to assist you on your path and see the immediate next steps, like a window to tomorrow. But we cannot see the end result, or influence it in any direct way. All we can tell you is that with Daniel holding his shield, and you using the ring and concentrating on following your spirit, you will be taken to the location of the sword where a great battle will take place. The rest is up to you."

"You're telling me the fate of the world rests on two kids?" Allie said.

Her mom's worried eyes moved to Principal Eisner, as if asking for any other way. But the principal nodded her head and placed her hand on Allie's shoulder.

"You aren't just kids," Principal Eisner said. "Not anymore."

Allie knelt and picked up the ring. It felt heavy in her grip, the silver cold against her skin.

"This means I'll miss soccer practice," she said.

"And me, baseball," Daniel said, with a nervous smile on his face.

Allie grinned and reached for his hand, but before she made contact her mom swept her into her arms and embraced her. With a kiss on her forehead, her mom squeezed her hand and said, "I'll be praying for you."

"I love you," Allie said. "Tell Ian and Dad the same."

"I will. I love you, too," her mom said.

"Wait, what will you tell them?"

Her mom looked for confirmation from the other two adults, then smiled. "I think it's time we told them the truth, see if they can handle it."

"Good luck!" Allie said, reaching for Daniel's hand.

She felt the warmth emitting from his fingertips as they touched. It was as if fire burned around them, warm and comforting, engulfing them in flames of the heavens. Light shot through the room, wrapping around their limbs and blowing their hair like the wind, gently caressing their skin like a pleasant bath. It brightened to a blinding glow, and they were forced to shield their eyes.

When the light finally faded, Allie and Daniel stood in a field of deep green, a line of trees in the distance and a stone tower atop a hill. Rays of dim light sprinkled the ground, escaping through leaves, and the thick clouds were turning pink and red.

"Can you believe this?" Daniel asked, his hand clenching hers.

"Not at all." Allie glanced down at their hands.

"I always wanted to visit Scotland, but not like this." Daniel took a step back, then looked up to the tower. His eyes darted to Allie, and she nodded in return.

"I don't suppose the sword could be anywhere else," she said.

They trudged across the field. A sweet smell of meat cooking carried in the morning breeze. Two words stuck in her head as she marched: Great battle. They'd escaped from the army of Strayers before, not stood in its path and tried to fight them. She gulped, suddenly wishing Daniel was still holding her hand.

The sun rose in the sky as they walked, but the chill remained. Allie noticed Daniel shaking his head and muttering to himself occasionally.

"Haven't accepted it yet?" she asked.

He glanced up and scoffed. "How can I?"

They reached the tree line and started carefully working their way around a string of muddy puddles, then descended to a valley very similar to the one where they'd first felt the effects of the stone that now fitted snugly in Allie's ring. She crossed a log and reached back to help Daniel, but was surprised to see him maneuvering it with ease in spite of the shield on his arm.

"You understand what they're saying?" he asked. "You'll be up there with people like Julius Caesar, Alexander the Great, Charlemagne, and the rest of the Nine Worthies. And I can say I knew you way back when."

"Shut up," she said. "If I hadn't seen what we did in Kyrgyzstan... I don't know." She remembered how Daniel had used the shield in the caves of the Throne of Solomon, how he'd put himself in harm's way to give her time to find her mom, and thought at that moment that if anyone were to stand by her side, she wanted it to be him. "I wouldn't be here if it weren't for you."

"You're stronger than you think," he said as they began the ascent up the other side of the valley.

The ground rumbled slightly and a flock of birds took off from a nearby tree.

"Come on." He quickened the pace.

Moments later they crested the valley and saw houses in the distance. Western style houses, but slightly different from those in the U.S. They were older. Some had flat roofs and many were made of brick.

"My dad used to take me to the Highland Games," Daniel said. "When I was young. I'll never forget the smell of blood sausage and haggis being prepared."

She cringed, but if that was the smell carrying in the

morning air, maybe she would be up for it. Anything sounded good at the moment. If she could get it down that is. Her stomach felt odd. Empty, yet ready to convulse at any moment and spew everything back out.

They were closer to the tower now and had reached a dirt road leading up to it from the west. A light layer of sweat covered Allie's forehead, but not from exertion. She wasn't scared, simply anxious.

Allie stepped on the road, and the ground shook. It kept moving, and soon the trees were swaying and the rocks grinding as the earth continued to rock.

"Get in the open!" Daniel shouted, reaching for her.

But Allie had seen something he had not. She spun him around and pointed to a spot between the houses and the tower. A dark whirlpool of dirt had formed in the ground. A great nothingness, with everything spiraling down into it.

"Get to the tower!" she said, and they took off running.

A stone tumbled down the hill toward them, then another. One landed two feet from Daniel, and then another came straight for him. He lifted his shield and Allie cringed as the stone clanked down on the metal.

"Under here," he yelled as he ran to her, holding the shield above both their heads.

They continued toward the tower, darting through the narrow entrance. In the shadows, Allie glanced back to see long wisps of darkness emerging from the hole in the ground. The hole widened as she watched, sending the darkness flying into the air, formless shapes that she knew had life to them. Allie pulled Daniel up the first stairs as the entrance caved in behind them. By the glow of her ring they were able to make it up the stairs, two at a time.

The tower swayed, shaking them off balance as they ran. When they reached a window, Allie paused to catch her breath, staring out in disbelief at the approaching forms. Winged shadows, dark and menacing, turned the air and everything around them to blackness.

And then she realized they weren't just coming out of the hole. They were pulling the world around them into it!

"Move it!" she cried, yanking Daniel up the stairs.

The tower shook, knocking them both to their knees. Daniel yelled and began to crawl up the stairs, the shield slung around the back of his right arm. Allie followed, the inside of her stomach tense with fear and her heart beating wildly. She thought of her mom, and a wave of guilt hit her. How could Allie have been mad every time her mom had left—had this been what she was up to?

The stone walls were collapsing all around them, leaving a gaping hole in the side of the tower, but the stairs remained. Suddenly, the whole wall gave way, and only the interior of the tower remained with them. They clung tightly to the stones.

Bright golden rays of the morning sunrise seemed to be battling the darkness, and losing. But then the yellow of the sun crested a far off hill and glinted off nearby steel—the sword!

"There!" Allie shouted.

Daniel looked where she pointed, across a gap formed by falling stone. He stood, about to leap, when something darted past him, landing on the other side.

"Chris!" Allie yelled.

Only his eyes weren't Chris's. They glowed red, their pupils black.

THE SWORD

C hris ran past them, an evil smile spreading across his face.

"Come on!" Allie said, watching as Chris closed in on the sword.

She took Daniel's hand in hers, and they leaped across the gap in the stairs. But Daniel lost his footing and started to slide down the wall. Allie held his hand tight and pulled him back up to safety on the ledge on the other side.

When she looked up, Chris's hand was wrapped around the sword, which was set deep into a stone altar. Daniel ran for him while Allie lifted her ring, sending a blast of light.

But it was too late. With sword in hand and free from the stone, Chris parried the light back at them. He sneered and rumbled a low, growling howl.

He pulled the sword back again, ready to thrust. Allie remembered that day at the cafeteria, when she had stood up for Daniel, and she hoped he did also. She threw herself behind Chris, calling for Daniel to shove.

Daniel nodded and smiled grimly. With a mighty push of his shield, he collided with Chris before the sword could strike. Chris growled in surprise as he stumbled backwards, over Allie, and toward the open sky. He screamed as the shadow left his eyes and the sword dropped from his hands.

Daniel caught the sword while Allie reached out to catch Chris, but she was too late. She pulled back and cringed at the thud against the ground far below. Turning back to Daniel, she saw the shield glowing a dim green on his right arm, the sword in his left hand held high in the air as if it weighed nothing. For a moment, his eyes held the glory of victory. Then he looked and saw Chris, whimpering on the ground below.

"I tried," Allie said.

She stood beside Daniel, fighting for balance. The earth still shook as the darkness consumed increasingly more land.

"The sword is ours," Daniel shouted into the sky, waiting to see if the darkness would stop its onslaught. It did not but continued to suck the world around them into a whirlpool of black nothingness. He lowered the sword, his expression defeated.

The shadows reached the base of the tower, and then Chris.

"What now?" Daniel shouted as Chris disappeared into the darkness.

Allie grabbed hold of him and moved close to be heard over the roaring of the whirlpool and the thundering of the earth. "We can escape, return home, and hope this is all over. Or we can jump, go find Samyaza in his world, stop this once and for all. Maybe save Chris, even Paulette. The entire world."

Daniel looked at her, eyes wide with fright. The tower began to sink, more stones breaking off and swirling around in the darkness, spiraling inward. A terrible sucking sound filled the air.

"I need you with me," she said.

He looked down at the darkness, then to the sword and shield in his hands. "We jump, together."

He nodded as if to convince himself, looked at her, then ran and sprang from the stone. The darkness took him at once, pulling him into its depths.

Allie followed close behind, hoping she wasn't making a terrible mistake. The darkness felt like a cold lake, enveloping her. She felt it pulling at her as if to rip her apart, but then she focused on their mission—a world without the darkness, without Samyaza. The beast that had overcome her fellow students and almost taken her mom.

She would not let it take Daniel.

The ring glowed brightly as she descended, enveloping her in a circle of intense light. Daniel swirled before her, and she focused her trajectory toward him. He held firm to the sword and shield, a dim glow of his own surrounding him, and she realized that he looked so much older than his twelve years at that moment. Maybe he didn't need her as badly as she thought.

When he saw her coming, he moved toward her, joining the circle of light with his own glow. The glow grew around them, yellow and green and blue brilliance. They no longer swirled with the darkness, but moved along their own path toward the center of the spiral, as if floating in water.

They felt ground beneath their feet as they landed. Beyond their circle of light, everything was pitch black, the ground shaking and the darkness roaring around them.

"We're in his world now," Allie said. "Let's make this worth it."

Daniel set his jaw and lifted the sword above his head. He stuck out his chest and yelled at the top of his lungs, "Show yourself, Samyaza!"

The noise stopped. The swirling and the shaking stopped. All was silent and black.

Then a barely audible noise came from nearby, almost a whisper. Daniel swung his sword in the direction, the glow of the sword illuminating the form of Chris lying on the black ground.

"Wait!" Allie lunged for Chris. She held his face in her hands and looked into his eyes. They were light blue, the black and red gone. He stared back, pupils dilated, pulsating, terrified. "I think it's really him."

Daniel stepped forward and assessed his longtime friend. Finally, he nodded and knelt down. "Are you okay?"

Chris whimpered. "I... I didn't mean to...."

Daniel shook his head. "We know. Are you okay?"

"I'm so sorry," Chris said. "I never meant for this to happen. I didn't know."

Allie stood and touched the ring to his forehead, closing her eyes and focusing on her living room. The light filled her mind, swirling around and then engulfing Chris. She opened her eyes to see the light fade and along with it, Chris.

"What'd you do to him?" Daniel said.

"I sent him home, to my mom. They'll know how to take care of him. We have to focus on finding Samyaza."

A laugh echoed through the darkness. A deep, guttural laugh.

"Find me?" a voice said from all around them. "Why, I am everywhere! I envelop all that is, all that ever will be."

"Show yourself!" Daniel said.

"Why, can't you see me?" the voice said. "Open your eyes and look around, or close them and see me there, too. For I am the darkness!" The voice laughed again, a laugh that pierced their very souls.

Allie moved to Daniel's side, holding her ring and concentrating on keeping the light around them. But it took all her energy, and she felt she couldn't make it last forever.

She looked to Daniel, relieved to see his shoulders rolled back, his jaw clenched in determination. He was so brave—but was she? She didn't feel it at the moment.

"This way," a soft voice said.

The darkness pulsed, angry, swirling. "Quiet!" Samyaza said. "You cannot defy me!"

"Over here," the voice said again.

Allie felt the power of her ring weakening, her concentration waning. She took a step toward the soft voice, recognizing it from somewhere. By the glow of green and blue light beside her, she knew Daniel followed.

"Allie," the voice urged. "Allie!"

Paulette!

Allie came closer to the voice, and sure enough, there in the darkness was the girl she had met at orientation day. Her hands were chained to the darkness, wisps of shadow covered her eyes and moved around her.

"Paulette?" Allie moved in with caution. When she drew close, Paulette's face contorted, as if she was fighting for control of her own voice.

"Run! Run from here, now!" Paulette screamed, herself for a moment. "Get out while you can!"

The darkness strengthened and Allie felt her spirit being crushed. Her will weakened, as did the light from her ring. She felt herself growing dizzy, and began to sink to the floor.

A loud noise filled the darkness. Daniel stood beside her, shouting as he swung the sword at the air. He yelled and lunged at the nothingness, pulled back and struck again.

With each strike, the darkness retreated, twisting

and shrieking. Following its path, Allie saw the form above Paulette, almost like the shadow of a large man, wings sprouting from its shoulder blades and long claws on its hands.

"There!" Allie yelled, pointing.

Daniel lunged, striking at the spot where the shadow figure had been. Light burst from the tip of his sword, a flow of pure, ethereal blues and greens. The shadow pulled back, hissing, and the darkness lifted. All that remained was a barren wasteland with a massive fortress before them, a dull red glow over it all. Paulette sat on the ground, whimpering.

"You must find the helmet," Paulette managed. "Within the fortress. Find it, and with that sword destroy the evil that protects it. Only then can you bind him from this world, only then can you fulfill your destiny."

With her last words, Paulette collapsed to the ground, unconscious. Allie approached and, as she had done with Chris, she touched the ring to Paulette's forehead. A moment later the girl was gone.

Allie turned to Daniel and waited.

"We have no other choice, right?" he said.

"Not if we want to win, to be done with this thing."

"Lead the way," he said, his hand firm on the hilt of his sword and his eyes set upon the fortress in the distance.

She nodded and took the first step.

29

THE FORTRESS

The fortress stood tall above Allie and Daniel's approaching forms. Thick stone walls spread for miles in each direction and reached high into the sky. As they grew closer, the entrance appeared more menacing, with carvings of tortured souls and huge beasts, and gargoyles hanging from parapets and lurking in dark corners. From the overhangs, stalactites hung like myriad teeth, and in the garden (if it could be called that), black withered flowers rose out of the red soil, their scent like forgotten swamps.

Rust covered the massive door, streaked with long lines of green sludge. A constant drip sounded from somewhere, unending and maddening. Allie remembered days at the fort on Whidbey Island, where her brother and she had joyously run along the dark tunnels. They had giggled and hid in corners to scare each other. But a giggle was the furthest thing from her mind now. She had really enjoyed those days, and wished with all her heart that this was a simple game with her brother.

Instead, she was about to find the fight of her life, the moment that would decide whether other children throughout the world would ever feel the joy she had once felt. It was time to destroy Samyaza.

She assessed the massive door, then turned to Daniel. "This is it."

He gripped the sword tight, and she could see the muscles in his hand clenching and unclenching, red blotches around his fingers.

"Are you ready?" she asked.

"You heard Paulette. This is our destiny. It's time we accept it."

She nodded, turned to the door and held out her ring. She concentrated all her will, but nothing happened. She looked at the stone, shook it several times, then tried again with the same effect.

"We didn't come here to turn away now!" Daniel shouted as he kicked the door, startling Allie. "Open up!"

To their surprise, the door creaked open.

"Huh," Daniel said.

They peeked past the door into the darkness. Musty, rank air seeped from inside. Daniel strode forward, sword held at the ready. At that moment, Allie saw him as an archangel come to wreak havoc on all that was evil. She followed him in, feeling almost safe in spite of the insurmountable odds against them. Together, they could do this.

They entered an immense foyer, completely dark now but for the glow of Daniel's shield and sword and the faint glimmer from Allie's ring. As they walked, the glow illuminated massive stone carvings of beasts in armor, fanged and horned, carrying axes, spears, and halberds. The floor beneath their feet echoed with each step. On one wall they found frames where pictures may have hung, but instead pure darkness swirled within, each one like its own pool of midnight-black water.

Allie felt a chill run down her back. Without thinking, she walked closer to Daniel as they explored deeper. They moved forward, down a passage with thirty-foot ceilings arching above them and chandeliers of spikes dangling down. At the end of the passage, they found the door to a second room.

When they entered the room, even their combined glow didn't reveal what lay behind the ocean of darkness. Heavy breathing echoed off the walls, growing deeper with each moment, vibrating through their bones.

"What is it?" Daniel whispered, startling Allie with the sound of his voice so close.

Then something brushed against her, followed by the sound of wings. She took a step forward, holding out her ring, but the dim glow did nothing against the immense darkness.

She was wondering what they should do next—just

head into the dark?—when a raspy voice filled the room.

"Welcommmme," it said.

"Show yourself!" Daniel called, and took a step forward.

"With pleasure!" the deep vibration was accompanied by flames of purple and black rising along the walls, casting an eerie glow on hundreds of bent forms across the floor. Allie took a step toward one, then pulled back in horror at the form huddled on the floor. It wore torn black rags, its eyes sunken and skin pulled tight across its face. She saw Chester, and other faces from the Strayers she had encountered. And was that Yuko, the Japanese girl from training?

"Was Yuko…?"

"What's happened to them?" Allie whispered, pulling close to Daniel.

Movement came from the back of the room, from a raised ledge with draperies hanging behind it. It was the form they'd seen outside, its massive shadow wings spread to cover the breadth of the room. It hovered in the air, the blank darkness where its eyes would have been staring into her.

"They are mine," Samyaza's voice shook them. "Through their shadows I have taken their souls, while their shells of bodies fight on for my cause. As they have become mine, so too shall the rest of the world." Samyaza flapped his wings and sent a putrid smell of death through the room, met by the whimpers of the helpless beings that had once been Strayers.

"It won't happen," Daniel said. "We have come to destroy you!"

Samyaza laughed. "Destroy me? Me! You have brought me what I most desire. If anything, you have begun the earth's demise! With the armor reunited, I will be all-powerful. With the ring, I will be unstoppable!"

Again he laughed, and the walls laughed along with him as the souls of the Strayers cowered, powerless. Samyaza reached out his shadow hands, his claws glistening in the purple glow of the fires. He brought his hands together with a massive clap. A thud sounded behind Allie, from the direction they'd come. Then another thud, and soon the walls were shaking with the sound.

Through the darkness, four forms moved with great speed in their direction—the stone figures from the entry room, their weapons glinting with each step.

"Daniel!" Allie screamed as the first stone demon attacked, bringing its halberd down to strike Daniel's head.

Daniel dodged left, parrying the attack with his sword. A second figure swung a spear at him, but Allie didn't have time to watch as a second halberd came for her own midsection. She flung herself to the ground and out of its way, then spun in time to see a demon wielding an ax, horns from its head aimed at her as it charged. She yelped and ran for it, dodging the ax and sliding beneath its snout at the last minute. She scrambled to her feet and stood to see the last demon colliding with one of the others. They disentangled themselves and turned to her.

Just past the two beasts she saw Daniel, warding off attacks with his sword and shield. The demons were ten times his size, but for the moment he was managing, moving with the grace and speed of someone who had practiced with the sword for years. Watching him, Allie felt even more inspired to fight. She tried her ring again, but its glow was dim, its powers seemingly useless in this horrible place.

Then the light of her ring flared as a massive force slammed her, flinging her forward. She recovered, her face a mere foot from the dark flames. Again Samyaza's laughter echoed in the chambers. She pushed herself to her feet and saw that the attack had come from the hoof of one of the demons, now raising its ax for a blow. She readied her ring, and saw Daniel running toward her, his two assailants in pursuit.

"Allie!" He collided with the ax-bearing demon, bludgeoning its leg with his shield. Next he whipped his sword around to cut the demon's leg in two.

Allie ran to Daniel as the demon flailed around, wailing in pain. The second and third demons were almost upon them, while the fourth was thrusting its spear at Allie and Daniel. There were too many of them, but she had seen what her friend could do and it gave her hope.

"Get me to Samyaza!" Allie yelled, and Daniel nodded.

The fight continued, Daniel blocking and slashing

as they worked their way backward through the Strayers. No longer helpless, the Strayers were rising from the ground. They began to reach and tear at Allie and Daniel, their eyes fluttering between normal and bright red. Allie pushed them back as Daniel sliced a demon's hand off with a swipe of the sword, its heavy weapon falling to the ground with a loud clang. He then turned the point of his sword on one of the Strayers.

"No!" Allie shouted, pulling him back. He looked at her with wild eyes, but she held his arm. "We have to save them."

His expression melted as he understood. Like Chris and Paulette, these people had not been themselves. They had been under the control of Samyaza.

Daniel turned back to attack, but too late—the one-armed demon struck at him with a back-hand, sending Daniel flying into the Strayers. The pitiful forms in black rags jumped on Daniel, covering him as he pushed back. But they were too much for him, and soon all Allie could see was a pile of writhing Strayers.

The demons advanced, their stony faces glaring down on her. They had her.

"What do you have to say now?" Samyaza cackled. "You are defeated. The light of your life shall soon be expelled from existence."

A demon struck with its spear, slamming the ground when Allie dodged. Allie took her chance and grabbed onto the weapon, holding tight as the demon pulled back, then using the leverage to kick off from the demon and jump. She landed with a roll just short of Samyaza and caught herself on one knee, her fist on the ground. Slowly she looked up at Samyaza, his face solidifying with eyes of flowing red lava within his shapeless head.

"You forget," she said. "It's darkness that fades in the light, not the other way around."

She lunged for him, pulling back her fist and then striking with all her might. The ring on her fist entered his shadowy form. Dead-cold engulfed her. Samyaza shrieked, writhing and changing form before her eyes. At one moment he was the shadow creature, then Paulette and then Chris, then he took the form of a stone demon, then a massive beast of fire. She looked away, but dared not pull back her fist and the ring. The demons behind her were crumbling to pieces, the Strayers pulling back, terrified. Samyaza's shape pulled into the ring, growing dense around it, then sizzled like water on a flame.

The light of the ring dimmed, but only for a moment. It grew from within Samyaza, and his fiery eyes faded and his form shuddered and vanished as the light exploded through the room.

When Allie looked down, she saw before her a snake, curled around a glowing gold helmet. It circled the helmet and hissed at her, its long tongue flickering across its exposed fangs. The only other sign of Samyaza was a pair of wings spread across the floor, black as if covered in tar.

A footstep sounded behind Allie and she turned to

see Daniel, his clothes torn and blood dripping from his nose and mouth, but otherwise unharmed.

"Not very impressive, is it?" Daniel said, pointing the tip of his sword at the snake. The snake hissed and lunged, but Daniel sprang forward and thrust his sword into the snake's mouth. The snake split in two and, as it hit the ground, its two halves turned to dust and dissolved into a shadow on the stone.

Daniel collapsed to his knees and Allie threw her arms around him.

"We did it," he said.

She pulled back, looking at him, her savior. Then she turned and saw the Strayers, slowly recovering and standing, their eyes searching their surroundings in confusion. The flames died around them. From the glow of Allie's ring, she saw they all appeared normal, their shadows at their sides.

"We're not quite done," she said, then picked up the helmet and turned to Daniel. "What was that they said about destiny?"

He remained kneeling as she stepped forward and placed the helmet upon his head. It fit perfectly. As it settled, a golden ray of light shot from the helmet to the sword and then to the shield, forming a golden triangle. It lit into a flame and moved towards his heart, passing through his clothing and entering his chest.

He breathed deep, then exhaled, and when he looked up she saw in his eyes a new man. He stood and turned to the former Strayers as the walls began to shake.

"Let's get them home," he said.

She smiled. "Let's get us home, too."

Stones began to fall around them. The wall on the far side tumbled inward and a massive rumbling came from above, as if a dozen voices chanted from the heavens. Where walls once stood, shadowy wisps like giant beings hovered, looking down on Allie and the others with red, glowing eyes.

"Give us the armor, give us the ring," a voice said in a whisper that echoed throughout the crumbling fortress.

Allie stepped forward, but Yuko jumped out from the recovered Strayers, not looking nearly as sickly as the others. She snatched the black wings from the floor and held them high. As she did so her body spasmed and a moment later the wings sprouted from her back like black fire.

"Take it!" the whisper of a voice commanded.

Yuko lunged, flapping in the air around Allie, but Allie protected the ring as Daniel pushed Yuko back with his shield.

"What do I do?" Daniel asked, frantic. "I don't want to hit her!"

"Stall," Allie said, and then she knelt.

She clasped her hands and closed her eyes. She focused on the ring, and on the people around her, knowing that she had to forgive them and save them from the destruction that would soon befall this fortress. She thought of her family, and her mom, and wondered if this was the end of it all, if she could be so fortunate. Then she decided that no matter what, with Daniel fighting by her side, she could handle it.

With a surge of light she opened her eyes and stood. The light spread across the room like a wave, halting the stones as they fell from the ceiling, halting time and space. Yuko screamed and vanished, as did the shadow creatures above. And then, with a mighty swooshing sound, Allie and the others were gone, pulled from the fortress and soaring across the world, across the ocean, and back to their homes.

Allie watched as Mount Rainier grew closer, the guiding light of Washington State. As they soared over the trees, the sun rising with their approach, one by one the former Strayers sank down to houses. They waved good-bye and called out their thanks. Allie smiled at Daniel and took his hand as they flew toward their apartment complex.

"I guess this means Chris is back, huh?" she said.

He nodded, then looked at her with worry. "And Paulette."

"Yeah, the real her…"

"But Allie," he said as they began their descent. "What about the soccer team? Your position?"

She shrugged, realizing that sometime in the last few hours she had come to understand there were more important things. "I suppose we'll have to see."

They landed in the parking lot and she hugged Daniel.

"See you at school," he called out, walking toward his apartment.

She looked at the yellow sky, the sun now plainly visible. "Yeah, I hope so."

In front of her apartment, she paused with her hand on the doorknob, surprised to hear yelling inside. She opened the door slightly, readying her ring for whatever awaited.

30

THE END

Allie put her ear against the crack of the door and was stunned to hear her dad yelling.

"I just got you back!" her dad said loudly, almost angrily. "And now our daughter's missing?"

"She's not missing," her mom said calmly. "I told

you, the ring, the stone that used to be in my necklace, it has powers and it—"

"Where do you come up with this stuff? First Allie, now you. I don't—"

Allie had heard enough. She burst through the door and went running to her parents, calling out to them that she had returned and was safe. Her mom turned and clasped her mouth as tears of joy filled her eyes, then ran and threw her arms around her daughter. Her dad stood with his mouth open.

"I thought you said she was off saving the world?" he said.

"I did, Dad," Allie said, beaming. "I'm back."

"Like I said." Her mom kept one arm around her daughter as she turned to face her dad. "The ring chose her. I knew she would be all right."

"Now hold on a minute!" her dad said, his voice rising again. "You put these ideas in your daughter's head, playing these games, and she starts to believe they're real. We can't be…."

His voice trailed off as Allie lifted her ringed finger and created a circle of light around herself. He took a step back, then watched as Allie used the light to lift herself off the ground. She landed with a smile, staring expectantly at her dad.

"Well…I—I, well…." He stared, hands on his hips. Finally, he put his hands in his pockets and stared at Allie and his wife wide-eyed. "So, you saved the world, huh?"

"Yup," Allie said.

"And that's what you were doing, before?" he asked his wife.

"That's right," she said.

Her dad rubbed his eyes, then his ears. He moved to his daughter in one step and knelt down, hands on her shoulders. "And everything's safe now?"

"We stopped the bad guys," she said. "We got more of the armor, and kept the ring."

"And it's all over now?"

She cocked her head, pondering his question, then turned to her mom. "We stopped him, turned him into a snake, then Daniel stabbed him and he died. But… someone escaped, with Samyaza's wings. We're not done, are we?"

Her mom shook her head, sadly. "I'm sorry it has to be you, but no. The Bringers of Light are never done. If it's not Samyaza, another evil force will challenge the world. The twelve fallen kings will see to that."

Allie felt her heart freeze. "The twelve fallen kings? They wouldn't happen to have red, glowing eyes? Appear as kind of shadow wisps or giants?"

"So you've seen them…." her mom said, face pale.

"Is that a bad sign?"

"It may be, or maybe not. It may even be that in your lifetime the ultimate battle between good and evil may not happen, but we don't know. No one knows. You must always be there, ready to stand for what's good. Can you do that, Allie?"

Allie thought back over everything she had been through, the battle at Kyrgyzstan, traveling the world, fighting demons in an otherworldly fortress. And only one question came to her mind.

"Will Daniel be with me?"

"He will," Her mom said. "As long as you both keep hope, and know what you are fighting for, together you will stand victorious."

"Then I'm ready for whatever the other guys can bring at me."

Soon though, Allie had the opportunity to face a different sort of opponent: The coach gave her a shot at the soccer team.

She stood in her soccer jersey, jumping from side to side to warm up and looking back at Daniel on the sidelines. The whistle sounded and it was time to move. She ran for the ball. A tall girl passed it to a nearby girl with pigtails, and Allie sprinted with everything she had. The girl spun, then faked with the ball, moving right past Allie. But Allie wouldn't give up so easily. This was her chance! She about-faced and ran after the girl, catching up with her mid-pass and blocking the ball in a perfect steal.

Several cheers came from the small crowd watching, and she knew it was her family and likely Daniel as well. The thought of them watching motivated her, gave her extra energy. She juggled the ball and ran for the opposing team's goal. Brenda was open and, in spite of her wish not to, Allie saw she was blocked off and had to pass. She ran alongside Brenda, and then she was in the open, the goal in front of her. Brenda passed the ball back. Allie caught it with her instep, then kicked it forward, juggling it across the field. She ran and pulled back her leg, then let the ball fly. The goalie didn't stand a chance.

Her teammates' cheers erupted and Brenda gave her a high five, which felt quite odd to Allie. Brenda had always felt off to her, and she was never really sure if she knew any of the players. But she knew after a kick like that, she must have made the team. Her worries were behind her, and now she could live a normal, soccer-filled life.

Until the next world-threatening crisis arose, that is. She knew it wasn't over with that Yuko girl or the twelve shadow creatures, but she had made a promise to herself and Daniel to wait and ask Principal Eisner about that later, after they had enjoyed their normal lives for a while.

For now, she welcomed the cheers of her new teammates. She laughed at the corny wink her dad gave her and waved back to her mom and Ian. Paulette stood nearby, somewhat bashful.

"Hey Allie," Paulette said. "I hope... I hope you know I would never have done any of that stuff..."

Allie looked around, not wanting to leave the joyous moment, but Paulette stepped close.

"It was like being in a car that you have no control over," Paulette said. "Like I was trapped inside, screaming to get out, but I couldn't."

Brenda joined them, but they fell silent as a tall ninth-grader approached them. She wore a soccer uniform with a nice white sweater tied over her shoulders and walked with confidence.

"Oh my god," Paulette said. "Is Cindy Valldee coming this way?"

"Who's she?" Allie asked.

"The most popular girl in the school, are you serious?" Brenda said. "She's captain of the varsity team. Oh my god, she must have been quite impressed…"

"Hey," Cindy said when she stopped within ten feet, arms crossed. She tossed her blond ponytail back and stared right into Allie. "Nice stuff there, new kid. Me and some of the girls are getting together to discuss plans for the team, maybe go out for ice cream. You should join."

Brenda and Paulette stared at Allie expectantly, the shock clearly visible on their faces. Allie couldn't believe it. This was everything she had wanted—the soccer team, befriending the cool kids. She had it made!

"Sure," she said coolly. "Why not?"

"Alright, come on," Cindy said as she spun on her heel to head back to the school.

Allie took a step and looked back to wave bye to her family. They smiled after her, but Daniel stood by himself. Allie paused. She looked back at the three girls who now waited for her.

"You coming?" Cindy said with a hint of irritation.

"Maybe later," Allie said.

Paulette glanced toward Daniel, where Allie had been looking. "You aren't seriously going to go hang out with him?"

"He's really cool," Allie said, knowing it was true. "And if you're lucky, maybe all of us can hang out sometime. But for now, I'll see you all later."

And with that she jogged over to Daniel, who stared at her in surprise as she approached.

"Where's Chris?" she asked.

"Off with some other friends, trying to be cool, I guess. Will they ever learn?"

She laughed. "So that wasn't part of Samyaza's powers on him?"

"Afraid not." Daniel laughed.

"Come on," Allie said, throwing her arm around Daniel's shoulders. "Let's go get some ice cream, maybe see if my family wants to come?"

"Sure!" Daniel said. "And maybe I'll call my dad and see if he wants to join?"

"Sounds great."

As they walked toward her family, Allie couldn't help thinking about how she now saw her mom in a new light. How all those times Allie had thought her mom was abandoning them, she was actually working to save the family, even the world.

And now the responsibility was Allie's, with Daniel's help, of course. She wondered how two kids were going to handle it, but then she looked over at Daniel walking beside her and she knew.

The bad guys didn't stand a chance.

BOOK THREE

ALLIE STROM AND THE TENTH WORTHY

NO REST

Allie stood in the middle of the field, her opponents running right for her. She had fought worse than them, and didn't even flinch. Taking a focusing breath, she lunged, pulled back her leg, and kicked—sending the soccer ball flying into the goal for the winning shot!

The crowd in the bleachers went wild, and her whole team surrounded her, high fiving and patting her on the back.

"You did it!" one girl said.

"We won!" others were shouting. "We won!"

Allie walked to the sideline, grabbed a cup of water, and looked to the bleachers. Sure enough, her mom and dad were there, smiling and waving. Half of her wondered if they were actually happy to see her playing soccer, or just happy to know that she wasn't out risking her neck to save the world at that moment.

So far, she and Daniel had found the Ring of Solomon, the Sword of the Spirit, the Helmet of Salvation, and the Shield of Faith. But they'd failed to get a fifth item. She had no way of knowing which one it had been—or where it had gone. What she did know was that they were still missing the Belt of Truth, the Breastplate of Righteousness, and the Sandals of Peace.

She had been told that the person to collect these items, "The Armor of God," as Gabe called them, would become The Tenth Worthy, and therefore gain immense power. If this meant going up against those shadowy figures from the underground fortress of Samyaza, then she wanted to run in the opposite direction. Their whispery voices still echoed in her ears, along with the image of Yuko trying to snag the Ring of Solomon from her.

"Way to bring it home," Paulette said with a smile.

She leaned in close and lowered her voice. "Didn't use any of your extra powers, did ya?"

"Of course not," Allie said.

"Yeah, right." Paulette stared at her, and Allie knew the older girl was wishing she still had her old powers, that she could still train. But she had been forbidden to.

Once a dark one was allowed access to your brain, it was that much easier for them to do so again in the future, Principal Eisner had explained. So since Paulette had been possessed by Samyaza, she could not return to training.

Allie smiled at the awkward silence, then turned to find Daniel in the crowd.

He was standing in the bleachers, just about to head in the opposite direction. She said goodbye to her parents, then caught up with him.

"Where you going?" she said.

"Hey." He greeted her with a surprised smile. "Thought you'd want to hang out with your cool friends today."

"Come on, you're my friend."

"I mean, Allie… you're the most popular girl in school now. With so many of the kids knowing what you did, and those girls helping you out on the field…."

"Does Chris feel this way?"

"Chris doesn't think about it like that. He's busy drinking the 'I love Allie' juice just like everyone else out here."

"Everyone but you."

"Hey, I—"

"Wait, you just said Chris loves me," she teased. "Wow, this is big news."

Daniel laughed. "Hey, I saw the way you ogled him when you first met."

"Yeah, but that was before he tried to kill us both and take the ring for…." Allie glanced over her shoulder at Paulette. "You know."

Daniel shrugged. "They couldn't help themselves. We can't linger on that."

"Still, I'm not ready for Chris's love."

Daniel hit her playfully. "You know what I meant."

"Okay, well I'm gonna get changed up. You and Chris want to hang out after? Maybe at my place?"

"Yeah, I'll check with him."

Allie couldn't ignore her annoyance as she watched Daniel walk away. After everything Daniel had been through with her, Allie kind of expected they would be best buddies now, not this weird third wheel situation they seemed to be headed in. To make it worse, she wasn't sure who the third wheel was at this point: Chris or herself.

"Let's go, girls," the coach said, and the team began filtering off to get washed up.

Allie meandered over to the locker room, but her arm was throbbing. It had been doing that more and more lately, and it was starting to worry her.

She found her towel and was heading to her locker when Brenda walked by.

"Hanging out with your boyfriend again today, Strom?"

"Sitting alone at home by yourself again?" Allie snapped. "Maybe if you weren't such a snot, you'd have some friends to hang out with."

Instantly Allie regretted saying it, having no idea where that came from. Brenda stared at her, wide-eyed, then turned on her heel and stomped off. Allie opened her mouth to apologize, but couldn't do it. She just watched Brenda turn down a row of lockers and disappear.

"You feeling okay?" Paulette asked, throwing her gear into the locker next to Allie's.

"Yeah, I think so." Allie quickly changed, then started for the door.

"We're not boys," Paulette said with a laugh. "You don't have to be shy about showering."

Allie instinctively put her hand over the sleeve of her shirt, to make sure the pattern was covered.

"I'm not," she said, glancing back with a forced smile. "I'm just in a hurry."

Outside, she pulled up the sleeve and looked at the pattern. It itched, but she did her best not to scratch it. She rubbed it gently on her jeans, then felt her stomach lurch—the pattern seemed to have moved, writhing like a snake.

She was going to have to tell someone about this, but... not yet, she thought, walking to where Daniel and Chris waited. She returned their waves and decided that no matter how much her arm itched, she wasn't going to snap at these two.

"Ready for Christmas break?" Chris asked. "Any

big plans?"

"Just hanging out here," Allie said.

"Talk about going out with a bang." Chris nodded back at the soccer field. "Really upped your game, huh?"

"Maybe I was always that good."

"Yeah, but something seems different about you."

They laughed, and Daniel held up his fingers as if counting. "Let's see, she saved you, saved me…."

"I had your help," Allie said, nudging Daniel with her elbow.

He shrugged and gave a nervous glance Chris's way. Chris was looking off, a distant look in his eyes.

"You okay?"

"Huh?" Chris looked back at them and forced a smile. "Yeah, of course."

Allie frowned, confused. "Something going on?"

Chris took a moment, staring at the ground, then sighed. "It was tough, you know. Like I was in two places. And when I think about it, I start to feel pulled apart again. I don't know, it's stupid."

"No, I get it," Daniel said.

"Don't see how you could," Chris replied, irritation growing in his voice. "You weren't really taken over, were you?"

"Not exactly, but—"

"That's what I thought."

After an awkward silence, Chris mumbled something about seeing them later and walked off.

"Come on, Chris," Daniel called after him. "Chris!"

But Chris was already walking back inside, the green doors swinging behind him.

"Sooo…." Allie waited.

"I don't know." Daniel stood with his hands on his hips, staring at the doors. "He kinda gets that way sometimes. Ever since…. But it's over now, and you'd think he'd get over it."

"It's a lot to get over."

Daniel nodded, turning back to her. "Yeah, you're right." He allowed a smile to return. "So, to the mall for free hot cocoa?"

"Of course, but I'm *not* going near ice skates."

"Deal."

They headed over on foot since it was only a twenty-minute walk. The whole way, they talked about how great it was to be living normal student lives again. She was sure she'd done horribly on the day's midterm exam, and he complained about striking out at the worst possible time in Vigil Junior High's recent baseball game. But they laughed about it because no matter what, these kinds of problems meant nothing when compared with the chaos of the fallen angels and that side of their lives.

At the edge of the outdoor skating rink, Daniel finished his hot chocolate and fished for a marshmallow with his fingers.

"You don't have to catch 'em all," Allie said with a laugh.

"Growing up, my dad would make me lick the pasta sauce from the plate, not wanting to waste anything.

Call me silly, but a marshmallow's way more valuable than pasta sauce. So I refuse to give up."

Allie scoffed, then said, "Get it, get it, get it," in a mock chant. When he succeeded, she cheered, and a couple of kids skating by looked at her like she was a dork.

But Daniel beamed at her. "Hey, at least we're dorks together."

"I'll take it."

They went into the mall to look for some last-minute Christmas gifts. After a trip to the Hallmark store and Macy's, they decided they'd come back later and figure it out.

"Is that Chris?" Daniel asked, stopping next to the big wreath at the entrance to the food court.

Sure enough, Chris was entering the movie theater with a girl. The girl laughed, then tossed her hair back.

"With Paulette?"

"Wow," Daniel said, his tone sounding as flabbergasted as Allie felt. "I mean... wow."

"Since when are they hanging out?"

Daniel shook his head, biting his lip in thought. "Didn't even say anything to me about it."

"We don't need them," Allie said as she held the door open for Daniel. "Come on, you promised you'd help me with soccer, right?"

"It's getting dark," he said, but at her look added, "But of course."

They walked for a bit in silence before Allie said, "Maybe they get each other, you know?"

"Daniel and Paulette?"

"Yeah. I mean, after both being possessed or what-ever you call it. Maybe they're like people who lived through traumatic events, only other people who went through it get it?"

"Or they're possessed again, and—"

"Don't joke like that," Allie said, and walked along in silence, trying to think about what Chris was going through.

That evening, Allie and Daniel met in the woods by their house to kick the soccer ball around, but soon they found themselves practicing their training instead.

"Come at me," Allie said, and blocked two punches and a kick from Daniel before he connected with a mock-elbow blow to her head.

He smirked, then motioned for her to come at him. She did, but after he dodged her first few strikes and ran, she spun, foot dragging to create an arrow in the dirt surrounded by a crescent. A burst of energy threw her into the air and after him.

"Whoa!" he said as she landed before him, his tone scolding. "What're you thinking?"

"What?"

"Someone could've seen that!"

She glanced around at the dark woods. "Come on…."

"Allie, we're not supposed to play around like that."

She stared at him, unsure until he lunged, both fists stopping inches from hitting her.

"Got you," he said. "As if I'd care about being discovered. We could just pass it off with some sort of magic, right? Like the earthquake thing."

"Not sure how that works," she said. "But I think you're right, we should be careful."

"If I'd had the helmet, no way you coulda caught me."

"Sure I could've. I'd just summon my eagle and have her take you down."

Daniel laughed, and they sat for a moment, considering.

Allie picked up a pinecone and flicked it against a tree.

"With Samyaza gone, what's the point of all this training?"

"It's fun though."

"True."

"Michael have you practicing the whole summon-an-eagle thing?"

"Yeah, but honestly it's still iffy. Half the time I call the eagle and it comes, the other half... nothing."

Daniel shrugged. "But hey, not like you need powers or spirit animals lately anyway."

"Right," she said, hoping that was true. She couldn't count the times in a day when that hope crossed her mind.

Samyaza was gone, for sure. But she couldn't erase the images of those dark beings she'd seen as Samyaza's fortress collapsed around her. The look in Yuko's eyes when she'd tried to snatch the Ring of Solomon still haunted her.

"Come on," she said, standing. "Best get to bed. We have a big day of finding Christmas presents ahead of us tomorrow."

Christmas Eve came, and Allie and Daniel agreed they'd meet up the next day, after opening presents and spending some time with their families. They hadn't seen much of Chris, but Daniel said they'd chatted and Chris had told him more about hanging out with Paulette.

"I get it," Daniel said from the other end of the phone.

"If you do," she replied as she finished wrapping the book titled *Mohira,* that she'd bought for her mom, "that's good enough for me."

"Alright, Allie. Merry Christmas."

"You too!"

They hung up and Allie dashed to the living room to add her present to the pile of others under the tree. Some families didn't bother much with a Christmas tree, or there was the situation like Daniel's, where his dad didn't see the difference between going all out and just throwing some decorations on one of their house plants.

But in Allie's house, the Christmas tree was like

their country flag. It represented her family, or she felt so, anyway. It started with the first Christmas her mom had to miss because of the "Army," or what Allie now knew to be her work as a Bringer of Light. Not having a lot of money at the time, her dad had worked some favors with friends to get the biggest tree he could find, visited the dollar store and secondhand stores for ornaments and lights galore, and he'd done his best to make sure the living room sparkled and shone in red, green, and gold.

Now with her mom back, the tradition continued. The only difference was that now they'd been accumulating ornaments over the years, and nice ones too. When they visited Allie's grandparents on Whidbey Island, they'd picked up a hand-crafted wooden Santa ornament. On their trip to California one year—a drive that Allie wanted blocked from her memory—they'd found a Santa-on-the-beach ornament that took a prominent spot on the tree. The list went on. Allie sat back on the couch, watching the lights transition from white to color.

A thought hit her—over-decorating to make up for a family member's absence would be about her from now on. If what Principal Eisner said was true and that the war was far from over, she'd eventually have to get back out there to find the rest of the Armor of God. Allie sighed, hoping that day was far off in the future.

"There she is," her dad said, plopping down on the couch next to her with a candy cane between his lips. "You guessed all your presents yet?"

"Not even close," she said, motioning toward a large one in the corner with her name on it. "But I know which one I want to open tonight."

"That one?" he said with a casual wave of his hand at the big box. "Not your best choice."

"No?"

"You always go for the biggest box. How many times has that been the best gift?"

She thought back, testing the implication. "Huh…"

"Exactly," he said triumphantly. "Huh. Never."

"Oh, the one year when I got the Costco teddy bear," she said, finger in the air.

"Doesn't count. It was too big to be wrapped."

She laughed, remembering how they'd simply put a box over the bear's head, the body left in plain sight next to the tree.

"Okay, you win."

He shook his head. "Not until I get my Christmas Eve hug."

"Daa-ad." She rolled her eyes but gave him a big hug.

Just then, her mom and brother walked in.

"Ahhh," Ian said.

"You owe me one too," their dad said. He pulled Ian in as Allie maneuvered her way out of the hug.

"Can we get to it then?" Ian asked. "I kinda… I got a date tonight."

"On Christmas Eve?" their mom said.

Ian shrugged. "I take what I can get."

"You're not going anywhere until dinner and at least one glass of eggnog," their dad said.

"Deal."

They enjoyed a delicious ham dinner that her dad had made, with homemade marshmallow-topped yams by her mom. It was fun, being a regular family and talking about normal stuff like who Ian's date was and how he'd met her. Anything to get Allie's mind away from the images of demons and Strayers that still haunted her dreams.

"Okay," their mom said to Ian as they were finishing dessert and eggnog. "One present for each of you, then you can go."

Allie sat down to open the big one, then changed her mind. She reached for a smaller, narrower box, and glanced at her dad. He winked, and she went for it.

She tore the paper off, about to see what was within, when a low rumbling sounded. She turned to her family as the house started to shake, Christmas decorations swaying with the rumbling of an earthquake.

"Mom?" she said, her voice cracking.

"With me, quick," her mom said as the earthquake died down.

They ran into Allie's room as Ian said, "Not a big deal, it was just a little earthquake."

But Allie's mom's eyes showed the same worry Allie felt.

"Check on Daniel," her mom said, pulling out her phone. "I'll get ahold of Principal Eisner."

Allie looked out the window as she pressed his contact icon on her phone, but everything looked normal. A few people had stepped out of their apartments, looking around to see if there was any damage. But there was none—just a normal evening, aside from the ugly Christmas sweaters one family was wearing.

"You think it was the fallen angels?" Daniel asked after saying he was fine.

"Let's just be on our guard," Allie said. She said good-bye and turned to her mom, who had already finished her phone call and shook her head with a look of relief.

"Eisner said it looks like it was actually just an earthquake this time."

"Well bloody-hell."

"Allie!" her mom gave her a semi-scolding look. "Come on, language."

"Does it count if it's not American-English?"

"It always counts, even if it's Japanese."

"I just—"

"I know." Her mom took her in her arms and Allie didn't maneuver out of this one. She leaned in and breathed heavily, eyes closed.

"Want to get back to your present?" her mom asked after a few minutes.

"Not yet," Allie said. "Let's let Ian wonder why we freaked out. Let him think we're weirdoes."

Her mom laughed and held her tighter.

That night when she went to bed, she clutched the new doll from her dad to her chest. At first she'd scoffed, wondering why he thought a doll was a good gift for a twelve-year-old, but then she'd seen that it was the exact same doll she'd lost when she was three, that she always saw in the pictures of her as a child and wished she still had. She couldn't explain why it meant so much to her, but clutching it close she could almost be a little girl again. Not a care in the world. She wished she could just enjoy Christmas like a normal girl, not worrying about demons or fallen angels just because there was an earthquake.

WAR BEGINS

Christmas break came to a close, and on the first day back, Allie's mom and dad both insisted on driving her to school. "To make up for you not spending any time with us lately," her mom said.

"Come on, Mom." Allie accepted the bag lunch her mom had prepared, secretly liking the idea of being dropped off but refusing to admit it. "You know I'm busy saving the world."

Okay, so she'd spent most of the break hanging out with Daniel kicking the ball around or helping him practice baseball... with the occasional pattern practice in the woods. She'd even managed to conjure up the eagle once, but it had flown into the clouds, realized they weren't in any sort of danger, and vanished.

"Busy what?" Her Dad opened the door and Allie followed them to the car. "I thought you were busy being the coolest kid in school now."

"Hey, it's not my fault everything's calmed down since I kicked Samyaza's butt."

Her mom gave her a look that said "Let's not talk about that" as they got in the car and headed to school.

"You know we're blessed to have you safe and sound?" her dad said, glancing at her in the rearview mirror. "This stuff about the Bringers and Guardians.... I still can't believe it."

He wrapped an arm around Allie's mom and gave her a quick kiss on the cheek.

"Hey, eyes on the road or we won't have anything to be happy about." She leaned into him and Allie couldn't help but beam, loving how close her parents were. Sure, it made her a little uncomfortable to watch them get all snuggly, but she'd take that any day over the alternative. They pulled into the school parking lot, which was bustling with other cars, busses and students.

"Hey!" Daniel said, running over.

Allie gave her mom and dad a quick hug, then ducked away from the car so no one else would see her with her parents.

"What up?" she said. "Ready for another normal day at school?"

"Do we ever have those?"

"From now on, I hope we have *only* those."

Daniel glanced around, then leaned in with a whisper. "But after that quake, if that's what it was, I started wondering... about that business with Yuko and—"

Allie held up a hand. "Not our problem. At least, not until we hear something."

"Yeah, I guess."

With a wave back to her parents, Allie led the way to the school entrance.

"Where's Chris?"

"You know him, doing his thing." Daniel leaned in close, lowering his voice. "Probably with Paulette again."

"Those two've shared something… something we don't ever want to experience."

Daniel shared an understanding look with her, then nodded.

In school, everyone had their faces buried in their cellphones. This wasn't odd for the nerds and punk kids, but for the social types to not be chattering away, something had to be up.

Allie found Troy in the crowd and tapped him on the shoulder, eager to see his warming smile. But when he glanced up from his phone, his eyes were tense and worried.

"Allie!" he said, managing a smile for a moment. "Oh, and hey Daniel."

"Sup," Daniel said in an annoyed tone.

"What's going on?" Allie asked.

"Where've you two been hiding?" He looked at them with a frown. "You really haven't heard?"

"Heard what?" Allie asked, snatching his phone out of his hands. "What's this?"

She watched as a video showed buildings collapsing

and people running and screaming. Everything was shaking.

"Damn, I thought everyone was watching this." Troy took back the phone and scrolled down, showing her the headline: *Massive Earthquake Shakes Japan.*

"It must've been pretty bad," Daniel said. "I mean, don't they have earthquakes like every day?"

"Not like this, man." Troy shook his head. "They're saying the death toll is already up there with the worst." He looked at them with doubt, then added, "And some of us are wondering… after what happened with our 'earthquake' here…."

Daniel gulped, sharing a worried look with Allie. They both knew he didn't mean the one on Christmas Eve. No, he was talking about the cover-up, when the school had been attacked by a fallen angel and they'd had to rescue Daniel.

"You think it could be another spiritual battle?" Allie asked.

He shrugged. "Who knows, but I'm wondering."

"Yeah, me too, now. Thanks."

Most of the students were still gathered around their phones, and none of them even looked up to say hi. Allie frowned in Paulette and Brenda's direction, but a hand on her arm drew her attention to Principal Eisner, whose worried expression was only inches from Allie's face.

"We have to hurry," Principal Eisner said, pulling Allie with her.

"And us?" Troy asked.

She glanced back, barely noticing him. "Yes, yes, just hurry."

Allie looked at Troy and saw real panic on his face. Daniel, on the other hand, looked almost excited. They made their way past the students and down the stairs to the familiar door—the portal to their training grounds as Guardians and Bringers of the Light.

The bright light took a second to adjust to, but when she stopped seeing spots, Allie saw that other kids were pouring into the training grounds. They looked to be from all over the world, and the group was much larger than she had ever seen. Older students were there, too, along with some young adults who must have graduated recently. She even saw several large groups of adults, some wearing colored sashes across their chests.

"Who are they?" Allie asked, gesturing to the adults.

"The Elite Guardians," Principal Eisner said. "You're not supposed to know about them yet, but...."

Suddenly, the large doors to the inner training chamber creaked open and Michael came out, his brow furrowed and lips pursed. He seemed to barely notice everyone gathered around, his eyes glued to his shoes. When everyone was quiet, he finally looked up, his eyes resting on Allie for a moment before moving on. She thought she saw worry there, and realized how fast her heart was beating. She told herself to breathe and, like the rest of those gathered, stood in silence, waiting.

"By now you've all seen the videos or heard about what's happened in Japan," Michael said. He waited to make sure everyone was listening. "It's worse than you could imagine."

With a sign from Michael, Gabe stepped forward and pressed a button on a remote, which brought a large screen down on the side of the training ground hall.

"Ready?" Gabe asked, and then pressed a button when Michael nodded.

The screen came to life. It was the same video Allie had seen on Troy's phone, only….

"What you see here is not protected, it is not veiled to hide the truth," Michael said.

On the screen, amid the screaming Japanese, a hole opened in the ground and a shadow-beast leaped out of it, forming into a giant, robed creature with a helmet on its head and glowing red eyes. A gasp carried through the gathered crowd, and then two more holes opened in the ground and two similarly clad creatures emerged. As the three drew fiery swords, more dark images began to fill the streets—Strayers. An army of darkness.

Gabe turned off the screen, and immediately everyone began talking over each other.

"Quiet!" Michael commanded, his worry now transformed to determination. "This is not the time for panic; this is the time for action."

"There are more than one of them, attacking at once?" a voice called.

"Yes."

"We can't fight that many!" another voice said. "We're doomed."

"We can, and we're not." Michael held up his hands to stop further outcries. "Ladies and gentlemen… boys and girls…. What you've just witnessed is a declaration of war. Them against us, good against evil."

33

BURNT WINGS

Principal Eisner ushered Allie and her friends into a corner of the training grounds, where they formed around her in a semi-circle.

"What does this mean for us?" Allie asked, heart racing.

Principal Eisner glanced around, making sure the others weren't eavesdropping.

"Many of the others will be going to full-on war," she said. "Some of them may not make it back…." She glanced over at Gabe, who, prepping his own team, gave her an encouraging nod, then turned back to Allie and breathed deep. "Okay, listen closely. We have some who are putting together strike forces—others, teams of Guardians to make up the frontal attack while Bringers of Light summon spirit animals and do what they can with patterns. But Troy, Brenda, Allie, and Daniel, I need you on a special team. To get to Yuko."

"The Japanese girl who took the wings," Daniel said when Brenda looked around with confusion.

"I know that," Brenda said. "But why?"

"She tried to get the ring," Allie said. "She may be connected to all this."

"Not maybe," Principal Eisner said. "Most certainly. Though we're not sure exactly how yet. Come, we have to get moving."

"Already?" Daniel said. "What about our families? What do we tell them?"

"I'm sorry, Daniel. There's just no time for that."

He nodded, understanding, and tapped his backpack. "Thank God I keep the armor in here."

"If you didn't have the enchantment to make it fit and weigh practically nothing when not on, I'd have to wonder how you do it."

"Hey now," he countered, trying to smile, "it's still very cool of me."

"Of course." She forced a laugh, in spite of the situation.

Allie wondered if her own expression looked as gloomy as her friends' did. They all followed Principal Eisner, passing students and adults who were donning armor, practicing sword strikes, and forming patterns in the dirt. Some were petting spirit animals, and a lion followed Allie with its eyes, giving her the shivers.

They climbed the stairs and went to the walkway of doors. Principal Eisner opened one that had a red, Japanese styled tori gate over it.

"Remember," she said, hand against the red door.

"Find out how Yuko's involved, and do what you can to stop her. Peacefully, if possible."

With that, she stood aside and gave them each a handshake before they stepped into the portal.

It was dark, and howling wind brought the smell of metal and dust.

"Where are we?" Daniel asked.

"Over here," Troy's voice said from nearby, followed by a clang. "No, never mind."

"I think I found something," Brenda said, and a moment later light flooded in to reveal a cramped room, its walls made of metal.

"Weird place for a portal opening," Troy said as he followed Brenda into the light.

Allie was the last to exit, and turned around to see that they'd just emerged from a giant Buddha statue.

"A Daibutsu," Daniel said, glancing around. "Looks like the one in Nara, near Osaka." Seeing everyone staring at him, he shrugged and said, "I was looking online. I've always wanted to come to Japan. This is going to be awesome!"

"Um, except the part about a war with fallen angels or watchers or whatever those things are," Brenda said with a scoff. "You are truly a nerd."

"And his nerdy knowledge will probably save your butt," Allie said, nudging Daniel in the side.

"Thanks, I think?" Daniel said.

Allie turned to take in their surroundings. Gold Buddha statues, incense, flowers, and an intricately carved wood ceiling.

"Hey, guys." Troy motioned toward some tourists on the other side of a small fence. They were looking at them and pointing, and past them, a security guard was coming their way. "I get the sense we shouldn't be back here."

"Come on," Brenda said, and she led them away from the guard, who shouted something in Japanese.

"Anyone speak Japanese?" Troy asked with a glance at Daniel.

"Not really," Daniel said. "But I'm willing to bet he said something about us being in trouble."

They ran around the back of a large wooden structure—a temple, Allie guessed, by the gold statues and incense and the way the roof curved upward. They ran past a grouping of trees, the cold wind blowing red and orange leaves around them, and sprinted past a pond where a crane stood still as a statue. Several deer turned their heads at their passing.

Finally, they came to a small hill and a series of connected buildings with tiled roofs that tilted up, much like that of the temple, but in need of repair.

"Over here," Troy said. They climbed up and over the hill, then turned to look back at the tall building that housed the large Daibutsu on one side of the trees, and the series of Japanese houses on the other. Allie was amazed by the exotic view: the close-set houses, moss-covered stone lanterns, and the odd writing on the Japanese street signs.

Brenda, however, didn't seem to care about any of it. "So what now?"

Daniel pointed to a wide walkway leading away from the temple. "I imagine we follow that and figure out how we're going to find Yuko."

"Wouldn't the portal have sent us to her?" Troy said. "I mean, it's not like we can just use our American dollars and bribe people to tell us where she is."

"He has a point," Allie said, hating to admit it. She pulled out her cellphone. "And, of course, our phones don't work here, either."

Brenda was looking around, deep in thought. "So you guys are saying Yuko might be here, somewhere?"

"I think she has to be," Troy said.

"Split up and look for her?" Allie suggested.

"Okay." Troy nodded to Brenda. "We'll wrap around back past the Dai-buddu—"

"Daibutsu," Daniel corrected him.

"Yeah, what I said. If you hear something…." He looked at his phone with a frown. "Yeah, just shout I guess?"

Allie laughed, looking at the immense temple area. "I guess we have no choice."

She led Daniel down the large walkway, figuring they'd start at the entrance and work backward, to meet Troy and Brenda at the midpoint. But they hadn't gone far when a small earthquake threw them off balance.

"There!" Daniel said, pointing to a black blur in the distance.

"What'd you see?"

"Strayers, disappearing past those trees," he said, and started running. "Let's go!"

She sprinted after him, rounding the trees. She smelled the smoke before she saw the fire, and they both halted at the sight of a house, covered with flames and burning brightly.

"This has got to be it!" Allie said.

Daniel looked at her with worry. "How does a burning house help us?"

A shriek from the direction of the house made him turn.

"Someone's still in there," Allie said. "It could be Yuko...."

"And you want to run into the flames?"

"No, but I can't let her burn, either."

She took a step forward, but Daniel grabbed her arm.

"Allie, that girl attacked us."

"And she was possessed, right? I refuse to let her die when we're right here to help."

She pulled herself free and dashed for the house, hoping Daniel was close behind.

A crowd of people had gathered around the house. They pointed and shouted when they saw Allie go running by, Daniel on her heels.

The wall of the house had collapsed, leaving an opening for her to rush into. She quickly performed a protection pattern in the ashy floor, then turned to see Daniel beside her.

"Stay close."

The fire seemed to have started at the front, and the flames hadn't destroyed the back part of the house yet. Allie ran deep into the smoke, shouting for Yuko. A burst of flame came through a door when Daniel opened it, but he jumped back just in time.

"Careful!" Allie shouted.

A scream came from upstairs, and Daniel pointed.

"There!"

The small set of stairs was almost hidden in a small doorway, and Allie threw herself up them.

"Where are you?" she yelled. "Daniel, how do you say it in Japanese?"

"I don't know! I just looked up where to go.... Something like 'doko'?"

"Kotchira! Kotchira!" the voice shouted, coming from behind a sliding screen door.

Daniel reached the door first, and when he slid it open, a burst of air knocked him back. Dark wings followed, holding Yuko in the air as she flew out with a kick to his chest.

"We're here to help!" Allie shouted.

But Yuko had turned on her.

"It's a trap!" Daniel said, trying to catch his breath.

"You think I don't see that?" Allie replied as she dodged a sweeping attack from Yuko.

The next strike caught Allie in the back of the head, sending her sprawling forward. She turned just in time to see Yuko falling from above, fist held at the ready. The winged girl landed with a punch to the floor that cracked the wood plank.

"Yuko, it's us!" Allie said. "We've come to get you out of here!"

"You can't!" Yuko said, spinning in a circle so that her wings knocked Allie over. She leaped at Allie, fists raining down. "Nobody can help me!"

Daniel tackled Yuko off of Allie, holding her to the ground. She stared up at him with confusion.

"Your English has gotten better," he said.

She looked insulted, then punched him in the chest, sending him rolling to the floor.

"Give me the ring!" she shouted at Allie.

"You know I can't do that." Allie lifted her hand with the ring and focused her energy. "But I can do this."

With a crack, the ring sent forth a burst of energy that wrapped itself around Yuko, constricting like a snake.

"Ahhh!" she shouted in pain. "Make it stop! It's just me, it's just…."

"Stop it, Allie!" Daniel said. "You're hurting her!"

Allie tried, concentrating on pulling back the light, but nothing happened.

"I—I can't," she said.

Yuko screamed again. "Enough!" she said, before allowing another anguished yell.

The light grew brighter as it squeezed, and Yuko let out yet another piercing scream as her wings fell to the floor.

Yuko collapsed, unconscious. Daniel ran to her side and lifted her with great effort.

"We have to get out of here," Allie said.

"And we're not leaving her," he replied. "Help me!"

Allie hesitated, but when flames tore at the stairway nearby, she darted forward. The two helped Yuko to her feet and started toward the exit.

As they ran through the fire, Allie turned back to see the flames take the wings. A plume of black smoke puffed into the air as the wings shriveled and then were gone.

34

ESCAPE

A llie kept running until Daniel finally stopped her, bent over in exhaustion.

"Okay, I think we're safe," she said with a glance over her shoulder.

Yuko, who had been struggling to keep up, panted with arms raised above her head as she struggled to catch her breath.

"What in the world happened back there?" Allie asked. She looked at walls of houses surrounding them. "And where are we?"

Allie and Daniel turned to Yuko, waiting.

"They…. They have my family," Yuko said. She looked exhausted, with bags under her eyes as if she hadn't slept in months.

"What do you mean?" Daniel asked. "Who?"

"The Strayers." She took a step but wobbled, and Daniel had to help steady her. "They took my mom first. Then, when I didn't do as they asked, my dad and grandmother."

"And what did they ask you to do?"

"The ring…." Yuko looked in awe at the ring on Allie's finger. "They said I had to put on the wings, get the ring from you, and bring it to them."

"You know that can't happen," Allie said, covering her ring with her other hand.

"No, of course. Not now."

"Not ever."

"That's not what I mean," Yuko said, looking to Daniel for help. "It wasn't me. The moment I put those wings on, I felt the pitch-black eating at me. It was like looking out from a smudged window, not able to control what I was doing but watching it with horror."

Allie sighed, allowing herself to relax. "Yeah, we've seen that before."

"Paulette," Daniel said with a nod of his head. "Samyaza, he has the power to do that."

"But we destroyed him."

"Samyaza was only one of many," Yuko said. "I overheard the Strayers talking… and now that Samyaza's out of the picture, it seems the other twelve fallen angels are stepping up to see which of them will take his place."

"Wait," Daniel said, looking around quickly. "You're saying there are twelve of those evil beings out there? Each just as bad as Samyaza?"

"That's what it sounded like," she said.

"Wow." Allie ran her hand through her hair, trying

to process this new information. "But, you…. Are you with us now, I mean like one-hundred percent?"

"I don't know how to convince you," Yuko said. "But yes, I am."

Daniel gave Yuko a compassionate look, then turned to Allie. "We're kind of at war, right? What choice do we have?"

"I guess you're right." She looked around and saw the temple in the distance, the one with the big Buddha. "Let's meet back up with Troy and Brenda and figure out the next step."

"What was the plan?" Yuko asked, taking a step on her own to see if she was able. "I mean, after coming for me?"

"We were kind of hoping you'd know."

They started walking, with Daniel lingering next to Yuko to make sure she kept up.

Yuko thought for a moment, then said. "When they took my family, the Strayers made me get something they called the Belt of Truth. I wore it—and that was how I was able to wear the wings."

"Wait, you mean the armor? That was you in Tulum, taking it when we got there?"

Yuko nodded. "Yes. And then they took it from me, and left me just the shadow wings, at first… then they sort of grew on me." She shuddered at the memory.

"Okay, so they have the Belt of Truth." They had all stopped, and Daniel was pacing as he spoke. "That leaves two—"

"No. It's one." Allie scrunched her nose. "I mean, I'm

not sure, but I think they managed to get the Breast-plate of Righteousness. That's my guess."

"If we go with the assumption, then yeah... that leaves the Sandals of Peace."

"Kinda ironic, huh?" Allie said, trying to smile. "I mean—"

"Yes, Allie." Daniel waved her off. "But they could be anywhere!"

Yuko looked at the two, surprised. "You mean you don't know?"

Both Allie and Daniel shook their heads.

"Why do you think the war is happening here? They knew you'd be after the last item, and they don't know exactly where it is, but they know it's in Japan. My guess, somewhere around Tokyo. So you have to find it first. And if you can find the Sandals of Peace, then you would be powerful enough to rescue my family."

"Let me get this right," Allie said. "First we find these sandal-things before the bad guys do, then we use whatever extra strength or power or whatever they give us to rescue your family?"

"Exactly." Yuko looked just as sick as Allie felt. "And the Strayers holding my family have the belt."

"And getting the breastplate?" Daniel asked. "Any plan for that?"

"That's where it gets complicated."

"You think? All we have to do is conquer this army of fallen angels and then it's ours. Only problem is, we need it to fight them."

"But it's the only way."

Allie massaged her temples, trying to work through this. It's not like she had thought their chances were great before. She made up her mind.

"Well, what're we waiting here for?" she said. "First stop, try to figure out where those sandals are."

"Guys!" a voice called.

They spun to see Brenda and Troy running toward them, followed by figures in black not far behind.

"Guys!" Troy called again, grabbing Allie's arm as he hurried past the group. "Time to run!"

"Strayers?" Daniel asked, falling in step behind him.

"I don't know," Troy said between breaths. "They're wearing black, but—"

"Yakuza," Yuko said with a glance over her shoulder. "Yeah, they're with the Strayers. Always have been."

"Damn!" Daniel said, his face going pale. "This is bad!"

"Wait a sec," Allie said with a scoff. "You look more scared now than when we were talking about fighting an army of demons and fallen angels!"

"Yeah, well, these guys are insane!"

Allie shook her head, running all out. A few shouts in Japanese sounded close behind them.

"Yuko, right?" Brenda said. "Any thoughts on where we can ditch these guys?"

"Your ring," Yuko asked Allie. "Didn't it work like a portal or something before?"

"Why didn't I think of that!" Daniel said, whipping his enchanted backpack around in front of him. As they ran, he pulled out the shield, but suddenly slowed under its weight. "We're gonna need somewhere to stop!"

"There!" Troy said, pointing to a small park with a circle of sand for kids to play in. "Get ready to make some patterns!"

As soon as their feet hit the sand, Troy and Brenda began making patterns in it—defensive circles with squiggly lines through the sides that faced their attackers. Daniel had the helmet on now, the shield on his left arm, and the sword in his right. Allie held the ring at the ready.

"How do you make it work?" Brenda asked.

Daniel and Allie looked at each other, not sure.

"What'd we do last time?" he asked, as a bullet ricocheted off of the invisible barrier created by the pattern. In the process, that section of the pattern was swept away, and Troy had to quickly redraw it.

"This won't hold them for long!" Troy said, his feet moving rapidly through the sand. "Allie, do you know how it works or not?"

"Not really," she admitted, flinching as everyone turned to her with shock and fright. "Last time we just had the shield and the ring, and we held hands."

Brenda and Troy looked at her like she was nuts, but then Troy shrugged and took Brenda's hand in his left and Daniel's in his right.

"Let's do it then," Troy said.

The yakuza men swarmed upon them. The first tried to attack with a blade, but the barrier threw him back onto the ground.

"Hurry!" Troy yelled.

Everyone joined hands. For a moment, nothing happened, but then the ground shook. More yakuza attacked and the pattern in the sand began vanishing, sand flying in all directions. The shield started to weaken, and then light swirled out of Allie's ring and engulfed her group….

With a blast of wind, they were gone.

35

MT. FUJI

hen Allie opened her eyes, she saw they were passing over a lake and heading toward a large mountain capped with snow. Wind blew past them like they were skydiving, but they weren't descending—they were arriving. Then, with a flash of light and one last gust of wind, they found themselves landing on a grassy walkway on the side of the mountain, where patches of snow matched the chill in the air.

"Where are we?" Brenda asked, rubbing her arms for warmth.

"Even I know that one," Troy said. "This is Mt. Fuji."

Daniel nodded with excitement. "I've always wanted to try to climb it."

Brenda shot him a glare. "Well, lucky us. So the item is supposed to be right here?"

"Not exactly," Allie said. "The other time, it was

more like the items were a loose magnet. We were close, but not right on it."

"But there was the tower that time, so it was pretty easy to figure out."

"Aside from the whole near-death thing and all that."

"Right…."

"Actually," Yuko said, "I have a thought."

"As to where the sandals are?" Daniel asked.

"My guess would be in one of the shrines near the top."

"This isn't going to be fun," Allie said, looking at the steep slopes ahead of them and the snow on the side of the mountain. "Where're all the tourists, anyway?"

"Can't come this time of year," Yuko said. "Too cold for climbing."

"Big surprise," Brenda said with a roll of her eyes. She rubbed her shoulders, shivering. "Maybe I wait here for you all?"

"We don't have time for that," Allie said. She glanced at Yuko, and Brenda got it. "I wish we could have thought of that before, and brought warm-weather clothes. But… maybe we can figure something out with the ring's magic."

"Yeah, okay." She started up the path. "Best get started then."

The walk was grueling and seemed to go on forever. The broad path turned into a narrow winding one, and soon the soft dirt became rocks and loose rubble covered with patches of snow. They knew they had to hurry to save Yuko's family and stop the war below. But when they rounded a bend on the mountain, the reality struck home: black smoke rose far off in the distance below, beyond the stretches of trees and lakes.

"Think that's the fighting?" Yuko asked.

"Definitely." Daniel walked next to her and lowered his voice, but not so much that Allie couldn't hear. "With everything going on... I mean, I knew it must be tough. You doing okay?"

Yuko shrugged. "Try being controlled by fallen angels and having your family's lives at risk sometime.... See if you're okay then."

Daniel continued in silence for a few minutes after that, then said, "You know, it wasn't like it was your fault. Samyaza tried to get to me through my dad, too."

"Yeah?"

"Me and Allie though, we stopped the Strayers, and saved my dad. Just like we're going to save your family."

She looked at him hopefully, then back to Allie, who smiled awkwardly. Talk about pressure.

The path turned from a gentle slope to areas of steep, stone steps. Everyone focused on moving forward, too exhausted to talk much.

Daniel, though, continued trying to comfort and distract Yuko, and Allie had to smile at how silly the two were.

"This is *kowai*," Daniel said at a stopping point, pointing to a pink monster on an ad for some sort of green tea chocolate.

"Not *kowai*," Yuko said. "That means scary. *Kawaii* means cute."

"Well," Daniel said with a shrug. "In this case it kinda works."

The two laughed softly, forgetting their fears for the moment. They went on, everyone feeling very happy that Yuko had some Japanese yen to pay for food when they found a small food depot station for hikers. It was closed and they had to break in, but they left the money on the counter and took some water bottles, snack bars, chocolate, and dry ramen noodles.

"Check this out," Daniel said as they reached a tall gate. It was made from two poles on each side and a curved one laid across the top. He was reading a guide-book that he'd apparently taken from one of the hiking stations. "This is gate eight, and according to this, everything from here up is technically considered part of the shrine."

"How many gates in total?" Brenda asked.

"Nine."

Allie turned to Daniel. "So technically, if these Sandals of Peace are in a shrine, they could be anywhere from here on up?"

"Just keep your eyes open for anything suspicious," he said, putting the book back into his backpack.

By now the snow was a few inches thick, and Allie wished they had dressed warmer. Of course, she'd had no idea where they were going. She had on a sweater and jeans, but would have preferred a parka and three layers of long underwear.

They soon reached the top without any sign of a pair of fancy sandals. As the sun began to set, they passed under a gate that had two stone lions, or dragons, or some mix in between, guarding each side. The setting sun cast a red glow on the snow. Breathing was a struggle, but still Allie wondered if she'd ever breathed air that smelled so fresh.

"Whoa," Daniel said when he nearly fell, but Yuko caught him by the hand. Neither let go, even after he steadied on his feet. "Thanks. I mean, *arigato*."

She smiled and slowly pulled her hand back.

At the top of the mountain stood a building, a lookout point, some vending machines, and a giant crater. With the snow surrounding them, the crater felt more like a perfect place to go sledding than a place where lava had once poured forth.

"What's going on there?" Daniel said, staring at the base of the crater.

Allie strained her eyes, but couldn't see anything out of the ordinary. "What do you mean?"

"Steam," he said. "Look!"

"That shouldn't be happening," Yuko said. "Maybe we should go into the buildi…."

But she didn't finish her thought, because at that moment the steam gushed out, followed by a spurt of lava.

"You have to be freakin' kidding me!" Brenda said, all color gone from her face. "We just climbed into a volcano?"

"No, it couldn't be," Yuko protested.

"It's not," Daniel said, pointing. "Not exactly."

They watched as more lava poured forth and the opening widened. The mountain shook, but there was no eruption. Instead, the lava shot into the air, swirling into thick darkness until a giant creature made of blackness stood before them, its black core surrounded by a shroud of glowing hot magma.

"It's a trap," Yuko said, her voice a quiet realization.

Brenda had already turned to run, but Allie and Daniel were getting in fighting positions. Troy looked at them nervously, and began moving about to form patterns in the snow at their feet.

"What're you doing?" Yuko asked.

"Saving your family," Allie replied. "Gotta start somewhere."

A group of Strayers emerged from the nearby building, and Brenda doubled back to rejoin the group.

"Looks like the only way out of this is the way we came," Brenda said.

Daniel shook his head. "We go running that way, we'll be falling to our deaths. No thanks."

"You'd prefer your chances against that thing?"

Allie and Daniel shared a look, then both said, "Yes."

Where the being had only darkness for a face moments before, red, burning eyes now glared down at them. A mouth formed, and its voice rumbled, "Bring me the ring."

The Strayers charged.

"Keep them off of us," Allie said to Brenda. "Daniel

and Troy, you fight him. I'll find the sandals, and then we can get out of here."

Daniel beamed as he placed the helmet on his head. In spite of his shaky legs, he stepped forward and raised the sword. Troy and Brenda began sketching patterns in the dirt, and Allie looked around, bracing herself.

"That's one of the twelve up there," she reminded Daniel. "In many ways, just as crazy and powerful as Samyaza. Be careful. Ready? Yuko, you're with me."

The Strayers hit the fields of protection Troy and Brenda had set up, falling back. In that moment, Allie and Yuko charged for the building.

"Is there a plan?" Yuko asked, eyes wide with terror.

"Search everywhere," Allie said, diving through a doorway as a bullet tore through the wooden frame. "And do your best to survive."

"Great plan."

Allie slammed the door as best she could, despite the splintered frame. Through the crack, she saw a couple of the Strayers had turned back to follow her and Yuko. Daniel was using his shield to hold off blasts of lava from the being in the sky, while Brenda and Troy furiously worked on patterns of protection and, in case they'd need it, healing patterns as well.

"You take downstairs," Allie said. "I'll get this floor."

Shouting came from the front door as Allie darted into a nearby room. Nothing but a few beds, some flowers in a vase and a bowl of fruit. The décor seemed odd, but not the point at the moment.

The door started to open, and she threw herself into the corner. A sliding shelf was big enough to hide her, and the Strayer seemed to be in too big of a hurry to bother checking it. He hastily scanned the room, then walked out.

Outside, Allie heard the sound of fighting, and Daniel yelling something about hurrying up. Then Allie heard Yuko scream and dashed out to find two Strayers, one male and one female, pulling at Yuko and trying to drag her down the hall.

"No sign of them," Yuko said as she stomped on the foot of one Strayer and elbowed the other.

Allie plowed into the female Strayer, knocking her down so that she hit her head against a stone wall.

"Where else can we look?" Allie said, glancing around as the second Strayer started to recover. She took a stone lion from the corner and hit him over the head with it.

Yuko was about to respond when Daniel called out, "Watch out, he's coming for you!"

Daniel grunted loudly, and then the walls were evaporating, giving way to hot magma.

"We gotta get out of here!" Allie shouted, pulling Yuko back toward the door they had come in. But more Strayers were entering, and it seemed hopeless to try to go that way.

Yuko tugged at Allie and shouted in Japanese while pointing to the side walls.

"What?" Allie yelled, frustration seeping into her voice.

"There are sliding doors over here! The screens!"

Allie and Yuko ran, escaping just as the room behind them collapsed in flames, taking some of the Strayers with it.

"That was close," Yuko said.

"Next time, English?"

"Gomen." Yuko blushed. "I mean, sorry. When I'm freaking out, it just happens."

A light from behind suddenly highlighted her face red.

"Time to freak out now?" Allie asked, and Yuko nodded.

They both ran as the being crashed through the collapsed shrine. Daniel appeared, darting in between them with shield at the ready. A blast of lava sent him back, nearly knocking the shield from his hands, but he held tight. Then the being lifted both hands and slammed them into the ground, sending a shock wave that pushed Daniel into the air and sent him flying to crash into a nearby rock wall.

"Daniel!" Allie said, running after him.

Yuko ran too, and Troy and Brenda joined them. Quickly, they started making patterns again, covered in sweat in spite of the cold. Troy moved to a circle with an infinity sign that Brenda had made, then he bowed his head and made the clawed pattern of his spirit animal. A gleaming gold tiger leaped from his outstretched hands, taking down three Strayers and then leaping for the being. But a burst of lava sent the tiger to retreat into the pattern on the ground. Troy fell back, as if he'd just been gut-punched. Brenda moved past Daniel, where he still lay on the ground, and made a new pattern—three wavy lines like a river. When the next siege of Strayers hit them, their fists and knives were swept aside as if by a strong current.

But the patterns weren't holding.

"We can't keep this up," Allie said. "We have to retreat."

Daniel recovered, his eyes groggy, and then he turned to the crater not far from him.

"The portal he came through," he said, pointing to the bottom of the crater. "It's still open, and we can use it."

"We have no idea where that'll lead!" Allie said.

"I'm willing to bet it goes either to the streets of the ongoing war or to Yuko's family. Maybe both."

"Fine," Allie said with a glance behind her. The being was shooting lava into the sky as it rushed towards them. "Go!"

She was the first to jump. The others followed close behind, all of them sliding down the snow in what would have been an amazing sledding adventure, if there hadn't been a group of Strayers and one of twelve fallen angels determined to kill them so close by.

"Yes!" Daniel was cheering behind her. When she looked at him, he almost laughed. "We did it!"

"We failed!" Allie screamed, the bottom of the crater zooming up to them. "What're you talking about?"

Daniel winked and, careful not to drop them, held up a glimmering pair of what looked like a cross between sandals and boots. The front part had a sole and straps to slide the feet into, and the top was like a golden shin guard.

"Are those….?"

"When I dove behind that prayer stone up there, the sword fell and cut right through the stone at my side. And voila!"

"Well, I hope we live through this, then, so we can celebrate!" Allie called back.

Daniel looked down, then rolled onto his back so that he could slip the sandals on over his shoes as he slid down the slope. When he rolled back, he gave Allie an adventurous 'here goes' smile and leaped up. She wanted to shout at him, ask what in the world he was thinking, but instead, she watched with wonder as the sandals gleamed extra bright and Daniel landed on his feet, sliding as if roller skating down the snow.

"I think we'll be fine!" he said.

"Speak for yourself!" Troy shouted as he approached the bottom. A sharp rock jutted into his path, looking like a claw ready to tear him to shreds.

Daniel ran on top of the snow and grabbed Troy, rolling with him to narrowly dodge the rock. It tore at the back of Daniel's shirt, but otherwise they escaped. With a helpful shove, Daniel pointed Troy toward the portal, then looked around to make sure the others were safe.

But Allie saw what he hadn't yet. The portal was starting to close!

"We're losing our chance!" Allie shouted, pointing.

Daniel ran to Yuko, whose slide down the snow had already started to slow. He grabbed her hand and slid next to her, tugging her so that within a second they were beside Allie.

"Give me your hand!" Yuko shouted, and soon they were all holding hands, catching up to Troy.

Lava landed nearby, sizzling through the snow. The portal looked smaller as they approached, but Allie remembered she hadn't tried everything in her power yet. She aimed her ring at the portal and closed her eyes, feeling the two powers clash—but a moment later she was flying through open space, the portal closing above their heads. They'd made it.

36

THE TOMB

Falling through empty space was hard on the mind, especially when all you could see was gray mist and the occasional burst of light.

"What now?" Brenda asked, glancing with a grimace at Troy and Daniel holding her hands.

"My family," Yuko said. "We can use the added magic of the Sandals of Peace, rescue my family, and get the Belt of Truth."

"They could definitely help," Daniel said. "They make my feet feel light, energized. Maybe I could run super-fast in them?"

Allie nodded, wondering if the other armor items would have their own powers as well. "The helmet, does that do anything?"

"I'm not sure yet, but I felt like I could sense attacks coming. Wasn't sure if I was imagining it or what, but yeah... now that I think about it."

"That's all cool and all," Troy said, legs kicking as he

tried to get used to floating. "So why not focus on the breastplate and go straight for the main battle?"

Yuko stared at him with hurt in her eyes. "My family."

"Right, but I mean—"

"No, Troy," Allie interrupted. "Besides, I don't think it works that way. It's like a hierarchy, maybe. One item leads to the next. For all we know, we could close our eyes and focus and end up at the breastplate, but then who knows if we'd be ready for that fight without the belt."

"So it's decided then," Daniel said, nodding firmly. "We rescue Yuko's family and get the belt, first."

"Everyone, close your eyes," Allie said.

The falling sensation stopped with a jerk. Even through her closed eyes, Allie saw blasts of light intensify until they were surrounded by white light. Next thing she knew, they were tumbling onto the floor of a train.

They recovered, standing to see two doors, one in front of them and one behind them, at either end of the car. A few people were seated in the shiny, leather seats, and trees and houses sped past the small windows.

"Shinkansen," Yuko said. When the others stared at her in confusion she said, "Bullet train."

"Okay, then," Allie said, checking the doors again to make sure no one saw their arrival. "Be alert, you guys."

One of the doors opened, and an old lady entered with a cart full of Japanese chocolates and some curry plates. She exchanged a few sentences with Yuko, and then continued down the car.

"I coulda used some of that," Daniel said. "The ramen from Fuji-san was definitely not enough."

Yuko smiled. "Sorry, no money. But you know to call Mt. Fuji 'Fuji-san.' How?"

"I just listened to you enough times," he said, blushing.

"Wow, calm down you two," Brenda said. "We should be checking the train, not batting eyelashes at each other."

Daniel's face darkened a further red. Yuko turned away shyly, but she couldn't hide her smile from Allie.

They split up again, Troy with Brenda to cover the front of the train while the rest checked the back. Allie was amazed at how clean it was, everyone in comfortable seats either sleeping or watching videos on their phones or tablets. Two Japanese children were playing a game, and a tanned man that looked to be American stared at Allie and her friends before turning away.

"Are there a lot of Americans here?" Allie whispered to Yuko.

"Many, yes. Why?"

"Probably nothing," Allie said, not sounding sure at all.

At the end of the car, she turned back to see the man was looking at her again.

"Hang on. I want to just be sure…." Allie whispered to Yuko. She walked back toward the man, but just as an announcement sounded, someone tripped her and she fell hard in the aisle.

She jumped up to look for the man, but she didn't have to look hard—he and two Japanese women in black were standing over her.

"Take her and the other girl," the man said, and the two Japanese women lifted her.

A lurch of the train threw Allie off balance before she could prepare for a fight. Someone shoved Yuko against Allie, causing them both to stagger, and then the women lifted their arms and a black shroud fell over the two girls. Allie could see Daniel through the shroud, but even as he raced to get to them, he became darker and seemed to vanish.

When the shroud came off, though, it was clear that Allie and Yuko had been the ones to vanish—Daniel, Troy, and Brenda were apparently still on the train, with no way of knowing where the two girls had gone.

"Where have you taken us?" Allie demanded, taking in the stone walls, the cobwebs in the dark corners, and the arched doorway that led to another room. She didn't have to wait long for an answer, though, because Yuko was running to an old woman who had just appeared in the doorway.

Yuko grabbed the old woman in a hug and then explained to Allie, "This is my grandmother." The two exchanged quick sentences in Japanese, and then Yuko said, "My family, they're still safe. We have to get them out of here."

"Lucky for these guys," Allie said with a glare at the

people who had brought them there. It was only then that she noticed they hadn't moved. They were standing at attention, as if awaiting someone.

Footsteps echoed in the chamber. The shadows darkened.

A robed figure stepped in, ducking under the arch. When he looked at Allie, she saw no face, only pitch black and glowing red eyes.

"You've brought me what I asked for?" a deep voice said from within the darkness.

One of the women nudged Allie and said, "Right here."

"Where?"

The woman looked at Allie, waiting.

"You want the armor?" Allie asked.

The robed figure's breathing grew louder, filling the room. Yuko huddled against her grandmother, trembling with fear.

"Where?" the deep voice bellowed, its eyes flaring with red. "You will give it to me!"

"He's a demon, a dark angel," Yuko said.

Allie nodded grimly at Yuko, already aware of the danger they were in. She cautiously slipped the ring into her back pocket, for once glad that Daniel wasn't there with them. The magical armor and weapons had made Daniel stronger, but she wasn't sure he was strong enough to defeat this foe.

"Allie!"

It took Allie a moment to believe what she was hearing. She spun to see Daniel appearing through a portal in the wall, the shield and sword held high and the sandals and helmet glowing gold and bright in the dim room.

"Come on!"

It wasn't his fault, he couldn't have known… but she wanted to punch him for bringing the armor right into the enemy's hands.

The dark angel made a pleased sound, then reached out a robed hand and pulled Daniel toward him. With each step closer, the armor began to rise off of Daniel.

"Allie!" Daniel shouted with worry. "We gotta go, now!"

She shook her head with a glance toward Yuko. They couldn't just leave her family here like this, captives of the Strayers.

"No retreat," she said as she pulled the ring back onto her finger and ran. She propelled herself into the air and spun, using the magic of the ring to pull the floating armor onto herself. The helmet landed on her head with a dull thud, the shield came to her ringed hand, and the sword flew into her other hand. When she landed, the sandals were in place on her feet.

Daniel stared in amazement.

"That was—" the dark angel started, but Daniel finished by saying—

"Amazing!"

"No. It was foolish." The being reached up and pulled back its hood, then cast the entire cloak to the floor. Its skin was cracked like a dry lakebed. In places where there was no skin, fire burned bright.

The dark angel looked at Allie like it was about to attack, but then tilted its head and smirked instead, showing pointed teeth. It reached for her and began a chant.

Allie felt the familiar pattern etched in her arm stinging, and then the shadows around her arms began to swirl. With a command from the dark angel in an ancient language, Allie spun and struck at Daniel!

"What're you doing?" he screamed, diving back and barely dodging her blow.

"I don't know!" she said. Her sword arm struck again, but she still had control of her other arm. She threw the shield to Daniel, which he caught and held in place to block her blade. "He's controlling me somehow."

"Make him stop!"

The chanting grew in volume, and Allie was pulled forward by the sword, its point aimed straight at Daniel's chest. He dove out of the way, blocking as best he could, but the strike hit his shoulder and drew blood.

"Fight it!" he shouted.

She felt her arm pulling back, ready for the slash that she was sure would end Daniel's life. If only she'd told someone about the marks on her arm, if only she had found some way to get rid of them before now. Closing her eyes, she focused on Daniel, their friendship, and on the ring that had once been part of a necklace that had belonged to her mom.

Her mom—what would she do if she were here? Not let her friend be killed, that was for sure.

Allie put everything she had into her ring, focusing on its positive energy instead of the negative energy flowing from the black marks on her arm.

With a blast of bright light, she pushed back on the force that was controlling her. She felt like a strong wind had been blowing over her, and then suddenly stopped.

The dark angel stared at her with its fiery eyes and again started a chant, but this time nothing happened. Allie took a relieved breath, but then something slithered on her arm. Above the marks carved into her skin, three black snakes were circling her arm, one preparing to strike. She knocked them off her arm and shot them with a bolt of fiery light from her ring.

"The sword, Allie!" Daniel said, hand outstretched.

His voice was urgent, and with a glance around the room, Allie understood why. The walls had begun to shift, revealing myriad spiders emerging from the cracks. Even the Strayers' eyes shifted at the sight.

She tossed the sword to Daniel and, running with her ring pointed in front of her, created a path of fiery light through the spiders.

"Where's your family?" she shouted as they reached Yuko and her grandmother, pulling them along.

"The back room, but it's blocked. We can't get through."

"Blocked how?" Allie shouted as she pulled to a stop, seeing the answer for herself.

The back room had been a tomb, but now the cement blocks were moved aside, and the undead that had once rested in its darkness were shuffling toward the group.

"Under different circumstances," Daniel said, preparing his sword. "I'd have thought this was cool."

Allie shook her head. "You'd have been wrong. In all circumstances."

He smiled, then charged. Allie ran beside him, staying between the bodies and Yuko. As Daniel hacked, she shot white blasts of light at the walking corpses. Each strike caused them to vanish into thin air, leaving behind floating dust.

"Yuko-chan!" a voice called from farther back. "Hayaku!"

"We have to hurry!" Yuko said, running out in front of Allie.

"Wait!" Allie said, but too late. One of the undead had grabbed Yuko and pulled her down, teeth bared for her neck.

A swipe of Daniel's sword turned the undead into dust that flew across Yuko. She looked like she was about to be sick, but shot him a grateful smile.

"Yuko-chan!" a woman yelled again as she ran out, helping Yuko to stand. Allie assumed she was her mother, and the man who joined to help on the other side, her father.

"This way," Allie shouted, leading them back toward the arched entryway.

"Are you crazy?" Daniel shouted.

"Yes, but as far as I can tell, it's our only way out."

The dark angel and his followers were waiting in the room, and more undead stumbled after the group from behind. The dark angel held up a hand, and silence fell over the room.

"You can't ignore fate," the dark angel said. "Join us. Fulfill your destiny."

"My destiny is to become the Tenth Worthy and destroy you!" Allie shouted.

The dark angel laughed, shaking the stone walls. "Is that what they've told you?"

She gulped, glancing at the exit.

"Now the time of truth, little one." The dark angel waved a withered hand in the sky and a glowing sphere appeared. In it were the shifting shapes of various men on horseback, always with armies at their back.

"The Nine Worthies... each with great power. Many cut down before their time." The images showed Julius Caesar being stabbed, Alexander the Great on his deathbed. "They were invincible when on our side, and only when they turned on us were they betrayed, their lives ended. Don't you see, Allie Strom? The path those so-called Bringers of Light would have you travel ends in your demise, but on our side you have an army of the gods, the power to change the world for the better."

She stared at the flashing image, which now showed her standing atop a green hill with men and women dancing around her, smiling. The ring glowed on her finger and the Armor of God glimmered in the moonlight.

"Why do you fear us, Allie?" The dark angel made the image bigger, and now it showed him and eleven others. Their skin was restored to a shining silver, white wings flowing from their backs. "Restore us to our rightful place, and together—"

"No," she said defiantly.

"You are wrong." The dark angel looked at her sternly. "You've been lied to, misled."

"I agree, but only by you." She looked to Daniel for confirmation and he gave her a nod. "I'm not fooled by you. My mom fought you and Samyaza, and I'll continue the fight."

The dark angel pushed the ball of light toward Allie. It exploded, but not before Daniel stepped forward and slapped it back with his shield. The light missed Allie and instead threw the Strayers onto their backs.

"Destroy her!" the dark angel shouted. It raised a sword that glowed red with jutting spikes.

The Strayers and undead moved forward. One caught Allie, pulling her to the ground and sinking its teeth into her shoulder. She screamed, trying to focus on her ring to send them back in flames, but there were too many. They began to pile on top of her, and all she could think of was her next breath. She tried to pull herself up, so she could breathe ….

She could hear Daniel hacking at the undead and blocking strikes from the dark angel's sword, but he was getting pushed back. Yuko's family was screaming, but Allie couldn't see them. All she could see was rotting flesh and gnashing teeth.

"Allie!" Daniel shouted. "What do we do?"

She opened her mouth to shout, but a clawed hand fish-hooked her cheek and she felt her stomach lurch. Instinct fueled by panic took over, and suddenly she was clawing her way out from under the pile. Forget the ring, this was time for crazy Allie. She found a hole in the assault, and finally pushed her way out. Kneeling at the edge of the lumbering corpses, she spun back and blasted the undead so that limbs went flying.

A swipe of the red sword came down at her head, but she dove and ducked it. Rolling to her feet, she aimed at the back of the dark angel's head and sent everything she had left into a blast that threw it sprawling forward and right into Daniel's well-placed sword thrust.

With a shriek, the dark angel hissed and spun, releasing a string of otherworldly curses, and then it fell to the floor, grasping at the open hole in its chest. Flames burst forth from beneath its skin as it hissed and spasmed in pain. The Strayers stared in horror as the dark angel convulsed one last time, and then dissolved into black smoke.

Allie turned on them, ready to finish the fight, but instead one of the Strayers knelt and pulled back a wig, revealing a shaved head covered in black patterns carved into her skin.

"They're here!" the kneeling Strayer shouted, and the dark marks begin to shift like snakes, glowing in a purple light. "Come, great lords."

The other two Strayers joined her, revealing their

own dark marks and chanting. As they did, a portal began to open in the floor, and through it, red eyes glowed. Allie could see at least three more dark angels, just like the one they'd just killed, about to come through the portal.

Allie glanced at Daniel, then to Yuko and her family, weighing their chances.

"Retreat," she said, and they all escaped through the arched entryway.

REGROUP

Allie and the group exited into a grassy field in the middle of a densely populated residential neighborhood. They saw restaurants on the corners and a shopping center not far off. They ran through narrow streets, past glowing vending machines and red lanterns. More than once, they had to slow down for Grandma. Their focus was on each step and making sure they were as far from the tomb as they could get.

Yuko's mom shouted something in Japanese.

"In here," Yuko said.

Heart pounding and gasping for each breath, Allie didn't argue. She glanced back to make sure no one saw them. She continued, the last to enter, and slid the shoji screen door shut behind her.

"Where are we?" she asked, looking around the tight enclosure. She saw a counter with stools before them and a large metal cooking pot.

"A ramen-ya," Yuko said. "Come, we know the owner."

They went through the back door and found an old man in his underwear and a tank top walking down some wooden stairs. Yuko's parents exchanged quick words with the man. With a look of doubt, he motioned them to follow him up the stairs. He led them to a back room with one window and a balcony, where Allie positioned herself as lookout. Her eyes scanned the shadows of the street while the others talked in hushed tones.

She was glad to see everyone was safe, and very glad to receive some ointment and gauze from the old man to treat her wounds where the undead creature had bitten her. Daniel sat beside Yuko, asking if she was okay, and Allie noticed the slight smile Yuko showed at the way he was catering to her.

Outside, the sky was dark and the wind was strong, rattling the window and howling. At least, Allie hoped it was the wind that was making the horrible noise. Black wisps went by and she ducked back behind the curtain, certain that she would be in trouble if they sensed her.

She wondered what had happened with Troy and Brenda back on the train. If they had escaped, she doubted they would have any way of reconnecting, so they might not see them again until this was all over.

A noise startled Allie, but she turned with relief to see it was just Daniel coming to check on her. He studied her for a moment.

"You could've told me, you know." He sat beside her and checked the wound.

"About what?"

"Allie…." He looked at her arm and the dark marks Paulette had carved there. "Maybe I could've helped?"

"I… I'm sorry."

"Next time, don't let there be a reason to say sorry, right?"

"I may just chop it off," she said with a glance at her arm.

"Let's not let it get to that." He smiled grimly and looked back at Yuko.

"You like her, huh?"

"What?" He glanced back at Allie, caught. "What'ya mean?"

"Daniel, come on. I've seen the way you look at each other."

"No different than how you've been looking at Troy."

"Hey."

He blushed, cocking his head. "Don't suppose it matters though, huh?"

"What do you mean?"

"If we don't beat the fallen angels to the rest of the armor, none of this matters. And right now, our chances are looking a bit bleak, right?"

She considered the golden helmet on his head, the shield and sword on the floor. The realization hit her, and she slapped her forehead with a groan.

"The Belt of Truth!" she said. "We completely forgot."

"That's what I mean," Daniel said. "Now there are three of those fallen angels waiting for us. Can we really go back in there against them?"

"We could try."

"You don't have to," Yuko said as she sat down beside them, beaming. "My mom managed to swipe this during the fight." She held up a belt with strips of gold-studded leather dangling from the front.

"Wow," Daniel said, then leaped up and gave her a hug. Stepping back awkwardly, he took the belt and tried it on, hanging his sword in the loop on the side.

"Maybe we're not in as much trouble as we thought?" Allie said, but then the house shook and an explosion sounded nearby. "Or at least, we're closer to succeeding than we thought."

As if in answer, the building shook again, followed by a series of crashes. Allie looked outside and saw a building down the street collapsing. Flames licked the sky from another building that had caught fire, and even as they watched, another tremor shook them.

"We can't stay here," Allie said, making eye contact with the old man and Yuko's family. "We're putting everyone at risk."

"We're all at risk anyway," Yuko said.

Daniel looked like he was about to agree with Yuko, but then shook his head and stood. "No, Allie's right. We have to get out there and fight this thing. We only have to find one last piece of the armor, and then…."

"Then what?" Yuko asked, defiantly. "You win, like that?"

"Well, no," he admitted, looking to Allie for help.

"But we have a fighting chance, at least." Allie stood beside Daniel. "You all, stay hidden. Daniel and I have to carry on this fight."

"Then I'll come with you," Yuko said.

Allie shook her head.

"I have to, I can't just—"

Daniel took her hand, eyes pleading with her. "Yuko, you've already been compromised, okay?"

"Well, yes, but—"

"And your family needs you."

This got to her, and after a glance at her family, she nodded. "But you... you'll be safe?"

He laughed. "I'll do my best."

"And when it's all over?"

"I'll come back for you."

Allie raised an eyebrow at that, surprised at how serious he sounded.

"I'll miss you," Yuko said with a kiss on Daniel's cheek.

"You too," he said, blushing. With a glance at her dad to make sure it was okay, he kissed her hand and then gave her a big hug. He stood tall, proud.

"Where to, Allie?"

"Maybe back to the school," Allie said. "To regroup. But I'm not sure how...."

Daniel assessed the ring. "In the past, you've focused on the ring while concentrating on locations, right? Like with me in the forest that first time, or Kyrgyzstan with the globe? So let's try that."

He had a point, so they knelt together. Daniel put his hand in hers, flashed a comforting smile at Yuko, and then they both closed their eyes and focused.

A sudden warm blast of air surrounded them, and when they opened their eyes they were in the light of the school training grounds.

Principal Eisner was standing there, back to them, staring at the screen where the briefing had taken place. On the screen, Bringers of Light and Guardians were in retreat. Tokyo was in ruins, and Principal Eisner cycled through the images to show other cities also in ruins. Strayers in their black robes were causing fires to erupt and earthquakes to bring down buildings.

"It's horrible," Allie said, standing next to Principal Eisner.

The principal spun to Allie with a look of surprise. "You're still alive!" She took Allie in an embrace, holding her tightly for a long moment.

"Barely," Allie said, with a nod toward Daniel. "Saved by my Guardian again."

Daniel blushed but shrugged in agreement. "Saving each other, right? It's our thing."

"Well, I'm glad," Principal Eisner said. "I was starting to worry." She gestured toward the screen and then lost herself in the images of destruction for a moment.

Allie asked hopefully, "Have you seen Troy or Brenda?"

Principal Eisner spun back on her with worried eyes. "You mean they're not with you?"

Allie shook her head.

"That's not good," the principal said. "Where were you separated?"

"On a train heading toward Tokyo, I believe."

The principal turned to the screen with a frown. "Let me see what I can find out, and in the meantime...." She looked over her shoulder to them, finally showing a hint of a smile. "Your parents are here, in the teachers' lounge. You can go see them."

Allie and Daniel broke into smiles and rushed from the room, running through the halls and into their parents' arms.

"Tell me everything," Allie's mom said. Allie's dad listened intently as she recapped as best she could, a shine of sweat on his forehead.

"You don't actually mean to go back out there?" he asked, fear and anger mixed in his voice.

Allie's mom put a hand on his shoulder and closed her eyes. "I know it's crazy, but she doesn't have a choice."

"You mean you're okay with this?"

"Of course not!" She opened her eyes, and they shone with tears. "But I was in her shoes once, and I remember what it means. If she were to walk away now, we'd all be dead."

"Or enslaved," Principal Eisner said as she entered. She shot a strong stare at Allie. "Like your two friends have been."

"What?"

"Troy and Brenda.... Let me show you."

Principal Eisner waved her hand in the air, much like the dark angel had done in the tomb, and an image appeared of Brenda and Troy. A dark shadow loomed over them and their eyes looked blank.

"The Strayers got them, and they've been taken over by two of the Fallen Angels."

"No...." Allie said, not wanting to accept it. "We were just with them."

"You'll need those two if you hope to retrieve the Breastplate of Righteousness. Which means your first step is a battle in the ethereal plane."

"I'm not following," Daniel said. He shrugged sheepishly. "For once, that is."

Allie rolled her eyes, but then nodded in agreement and looked to Principal Eisner with curiosity. "Yeah, none of what you said makes sense."

"There's a place out there—call it our subconscious, call it another plane—where the angels and demons can affect us on a mental level. When people become possessed, as with the current situation, this is where the true battle must take place to set them free. You've been there before, when you defeated Samyaza."

"That wasn't the underworld?" Daniel asked.

"Not in physical reality. It was in your mind, in a way. Or on a different plane. However you want to look at it."

Allie blinked, then decided she could ask Principal

Eisner for a lesson on ethereal planes later. "Just tell us what to do so we can get it done."

Daniel glanced at her and narrowed his eyes, determined. "Right."

"Wait just a minute," Daniel's dad interrupted. "Allie has to do it, I get that. But my son, too?"

Principal Eisner bit her lip. "He has a point. Daniel, if you don't want to go, there's nothing to say you have to."

He looked at Allie, shaking his head. "I could never…."

"It's okay, Daniel." Allie did her best to put on a smile. "You watch out for everyone here. I can take care of this."

"NO!" Daniel put his hand on the hilt of his sword. "If you went out there and never came back, I wouldn't be able to live with myself."

"Don't put your life at risk over pride or guilt, or whatever."

"I'm not," he insisted. "I'm putting my life at risk to be there if you need me. To save you if necessary, so that you can save the rest of us. All of us." He glanced to his dad with a smile, and then looked down with a worried expression.

Allie knew he was thinking of Yuko, and also knew then that there was no stopping him.

"I'll be glad to have you with me." Allie turned to Principal Eisner. "Okay, how do we do this?"

"Your best bet is for me to open a portal to Brenda and Troy," Principal Eisner said. "When you get close to them, you'll see the way open up, as you did with Chris when you entered the plane to confront Samyaza. But, before you go…. Daniel, Allie will have to wear the armor to become The Tenth Worthy."

"Leaving him unprotected?" Allie asked, appalled.

"You are the one chosen for this fight, and you must be the one to wear the armor to be victorious and fulfill your destiny."

"He keeps the sword," Allie said, with a look to Daniel.

"For now." Principal Eisner's brow creased with worry. "But when you get close to the breastplate, make sure you're holding the sword, too, and wearing all the armor. Now, let's get on with it."

As she created a portal and Daniel took one of the school swords, Allie donned the armor. The helmet was surprisingly heavy, but when she put on the belt and the sandals, she felt a new vigor. The shield was also heavy at first, but then it adjusted to her size and grip.

"Allie," Daniel said, with a glance at the dark marks on her arm.

Allie shook her head and mouthed 'no.'

Allie hugged both her parents, clinging extra tight to her dad and then kissing her mom on the cheek, and then stepped into the portal with Daniel close behind.

DREAM WORLD

They stepped out into chaos. Buildings smoldered in ruins, and scattered fires sent black smoke into the night sky.

"Where do we start?" Daniel asked.

"This way," Allie said as she started walking. She was sure they would come across Troy and Brenda, somehow. She hadn't been able to tell Daniel, but when she saw Troy on the image at the school, knowing he'd been taken by the fallen angels, she'd been surprised by the depths of her fear. Maybe what Daniel had said before, about the way she looked at Troy... maybe it had some merit. Maybe she did care for him as more than a friend—like how Daniel seemed to care about Yuko. She wasn't sure, but she was certainly sick of people around her getting hurt.

She looked for signs of nearby fighting, then turned to Daniel. The desperation in his eyes caused her to miss a step. She wasn't used to such despair, not from him.

"About what you said back there," Allie started, probing gently. "About saving all of us. I know how you feel about Yuko. It's okay, you know."

"I know."

"You like her. It's cool."

"It makes me jealous of Chris, sometimes, is all."

"He was Samyaza's prisoner," Allie said, confused. "What's there to be jealous of?"

"No, I mean, now he gets to stay back and be a normal kid, right? He and Paulette have been hanging out a lot. I imagine it's kind of nice, not having this responsibility on your shoulders."

"Yeah, I guess." She walked in silence for a minute, eyes searching the collapsed buildings and a group of trees in the distance. Would she give it up if she could? Leave it all for someone else to figure out? But that would mean trusting her family's fate to the competence of others.

"But don't forget, if we fail, they'll be either killed or enslaved, so...." Allie stopped, unsure.

"Better to have some influence on how it all goes down?" he said, eyes distant.

"Isn't it?"

"Yeah, I suppose I get that. Though ignorance certainly has something going for it."

Allie laughed. She had to agree there, and would almost give anything to go back to how it was when she had no idea this crazy spiritual war was going on.

"Look," she said, pointing to a flutter of birds that burst into the sky.

They sprinted over, careful to avoid sparking power cables and maneuver around a pileup of cars. They reached a small park that was relatively untouched in the havoc, and came to a stop behind a short, granite wall to hide and get a good view.

Next to the swings, Michael was using his fiery sword to deflect blows from Troy, Brenda, and several Strayers. They had him pinned down, in part because he refused to strike Troy and Brenda.

Michael parried a strike from Brenda, then blocked a blow from Troy and shoved him back.

"Return to me, Troy!" Michael called, then moved aside as Brenda came back at him. "Brenda, you must fight it!"

From their hiding spot, Daniel looked at Allie with wide eyes. "Plan?"

"Let's just try to help Michael, and not hurt Brenda and Troy." Allie pulled the heavy helmet down over her brow and charged.

As they approached, the wind began to swirl up around them into an upside-down tornado, pulling in trees and grass. It was much like how the ground had seemed to give way when they'd confronted Chris over the Sword of the Spirit. The Strayers braced themselves against the toys in the playground.

Troy turned on Allie with wild eyes and struck with his sword, but then something interesting happened. Allie felt the helmet pull her, gently, telling her to move to the left. Almost instinctively, she did—right out of the sword's strike. But when Brenda came in with a kick and Allie ducked, again feeling the nudge of the helmet, she moved too slowly. Allie took the kick in her chest and went sprawling onto her back.

Daniel parried a strike from Troy and pushed him back. Then he turned as Brenda swung at him from behind.

"Look out!" Allie screamed as Troy started to rise to his feet. Daniel looked in her direction, then side-stepped Troy just in time for the swirling vortex to pull Troy up and out of sight. Brenda charged, infuriated, but Allie rolled away from Brenda's heel—prompted again by the helmet. She kicked Brenda in her stomach, knocking her off balance and into the portal as well.

"Go after them!" Michael said as he held off a wave of Strayers.

"What about you?" Daniel asked.

"I'll keep the Strayers at bay, and ensure this place is safe for your return." He held their gaze for a moment, then added, "And you must return."

Allie felt a shiver run down her spine, but there was no time for fear. She leaped forward, into the portal.

Gusts of wind grabbed at her, pulling her up and spinning her in all directions, like a doll being flung around by a dog. Daniel appeared next to her and bumped into her side, and they held onto each other as they tumbled down, both too frightened to speak.

They hit the ground in a strange land. Wind flowed

past them like colors in a painting, and tall grass brushed their cheeks like a gentle mist.

"We're there," said Allie. "In the mind-world that Principal Eisner was talking about."

"Whose mind could this be?" Daniel asked.

"I don't think that's how it works," Allie said, standing unsteadily as her feet sank slightly into the ground. "It's another plane, a place like a spiritual realm."

"Yeah, okay," Daniel said, still looking a little confused. "So, let's start with figuring out where we go from here."

They were in a valley, trees covering the surrounding hills, and the curved roof of a temple visible halfway up one hill.

"To the temple?" Daniel asked, with a knowing look.

"Sounds better than wandering around the trees," Allie said, already walking in that direction.

As they climbed, the trees grew dense, the branches almost blocking out the sky. Rays of sunlight provided some visibility, but the woods were still gloomy. They made their way around a rock formation and up a steep path, using ferns and tree roots to pull themselves up. Then a shadow passed overhead, and Allie and Daniel shared a worried glance.

"In the normal world, I would say it's a bird...." Allie said.

"Maybe an eagle?"

"Actually...." Allie's heart raced at the idea of putting her spirit animal to good use again.

"Can you summon in this place?"

"Only one way to find out." She closed her eyes and focused, moving her hands in front of her body in a pattern that first formed a body and then spread out like wings.

A burst of warmth came over her, and a moment later the screech of her eagle sounded from above.

"What's it see?" Daniel asked, eyes wide with excitement.

"Wait," she said. "I have to focus on it."

But before she could finish the thought, another screech came from above, followed by a loud howl. They heard a rustling of leaves, and then a large shadow loomed over Allie and Daniel.

"Move!" she shouted, diving to push Daniel out of the way and grateful again for the helmet's helpful nudges.

With a crash, her eagle slammed a winged beast into the ground, skidding to a stop at a nearby tree. The beast's head cracked against the tree trunk and sent a spray of pinecones down on it.

The eagle hopped back, looking at Allie triumphantly.

"Um, thanks," Allie said, brushing off pine needles and dirt.

"That was awesome!" Daniel said, approaching the eagle. He craned his neck at the large bird. "You give her a name yet?"

"Should I?" Allie looked at the eagle, and it cocked

its head as if waiting. "I guess that makes sense, us being linked and all."

She closed her eyes and felt a warm breeze flow over her.

"Trellon," a voice whispered in the back of her head, and when she said it out loud, the eagle nodded as if in a bow.

"Sure coulda used Trellon when we were fighting Samyaza," Daniel said.

Trellon gave Daniel a narrowed look, spreading his wings, and Allie understood why.

"In a fortress like that?" she said. "He wouldn't have been able to do so well, with the enclosed walls and all."

"Good point. Anyway, I wish Guardians could summon spirit animals like that." He nodded to the eagle in respect, and then bent down next to the fallen beast with a whistle. "You gotta see this."

Allie had been keeping her distance, but her curiosity won out. "Okay, Trellon," she said, patting the eagle's wing, "be ready in case something happens."

The beast on the ground had a wolf's body and large wings with hooks, like those of a bat. The fact that Trellon had taken it down gave Allie an immense appreciation for the eagle.

"So, this isn't Kansas?" Daniel said. "Is that how the saying goes?"

"Close enough," Allie said. "Though I still don't get how you can be such a history buff and know so little about real culture. Can't even get that quote right."

"Right," he teased back. "I know plenty of what

matters, though. Let's get moving before more of those things find us."

Allie sent her eagle into the sky to be on the lookout, and the two continued to the temple. Each step reminded Allie of how little rest they'd had since the war broke out. She still hadn't recuperated from the Mt. Fuji climb, and she hoped that the oily feeling in her hair would wash out—if she ever had the chance to take a shower.

"What was that?" Daniel said, spinning around and eying the trees.

"Where?" Allie's stomach jumped.

"Wait, it's gone. I guess. I'm sure I saw something…."

Allie pushed forward, trying not to give in to her growing anxiety.

They stopped for a rest, and she noticed long, curving marks in the ground. They were everywhere, crisscrossing and forming patterns, moving in a circle, closer and closer, as if closing in on its prey.

Like a snake, Allie thought.

"Snakes," Daniel said, echoing her thought.

"No way." Allie knelt and put her hand in one of the shallow ditches. It was at least three hands across, two deep. "That would be…." She couldn't even think it and closed her eyes with a shudder.

"This isn't our world," Daniel reminded her. "Anything's possible."

Allie stood and pulled the helmet down firmly on her head, then made sure the sandals were on tight. If things got dicey, she wanted to be ready. They started walking again, and she noticed that Daniel had his hand on the sword. She wasn't sure if it should worry or comfort her.

When they were within a few hundred feet from the temple, Allie suggested they stop for a break. Her neck was starting to ache from the helmet, and while the sandals made her move fast when she wanted, this slow march made her feet ache.

"How did you wear this armor all the time?" she asked, turning her head and rubbing her neck.

"I'm just a manly man," Daniel said. He glanced down at the sword and the belt he wore. "You know I can help if you need it. I mean you don't have to *always* be wearing it."

She considered the offer but knew she had a responsibility. "No, Principal Eisner wanted me to train in it, and be prepared."

Daniel nodded, then turned and looked back at the way they had come. "You see this?"

When Allie stood beside him, her jaw nearly dropped. Now that they were on higher ground, they could see what had been hidden from below. Beneath a sky of swirling colors, she could just make out the tops of pyramids like she'd seen in books on Egypt, peeking out from behind a hill. Beyond those, on another hill higher even than the pyramids, stood an ancient temple of marble, like Allie imagined they would find in Greece. Above it all and past the temple, mountains rose into the sky, a swirling cloud of dark gray at the highest peak.

"I'm kinda glad we didn't head that way first," Daniel said.

She nodded, and for a long while neither could move. When they started walking again, Daniel kept looking back at the pyramids, eyes full of curiosity.

"My dad used to read me stories about Egypt," he said. "Stories about the sun god, adventures with mummies, and cool stuff like that."

"Cool's a relative term there."

"No, no way. I mean, yeah, it's not cool in the risk-your-life-by-driving-a-motorcycle kind of way, but in the 'it's freakin' awesome' way. Not debatable."

"Okay...." She meant to ignore the topic, but after a few beats of silence she asked, "What exactly?"

"Oh, man." He grinned, won over with the question. "You want to talk about nerdy awesomeness. You know the stuff about Ra's Al Gul in Batman, with the Lazarus Pits and how he could regenerate and lived for centuries, but later in the comics they tried to use the power to bring someone back to life in the body of another girl? Just like in that *On Stranger Tides* book, with the pirates trying to resurrect people. That stuff?"

"Dude, do I look like I'd know all that?"

"Yeah, well, Egypt had it going on way before those writers."

"And you like those kinds of stories?" she asked. "I mean, that's what gets you excited?"

"How could it not?"

"It's just so...."

"Unrealistic?" He laughed, motioning around them.

"Look at us, Allie. Tell me what's realistic and not, please. Because I have a hard time understanding the difference lately."

He had a point there, and she nodded, giving the moment to him.

"What about you?" he said. "What floats your boat?"

They reached the entrance to the hillside temple and paused, looking into the light glow of flickering candles. On both sides of the door stood large wooden warriors carved in flowing stances, each with an imposing spear. She brushed her fingers across one of them, making sure it was wood and not about to come alive, and then turned back to Daniel.

"Me?" She thought back to her brother's Dungeons and Dragons stuff, and all the awesome '80s movies her dad had made her watch until she loved them as much as he did. But at this moment only one answer came to her.

"Curious George."

"What? No, I don't mean when you were a kid."

"Me neither." She shrugged, refusing to be ashamed of it. "I don't know, I remember watching it with my brother when we were both really small, and I loved that. It was just... special. So sometimes, when I'm not feeling so spiffy, I'll throw on a little Curious George until I feel better."

"That's kinda sweet." Daniel took the first step into the temple, waiting for her to follow. "If I run into Mr. Curious in here, I'll let you know."

"Hardy har."

"Hey, in this place, you never know."

She looked back with a nervous glance at the trench-like marks in the ground, then followed him into the dim light of the temple. She somehow doubted they would meet Curious George in there.

THE TEMPLE

A gentle orange light highlighted paper shoji-screen walls. Allie wanted to turn and run after one look at the dark corners and multiple passages ahead, but she pushed forward. It was entirely possible that either Troy or Brenda would be held here, if not both of them.

Her footsteps creaked on the tatami mat floors. A few steps in, they came to a stop at several sliding paper doors. Allie hesitated.

"What do you think?" Allie asked.

"Always the middle door," Daniel said.

Allie scoffed. "Not if you played D&D with my brother… that door always got you killed."

"So…. Left then?"

She felt a nudge from her helmet. Looking at Daniel, she shook her head and opened the door on the right. Inside was another dark hallway, which they followed until they found a large chamber. A scuffling sound behind them made Allie turn.

"Did you see that?" she whispered.

Daniel stopped walking. "No," he said. "But that doesn't mean there's nothing there."

She looked around nervously as they continued on, past the room and into what seemed to be an outdoor courtyard. The sky was dark, which was strange since it had still been light outside when they'd entered.

"See," Allie said, "alternate reality."

"Exactly."

They walked on, careful not to stray from the stone path that was surrounded by small, glimmering pebbles. Pillars of rock rose up around them, with draperies and ancient Japanese paintings flowing from them. Tall clumps of bamboo grew between the rocks.

A soft flute carried in the wind—a tune like something out of Zelda, perhaps, Daniel pointed out. She told him she'd just have to trust him on that one.

This time, they both saw the eyes. And then a snarling that even Daniel couldn't deny.

"Not that way," Allie said, looking for a new path, one that was not in the direction of the sound. She pointed to stepping stones leading off to the right.

They skipped across the stones and hurried toward a stairway. Daniel screamed, and Allie looked up to see a winged wolf like the one from outside sitting atop one of the pillars and looking down at them as if ready to pounce.

Daniel readied his sword, but Allie ran back and pulled him with her.

"It hasn't attacked yet!" she said, but she spoke too soon.

The wolf leaped, diving into their path. Urged by the helmet, Allie stepped back, but she tripped on the stepping stone and landed in a scattering of shiny pebbles. Almost immediately, her skin began to burn. But the beast's claws were coming for her, and she didn't have time to worry about anything else at the moment. She rolled aside as Daniel lunged with his sword, narrowly missing the wolf creature. Allie pulled herself up and aimed her ring, sending out a shot of light that knocked the beast back and into the pebbles, where it writhed in pain.

Daniel stood above it, sword raised, but then looked at Allie with hesitation.

"Do it!" she yelled.

His eyes narrowed and he stared at the beast again, then let the sword fall to his side. The beast stared up at him with frightened eyes.

"Let's just keep moving," Daniel said.

She stepped forward, ring raised, thinking she'd do what Daniel couldn't so that the beast wouldn't inter-fere again.

But she couldn't do it either. Her arm felt heavy, and her whole body seemed drained of energy. Some-how, attacking the creature didn't feel right.

"Yeah," she said, hanging her head. "Keep moving."

They left the winged wolf behind and found them-

selves in walkways of more shoji-screen walls, a cavern
with a rock ceiling high above them. More than once,
Allie was sure she saw the winged wolf clutching onto
a stalactite, staring down at them. But then she grew
more worried about the fact that every turn they made
just seemed to take them back in a circle, no matter
which way they went.

"Some kind of maze?" Daniel asked.

"Let me guess," Allie said. "You think it's cool?"

"I would if I wasn't so freaked out right now."

"My thoughts exactly."

The two walked on, side by side. Allie heard a loud
flutter behind her and looked up to see the wolf's red
eyes, trailing them. She shuddered and tried to focus
on the way forward, but the fluttering sounded again
and a chill went up her spine. She turned, ready for
anything…. But the winged wolf seemed to motion
with its wing before flying to another stalactite to their
left. She frowned, considering the situation.

Maybe it was somehow trying to help? She kept her
eye on the beast, moving in the direction it had indi-
cated as best she could in the maze.

"Remember the wolves in Kyrgyzstan?" she asked.
"On Solomon Mountain?"

"Yeah, but I thought we agreed those were Chris's
weird form of a spirit animal, trying to help us." He
glanced up at the winged wolf. "This feels a bit
different."

"Just thinking out loud, but watch…."

Again the wolf motioned, this time in a different

direction. Allie followed, Daniel at her side. Now when they looked back, she could tell they were definitely farther from where they had entered, and making progress through the maze.

"You gotta admit, something's going on here with that wolf-thing," Allie said.

"When we're out of here safely and it hasn't bit off my head, then yeah, sure."

They continued down the passageway, following the wolf as it flew, and soon they took a left that brought them to the opposite wall from the one they'd started. At its base, they found a small door that was only as tall as their knees.

They looked up to see if the wolf would lead them somewhere else, but it seemed to have vanished.

"So, you have a drink or a cake that will shrink us or something?" Daniel asked.

Allie knelt down and opened the door, peering into the darkness. She looked back up at Daniel, and he backed away, hands raised as if to ward her off.

"Nu-uh, I'm not crawling through that!"

"Don't know that we have a choice," she said. "You wanna stay in the maze instead?"

"Yeah, kinda."

She jutted out her lower jaw and raised her eyebrows, doing her best impression of her mom whenever she was serious about something that Allie didn't want to do.

"Come on, Allie." Daniel knelt and looked into the narrow passage. "It's dark, it's…. it's like a…."

"A casket?"

"Ugh. I was gonna say MRI machine, but yes, now that you mention it." He looked at her, eyes wide, but then nodded. "Can you at least make your ring glow or something while we crawl?"

With a nod, she agreed. She got down on all fours and, ring glowing, inched her way forward and into the tunnel. It was a struggle, especially since having the ring glow forced her to concentrate, and drained her energy. The ring's white glow illuminated what seemed to be a long tunnel with dirt and rocks surrounding them, nothing more.

They crawled through without incident, and she was as happy as Daniel looked when they emerged to find themselves in a new room. Several thick, wooden beams led across to the other side, with an open area below them. The glow from Allie's ring showed the bottom faintly, the glow reflecting in what appeared to be moving water.

"Why's it moving like that?" Daniel asked. "Shouldn't water be still in a place like this?"

"You'd think." She started across the middle beam, not wanting to dwell on the waters. She hated the idea of falling, even if there was water down there to catch her, and she wanted to keep her mind on the beam—and getting across.

A creak sounded from behind and she turned just in time to see Daniel struggling to keep his balance. Her hand nearly missed his, but she was able to grab it to help steady him. Just as he was firmly on his feet, a hissing sounded from below.

"You gotta be kidding me," Daniel said, jumping back. A second later, gleaming eyes appeared and teeth reflected the glow of Allie's ring as a snake chomped at the spot where Daniel's foot had been a moment ago.

"Now you're afraid of snakes?" Allie said, heart thumping, hand trembling. "How cliché."

"Have you ever met anyone not afraid of snakes?" he asked, pointing at the slithering mass below. "Especially that many, with heads as big as ours?"

She shook her head, not wanting to talk again and give away how bad her teeth had begun to chatter. When she was young, her brother had snuck a garden snake in her bed. She had discovered it when she curled up to go to sleep, and she hadn't stopped screaming for at least an hour, sure the snake had tried to kill her. Even after her parents told her those little snakes couldn't hurt her, she'd had nightmares for years.

One foot in front of the other, she told herself. Each foot touched on the beam gently, careful not to risk her balance.

"Do we have to go so slow?" Daniel asked from behind.

She refused to look back, or even pause to answer. Just one foot in front of the other.

Daniel sighed with frustration, but continued behind her. Slow and steady.

Something growled, and Allie paused, listening.

"What was that?" she whispered.

A small chuckle. "I think it was my stomach. I'm starving back here."

"You can think about food at a time like this?"

"Not me, but that doesn't mean my stomach wasn't. This little guy has a mind of his own."

She risked a glance back so she could glare at him. "Just focus on staying alive, okay? And ask your little belly friend to shut up."

He half-smiled, but then glanced down again and the terror returned to his face.

Finally, they made it to the end. This time, they were happy to see a normal-sized doorway. But there was no door in it, just a doorway that led to a drop, the ground not far below. Now Allie's stomach was beginning to rumble as well, and she felt drained from using the ring for so long. But since there wasn't any other light source, she kept it on.

Daniel lowered her first, and then slid down behind her, landing with a thud. Allie turned to help him up, then felt her breath catch in her throat—they weren't in a separate room at all. They were surrounded by snakes, and several had noticed that they had company.

"RUN!" Allie shouted, already pushing herself away, Daniel's hand held tight in hers.

In spite of the exhaustion, she felt her feet moving faster than they ever had. At first, she thought it was the terror of being chased by snakes, but when she looked down, she saw the sandals glowing and remembered their special powers.

The cavern curved to the left. Ahead was a large opening, like a cave entrance, with beaded ropes hanging from the top all the way to the bottom.

"In there!" Allie shouted, knowing how stupid it sounded since there was nowhere else for them to go.

They neared the entrance, but a loud snarling echoed in the cavern and the winged wolf landed before them, teeth bared.

Daniel pulled the sword and prepared to attack, but Allie screamed "No" and pulled him aside as the beast leaped and attacked the snakes! Its claws ripped at the first snake's eyes, then it turned on the next with a howl and sank its teeth into the snake's neck.

Allie ran with Daniel and, brushing the beads aside, they entered the cave.

The sudden change made her stop abruptly. Where there had been chaos before, now there was only peace. A waterfall nearby brought the scent of lilies. Sunshine warmed their skin. Allie licked her lips, smelling freshly baked bread, and saw a tray of sweet-breads on the floor, surrounded by bright orange and purple flowers. Past that, seated with her legs tucked under her kimono and head bowed, was a woman with white face paint and her hair done up in the geisha way. Allie took a step forward, noting the floral pattern on the white kimono that matched the flowers on the floor.

"Were you expecting us?" Allie asked.

The geisha looked up slowly, eyes full of warmth. She smiled, lips never parting, and motioned for them to sit.

Allie and Daniel exchanged a nervous look, but both were too hungry and tired to resist.

"Thank you," Allie said, sitting across from the geisha.

The geisha motioned toward the food and bowed slightly.

Daniel took a piece of bread that looked like it had a pineapple crust and began munching away at it. With a jolt, Allie remembered all the stories where heroes found themselves in situations such as this.

"Wait," she said, a hand on Daniel's arm. He paused mid-bite, wide eyes looking at her. Allie shook her head, and Daniel lowered the bread.

"What's the problem?" Daniel asked Allie in a whisper.

"We have no idea what's going on here, or who she is."

"She's a goddess," Daniel said, staring ravenously at the geisha, his voice slurred. "So beautiful."

"And Yuko?" Allie asked. "Have you forgotten about her?"

Daniel shook his head, as if trying to clear it, then muttered, "Yuko...."

The geisha laughed, a low, haunting laugh. "You'll both be perfectly safe with me."

"We're looking for our friends," Allie said. "Troy and Brenda."

The geisha smiled, staring intently into Allie's eyes. Under that stare, Allie felt herself wanting nothing more than to lie down and take a nap. A long, restful nap.

She shook her head and repeated herself, "We're looking for our friends!"

"You've already found one of them," the geisha said, motioning behind them where the winged wolf stumbled in, licking a wound on its leg.

"You mean...." Allie stared in horror at the beast, then turned as Daniel let out a shout. He doubled over and, as she watched, hair sprouted from his face. Something started to work its way out of his back, and she covered her mouth and stepped back as he sprouted wings.

The geisha stood, tall and imposing. She held out her hands like she would take them all in an embrace, and then smiled wide.

"Allie, you belong with me. Don't you see? I can give your friends incredible strength. We can form an army from them the likes of which cannot be defeated. Join me, and together we can rule as goddesses. The men of your world will bow before us, swoon over us, cater to our every desire."

"If you knew anything about me at all," Allie said, stepping forward in spite of her hunger and exhaustion, "you'd know that none of what you just said means two craps to me."

The geisha's face contorted, no longer beautiful. Her skin pulled back against her skull and her eyes reddened, until the former goddess looked very much like the fallen angel they'd fought in the tomb when rescuing Yuko's family.

"She's one of them!" Daniel shouted, still partly himself but half winged wolf as well. "Allie, save yourself!"

He leaped for the geisha-creature, trying to pull his sword free. His claws made him clumsy, though, and he dropped it. The geisha spun on him and blasted him with a glow of red light, then hissed, "Kill your friend."

Daniel, his nose growing into more of a snout and his teeth protruding and growing pointy, struggled against the command, but then growled as his eyes glazed over.

He leaped for Allie, teeth bared.

Move left, her helmet nudged. She threw herself to the side. The other winged wolf—whether it was Brenda or Troy, Allie didn't know—collided with Daniel and they rolled, gnashing teeth and clawing at each other. The geisha held up a hand and they both fell from each other, bodies twitching, then turned on Allie.

Allie gulped, looking between the two winged wolves that she knew were her friends, or had been her friends before they had been changed by the fallen angel in front of her. A glimmer caught her eye —the sword.

Allie charged, relying on the speed of the sandals and the warnings from the helmet. She dodged under a blast of red light and snatched up the sword in time to see both wolves leaping for her. She couldn't hurt them, but she could use them. She leaped, hoping the sandals would help her to jump as well as run, pushing off of one of the wolves and onto the other, and then springing with all her might for the fallen angel.

The sword bit deep, cutting right through the kimono and pulling down as gravity worked its magic. Screams filled the room as red light shot forth from the slash made by the sword, swirling around Allie and the winged wolves.

"You can't stop us all!" the fallen angel screamed, reaching a clawed hand for Allie. "We're too powerful, we're too much for you!"

Allie, feet now planted on the floor, felt the energy of the ring push through her. With a final surge of strength, she spun and chopped off the clawed hand before plunging the sword deep into the dark angel's chest.

The screams erupted into a piercing screech, and then the room exploded in a mixture of red and white light, fading slowly.

Allie knelt on the grass in the woods, no temple in sight. Daniel and Brenda were back to their normal human forms, lying beside her, panting, thin lines of blood and scratches covering their skin. But they were safe.

Still trembling, Allie stood and blinked, trying to pull herself together.

"Missing boring old history class about now?" Daniel said, propping himself up with his elbows.

"Missing a whole lot of stuff right now," Allie said.

"And yeah, I'd even take history class over this. Any day."

"Daniel?" Brenda said, eyes wide at their surroundings. "Allie? How did we get here?"

"They had you," Allie said. "Daniel for a minute there, too."

Daniel hung his head in shame. "It was horrible. Sorry, Allie. You know, for attacking you."

"As if you had a choice." Allie shook her head, processing it all. "We still have to rescue Troy, and I'd prefer you have a weapon so I don't have to do it alone again."

"Any idea where to begin?" Brenda asked.

"Well, if we find ourselves a winged wolf, that'd be a start." Allie turned, looking at the Egyptian pyramids. "Otherwise, that's as good a place as any."

40

EGYPTIAN GODS

T he walk went on and on, especially now that they were exhausted and the armor weighed even heavier on Allie. The winds had shifted, and where once the air had felt fresh, now it carried with it the thick scent of sulfur, at times gusting with sand so that the trio had to cover their faces and wait it out. Finally they crested a hill, and found only desert and pyramids before them, a wide river cutting through the sand and leading to the hill of ancient Greece in the distance.

"You mean, I was… like a werewolf?" Brenda said, not fully understanding.

Allie nodded, wishing they could just continue the walk in silence.

"More like some other kind of creature," Daniel said. "But yeah."

"Eck!" Brenda walked slower for a bit, then caught up. "Sorry for that back there."

Allie found herself rattled as they grew closer to the first pyramid. She expected it wouldn't be any different from the temple. More bad guys, more fighting. More near-death experiences.

"It wasn't your fault," Allie said when she noticed Brenda staring at her.

Brenda gave her a half-smile, then turned and looked at the pyramid above them.

"Quite the sight, huh?" a voice said. They spun to see a man, nude but for a golden cloth wrapped around his waist and wearing a dog-mask over his face. He stood in a boat at the side of the river, a long staff stuck in the water to hold the boat in place. "Quick, follow me."

She noticed the way the mouth moved, and Allie realized that the dog face was no mask.

"Who are you?" she asked, backing away and

motioning for her friends to be ready.

"I'm called Set," the man-dog said, then motioned again. "If you want to avoid being eaten by the serpent Apep, I advise you do as I say."

Allie looked about and saw something move in the sand. Suddenly, the massive serpent leaped from the ground, cresting over them.

"I say we go with him," Daniel said, but Allie was already running.

"Smart choice," Set said as Brenda trailed the other two onto the small boat. He lifted the staff and pushed away from the shore just as the serpent lifted its head from the sand and snapped at them, red eyes burning like the sun. A whap from Set's staff sent it back, and soon they were out of striking distance.

"I'm getting sick of those things," Allie said.

"Oh, you've not seen one like that before," Set said, his dog eyes staring at her intently. "No, that is the form of Apep, the god of chaos. If you'd seen him without my presence, I'm sure none of you would be alive at this moment."

"We've dealt with worse," Daniel said with a cocky frown.

"No, you haven't." Set steered the boat to the point in the river with the strongest pull, and then motioned ahead, to the largest pyramid of them all. "It's only by the grace of Ra that I've come to lead you and protect you from that evil."

"Even here?" Brenda asked. "I mean, there's another

battle of good and evil apart from the one we're fighting?"

Set nodded. "There always has been, and always will be. The day this war ends, you'll either see eternal tears and suffering or eternal peace."

"So then… this Ra?"

"He means to bring this all to an end, and soon. He is the real Bringer of Light, the one true God of the Sun."

"We weren't told any of this," Allie said, frowning.

Set looked at her, staring deep. He seemed to be considering how much he trusted her, then nodded.

"You shall see soon enough."

With several thrusts of his staff into the water, Set brought them to a spot at the riverbank where reeds grew in lush groupings, and flowing silks covered a walkway to the pyramid.

"Um, aren't the pyramids places of the dead?" Daniel said with a worried glance to Allie. "Maybe we shouldn't be following this guy?"

Set turned to him with a growl, but then stepped aside for a man all in white who was approaching, a short, curved cane in one hand and what looked like some sort of whip in the other.

"The Bringer of Light?" Allie said, skeptically.

The man in white chuckled and gave them a slight bow. "But a humble servant of his, I'm afraid. Osiris is the name."

They nodded their heads in turn.

"Quickly, the attack will soon begin," Osiris said to Set. "We must get them to safety."

"Mind telling us what you're talking about?" Brenda said. "I'm not going in there unprepared."

"Of course, my apologies. The gods of the hill," he motioned toward the hill with the Greek temple, "they mean you harm. But we are here to protect you, you have my word."

"There's no such thing as gods," Daniel said with a scoff.

"No?" Set said. "Then what do you think we are, boy?"

"Some sort of…." He looked to Allie for help, but she just shrugged. "Figments of our imagination in this weird mind-world at best, demons at worst."

"Not how it works here," Osiris said with a shake of his head. "You see, I'm the god of the dead, and Set here is the god of the desert, charged with repelling Apep. But he isn't our only worry. The gods of those temples mean us harm. They're jealous of Ra's power, and they mean to use you against us, if possible."

"And that?" Allie said, pointing to the mountain surrounded by the swirling storm.

"Yes, there is also that…." Osiris and Set shared a nervous glance. "Apep and all others of his ilk … that is where they come from, and where the world would go if we fail."

"Now, if you would, please," Set said, motioning toward the pyramid door.

Brenda and Daniel looked at each other, then turned to Allie, waiting.

"You guys believe this?" Allie said. "Think we should trust them?"

"No," Daniel said, with a look at Set that said he didn't care if he heard them. "But it's the path ahead of us."

"And it seems like we keep ending up where we're meant to be," Brenda added.

Allie didn't like the idea of following these beings that claimed to be gods. It rubbed her all wrong and made her stomach clench up. But if they were going to find Troy, she would probably have to do a lot of things she didn't like.

"Lead the way," she said.

Osiris bowed low, spun on the heel of his sandal, and led them into the pyramid.

Walking into the pyramid was like nothing Allie had ever expected. She'd seen pictures of them on TV, but she had never seen one so grand, decorated with spiral staircases, flowing palms, and immense, intricately carved vases. Draperies hung from the gold ceiling, and in the center was a raised throne. A man sat on the throne, a single shaft of golden sunlight from the peak of the pyramid shining on him. Other gods and goddesses stood or sat nearby, all turning to see the group as they walked in. One had the face of a falcon, a disk of glowing light behind his head. Allie knew that one to be Horus.

"I give you the Bringer of Light," Osiris said,

gesturing to Ra as he bowed and stepping back so that the path was clear. "Advance."

Allie saw a look of doubt and worry on Daniel's face, but she tried to hide her own as she stepped forward.

"If you're the Bringer of Light," Allie said, challenging, "why aren't you on Earth, fighting the Strayers and the fallen angels?"

The man stood, and the sunlight moved with him. Allie couldn't make out his details—the light was too bright.

"My child," he said, arms outstretched. "Welcome home."

The pyramid filled with murmurs of interest.

"Answer the question," Allie said, adjusting her ring with one hand, other readying her sword. She was ready for anything.

"You demand so much of your god?" Horus asked. It was so weird watching words come out of a bird's face.

Ra laughed, waving him off. "Don't worry, children. I'm not mad at you. The problem, you see, is one of perspective. When you were a child, how often did you believe with all your heart that you were right and your mom was wrong, only to grow older and realize that she was right all along?"

Allie frowned, not liking where this was going.

"You see," Ra continued, "this is what we're seeing right now on Earth. These Strayers, they don't mean ill to begin with, but their confusion corrupts them. Likewise, the men and women you have allied yourself with don't see the full picture, so they attack when they should ask questions, learn."

"And the fallen angels?" Allie asked. "The Grigori? The Watchers?"

The beam of light seemed to glow brighter at this.

"Tell me, Allie Strom," Ra said in his beaming voice. "Have you ever been misjudged? Who told you this is what we are?"

"We?" Allie fumbled at her ring, heart racing.

"Yes, Allie, 'we.' We are none of those things. We are the gods you see before you. We always have been, always will be. They call us fallen angels. They worship *him,* but why? What do they have to show for it? They have nothing! No proof, no power! But look at me, Allie, look at me! I stand before you, my fellow gods and I, and we are real."

Ra stepped forward and out of the light, and Allie and her friends gasped. Indeed, he looked every bit like an ancient god should, with his muscular body and glimmering gold clothing. But the look in his eyes, a fiery red, told them everything they needed to know.

"I don't accept this," Allie said. She took a deep breath, focusing on calming her nerves. "These claims of yours are nothing but lies."

"You dare?" Ra said, eyes flaring with red fire.

"You are no god. You're fallen angels sent to this plane to try and distract us. To tempt us, just like that one back in the Japanese temple. But guess what? We've dealt with your kind already. We've destroyed your brothers and sisters, and we'll do the same to you."

Ra's breathing filled the pyramid. Then he screamed, and blocks of gold fell from the ceiling.

"Destroy her!" he yelled, pointing at Allie. "Bring me the ring and the armor! You'll see, petty girl. I am the god of the sun! I am the Bringer of Light, and you shall be devoured by it!"

A god with bull horns and holding a glimmering sun disk charged, her eyes shining like polished steel. Allie sensed the attack, but not for herself, for Daniel. She shoved him aside and tried to shoot the bull goddess with her ring…. Nothing.

"I don't have the energy!" she shouted. Daniel recovered and struck at the goddess with his sword, and Allie turned to see two more coming at them. She had her sword at the ready.

"We'll have to do it the old-fashioned way, like we were trained," Daniel said, backing up toward her. "Unless you wanna give that guy your ring."

"No way." Allie spotted Set approaching from behind. She dodged his attack and connected with a kick to his stomach, then jumped with her sword to knock his staff free and into her own hand. "Okay, let's do it."

The next few strikes and blocks came with ease, Allie and Daniel fending the gods off. She wondered why it wasn't more of a challenge until she spun and saw Brenda doing her best to form patterns of protection and enhanced speed around them.

Horus thrust out his staff and it shot out a burst of red light, nearly singeing Allie's hair. She quickly dodged the next one, thanks to her sandals, and then she had him, sword tearing through the god.

A blast of gold light shot out from behind and whipped past Allie. She felt the wind like a punch to the face. She tripped, falling backward and barely catching herself, then turned to see Ra had joined the fight.

"You can't stand against all of us, child."

"We're sure going to try." She faced him, sword at the ready in one hand, staff of Set in the other. "Let's find out, shall we?"

With a heavy sigh, Ra rushed her, this time throwing her so she went flying backward into a dark passageway. Laughter filled the area behind her and hands clutched at her clothing, but with a sudden burst of light from her ring, she was free. She spun to attack again, but this time conjured nothing more than a glow. She bit her lip, then turned just in time for Ra to appear in a blinding flash of light right in front of her.

With nowhere to go, Allie knelt and propped the staff against the floor. Bracing it tightly, she lifted it just as Ra charged. He slammed into it with a sickening crunch.

Ra stood there, staring at her, his glow fading and the back of the staff sticking out from his ribs.

Allie stared in amazement as the light around him dimmed, leaving behind only a gray pile of dust that soon blew away.

A crash from behind pulled her back to the moment, reminding her that Daniel and Brenda were still out there fighting. She rushed back to see Set fall as Daniel swung his sword at the last of them, changing the horned woman into a pile of dust.

Daniel turned to Allie, and for a moment she felt she barely recognized him. The look in his eyes was so mature, so battle-hardened. But then he smiled, and the same old Daniel returned.

"Now we just have to find Troy," he said.

"Oh, I wouldn't worry about that," a booming voice said. The pyramid began to shake, stones and gold falling all around them as the top opened to reveal the mighty form of Zeus.

41

THE GREEKS

Zeus moved his hands apart, and the entire pyramid split open like a toy. Thunder rolled and clouds surged past his head, lightning crashing in his eyes. With a motion from his hand, the trio was flown into the air and whipped about in a circle before his eyes.

"The time for games is over," Zeus said. He motioned toward the Greek temple on the far hill. "There you will choose your fate."

Another gust of wind swept at them, and Zeus shimmered to the form of an eagle. The group found themselves swept along behind him as they sailed toward the temple in the distance.

"Are you one of them?" Allie screamed over the howling wind, trying to get his attention as she focused her energy on recharging the ring. "One of the fallen angels?"

The eagle turned to look at her, then swooped

down to the ground and returned to the form of Zeus. Now he stood at human height, albeit a towering human. He motioned around at the statues of different Greek gods carved from pure gold—Poseidon with his trident, Ares with his sword and plumed helm, and there was no mistaking Hades, with his hollowed-out face and chilling eyes.

"Do we look like fallen angels?" Zeus demanded. He paced before the statues, each step thundering through the temple. "We are gods. The gods! We've stood the test of time while your supposed God comes and goes, a fashion of the day."

"Sounds like you're trying to convince yourself," Allie said.

Zeus's eyes were like ice. He held her stare for a moment and then lifted his hand. In the middle of the room, a hole opened up and a stone table rose from the floor. Troy was tied to it in chains so that his limbs formed an X.

"Troy?" Allie said, sounding doubtful.

Troy's eyelids fluttered, and he managed to send her a terrified look before he passed out again.

"What've you done with him?" Brenda demanded.

Daniel aimed his sword at Zeus. "Just say when."

"You silly children." Zeus approached the table and looked down at Troy. "This one thought he could fight, too, when we took him…. Even managed to take one of Cerberus's heads in the battle…."

"A crime that will not go unpunished," a whisper said.

They spun to find Hades standing behind them. His three-headed dog had only two heads now, a piece of cloth draped over the spot where the other head would have been.

"Zeus will see to it, brother," another voice said, and they spun to see Poseidon with his mighty trident on the other side.

"The Egyptian gods were old," Zeus said, arms spread with palms toward Allie as if to show he meant no harm. "They were long-forgotten, powerless in comparison to us."

"We could still take you," Daniel said, raising his sword. "Right, Allie?"

She pulled at the power of her ring, feeling its energy, but didn't answer. In truth, she wasn't sure if this was a battle they could win. If Zeus spoke the truth, it might be better to avoid the fight and listen.

"What do you want?" she asked Zeus.

Zeus smiled and snapped his fingers. Lightning flashed, and then Ares, the god of war, stood over Troy with a sword to the boy's throat, a vicious smile on the god's lips.

"You see," Zeus said. "In an instant, your friend here could be dead. But I'll give you the choice, Allie Strom. You stay, and your friends may leave. Or they can stay, and you go. But if you try to fight us, he dies first, and then the rest of you."

"Don't listen to him!" Daniel shouted.

Brenda looked at Allie with uncertainty.

Allie had a duty: to finish the battle, to protect the

world. But she also couldn't let Troy die. The idea made her want to just lie down and give up.

"Let them go," she said.

"And you're ours?" Zeus asked.

"I'll stay, just let them go."

"No, Allie!" Daniel said, but already Zeus had motioned and a great wind was pulling them back.

"Him too!" Allie said, pointing to Troy.

"Of course." With a nod, the chains broke free and Ares backed away. The wind lifted a groggy Troy and set him down beside Brenda and Daniel, where they rushed to support him.

But Zeus had his eyes on Daniel now. "Of course, we'll be needing the Sword of the Spirit and the Shield of Faith."

"That wasn't part of the deal," Allie said, stepping forward. "I'm here. Take me and let them go."

"Of course, of course. But not without the shield and sword."

"For what? So you can claim the spot of the Tenth Worthy? You're no god; you're just some petty fallen angel, no better than the rest of them, no better than Samyaza was!"

"And you're a fool!" Zeus turned on her and swung. A massive spear appeared in his hands, crackling with lightning. He gestured with his hands, and the winds sent Brenda and Troy flying, but Daniel braced with the shield and stood his ground.

Zeus frowned, nostrils flaring and chest heaving,

but then he smiled. "This is how you want it? The two of you? Then let it be done."

"What do you mean…?" Allie said. But then she felt the sting of the marks on her skin.

Zeus was gesturing again with his free hand, as if coaxing the dark powers in her arm to do his bidding. The shadows returned, twisting around her arm like black snakes.

Allie turned to Daniel with a terrible feeling—she had to kill him.

"No!" she shouted, fighting the urge. "You won't control me!"

Again Zeus motioned, and the urge grew stronger. She took a step toward Daniel, who was backing up, shield raised and eyes wild.

"What are you doing, Allie?" Daniel said. "It's me, it's Daniel."

"I know!" she said, resisting the next step.

This time Zeus dropped his spear and pushed with both hands, surging dark energy into her blood. She felt it, boiling beneath the surface. She closed her eyes, trying to ignore the pain, trying to push back, but it was taking over. Her mind swam… darkness… pain….

A laugh came, somewhere from deep within. Her childhood, swinging in mom's arms. An image of her dad looking down at her with love. A brief memory of her and Daniel in the grass outside their apartments, that time when she'd yelled at the top of her lungs that he was her best friend.

With a burst of energy, she jumped into the air and

threw back the forces Zeus was sending her way. The weaving black light became a bright yellow, then white, twisting around her until it entered her body and shot out through her ring, throwing Zeus to the floor.

Recovering, he propped himself up and looked at her with interest.

"I see that I'll have to approach this from a different direction," he said, and then nodded to Hades and Poseidon.

The two gods charged Daniel and leaped in the air. But instead of attacking him, they both shifted to a dark, oily mist, then dissolved into his body.

Daniel took a step back, screaming. He fell to one knee, and when he looked up, his eyes had that same blank stare Allie had seen on Troy and Brenda when they had been taken over.

"Daniel, fight it!" she screamed, but he was already charging.

Allie lifted her ring to fight, but she had used up its energy on Zeus, and nothing happened. Daniel tackled her, slamming her to the ground. Allie raised her arms to protect herself—but he wasn't striking. Instead he was pulling the armor off of her and placing it on himself.

"You never deserved this, Allie!" He donned the helmet and then yanked the belt from her waist, securing it on his own. "I deserve this. You should have seen that from the beginning. Allie Strom, the Tenth Worthy?" He laughed, then pushed aside her arms, pinning her to the ground as he yanked the sandals from her feet. "I don't think so."

"Daniel, stop!" she screamed. "This isn't you!"

"This is more me than I've ever been," he said as he held down her wrist and slipped off the ring. He stood, placed the ring on his own finger, and smiled at Zeus. "Let's get to it then."

Zeus nodded, and in a blink of an eye, they were gone.

A shudder went through the ground, then another. The temple started to fall around Allie. An oil lamp shattered and tapestries caught fire. Flames roared nearby, but Allie couldn't move. She just lay there, devastated, staring at the stars visible where parts of the ceiling had fallen in. They'd taken over Daniel…. How?

More ceiling fell and a shot of pain coursed through Allie's ribs. Something had fallen on her, but she didn't care to check. It was over. She closed her eyes.

"Allie!" a voice shouted.

"Where are you?" came another.

It didn't matter, she told herself. They'd lost.

"Allie!" A chunk of rock moved aside to reveal Troy, scrambling to free her from the debris. "Thank God."

"Troy?" she said, weakly.

"We're getting out of this."

Brenda appeared beside him, helping to move the rocks. Soon they were carrying her away from the flames and the wreckage. They paused on the wooded hill, and watched as the large serpent far below created sand dunes around the destroyed pyramid, as if looking for its friends. The image of it thrashing about, slamming against the pyramids and fallen stones and retreating back beneath the sand only to resurface moments later, made Allie's skin crawl.

"I wish we'd never come here," she said.

"It's not over," Troy said, holding her hand with both of his. "We can still fight."

"How?" Allie asked. "They took everything."

"Did we train to fight them with rings and magic armor?" Troy asked. "No! Well, not exclusively. We trained our minds and bodies to be ready for this."

"We can fight them," Brenda said, nodding in agreement. "If we don't, no one will."

Allie struggled to stand, looking each of them in the eye. They actually believed this... and they were right.

"They took Daniel... and they'll hurt everyone we've ever loved. We can't allow that."

Troy and Brenda smiled, weary smiles that showed how hard the path would be.

"Of course," Troy said with a glance around them, "there's still the problem of getting out of here."

"Allie," Brenda said, eyes narrowed in the way they often were when she had an idea. "Your eagle, it's not entirely of this world or our own, right?"

"And maybe it can bring us home!" Allie hugged Brenda, for a moment forgetting the bad blood between them.

With a small pattern in the dirt, Allie called on her eagle, and a moment later it was circling them. A mist of lavender began to spread around them, hiding the surrounding hills and smoking ruins from view.

When the mist cleared, they were back in Japan, in what appeared to be a crowded train station.

"Why here?" Brenda asked. "I'd have thought it would take us back to school."

"I don't know," Troy said. "We haven't found the last piece of the armor, and that means it's still out there. And it makes sense, right? That's where they'd be keeping the breastplate… the most populated place on Earth, where they'd know you would want to avoid fighting."

"And that's somewhere in Japan?" Brenda asked.

Troy walked to a wall of glass. "That's right here."

The other two joined him and looked down at a massive intersection. People were running everywhere —dodging bursts of flames spouting from the ground as three shadowed figures shimmered into existence in the midst of the chaos. Then, in the middle of it all, Allie spotted an armored figure, red and black light swimming around him. In his hands he held a glowing red breastplate.

"Daniel!" she shouted, pounding on the glass. "We have to get to him, to stop him!"

"It's too late," Brenda said, her voice cracking.

All three watched as Daniel donned the breastplate and then rose into the air, hovering above the crowd. The chaos suddenly stopped, everyone staring at him in awe. The three shadowed figures removed their hoods to show angelic faces, a faint red glow vanishing from their eyes to be replaced by a piercing blue. One of them, looking very much like Zeus, raised his hands.

"Bow, people of Earth," the one calling itself Zeus said. "Your time is at hand. The Tenth Worthy has been proclaimed."

Allie took a step back, then collapsed on jelly-legs, staring at the face of what had once been her friend, but who was now the Tenth Worthy.

TWO WORLDS COLLIDE

Daniel was lost to them. He had been taken over by the fallen angels, had taken Allie's armor and her destiny to become the Tenth Worthy. That title was now his.

Where did that leave her?

Troy and Brenda were saying something, but all Allie could hear were the muffled voices of people chanting.

"Tenth Worthy! Tenth Worthy!"

"Let's get out of here," she said, reaching for Troy's extended hand.

But as she stood, Daniel turned and stared at her—a deep, dark stare that reached her all the way from the street below.

And then he was surging toward her, crashing through the window and placing the tip of his sword at her neck.

"I can't let you live," he said. "You'd try to take this all away from me, and we just can't have that."

She hated that tears filled her eyes, but to hear that from him was gut-wrenching.

"Stop it," Troy yelled. "It's still you in there, Daniel. Fight them, come back to us!"

Daniel turned on Troy and plunged the sword into his chest, laughing as Troy fell to the floor in a pool of blood.

"Soon there won't be an 'us' to come back to," Daniel said, turning on Brenda next and slicing her neck and shoulder.

Allie backed up, horrified, but someone shoved her forward. People in black surrounded her, and outside she could see doorways opening and more Strayers coming through, hungry to watch the Tenth Worthy destroy Allie.

"Don't any of you know what's going on here?" she screamed. "What this will mean for our world?"

The remaining three fallen angels appeared beside Daniel, and he turned on her, his glowing sword at the ready.

"It means a return to the old days," Zeus said, and the ground outside began to transform. In place of the billboards and tall buildings, old temples formed, an ancient Japanese castle in the background.

"It means a coming of better days," the second fallen angel said, and raised its hands into the air. Lush trees sprouted everywhere, with huge flowers in vibrant blues and pinks.

"It means the rule of our ways," the third one said in a singsong female voice. She wove her hands together, pulled a golden crown from thin air and placed it atop Daniel's head, where it melded with the helmet.

All the Strayers bowed to Daniel.

"Don't you see?" Daniel said, arms spread, accepting the praise. "We were lied to, Allie. This is the path we should have been on, this is what's right."

Allie stared at him, wondering if he truly believed that, if somehow he could be right. What reason did she have for trusting Principal Eisner and her mom and everyone, anyway? But those fallen angels had taken over Daniel's body by force, she reminded herself, and were controlling him. She pushed all doubts from her mind and stood her ground.

"I know that's not you in there," she said to Daniel.

"This has to stop, so I'm sorry for what I'm about to do."

He held her gaze, and the fallen angels laughed as she charged. They vanished and reappeared around her in bursts of black flames, raining down blows on her as she ran. Each one burned, but she deflected them, running for Daniel in a zigzag pattern and creating momentary defensive charms as she advanced. One blow knocked her sideways and onto shattered glass, but she recovered, performing a quick pattern that threw the glass into her attackers.

The fallen angels drew closer, and Allie leaped at Daniel, hoping to at least knock the weapon from his hand. His shield caught her, though, and threw her through the broken glass. Air streamed past her and her chest clenched as she fell, and then she slammed into the ground with a thump.

Strayers surged toward her, but stopped at a command from Daniel.

"She's mine," he ordered, his voice deep and unfamiliar.

Allie turned to look up, and then he was on top of her, sword raised.

"Don't do it," she said in a whimper.

"I... have no choice." For a moment his eyes flickered and she saw a tear form, but then the distant stare was back, the sword falling.

The steel felt cold as it broke through her, grating against bone and contrasting with the warmth of her blood flowing forth from her chest.

Grabbing the sword, she pulled it deeper. She clutched at Daniel's arm, fingernails digging into his skin, and drew him closer. He stared at her with wide, confused eyes as she grabbed the back of his neck and pulled—bringing him into an embrace.

Using all her will, she stood there, hugging her best friend as her body grew colder.

"I forgive you," she whispered into Daniel's ear, gripping him tightly to her. Her body shuddered and her vision darkened, but she held on, resting her cheek against his. She could feel his heartbeat, smell the sweat. But none of it was evil; it was Daniel, somewhere in there.

"No...." he said, then louder, "NO!"

He tried to push free, but she held tight.

"I forgive you."

Then Allie let go and slipped from the sword, collapsing onto her back in an agonized groan. Her eyelids grew heavy, and then it was dark.

Only it wasn't, not anymore. A gold light was shining through her closed lids, and warmth tingled through her body. She forced her eyes open and saw a bright light streaming from her to Daniel. The nearby Strayers and fallen angels pulled back, covering their eyes. The light exploded, and Allie was standing over Daniel, who lay unconscious with the armor scattered across the ground.

The Strayers and fallen angels stared, horrified.

Allie looked at the armor, then at the bloodied

sword, confused. Daniel now had the gaping hole in his chest, instead of her.

"Please, no," she said as she knelt beside him. She lifted him and looked around, searching for a patch of dirt. She spied one nearby, where the strange trees had sprouted at the fallen angel's command.

Still holding Daniel, Allie performed the healing pattern. But it didn't work. She tried again, and nothing.

Frustrated and scared, she wiped the stinging sweat from her eyes. Then she saw the glimmer of her ring on his hand. She had forgotten to put it back on! Gently, she removed the ring and slipped it back on her own finger.

This time when she performed the pattern, Daniel's wound started to glow. She performed the pattern again, and the scattered armor—corrupted to black and red—began to return to its golden hue. It floated up and attached itself to her, but unlike before, it felt weightless. As if it belonged with her.

The helmet was the last piece, and when it landed on her head, the wound in Daniel's chest healed completely. Golden light shone out from the armor in all directions, and Allie lifted off the ground to hover over the Strayers.

They stared up at her in confusion, and for a moment she searched for something to say. Then a portal opened before her, and Principal Eisner stepped out. More portals opened, followed by more

Guardians, Bringers of Light, and others she recognized from the training grounds.

Daniel sat up in bewilderment, and Allie felt relief wash over her. Then she saw Brenda and Troy, also sitting up as a fading, golden light shone from their wounds.

Principal Eisner gave her a warm smile. "Are you ready?"

"Yes," Allie said, taking a deep breath for whatever came next.

With a raised eyebrow, Principal Eisner spread her arms and addressed the crowd. "I give you, the Eleventh Worthy!"

Silence for a moment. And then, like a strong wind blowing away dirt, the Strayers scattered, trampling each other to flee.

The fallen angels pulled back, watching the chaos. Then Allie met their eyes and, hissing like snakes, they retreated with the Strayers, disappearing into one of the portals. Another thing that vanished, at least temporarily but she couldn't be sure, was the dark marks on her arm! The ones that Paulette had carved there back on that mountain in Kyrgyzstan... they were gone.

"Should we go after them?" Allie asked as she floated down to the ground beside Principal Eisner.

"Not yet," Principal Eisner said. "We've won the battle, but we must recuperate to finish the war another day."

"Then may I...?"

"Of course."

Allie ran to Daniel, who was standing now, eyes wide and glistening with tears.

"It was horrible, Allie," he said. "I can't even say how sorry I am, I just—"

She threw her arms around him, laughing with joy that he was alive and himself again.

"I don't care about that," she said. "We did it, we won. It's over."

He pulled back and looked at her, then laughed as Troy and Brenda joined them in the hug.

"It's over," Daniel said, closing his eyes.

Allie loved those words.

43

THE ELEVENTH WORTHY

A week later, Allie sat in the Principal's office with her mom and dad, staring in confusion at Principal Eisner.

"But what if I don't want the new training?" Allie asked, trying to keep her voice steady.

"You need this," Principal Eisner said. "You're the Eleventh Worthy now, and you'll be training with The Elite Guardians and Bringers of Light, not children."

"It was these children that saved the world," Allie said, annoyed.

Principal Eisner nodded. "I understand, Allie. But there's a lot more for you to learn, and some great teachers for you to be exposed to. You'll use the portal doors to get to training, so it's not like you're really changing schools. You can still come here every day, as if you were going to Vigil Junior High part time. You can even stay on the soccer team if you want, and come help out with your old P.E. class from time to time, but the door you'll go through will bring you to the elite training grounds."

"And when this war against evil is over?"

Principal Eisner shared a look with Allie's parents, then shook her head.

"Dear," Allie's mom said, a hand on her shoulder. "We're not sure it'll ever truly be over."

"Sure it will," Allie said. "We defeat the last three Grigori, then hunt down any Strayers that remain."

"And you think that'll mean the end of all evil?" Principal Eisner asked. "I wish it were so simple, but I'm afraid it's just not the way it is."

"And Daniel? The others?"

"We've seen that being taken over by darkness isn't a sound reason to stop them from training. They, along with Paulette and any others that wish to return to training, are welcome to."

Allie nodded, unsure what to expect from this new training, but accepting that her fate wasn't that of a regular kid anymore.

Troy was waiting for her as she walked back to her parents' car.

"Can I have a minute?" Allie asked, and her parents said they'd be in the car.

"I heard the news," Troy said when they were alone.

"Already?"

"Yeah, well...." He blushed. "I was kind of listening at the door."

"And why would that be?" she asked.

"Let's just say I want you to stick around... I like being around you. I mean...."

"I get it," she said with a smile.

"You do?"

"Yeah, you like me."

He turned even darker red, if that was possible. But his look of embarrassment turned into a smile, and he shrugged.

"Caught me," he said.

"Don't worry, we'll still be seeing each other." She gave him a peck on the cheek, and then spun on her heels and walked back to the car. Her dad glared past her at Troy, but her mom was giving her a corny thumbs up.

From now on, she told herself as she got in the car and ignored their questions about Troy, she wasn't going to sit around wondering and hoping. She was going to take charge. She had some great friends, even if Daniel had decided to study abroad for a year to spend some time getting to know Yuko and learning Japanese. Brenda had come over to hang out a couple of times over the last week, and she was actually turning out to be pretty cool.

Now Troy—and she really did like him. A lot.

Perhaps she would see where it went. But she would be happy no matter what, because she was in control. She was the Eleventh Worthy, after all.

ABOUT THE AUTHOR

Justin M. Stone is a novelist (*Allie Strom and the Ring of Solomon; Falls of Redemption*), video game writer (*Game of Thrones; Walking Dead; Michonne*), podcaster, and screenwriter. He has written on taking writing from hobby to career in his book *Creative Writing Career* and its sequel, and how veterans can pursue their passions in *Military Veterans in Creative Careers*. Justin studied writing at the Johns Hopkins University.

To receive other free stories and audiobooks, as well as future updates, sign up for Justin's newsletter.

www.JustinMStone.com

Newsletter subscribers can get a short story that follows this series as a little spin off.

ALLIE STROM AND THE RISING FLAME

And join my Facebook Group!

Facebook.com/groups/JustinMStone

Printed in Great Britain
by Amazon

44530703R00279